FANNING FIREFLIES

Book 3
The Limerent Series

LS Delorme

Copyright © LS Delorme, 2024

Published: 2024 by Limerent Publishing LLC
Florida, USA

ISBN: 979-8-9874880-4-1 – Paperback Edition
ISBN: 979-8-9874880-5-8 – eBook

The right of LS Delorme to be identified as author of this work has been asserted by her in accordance with sections 77 and 78 of the copyright, designs and patents act 1988.

This book is a work of fiction and any resemblance to actual persons, living or dead, or locations, is purely coincidental.

All rights reserved. No part of this publication may be reproduced or transmitted in any form or by any means, electronic or mechanical, including photography, recording, or any information storage or retrieval system, without permission in writing from the publisher.

The book is sold subject to the condition that it shall not, by way of trade or otherwise, be lent, resold or otherwise circulated without the publisher's prior consent in any form of binding or cover other than that in which it is published and without a similar condition, including this condition, being imposed on the subsequent purchaser.

Cover Design by Brittany Wilson | Brittwilsonart.com

This book is dedicated to my mother, whose brain was running a very different operating system from all those around her. It is also dedicated to her children and grandchildren who have inherited that gift.

Author's Note/ Trigger Warnings

This story takes place in the U.S. south in 1945. So, to begin with, I should state that I have NOT used some of the harsher language that was common parlance at the time. This is because these words can be deeply triggering and are a part of an evil that still shadows many systems unseen. So, I have tried to avoid such language while retaining authenticity.

This novel deals with intense themes such as racism, racial violence, discrimination, and graphic scenes of animal cruelty, set against a historical backdrop of socio-economic hardship. It is about violence, questioning its justification and necessity in various contexts, and how love can both mitigate and exacerbate these conflicts. The narrative does not shy away from depicting the brutal realities of the lives the characters and the times they lived in which includes significant racism and misogyny but these are crucial for understanding the characters' motivations and growth.

Chapter One

Dead and Dying One and All

The headless chicken charging toward Veronica Crane was clinging to life against all odds.

Her friend Lizzie shrieked, dropped Veronica's arm, and jumped back as the chicken ran between them. It was followed by a large, round, and sweaty Hank Price. He charged down his dirt driveway, panting, with a hatchet still in his hand, and blood on his apron. The chicken was now trying to run up the incline to Veronica's small mill house but, being headless, it was running without direction. Its only motivation came from whatever vestigial brain was left, and was screaming run from the predator behind it.

"Sorry ladies," Hank called, passing them. "Dang bird got away from me."

The bird had made it onto Veronica's porch and was now scrambling around, bumping into things, and dripping blood everywhere. In its own way, it was heroic. The fact that it was *sans* head, made its attempt even more valiant in a doomed hero sort of way. But these thoughts vanished when Veronica realized that she would be the one having to clean up the blood on her front porch later.

"That was an ugly kill, Hank!" Veronica called, as Lizzie clutched her arm and pulled her down the dirt road that they both lived on.

"Come on," Lizzie said.

"He should have secured it with something, cut its throat and let it bleed out," Veronica said, eyes still on the tormented chicken.

"Ugh," Lizzie said. "Let's go."

Veronica rolled her eyes.

"I know you do it in your family, but my brother does it ours. And we don't do it often as we mainly keep the chickens for eggs."

"When a chicken isn't laying anymore—" Veronica began but Lizzie shook her head.

"I know. I know. I know," she said, as she pulled Veronica onto the paved road that led to the city center.

There were no cars in sight as it was early Saturday morning, and most businesses didn't open until ten on Saturdays, but she and Lizzie had been lucky enough to get temp jobs at the draft office on the weekends, and they had to be at work by 7:30 a.m.

"Hey, did you hear that there was *another* cat hanging from a telephone line this morning?" Lizzie asked her as they started down the road.

"Ugh, how many is that?" Veronica asked, grimacing.

"Ten in as many weeks."

"When did it happen?"

"They must have done it last night," Lizzie replied. "But they found it this morning, first thing. My brother's wife's brother works for the telephone company—"

"You mean Teddy?"

Lizzie nodded.

"And they don't have a suspect for it?" Veronica asked.

"No," Lizzie replied, "but it's cats, you know. I guess Chief Bishop has other more pressing problems."

"Obviously," Veronica muttered.

"Ronnie don't be like that," Lizzie replied. "CJ's an okay guy, and his dad is an okay guy. It can't be easy to be chief of police."

"Of course not, Harrisville is such a teeming metropolis that it must be emergency calls twenty-four hours a day," Veronica said, thinking of the short, round police chief. Anyone who had enough food to get fat was never going to get her sympathy. "I bet he even has to skip meals occasionally."

"You know, people think you are snobby because you talk like that," Lizzie said.

"Like what?"

"Using big fancy words like metropolis," Lizzie replied.

"If anyone doesn't like my word choice, they don't have to talk to me," Veronica snapped.

"Wow you are grumpy this morning, did you have any breakfast?" Lizzie asked.

Veronica shook her head.

"Franklin needs the breakfast more than me," Veronica said softly. "Besides, I'm not really hungry."

This was lie, and Lizzie knew it. Veronica's mother had been sick a couple of days last week, and so they were low on money. Right now, there was nothing in their icebox and they were down to the last jar of preserves from the previous summer. Veronica did without so that her mother and brother could have a little more.

"Here," Lizzie said, pulling an apple from her lunch box and handing it to Veronica. Veronica didn't argue. She and Lizzie had known each other for too long to put on airs. Lizzie's family was far from well off, but they always had enough food on their table. The same was not true for Veronica's family.

"How *is* Franklin?" Lizzie asked her as they turned onto Broad Street with its tree-lined sidewalks.

"Fine, for the most part," Veronica replied.

"What do you mean, 'for the most part'?" Lizzie asked.

"He's already working full time at the pig farm, but now he just got on at the fire department—" Veronica began.

"Well, that's fantastic, Ronnie." Lizzie beamed. "He's always wanted to be a fireman."

"Well, he's not exactly a fireman yet," Veronica replied. "He's just helping out for the moment, but it could lead to a full-time job later, if he can pass their test."

"They have a *test* to be a fireman?" Lizzie asked, grimacing.

"Mm-hmm," Veronica responded. "But it's a written test, so I'm sure he can pass it and the fire chief seems really nice. I hope he is as nice as he seems."

Lizzie nodded, taking Veronica's arm again.

"The problem is that he's already working so many hours, what with the pig farm, and the factory on the weekend, that he barely has time to sleep. And they don't pay him as much because—"

"I know," Lizzie said, kicking a stone viciously. "It's not fair though."

"No, it's not," Veronica replied, as the sincere, handsome face of her brother appeared in her mind's eye.

They had now entered the part of town where the richer folks lived. The houses were large with wraparound porches. Veronica had always thought that they looked like gingerbread houses.

Even the smaller houses here were larger than Veronica's. Almost all of them had real front and back yards and about half of them had a second story. Veronica suspected that the people living in these houses had their own bedrooms.

A group of men who worked at the mill walked by and whistled at them. Lizzie laughed and flipped her hair. Lizzie Goodwin was an unquestionable beauty, and everyone knew it… including Lizzie. She was often compared to

Veronica Lake, as she had light blonde hair that she curled in waves. Despite her beauty, she wasn't really vain. Lizzie viewed her beauty as a tool to get her out of poverty by marrying up. Veronica couldn't rely on her beauty to get her anywhere. She was okay, but far from Lizzie's level of beauty. Her breasts were too small and her hips too wide to fit the traditional beauty standards. Her hair was a pretty auburn, but she had pale freckles across her cheeks and nose that she hated. Her only vanity was her slate-gray eyes, with a little ring of gold around the center. They were not as beautiful as the blue eyes of her brother or grandma, but they were nice.

As they approached Marvin Bear High School, they saw a group of colored men standing in the street in front of the school. In truth, they looked more like boys than men. They were huddled together, with their heads down. Some were smoking but most were simply talking.

"What are they doing there?" Lizzie whispered to Veronica, although there was absolutely no reason to whisper.

"I heard that we would be processing boys for some colored units," Veronica replied.

"I don't like it."

"You don't like that someone wants to fight for their country?" Veronica asked. She knew what Lizzie was implying, and it annoyed her.

"Well, they're not like us," Lizzie said. As Veronica had never met, let alone known, a colored person, she couldn't argue with this.

"You mean you aren't scared of them?" Lizzie asked.

"Of course I am, but not any more than any other man. Horrible comes in all colors."

"Well, the police chief thinks that one of the colored folks might be the ones killing the cats," Lizzie said.

"Who told you that?" Veronica asked.

"Ben," Lizzie replied, nodding knowingly. Of course, it would be Ben. He was Lizzie's longtime boyfriend and Lizzie took everything he said as gospel.

"Ben said that CJ also thinks it's the coloreds," Lizzie said.

The back of Veronica's head began to throb. The spot Grandma Janie used to call her "knowing spot."

"Of course, CJ would say that," Veronica muttered.

"What do you mean?"

"CJ has too much spare time," Veronica replied. "If he had to work as hard as we do, he wouldn't waste his time looking for reasons to hate people."

Lizzie laughed.

"Wouldn't you like to have that problem, though?" she said, poking Veronica in the side.

"Hi de ho, hi de ho!" came a loud voice from just behind them. Ben Morton, Lizzie's boyfriend, squeezed in between them and put his arms around both girls. "What a lucky guy I am."

Veronica hit at him with her purse and pulled away.

"Did I offend Ronnie again?" He laughed, releasing Veronica, and pulling Lizzie closer to him as they walked.

"I think your breathing offends Ronnie," Lizzie said.

"Ain't it always the way?" Ben said, grabbing at his heart. "The most beautiful dames are forever out of reach. So I guess I am stuck with you."

"For now... if you are lucky." Lizzie pulled her arm away from him.

"Ouch!" Ben said. "Hey, don't be like that, sugar."

"You are paying for my lunch today," Lizzie snapped.

"I always pay for your lunch—" he began, but Lizzie held up her hand.

"And Ronnie's lunch," she said.

"I thought Ronnie always brings her lunch—" he started, but at Lizzie's glare he held up his hands.

"And anything Ronnie wants to eat, of course. Jeez."

Lizzie smiled, winked at Veronica, and put her arm through Ben's.

"Are you taking me to a movie tonight?" Lizzie asked. This was a common game for them. None of them had the extra money for something as frivolous as a movie, unless it was a free film put out by the war department. Veronica was expecting the normal "Sure, baby" response that Ben always gave. Instead, his brow furrowed.

"I can't, there's going to be a pep rally tonight," he said, chewing the inside of his lip.

"Aren't you a little old for high school girls?" Veronica asked.

"It's not a school pep rally," Ben said, his voice softer. "It's a Knights of Harrisville rally and I'm hoping to be invited."

Lizzie rolled her eyes.

"Ben, when will you stop trying to be friends with those guys?" Lizzie asked. "They don't like you. You aren't a townie."

"CJ is a good guy," Ben replied. "The others are nice too. You just don't know them very well."

"Neither do you," scoffed Lizzie.

Veronica turned to go, but Lizzie called after her.

"Ronnie, meet us at the soda shop for lunch."

Veronica waved her hand and walked alone toward the entrance to the school gymnasium that had been appropriated on the weekends to process army recruits.

As she walked into the building, Veronica's mind drifted back to the headless chicken. In some ways she envied it. If you were headless, at least you didn't have to listen to fool's talk.

*

The gym was split into two halves by white screens on rollers. There was one opening in the screens on the right side of the room, and another opening on the left side of the room. In front of these screens were desks that had been arranged along each wall. At each desk was a chair, a typewriter, and a filing cabinet. On top of each desk was a letter tray.

Mrs. Cartwright, their supervisor here, stared at them as they huddled together. It was early May, but it was still cold enough outside to require a coat. The inside of the gym wasn't heated, and it was drafty. Veronica's hands started to ache, so she began to open and close them slowly at her sides. Lizzie ran in to join the group, earning a harsh glance from Mrs. Cartwright.

Looking around, Veronica counted eighteen girls. That was a high number for a recruiting office.

"Ladies, I need your attention please," Mrs. Cartwright said, as she walked in front of them. She walked and spoke like a military man. Veronica wondered if her husband or father had been in the military.

"We will be processing several busloads of recruits this morning. You will register them and fill in all the information needed on their cards and forms. You can all type, can't you?"

Most of the girls nodded but a few shook their heads.

"Ugh," Mrs. Cartwright said, rolling her eyes. "Okay. As they didn't specify that you needed to type, those who can't can just write in the information."

"Once you have processed them, you are to send them past those screens, where they will get their medical exam. But do make sure they go to the correct side."

"What do you mean the correct side?" asked Missy, a petite brunette who Veronica had known since kindergarten.

"I mean that we will be processing white men and colored boys," said Mrs. Cartwright. Several of the girls gasped audibly. "Every day, half of you will be working to process the white soldiers and the other half will process the colored boys. The next day, you will switch."

"Will we be safe?" Lizzie asked.

"There will be soldiers overseeing the operation, so yes, you will be safe, Miss Goodwin." Mrs. Cartwright's words were meant to be comforting but they were dripping with condescension. Lizzie was not making a good impression.

"Also, the military is seeing fit to pay you more on the days that you process the colored boys."

Missy raised her hand.

"Oh, I'll volunteer for both days," she said.

"The schedule is neither optional nor flexible," said Mrs. Cartwright, glaring at Missy.

Clearly it was better not to speak to this woman. Veronica's hands were starting to throb, and she desperately wanted to rub them, but she just put them behind her back and continued to open and close them.

"I'm going to separate you into two groups. Group 1 will register the white men today," she said. "Group 2 will register the colored boys."

As she said this, the doors opened, and five soldiers walked in. Mrs. Cartwright nodded to them. Four of the men went to stand at each corner of the room. The fifth came up to Mrs. Cartwright.

"This is Sergeant Deal, he will be overseeing operations today," Mrs. Cartwright said. "If you have any problems or feel any discomfort, feel free to raise your hand and get my attention or his."

"Looks like he got a raw Deal," Lizzie whispered in Veronica's ear. Veronica bit her lip and tried not to smile.

"All right, ladies, let's line up," Mrs. Cartwright said, clapping her hands.

They were lined up and numbered. Veronica and Lizzie were both assigned to Group 1, the white men.

"I'm not sure if it's better or worse," Lizzie said, as they all moved toward their desks. "I don't have to register the negroes today, which is good, but then I have to spend all night worrying about tomorrow."

Veronica shrugged and went to her desk. She didn't care much one way or another. Well, that wasn't strictly true. She agreed with Missy more than Lizzie—she could use the extra money. Her mind was practical that way.

Once the registration began, she didn't have time to do much besides process the men who came in an endless flow. Missy was sitting at the desk next to her. Veronica occasionally saw Missy sigh and blow her bangs out of her eyes. The gesture was both childlike and world-weary in equal measure, which was a good description of Missy. Her father had died when Missy was two and her family were just as poor, if not poorer, than Veronica's family.

At about 10 a.m., they were all interrupted by the voice of Sergeant Deal.

"Boy, are you deaf or something?" he bellowed at a group of colored boys in the line. They all cringed backward and cast their eyes downward. All except one.

"YOU! BOY!" the sergeant yelled, pointing at the one boy who was looking at him.

"Are you stupid or something? What are you doing standing in the colored people line?"

All the men froze, wide-eyed, as the sergeant strode toward the line, grabbed the boy out of it and pulled him to the center of the room. The boy he was yelling at was brown haired and tan, but his skin was much lighter than most of those around him and his hair was straight.

"Boy, you must be deaf," the sergeant barked. "Or are you just so in love with them coloreds that you have to stand with them?"

"I'm Brazilian, I thought—" began the boy, his voice softer and smoother than seemed right, given the fact that the sergeant was right up in his face.

"I don't care where you're from, boy," Sergeant Deal yelled, spittle flying. "Do you look like those colored boys? You don't, do you?"

The boy had adopted a more stoic expression, eyes down... but Veronica saw a slight smile playing at his lips.

"Get yourself over to one of those white ladies, right now and get yourself registered," the sergeant yelled, grabbing the boy by the arm, and shoving him toward their tables.

The boy walked over with much more ease and grace than should be expected in such circumstances and came to stand just in front of Missy. Up close, he had a very handsome face with a straight nose and wide-set, dark eyes. His lips were full but not to the extreme.

"I think I am supposed to register with you now," the boy said. Rather than looking down, the boy looked directly at Missy and smiled. Missy blushed.

"Okay, ummmm, what's your name?" Missy asked, turning to her typewriter.

"Caio. Caio Silva," he replied, sitting down.

"Do you have a middle name?"

"L."

"Does L stand for anything?" Missy ended the question with a little giggle and hair flip.

"No, just L."

Missy laughed and flipped her hair again. Veronica put her hand over her mouth to suppress a smile, but she didn't have any more time to watch what was happening with Missy, as her next recruit of the day approached. From that point on she had her hands full with the recruits who came through her. After a few hours of processing, Veronica's hands had stopped complaining and started screaming.

At around 11:30 a.m., she raised her hand to take a short break to go to the washroom. She didn't really need to use the restroom, but she did need to take a couple of aspirin for her hands. After she had taken the tablets, she held her hands in water as hot as she could stand for as long as she could bear it. After that, she wiped them gently with the towel on the wall and hurried out of the door—and ran straight into two young men standing in the hallway.

"Excuse me, ma'am!" exclaimed one of them. He was a young colored man and his facial expression was almost comically horrified.

The other was the boy Caio that Missy had processed earlier. Both were dressed in only undershirt and underwear. Veronica could feel her face beginning to burn. She had never seen a man in underwear, apart from her brother.

"This is George," Caio said. "He was just looking for the restroom."

"Oh, it's right there," Veronica said, pointing to the men's room, just behind her.

"No, ma'am. I am looking for the colored restroom," George said. "You have those here, right?"

Veronica nodded.

"Do you know where the nearest one is?" Caio asked her.

"I don't... I don't know," Veronica said, shaking her head.

"Don't worry yourself, ma'am," said George. He looked as uncomfortable as she felt.

"I can't go in the white man's bathroom," George said to Caio.

Before she could stop herself, Veronica blurted out, "Maybe you can go to the white woman's bathroom." She giggled. This wasn't funny and she knew it, but this whole situation felt unreal.

"I doubt white women would appreciate that," George said.

"I don't care what bathroom someone goes in, as long as they wash their hands afterward," Veronica said.

George and Caio stared at her for a moment, and then laughed out loud.

"That is very sensible of you, ma'am," George said. "I wish you were in charge."

Veronica smiled, waved at them, and then turned and ran back to her desk.

Have I just flirted with those boys? That just wouldn't do.

Still, they thought she was funny, and she had a little smile on her face when she sat down. She took off her shoes and settled at the typewriter.

Veronica's hands gave her a break for the next two hours. So much so, that when Mrs. Cartwright called for lunch break, she realized that she hadn't had any pain at all in hours.

As Veronica was putting on her shoes, Missy leaned over.

"Did you see where he went?" she asked.

"Who?"

"The boy named Caio," Missy whispered.

"Why are we whispering?" Veronica replied, in a softer whisper.

"Because he was handsome, wasn't he?" Missy said, biting her lip and giving a little shiver.

"Yes, but it was strange that he was standing with the colored boys,' Veronica whispered back.

"I know. I mean it was obvious that he wasn't," Missy said. "He said he was from Brazil. That's in South America, not Africa. So he is American."

Veronica laughed.

"But people would tease me if I said anything because they would have seen him go into the colored line. I mean, he clearly isn't colored. He looks almost Italian."

"How do you know what an Italian looks like?" Veronica asked.

"Hugh's family has Italian ancestors," Missy said.

Hugh's face popped into Veronica's mind... all white-blond hair and milk-pale skin and she laughed out loud.

"Hugh's last name is McBrayer, and he's about as Italian as I am." Veronica giggled. "He even gave you a Claddagh ring. You don't get much more Irish than that."

"He's Irish on his dad's side, silly," Missy said, but she was smiling. "He's Italian on his mother's side."

As far as Veronica was concerned, Hugh's pale, dark-haired mother looked no more Italian than his father did, but she thought it was time to let this go.

"Are you meeting Hugh for lunch?" she asked.

Missy nodded.

"I'm meeting him at the soda shop. You should get Lizzie and come," Missy said. "But don't say anything about that boy Caio."

"Not a word," Veronica said, pulling her finger across her mouth.

"He was really handsome, wasn't he?" Missy whispered, picking up her coat and purse.

"Yes, he was," Veronica replied softly, realizing with a shock that she had noticed it herself.

Before she had seen Missy blush while talking to Caio, she had never considered whether such a person could be attractive to her. The truth was that she rarely considered any man attractive. Her only real experience with men had been her family. Her brother, who was the most decent person she had ever known, was taunted and bullied for his differences from "normal" men. The only "normal" man she had known well was her father.

And he had taught her that having a man in your life was not worth the pain.

Chapter Two

Two Scoops of Stupid

As Veronica made her way up Main Street, she looked at her hands. Her hands used to be pretty, but they weren't anymore. Her knuckles were swollen, and she had little cuts all up and down her fingers. Some of them were oozing.

This is what came of working long hours packing cigarettes into boxes at the factory. The repetitive motion of it made her fingers ache, and the cellophane wrappers cut the skin on her fingers and palms if she wasn't careful. Still, she couldn't complain. She worked ten hours a day for five days a week, but she brought home twenty-four dollars a week, and the factory provided them with a house for as long as they worked there. Veronica knew that some factory workers lived in bad conditions, but the cigarette company was one of the good ones. They even gave away free cigarettes in the break room.

As Veronica had been looking at her hands, she didn't see the shockingly beautiful stranger until she was almost upon her. The woman was standing next to a parked car, wearing a simple black dress that accentuated her white-blonde hair. Her face was heart-shaped and her skin as pale as cream, but it wasn't her beauty that was striking, it was simply her presence. She looked like a movie star trying to mingle with the masses. Veronica would have been happy to stare at this woman for hours, just to watch her move. She wasn't attracted to her, per se, but she was riveted. At least she was riveted until the woman's companion stepped out of the car. He was a tall, dark-skinned man wearing a top hat with a playing card inserted into its maroon band. He had dark trousers, but they were overshadowed by something on the man's groin that looked like a codpiece from the Middle Ages. As the man approached her, the woman smiled at him. That smile conveyed so much emotion that it was both hard to look at and hard to look away.

Veronica glanced around and saw that she was not the only one who had been stopped by this couple. Several other people on the street were staring, but the woman and man took no notice.

They should be careful here, Veronica thought to herself, and she pulled her eyes away and continued up Main Street toward Woolworths.

"She's sooo beautiful," Veronica heard a girl tell the boy standing with her. "I bet she's a movie star."

"Then she's a beautiful, crazy movie star," the boy replied.

The girl glared at him and hit him on the shoulder.

"What?" the boy replied, rubbing his arm. "She's talking to herself."

Veronica faltered in her step for a moment. She looked back and, sure enough, the beautiful woman was alone, but talking—as if to someone else. Veronica shook her head.

This hadn't happened in a long time. In fact, the last time it happened was at her Grandma Janie's funeral, when Veronica was thirteen. She had snuck out of the service, only to find her grandmother waiting for her out on the church lawn. She had held her arms out and Veronica had run to her, throwing herself into her grandmother's all-too-real-feeling embrace.

"They said you were dead, Grandma," she had said.

"I am, child," Janie had said.

"Then why can I see you, why can I feel you?" Veronica had asked.

"Remember you are Furiae,"

"The fire gods?" she had asked, and her grandmother had nodded.

"You will see ghosts that have fire in them... like me."

"Come walk with me awhile before the adults come out," her grandma had said. She had walked and talked with her grandmother for hours. The sun had been almost setting when she had returned to the church to find her mother and the other adults in a panic over her disappearance. When her mother had asked where she had been, Veronica had told her softly that she had been walking with Grandma.

She had been unprepared when her mother slapped her across the face, but she hadn't cried. Veronica had never cried—or at least, not since she had been old enough to remember.

"Never talk like that—never," her mother had hissed.

The pastor had hurried over and taken her mother aside, while his wife came to comfort Veronica. Veronica remembered that the look on her mother's face had not been anger but fear.

Lizzie's voice shocked Veronica out of her reverie.

"Ronnie!" Lizzie was standing in the door of the Woolworths. "Hurry up, Ben is holding us some seats!"

Veronica glanced back once more. Now both the beautiful woman and the exotic man were gone.

*

Veronica ran to the entrance and both girls made their way through the crowd of people that was beginning to gather. The lunch counter at the Woolworths, commonly referred to as the "soda shop," was a long counter on one side of the store with stools where they served food and ice cream. It was popular enough during the work week. The food was good and relatively cheap. As a result, it was hard enough to get a seat for lunch during the week, but damn near impossible on the weekend.

Sure enough, Ben was sitting on a stool, with his coat draped across two other stools. Veronica and Lizzie pushed through the crowd, making apologies as they went. They hung their coats on the hanger at the end of the counter and ran over to Ben. Lizzie gave him a hug and a quick peck on the cheek.

"Whoa, it's about time," Ben said. "I was sure that I was about to be eaten alive by these cannibals."

He waved his arm around him.

"You're so dramatic," Lizzie said, laughing, as she sat down on the stool and put her purse in her lap.

Veronica sat down beside Lizzie. On the other side of her was an old man who she recognized as working as a janitor at the hospital.

She looked at the menu. The cheapest thing that she could get was a cheese or ham sandwich, which was thirty cents. She didn't like taking Ben's money, even though he had a good job working in his father's firm. Ben's family weren't rich but they had a lot more than Veronica's family had ever had. Ben's parents were second generation Scottish immigrants, and his father was a respected local accountant.

"So, what's your fancy?" Ben asked her.

"I'm getting a chicken salad sandwich," Lizzie said. Ben winced dramatically. "AND a banana split."

"You are going to ruin me," Ben said, putting his hand to his forehead.

"Listen, I don't need anything—" Veronica began, but Ben interrupted her.

"You might as well order," he said. "If you don't, then Lizzie will just order more, and we don't want her to end up fat."

Lizzie hit him.

"Just get me a cheese sandwich," Veronica said.

"And a chocolate milkshake," Lizzie said.

Ben nodded and raised his hand for the waitress.

"Ben told me that he made a reservation at the Grill on Main Street," Lizzie whispered to her.

"The super-expensive place?" Veronica asked.

Lizzie nodded. "Do you think he might be planning to ask me?" she asked in a whisper.

"It would be about time," Veronica replied.

"Ben Morton, you lucky so-and-so," a deep voice boomed. Veronica turned to see that the owner of the voice was Tommy Sawika. He was tall, and dark haired, with the clearest green eyes Veronica had ever seen. He was also a bully, inclined to torture anyone he viewed as weak or inferior. His father was the manager of the cigarette factory where Veronica and her mother worked, and he was constantly reminding her of that fact. He was the second-to-last person Veronica ever wanted to see.

"Did ya'll hear about the cat this morning?" Tommy asked. "My dad said that its eyes were popped out of its head. He said sometimes when they are choking, they—"

"Ugh," Lizzie said, scrunching up her face. "Tommy, we would rather not hear about that just before we are going to eat."

"Oh, right. The girls don't have the stomach for it," he said, laughing. He then turned to the old man sitting on the other side of Veronica.

"Hey there, old man. I think you got somewhere else to be," Tommy said, his voice softer but infinitely more menacing.

The man, who was probably 60 years old, moved away without a word. Tommy put one hand on the stool and raised the other.

"CJ, look who I found," he called out, loud enough for everyone in Woolworths to hear.

Veronica groaned inwardly. That would be CJ Bishop, son of the police chief. He was the last person she wanted to see. He was an average-looking guy of average height and bland brown hair, but what he lacked in appearance he made up for in cleverness. Like Tommy, he was also a jerk, but a subtle one. He had been harboring a crush on Veronica since high school.

"So, Ronnie, how's dad been treating you down at the factory?" Tommy asked, putting his arm around her.

"Fine," Veronica said, removing his arm from around her shoulder as if it were a poisonous snake.

When CJ walked up, Tommy stood and gestured for CJ to take his seat. This was going to be a glorious lunch. Tommy moved to take the seat of the boy sitting next to Ben.

"Don't let Tommy bother you, Ronnie," CJ said quietly, smiling and shrugging. "He doesn't understand that some of the things he says can sound offensive."

"Of course," Veronica said, as the man behind the lunch counter handed her a small plate holding her cheese sandwich.

"Excuse me, sir," CJ said, raising his hand to the man. "Could I get a ham and cheese sandwich and two slices of apple pie?"

"Excuse me, did you say two slices?" the man asked.

"Yes, that's what I said," CJ said, his words clipped.

"You must be awfully hungry," Veronica said, forgetting that it was always a bad idea to talk to CJ.

His eyes gleamed as he smiled at her.

"I *am* very hungry," he replied, "and if I get full, I am sure there is someone else here who wouldn't mind a piece of pie."

"Nice of you to think of Tommy," Veronica said quickly. CJ blinked quickly with his mouth open for just a moment, before returning his face to its usual bland calm housing dead-looking eyes.

"So about the cats they found," Tommy called across to Veronica.

"Don't be a buffoon," CJ snapped, as the lunch man brought him his plate. "I don't think Lizzie wants to hear about murdered cats."

"Normally I wouldn't, but there have been so many," Veronica said. "I would think someone would have been found by now."

"Well, the colored folk always stand up for each other, and so it's hard to get information out of them." CJ picked up his sandwich and taking a large bite.

"Why do you think it's them?" Veronica asked.

"Who else would do something like that?" CJ asked. Before she could respond, he turned to Ben. "Are you coming to the meeting tonight?"

"Oh, um, I thought it was by invitation," Ben stammered.

"It is, and I am inviting you," CJ said, with a regal sort of head bow. Veronica felt the urge to vomit up her sandwich. "Of course, you can bring Elizabeth as well. A lot of girls are coming."

"Great!" Ben said. "I'd love to go and I'm sure Lizzie would be happy to come along."

Lizzie shot Ben a look of both surprise and annoyance, before she realized it and quickly composed her face.

"What about you, Ronnie?" CJ asked. "Would you like to come?"

"Sorry, I need to get home early tonight," Veronica replied quickly.

"Listen, if you go out with him, I bet he'll buy you a nice dinner." Tommy gave her an exaggerated wink.

"I can get a nice dinner at home," Veronica replied, taking the last bite of her sandwich, and a sip of her milkshake.

"Sure, right," said Tommy, rolling his eyes.

"What does that mean?" Lizzie asked, but Ben jabbed her in the side.

"It means that Veronica's family doesn't have the money for the sort of dinners we have, right?" Tommy replied with a shrug.

"Most of us don't have the money for the kind of dinners your family has," Lizzie replied.

"Yes, but Ronnie here had a deadbeat for a dad and an idiot brother to look after," Tommy said.

CJ patted Veronica's hand, but she jerked it away.

"My brother is not an idiot," Veronica snapped.

"Your br-br-brother ca-ca-ca-can't t-t-t-talk," Tommy said, then laughed. "What is that, if it isn't an idiot?"

"It's a stutter and it has nothing to do with intelligence. Just like lacking a stutter clearly doesn't prove it."

Veronica stood up, put her purse on her shoulder and smoothed down her skirt.

"Thanks for the lunch, Ben. I'm going to head back to work now," she said as she grabbed her jacket from the coatrack.

"Hey, Ronnie, don't go," Lizzie called, but she had not moved from her seat.

"Ben, make sure that Lizzie gets back in time. She can't be late, or Mrs. Cartwright will eat her alive," Veronica called back, glaring at him.

Ben nodded, face tight and smiling like he had something stuck in his throat.

*

Once she got outside, Veronica walked far enough down the street to be out of sight of the Woolworths window before she stopped and let out a long breath. She probably should be grateful to Tommy because he gave her an excuse to leave before she had to say no to CJ. CJ had rarely approached her in any open manner, and she was worried that offending him might somehow come back on her or her family. The Bishops were very close to the Sawikas, and therefore any slight to CJ could have ramifications on the elder Sawika's treatment of her mother or herself.

She was lost in these thoughts when she glanced across the street and saw the beautiful woman she had seen before. She was with the darker-skinned man again and, this time, she was kissing him. She was kissing a colored man right in public, and the kisses weren't platonic. As Veronica stared, she saw the woman's white hair lift as if in the wind, but there was no wind. She was staring and she suspected that being seen staring would be unwise, but she couldn't help it. They looked so beautiful together. Beautiful and wild.

A group of colored men were congregated just in front of her, but none of them were looking at the couple on the other side of the street. Surely, they would be staring if they could see what she saw.

"Ronnie!"

Veronica turned to see Tommy running her way. When she turned back, the man and woman were gone. She turned and began walking quickly down the street toward the school.

"Hey Ronnie," Tommy said, coming up next to her and taking her arm. "CJ thought I might have upset you."

"That was perceptive of him," Veronica said coldly.

"Yeah, he is—wait, are you making fun of me?" Tommy said, voice turning stormy.

"No," Veronica said. This was true. Strictly, she was making fun of CJ.

"Oh, okay," Tommy said, smiling again. "So CJ was mad at me, but he is always trying to be nice to you and you are always freezing him out."

"I have to go, Tommy," Veronica said, turning to walk away. Tommy grabbed her by the hand. When she jerked it away, he grabbed it again.

"Don't turn away when I am talking to you," he growled.

"Sir, I don't think the lady wants you to touch her," came a voice from behind Tommy, where the group of young colored men were standing.

"Excuse me, what did you say?" Tommy said, eyebrows raised.

With a mix of horror and dread, Veronica saw that the speaker was none other than George, the boy she had met earlier at the gym.

"I said I don't think the lady wants you to touch her," George said. He was still standing in the road, but he had moved close to the sidewalk.

For a colored man to talk to a white man without first being addressed might be normal up north, but it was *not* normal here. For a colored man to admonish a white man... well, it was unthinkable. Veronica found herself frozen in place, staring at George. He couldn't have been more than nineteen. He wasn't much taller than Veronica and had fairly dark skin, and large, liquid, dark eyes. Like

Veronica, the other men around him had also frozen in place. For a moment, no one seemed to breathe. And then Tommy laughed out loud.

"Well, you're uppity, aren't you?" Tommy asked.

Veronica noticed that a few of the colored boys seemed to relax and go back to their conversations. Those boys were strangers here. Anyone who lived here knew that Tommy Sawika's laugh wasn't an expression of mirth—at least not a mirth that mentally stable people would understand.

Caio, the young Brazilian man that Missy had registered earlier, was walking up the street toward them.

"Where are you from, boy?" Tommy whooped. "Because I know you ain't from here?"

"Hey y'all, come see this uppity bastard," Tommy called to CJ, Lizzie, and Ben, who were heading down the street toward them. Missy and Hugh were now with them. Caio had arrived and was standing close to George.

When Missy saw Caio, she flushed slightly. If Hugh had been more attentive to her, this might have caused a problem, but his attention was focused on what was unfolding in front of them.

"Boy, let me explain something to you," Tommy said, moving closer to the colored boy.

"George," the boy said.

"What?" Tommy snapped.

"My name is George, not 'boy'," he said.

Veronica steeled herself for an outburst, but Tommy just laughed again.

"Okay, GEORGE," Tommy said as he stepped forward again. Veronica could not see the expression on his face, but George stepped backward.

"See, here in North Carolina, y'all don't interrupt when a white man is having a conversation with a white lady," Tommy said. His voice had become softer and infinitely more menacing.

"How about interrupting a pest who's annoying a lady?" asked Caio. He gently positioned himself between George and Tommy.

"You calling me a pest?" Tommy snarled.

"Are you annoying the lady? If so, that makes you a pest," Caio replied.

The words were barely out of his mouth when Tommy punched him in the face and blood sprayed as Caio fell to the ground.

The other colored men started backing away as more white people began to gather around them.

Caio was sitting on the ground, wiping his nose with his hand. He muttered something under his breath.

"What did you say to me?" Tommy snarled.

"I said that we should probably stay out of your way," Caio said calmly, as he stood up. His nose was dripping blood but his eyes were calm and cold.

"I got my eyes on you," Tommy said, shoving Caio to the ground again.

Veronica expected Caio to fight but he just shook his head.

"Do you feel better now?" Caio asked, looking up at Tommy with a strange smile. "Did that make you feel better about your—well, about yourself?"

Tommy advance toward him but as Caio stood, he grabbed Tommy's hand and did something that caused Tommy to jump and yelp.

"Sorry about that, I slipped," Caio said flatly, but Tommy suddenly backed away from him.

"Get away from me."

Missy stepped forward.

"Come on, Tommy," Missy said. "You have to get back to the factory to see your dad, and you don't want to show up all messed up."

"You saying this-this-boy could take me?" Tommy replied, advancing on Missy. Missy backed up but Caio moved forward, stepping onto the sidewalk. CJ stepped between Tommy and Missy.

"Missy's right, Big T," said CJ. "That piece of trash ain't worth the trouble."

Tommy turned and snarled at Caio, who just continued smiling at him—well, his lips smiled. His eyes were not smiling. They looked cold, flat, and dead.

"Killer eyes"—that's what Grandma Janie would have said.

Veronica turned to walk away, but Tommy grabbed her hand before she could go. His hand was wet in hers.

"Think about coming tonight," he said, with a wink. This expression was made all the more grotesque by the fact that there was blood on his shirt. In fact, the wetness on Tommy's hand was probably Caio's blood.

She jerked it away.

"I'll think about it," she said, before turning and walking away.

Veronica looked at her hands, and sure enough, there were traces of blood on them. She didn't have anything to wipe them with, so she would have to wait until she got to the restroom at the gym. In her imagination, she saw the blood on her hands seeping into the ever-present cuts in her fingers.

But that was probably just her imagination.

Chapter Three

Fire and Hunger

Veronica's fingers were throbbing as she walked home from the gym. The sun was setting, and the shadows of the trees were reaching their arms across the sidewalk where she walked. With no one around to judge her actions, she allowed herself to step over the shadows in her path. While she wouldn't call herself superstitious exactly, she didn't like to take chances when she could avoid them with so little effort.

The air was getting colder and with each step the cold sank into her bones making her hands hurt even more. Veronica's walk back home from the gym had been quieter than usual because Lizzie had left with Ben to go to the meeting of the Knights of Harrisville. In truth, these people were basically the Ku Klux Klan in their beliefs and ideologies. They believed that whites were better, immigrants were evil, and men were the masters of their households. The difference was that Klan members were largely lower-class white men, often farmers and factory workers. The Knights of Harrisville had based themselves on the Knights of White Camelia, and their membership mainly consisted of upper-class white people.

Veronica knew that Lizzie had zero interest in going but she would do whatever she needed to do to keep Ben happy. Ben was her ticket to a better life, and, despite their play fights, she deferred to him on most big issues. It wasn't that Lizzie didn't love Ben, she probably did, it was just that love couldn't be the primary motivator for marriage... at least not for people like her and Lizzie. Marriage was a more practical matter. The only way out of the marriage noose for a woman was to get enough education to get a job. This was why Veronica was working a full-time job and taking jobs over the weekend. She was trying to save whatever pennies she could so that she could afford to take an accounting class at the local college. She loved numbers, books, budgets, and everything math. These things were concrete and reliable, unlike people.

As she approached her house, she felt that mixture of nostalgia and pride that she always felt. Their house was small, but they kept it clean and tidy. It wasn't until she saw Franklin sitting on one of the metal chairs on their small porch that her heart sank. Franklin had his face in his hands, but even she could see that his shirt was torn. She picked up her pace.

"Franklin," she said as she trotted up their gravel driveway.

Franklin looked up and, sure enough, there was a bruise forming on his left cheek and his right eye was swollen. There was dirt in his dark hair.

"What happened?" Veronica asked, as she came to sit next to him on the porch.

Franklin shrugged.

"I made the mistake of being alive today," he mouthed to her. Franklin's stutter only affected his actual speech. He could have a completely fluent conversation if speaking to someone who could lip-read.

"Who did this?" Veronica asked, taking his hand.

"John Bilbo," Franklin mouthed. "And a couple of other Klan goons. They jumped me on the way home. But a couple of them look much worse than me."

Franklin gave her a little smile.

She could believe it. Her brother was six foot three and all muscle. What he lacked in communication skills he made up for in physical intelligence. There wasn't one sport that he didn't excel at, there was no race he couldn't win, no machine he couldn't fix, no animal he couldn't tame. This was why he was so valuable working at the pig farm. Of course, he often smelled like pigs, but you got used to it after a while.

"Aren't you going to the firehouse tonight?" Veronica asked.

Franklin nodded.

"Then you better get cleaned up," she said, standing and pulling him up.

"Okay, okay," Franklin mouthed.

"Nan works there, doesn't she?" Veronica asked.

"Nan is way too good for the likes of me."

"No one is too good for you," Veronica said, as they entered their small house through the back door. They never used the front door. No one did.

"Go get a shower and I will make you some eggs real quick," Veronica said.

"But we don't have enough—" Franklin said, but Veronica swatted him on the arm, and he left with a sigh and a grin.

He was going to say that they didn't have enough eggs for all of them to have dinner and then breakfast, but Veronica already knew that. She was the one that collected eggs in the morning. They had six birds at the moment, so that meant six eggs a day at best, but this time of year wasn't the best. It was still spring, so although their hens were laying more regularly now that the days were longer, they didn't always get eggs from all of them every day. In the winter, they kept a light bulb in the hen house, but in spring they turned it off to save costs. This morning, they only had four eggs, and one left over from yesterday. Her mother had already gone to work, and wouldn't be back until ten tonight, so she wouldn't eat.

Veronica pulled a cast iron pan from the small cabinet and added some oil to it. She cracked four eggs into the pan for Franklin. Her stomach growled at the sight of them, but she took a deep breath and forced it to be still. She wondered what it was like for people who were never hungry. Of course, there were people a lot worse off than she was, but that gnawing in the pit of her stomach was way too frequent for her liking.

When Franklin came back into the kitchen, his hair was still wet, but his face looked much better. Her brother had dark hair, clear, tanned skin, and blue eyes with naturally thicker and blacker lashes than any girl Veronica knew. If Franklin had been a normal speaker, he would have had to beat the girls off with a stick. As it was, most of them just looked away whenever they saw him. Nan Payne was different. Her father was the local doctor, and she was always very kind to Franklin. Of course, Nan was very kind to everyone, but at least that meant that there was one other person at the fire department who Franklin could "speak" with.

"How many eggs is this?" Franklin asked, staring at the plate.

"Three," Veronica lied.

"Liar."

"Just eat," she said.

She tidied the kitchen as Franklin finished his eggs. As usual, she made a point of not looking at the rust-colored stains on the ceiling, the ones she could never get out, no matter how hard she tried.

She suspected that the cause of those stains might also have been the root cause of Franklin's stutter, or at least the reason it was so bad.

Veronica pushed these thoughts from her mind, before anger took hold.

*

Franklin gave her a hug and a kiss before he left. For a moment, she felt the urge to run after him and tell him to be careful, but he understood the dangers of being who he was much more viscerally than she did.

With Franklin gone and her mother not due to be back for another three hours, Veronica went to the living area and arranged some paper and kindling in the fireplace. She could have used this time to get a shower, but she was uncomfortable showering with no one in the house. Having a shower was supposed to be a luxury that was provided by these houses, but Veronica hated them. In a shower, she couldn't hear what was going on in the rest of the house. Someone could enter and she wouldn't know until they were almost upon her.

Her mind, unfettered by activity requiring immediate attention, wandered back to what had happened in the soda shop. When Tommy had made fun of Franklin's speech, she had actively wanted to kill him. Even now, she would do it if she thought she could get away with it. He was a person who took the benefits that life or fate had awarded him and gave nothing back. Franklin, on the other hand, gave to people. He had been protecting her since he was small, and the truth of the matter was that just being his sister gave her protection. Despite his stuttering, or maybe because of it, he had learned to fight at a young age, in both the metaphoric and literal sense. He was tall and strong and unafraid in a fight. None of the men in town would ever have the guts to take him on in a one-on-one fight—at least, not since he was about thirteen. That's why his injuries always came from being jumped by a group.

For as physically tough as he was, he was unusually sensitive to the feelings of others. When Veronica was fourteen, Franklin had been the one to wash her hair after John Bilbo blew snot in it. Then he sat next to her, as she lay on her bed fighting back tears. He didn't try to get her to talk about it, and he never brought it up again. He simply made a point of staying a bit closer to her during lunches and breaks at school. Franklin was the probably only reason that she had any faith in men left.

The one good piece of news this evening was that Franklin would be able to spend some time with Nan Payne at the firehouse. He had been sweet on her since grade school but had never thought he was good enough. Veronica suspected that Nan was sweet on him as well, but she was too shy to talk to him. So, if they were put in close proximity to each other, Franklin might try. She smiled to herself as she pushed a few more wads of paper in between kindling.

Once the paper and kindling were set, she reached for a match but stopped. Instead of lighting it, she went and sat down on the sofa. She was alone now, but she didn't feel lonely. The house, particularly this room, would always remind her of her Grandma Janie. In fact, she had been sitting right here on this couch when Janie had taught her how to light a fire.

Veronica had been about seven when Janie took her to sit on the couch. She had then put paper and kindling in the fireplace. Then she came to sit next to Veronica.

"Aren't you going to light it?" Veronica had asked.

"Of course," Janie had said.

"Well, you'll need a match."

"I don't need no stinking match," Janie had scoffed. Then she had turned her gaze to the fireplace. For a moment, the air between them rippled and Veronica felt a wave of warmth surround her... then the paper was ablaze.

"Go put some more wood on it."

"I'm scared to... what if I catch fire?" she had asked, but Janie had laughed. "Child, you got no more reason to be scared of me than I have to be scared of you."

"What do you mean?" Veronica got the logs and threw them on the fire. Some of the flames were blown out. "Oh no, the fire went out."

"Don't you worry, little Ronnie. You just come and sit by me."

Veronica had cuddled up next to her. She could still remember how warm her grandma's skin had felt.

"Watch," Janie had said, turning her eyes to the fire.

In a second, the fire in the hearth blazed again, casting out the shadows in the corners and bathing Janie's fierce face in orange glow. The flames quickly receded, but all the wood had now caught. Janie smiled at her.

"Now you try." She kissed Veronica's cheek.

"I don't know how," she had whispered.

"It isn't a knowing, child. It is a doing. You don't know how to breathe, but your lungs do. You don't know how to pump blood, but your heart does. You don't have to know. You just bring the flame."

"Do I do it with my heart?" She had expected Janie to laugh at her, but she just smiled.

"It resides in different places in all of us. Just look at the flame and see what you can find inside yourself."

Veronica could still remember staring at the fire and how she had turned her attention inward. At first, she had found nothing. It had not been in her head or her heart or even her stomach. She remembered looking up at Janie who had been staring down at her. It was then that she had felt it. She had felt it in her throat, and it felt like beauty and love. At that moment, the flames in front of her roared again.

Grandma had laughed and clapped her hands.

"Well done, Ronnie. Well done," she had said, giving her a big squeeze.

"How can we do that? Can everyone do it?"

"No, dear, not everyone, only the Furies."

"What are Furies?"

"Furies are what we are," her grandmother had said, beginning to rock her in her arms.

"I thought we were part Indian," Veronica had replied. Her grandmother had regularly told her that her own grandfather had been Cherokee Indian and had taken the name of the county that they were in, Hall, as his last name. Janie's tanned skin and sharp features attested to this, but Janie's bright blue eyes had come from her Celtic ancestors. Veronica had often wished that she had inherited Janie's tan skin and bright eyes.

Janie had laughed and pulled her close.

"Furies means 'dark' in the old language but our people, my mama's people in Scotland, were warriors against the dark. Taking the name given to shadow things takes their power from them. We don't fear them. We are forged by fire, and we bring light to dark places."

"So we are fighters?" Veronica had asked, but softer now. Her grandmother's voice had always hypnotized her.

"Yes, and we are the descendants of fire gods," Janie had said. "I will say this to you only once, and you must never repeat it to anyone. They have tried to drown our kind one too many times, and you need to keep yourself safe. The silly Romans tried to turn us into demons who seek retribution for sins… probably because the only time they saw us use our abilities was when we were defending ourselves. But should you ever be threatened, or if your loved ones are ever threatened, remember that the flames that kill others are your friends. Don't hesitate to call them if you are scared, no matter who makes you scared."

In that moment, Veronica had understood that calling the flames was simple. You simply had to love them and the part inside you that contained them.

Now, sitting in a cold, dark house, Veronica closed her eyes and reached out to the beauty of the flames inside of her… and she felt a pleasurable shimmer run down her spine.

When she opened her eyes, the fire in the hearth was blazing.

Chapter Four

Shadows Get Faces

Lizzie was knocking at Veronica's back door before she was even dressed. Franklin and her mother were still asleep.

"Ronnie, you ready?" Lizzie called, opening the screen door.

"Yeah, I'm coming," Veronica said, hopping down the hall on one foot as she put a low-heeled shoe on the other.

"I have two hard-boiled eggs and a roll for you," Lizzie said, holding out a paper bag. "You can eat as we walk. We don't want to be late today."

Veronica took the proffered bag with no complaint, grabbed her coat, and followed Lizzie down the driveway. She hadn't even had time to check the chickens.

"It's too early for any decent Christian woman to be up on a Sunday," Lizzie snorted. As Lizzie was a good three inches taller than her, her strides were much longer and when she walked briskly, Veronica had to trot to keep up.

"It's only six forty-five, we don't have to be there until seven-thirty," Veronica said, as she began peeling an egg.

"Yes, but we'll be processing the colored men again today, and they get there early," Lizzie said.

"So that doesn't mean we have to do the same," Veronica replied, with a mouth full of egg.

"I know, but I want to get there before them because I don't like the way they stare at me," Lizzie said.

Veronica used eating as an excuse not to respond. Personally, she had no memory of any colored man ever even looking at her. Most of the time, they kept their gaze down in the presence of white women. Well, there was yesterday, when she spoke with the colored man. George... and Caio. And then later, well,

George had stood up for her, and Caio had been punched in the face for it. Lizzie put her arm through Veronica's.

"I'm sorry about what happened yesterday," Lizzie said.

"I hate it when they talk about Franklin like that," Veronica muttered.

"Oh, yes, that. Of course, that too, but I was thinking about how that colored man started harassing you," Lizzie said.

"What?" Veronica said.

"Tommy told us last night at the meeting," Lizzie said. "He said that the colored boy started trying to talk to you, actually talk to you. It was a good thing Tommy was there to help you. What did he say? Were you scared?"

"Lizzie, no one talked to me but Tommy," Veronica said. "Tommy was getting pushy with me about CJ. I was trying to leave, and he wouldn't let me. Geo—I mean, the colored boy asked Tommy to leave me alone."

"He didn't! He actually spoke that way to a white man?" Lizzie gasped. "That explains why Tommy hit him."

Lizzie was clearly confusing some facts and ignoring the rest, but before she could correct her, they turned the corner, and the high school gym came into view. On the street in front of it, a dozen or so colored men were waiting. Most of them were talking to each other, a few were smoking, but there was one who was sitting apart from the rest of them.

"Oh no, they are already here," Lizzie whispered, grabbing Veronica's arm. "I hope the guards are here. Maybe we shouldn't have come so early…"

Lizzie continued her rant, but Veronica's attention was drawn to the man who was sitting alone. He was sitting on his field pack, his legs spread, elbow on his knee and face in his palm. The man was staring at the ground, brow furrowed and eyes hooded. His body stance surely spoke volumes, but it spoke in a language Veronica didn't know. Someone called to him, and he stood up, smiled, and walked over to the group. His smile was warm and open.

"Thank goodness, it's Mrs. Cartwright," Lizzie said, grabbing Veronica's arm again and pulling her across the street.

When they entered the gymnasium, half of the girls were already there, and half of those had apparently heard Tommy's version of the events of yesterday as they crowded around her and pelted her with questions, all voiced in a tone of whispery dread.

"Did that colored boy talk to you yesterday?"

"What did he say?"

"Did he get close to you?"

"He didn't touch you, did he?"

"You're so lucky Tommy was there."

Veronica couldn't answer one question before another was asked. She had known most of these girls since she was in grade school, but now they were looking at her as if she had encountered a space alien.

"It wasn't really like that," she began, before noticing that Missy was in the crowd and strangely silent.

"Missy was there," Veronica said.

"Oh, I only came at the end, when Tommy hit Caio," Missy said.

"*CAIO?*" gasped Ann Vernon, a skinny, snaky girl that Veronica had never trusted. "You know a colored boy by his name?"

"Caio is not colored," Missy snapped back. "He is Brazilian, and I registered him yesterday… with the other WHITE men."

"So why did Tommy hit him then?" asked Ann.

"I heard that he was egging the other colored boy on," whispered someone else. Frustration, anger, and anxiety were doing a dance in Veronica's stomach, causing bile to rise in her throat. She was just about to speak when Mrs. Cartwright saved her.

"All right, ladies," she said, waving them away from Veronica. "I gather that Miss Crane must have escaped from the very jaws of death, by the way you are talking. But she seems very alive to me, so can we please start our day—with a little less drama."

She motioned sharply and they all organized themselves into a line.

"If you registered the white men yesterday, you will register the colored boys today," she said. "If you registered colored boys yesterday, you will register the white men. The sides of the room are the same, so please find yourself a desk and get yourself set up."

Veronica headed to her desk privately sending Mrs. Cartwright a little blessing. If she had been forced to listen to those questions any longer, she might have said something that she would regret. She was furious that Tommy had twisted his boorish behavior into something heroic. She was even more furious at herself because she didn't try harder to correct his presentation of the facts. That was cowardly of her, particularly when the consequences of his actions were likely to fall hardest on those who were simply trying to help her.

*

Luckily, she didn't have too much time to castigate herself, because the recruits were immediately let in and Veronica became busy fast. Despite the constant flow of people, she did notice that the man she had seen sitting on the duffel bag out front was now standing in line with the others. He was chatting with the people around him and smiling more than she had ever seen a colored man smile. Most of the colored people she had encountered in her life had never even looked at her, let alone smiled.

Veronica was at the desk next to Missy again today, but Missy was unusually quiet. Normally, she was a talker and would make chitchat with anyone around her in between recruits or even while interviewing them. But today, she had only nodded at Veronica with a smile before starting her interviews. It was about mid-morning that Veronica noticed that Missy's wrist was swollen and bruised.

"Missy, what happened to your wrist?" Veronica heard herself ask, between recruits, about a half second before her brain had engaged. When she saw Missy wince, she immediately regretted her words.

"Oh, it's nothing. I just fell on it last night after the meeting," Missy lied.

It hurt to hear this lie. There was a time when she had needed to come up with the same sort of lies. She remembered how uncomfortable it was and how she hated the knowing looks—and the pity.

"You should be more careful," Veronica said. "Maybe those meetings aren't the safest place for you to be... seeing as how you are accident-prone."

Veronica's voice sounded harsh to her own ears, but at least she didn't sound pitying.

To Veronica's relief, Missy smiled.

"Yes, I am really clumsy sometimes," she said.

"Hello, I am supposed to register with you," said a voice. Veronica looked up to see the soldier who had been sitting on the duffel bag was right in front of her. His skin was honey colored but with an ashy undertone and his brows were thick but well arched. A Clark Gable-style mustache graced his upper lip and his eyes were a light brown that looked almost gold. He looked very different from most colored men that she had seen. She wasn't sure why... maybe it was the fact that he was actually looking at her.

"May I sit down?" he asked with a smile. Veronica nodded, realizing that she had been staring.

"Of course, of course." Veronica turned to her typewriter. "Your name?" she blurted out.

"Lazlo Fox," he said, sitting down. When he looked up, his eyes caught hers and they went wide. He quickly looked down. She saw that his eyes were moving rapidly, seeming to search the floor for something.

"Do you have a middle name?" she asked, looking at her form.

"No... just Lazlo Fox," he said, eyes still on the floor.

"Where were you born?" she asked, eyes back on her typewriter. Her heart had started pounding in her chest for no good reason.

"Savannah, Georgia," Lazlo replied, looking up at her again. When their eyes met, Veronica felt a rush of energy.

"Really? How did you come to be in North Carolina?" she asked quickly.

"I came here for work after I turned eighteen," he said.

"So your family is still in Georgia?" This question was NOT on the list of things she needed to ask and Missy shot her an odd look.

"Yes, but I'm over eighteen so I suppose I don't need their permission to enlist," he said.

"Oh, sorry, I didn't mean to suggest—"

"No, no, I'm sorry. I didn't mean it to sound that way," he said. "I'm just not used to… well, I've never done this before."

He laughed a bit and smiled. She felt her lips smiling in return.

Stop it. Stop it. STOP IT.

"I guess one doesn't enlist in the military every day," she said.

"Of course, I was talking about the military," he said. He was still smiling but it was a small smile.

"You weren't?" Veronica asked. "I mean, talking about the military?"

"Uhhmm, well, yeah, I guess, umm, I suppose…" he said, then he looked down again. He seemed to be breathing faster.

"Oh, okay," she replied. "So what is your birthday?"

His eyes were now back on her and his gaze was intense.

"April twenty-third," he replied quickly.

"What year?"

"1923."

"So, you're twenty-one. You look younger," Veronica said.

"People say that," Lazlo said. "I'm not sure if that's good or bad."

"I guess the older you are, the better that gets." Veronica blurted out.

Lazlo laughed out loud. It was short and soft, but it was out of place here. People around them turned and stared. Lazlo covered his mouth, but he was still smiling.

"You know how to tell the truth, don't you?" he said.

"Yes, that's a problem I have, or so my friends tell me," Veronica replied with a shrug.

"That ain't no problem, that's always best," Lazlo said, smiling at her.

She smiled back.

For a moment, they just sat there.

"Veronica, he needs to go and get his physical now!" Missy hissed, poking her.

"Oh, right. You go right through those screens and they will get you... I mean you will have to take off... I mean, you'll have your physical."

"Is this desk yours?" Lazlo asked suddenly.

"No, why?" she replied.

"It says Marianne on the file folder," he said, pointing to a piece of tape stuck to the inbox on her desk.

"Oh, no. My name's Veronica," she said.

Lazlo smiled at her.

"It was nice to meet you, Veronica," he said, standing up.

Veronica heard Missy actually gasp beside her. She felt like she was standing in the headlight of some fast train. She should move off the tracks and out of the way, but stupidly, she couldn't. She just kept sitting there, staring.

Lazlo backed away a few feet before turning to leave. His eyes caught hers again and something flared deep in the pit of Veronica's stomach.

Oh, no, this is not happening.

"Veronica, stop staring," Missy hissed. "People will notice."

"I'm not staring," Veronica said as much to herself as to Missy, before turning her eyes quickly to the next recruit approaching her.

*

Despite what Veronica had told Missy, and what she had told herself, it was hard for her not to look around for Lazlo as the day progressed. She couldn't see much behind the screen that was set up, and it wouldn't do to be caught staring at an area where men were getting undressed. She thought she heard him speaking a few times and was surprised that she might be able to recognize his voice from one conversation.

At lunch break, she avoided the soda shop, and treated herself with a cheap sandwich at a diner further up the road. She got it to go and ate it as she walked down Main Street. She told herself that she was just trying to avoid Tommy and CJ. She told herself that it was because it was cheaper than the soda shop. She also told herself that she wasn't looking for Lazlo, and yet her eyes scanned every group of colored men that she passed.

This is ridiculous, she thought to herself. *It's not like I don't have enough problems without befriending some negro man. I'm going to just eat my lunch, go back to the gym, register recruits, and get paid. I'm probably just hungry, and it's making me crazy.*

Veronica was almost at the end of the street when she felt eyes on her. She turned and saw that the beautiful blonde woman she had seen before was sitting on one of the benches in the park. Her dark-skinned beau was sitting next to her, with his arm around her. The woman's platinum hair was moving on its own again… dancing against the wind and caressing the skin of her companion. Strangely, they weren't looking at each other. Instead, they were looking at a man sitting at a picnic table a few feet from them. When Veronica followed their gaze, her heart stopped. The man they were staring at was Lazlo. Lazlo didn't seem to see them… but he saw her all right.

For a moment their eyes met, and he smiled, but then he looked down at his hands. He didn't seem to have lunch with him. She wondered if he had eaten recently. She wondered if he felt hungry as often as she did. For a moment, she considered taking him half her sandwich, but then her common sense kicked in. He wasn't even allowed to look at her. That was the unspoken but enforced rule. So many of the layers of separation, so many of the rules put in place, were to keep black men from having any contact at all with white women. As a result, colored people were never more than shadows in her life, passing around her but never affecting her.

Veronica realized that she had stopped and had been rooted in place for over a minute. She turned and hurried back toward the gym but before she reentered, she glanced over her shoulder. Lazlo was gone.

When Veronica got back to her desk, most of the girls were still at lunch, but Missy was there, eating a sandwich.

"You should be careful," Missy said softly, as Veronica sat down.

"What do you mean?" Veronica asked.

"You were talking way too much to that colored boy," Missy said.

Veronica felt panic well up. Accusations brought out too many memories for her.

"I was just registering him," Veronica replied curtly.

"No, you were talking to him… like… well, like he was a white boy," Missy said.

Veronica took out her sandwich and took a bite out of it. She was banking a wave of anger.

Why should anyone care who she talked to? She wasn't married. She wasn't even dating anyone.

"Don't get mad, Ronnie," Missy said softly. "I don't care who you talk to but there are some people that do. People that you don't want mad at you."

People that you don't want mad at you. Did that mean the son of the police chief or the son of the factory manager?

Missy rubbed her wrist.

"Did Hugh do that to you?" Veronica asked, nodding at Missy's wrist.

"I already told you—"

"A lie," Veronica finished the sentence for her. "I know that kind of lie too well not to recognize it." At first, Missy's eyes widened but then quickly welled with tears. Veronica felt her stomach drop. That had come out harsher than she intended.

"I'm sorry, Missy," Veronica said, rolling her chair over to Missy's desk. Missy's head was down, and she was sniffling. Veronica put her hand on her arm.

"He didn't mean to hurt me," Missy said. "He was mad at me for… for… for watching that boy, Caio. We were having an argument about it, and I got mad and tried to walk away and he grabbed my arm. He didn't realize how hard he grabbed it. And I shouldn't have been looking at that boy anyway."

"How could you not?" Veronica said. "Tommy punched him in the face. We were all staring."

"Yeah, but it was different," Missy said. "I thought he was handsome, and I think Hugh saw that. So it was my fault, really."

"It's not your fault, Missy," Veronica said as she patted her arm gently. She was trying as hard as she could to keep her anger from bleeding into her voice.

You shouldn't do things to make your father mad.

He slapped you because you were disrespecting him.

If your father has had a bad day, just try to stay away from him.

How many times had Veronica heard statements like this when she was younger? She had only felt safe when Grandma Janie was in the house, because her father had been terrified of her grandmother. The day that he disappeared was the day she began to have some hope for her future.

"Thanks Ronnie." Missy sniffed. "I only wanted to warn you about talking to that boy because… because… well…"

"I know, Missy," Veronica replied. "But you don't have to worry."

"Okay," Missy said, pulling a handkerchief from her purse and wiping her nose. "Well, they'll all be gone tomorrow anyway."

"That's true," Veronica replied, but her heart cramped painfully in her chest. It made the pain in her fingers feel like nothing.

She rolled back to her desk, and as she did so she was hit by the realization that Lazlo was probably finished with his physical and wouldn't be likely to come back into the gym. She felt something like panic crawl up from her belly to her heart and finally settle in her throat, making her feel like she was suffocating.

When lunch break was over, and the recruits returned, she was able to bury the panic feeling in activity.

Still, her eyes kept searching for him without conscious intent.

Chapter Five

The Sound of the Train

When the day ended, Veronica slowly collected all the remaining registrations into a neat little pile to give to Mrs. Cartwright. Despite looking for him, Veronica had not seen Lazlo again. She was afraid that he had finished his registration and had left for the day. Of course, it wasn't a huge problem, but she just would have liked to have seen him again before he left for war. The way she had reacted to him earlier was probably just because something about him reminded her of Franklin, maybe it was his calm demeanor or his earnest expression. It could also be a reactionary response to Tommy's behavior yesterday. In addition, she couldn't discount that the whole thing could just be lack of food. She hadn't eaten much in the last few days, and she knew that hunger could affect a person in a myriad of ways.

Her stomach growled audibly, as if to underscore that point.

Besides, Lazlo would be gone tomorrow, so it wouldn't be an issue anymore. On one hand, it was a relief not to have to worry about her reaction to some colored man. On the other hand, the day seemed duller than it had before.

"Veronica Crane," said Mrs. Cartwright. "You didn't pick up your pay."

Mrs. Cartwright handed her an envelope with her name on it.

"Thank you," Veronica said, handing her the stack of registrations.

"You did a good job," Mrs. Cartwright said. "You aren't as silly as some of the girls, so I will put in a good word for you if you want us to keep your record on file for further opportunities."

"Thank you, I would appreciate that," Veronica said. Mrs. Cartwright gave her a nod and a tight little smile.

"Good, then. You should go on home now," she said, as she turned her back. "The other girls couldn't wait to get their money and run."

Veronica took her jacket and purse and began walking out of the gym. For some reason, she felt reluctant to leave, but she didn't want to examine that feeling for too long.

When she stepped out into what was left of the day, the air was crisp on her skin. The magnolia trees that were scattered up and down Main Street were in full bloom, and their syrup-sweet perfume was carried on the gentle breeze that ruffled Veronica's hair. It was 5 p.m., so the sun was still fairly high in the sky, but the shadows were lengthening quickly. Veronica turned and began walking toward home, but suddenly stopped. As this was Sunday, Franklin would be at the fire station already and her mother would be home. Somehow, Veronica didn't feel like seeing her mother at this exact moment. So, instead, she turned and made her way towards the town center. After a few moments, she found herself looking across Main Street at the small park where Lazlo had been sitting that afternoon. With a start, she realized that the blonde-haired woman and the dark-skinned man were still there—but they were sitting on a branch of one of the magnolia trees.

They were seated facing each other, in the way that children would sit two in a swing, but that was their only similarity with children. They were locked in an embrace and kissing each other deeply. With a shock, Veronica realized that the style of the woman's dress and their position meant that they could actually be having sex—right there and out in the open. She should have been disgusted or appalled. She should have at least turned away for propriety's sake, but she didn't. They were too beautiful not to stare. She felt herself drawn to them and she felt a heat spring to life in her belly.

"You can see them, can't you?" asked a voice from behind her.

Veronica jumped and whirled to see Caio standing there with a little smile playing at the corners of his lips.

"See who?" Veronica asked, although she knew the answer.

"The man and woman kissing over there," Caio replied. "Doesn't that strike you as unusual? A black man kissing white woman… and in public?"

"Yes," Veronica said, "and you can obviously see them too."

Caio laughed.

"Touché," he said. "So, you do know he is a ghost, right?"

"Yes," Veronica replied softly. "Is she one as well?"

"Kara is a lot of things, most of them you don't want to encounter," Caio replied. "I wouldn't be standing so close if she weren't so engaged with Dante at the moment. But she will come back to herself soon enough, and if I were you, I would be gone by then. I certainly plan to be."

"Why?" Veronica asked.

"Two reasons," Caio replied. "First, Kara and Dante don't show up in places where things are going well. They show up either just before a disaster or just after one."

"To do what?" Veronica asked.

"To clean up," Caio responded. "And you don't want to be something they need to clean up. So, as you seem nice, I am telling you that you and yours should leave town as quickly as possible. Our bus leaves tomorrow evening, so it's not too much of a worry for me, but it will be for anyone who lives here."

"You said there were two reasons I should leave. What's the second one?" Veronica asked.

"Because the person you are looking for will be leaving at the same time that I do tomorrow."

"I don't know—" she began, but Caio waved his hand dismissively.

"And if you hurry, you might find him walking down the train tracks right now," he said.

Veronica froze for a moment. Her heart screamed *run after him*. Her brain screamed *don't give yourself away*.

"But you'll have to run," Caio said. "I'm not sure how long he'll be there."

"How did you know?" Veronica whispered.

"I was watching you," Caio said. "Could you always see ghosts?"

"I've seen them before, but not a lot," Veronica replied. "I've seen more in the past twenty-four hours than I've seen in ten years."

"Yesterday, did you get my blood on you at some point?" Caio asked.

Veronica felt something in her stomach lurch.

"I don't think so," she lied.

"You look familiar to me," Caio said.

"I don't think we've met," Veronica said, but for a moment she had a weird choking feeling.

"Maybe not yet," Caio said softly. "But time is a funny thing, and it's something you are about to run out of if you want to catch Lazlo."

Veronica felt her heart suddenly spasm in her chest at the mention of his name. Without further thought, she turned and, throwing reason to the wind, ran down Main Street toward York Street.

When she got to Eddie's Ice Cream shop at the corner of York and Main, she slowed herself down to a quick walk. York was a dead end into the train tracks, which was sheltered by a concrete and grass embankment. It wouldn't do for someone to see her climbing through bushes to get to the train tracks. The only people who did that were children. But, despite the busyness of Main Street, there was only her on York Street, so when she stepped from the street and into the grass at its end, the only creatures that noticed her were the bugs that she displaced as she walked quickly through the grass, pushing her way through some bushes that had grown up on the edge of the embankment.

Once at the top of the embankment, she saw Lazlo immediately. He was walking right down the center of the tracks. His gait was long and relaxed. With shock, Veronica realized that she had never seen a colored man walk that way before. Even if he thought he was alone, a colored man could never be sure when he would be interrupted… or when he would be required to subjugate himself to some white person. He could be forced to speak when he didn't want to, forced to step out into the street to make room for a white person. This thought made her feel deeply sad, but it also called forth the voice of reason.

What are you doing? she asked herself. *No good will come of this for either of you.*

Despite her internal warning, Veronica walked gingerly down the embankment until she was right next to the tracks. Here she would be walking on grass and her footfalls were silent. Lazlo strolled slowly down the very center of the tracks, probably stepping from wooden board to wooden board. From the back, she could see that he had broad shoulders, but they were set on a slight frame. He wasn't one of those strapping, corn-fed, rich boys, like Tommy Sawika or John Bilbo, but his movements had grace. If boys like Tommy and John bulldozed their way through life, Lazlo moved as if he was a guest in someone else's house.

Veronica matched his pace, while she kept her eyes open for others who might appear. It would be bad for both if they were caught alone in the same space. It wouldn't matter that he was yards away and didn't know she was there, he would be blamed. She should definitely leave now.

Lazlo stopped for a moment, and Veronica's heart skipped a beat, fearing that she had been discovered. Instead of turning, he bent down and picked up a stone. He then threw it toward some bushes on the grassy bank in front of him. A dog burst from the bushes and scampered away. Veronica realized that her house was now just a couple of blocks off to her right. She could escape quickly if she needed to.

She heard voices in the distance, but Lazlo didn't react. They couldn't be caught here, but she didn't want to leave him. She wanted to see his face again, even if it was only for a second and from a distance. She heard the voice of a child; it was closer now.

Without realizing what she was going to do, she coughed into her hand. Lazlo immediately whirled around. When he saw her, he froze. Veronica saw his face and her heart spasmed in her chest. The voices of children were getting louder, but Lazlo wasn't moving. He was standing and staring at her. It was hard to see his expression from this distance but what she did see was hard to read.

"Bet you won't lie down on the train tracks," a boy's voice called. It was far too close.

Veronica waved quickly and then turned and ran up the embankment without looking back.

*

Veronica ran most of the way home, trying to calm her agitation. It was a good thing that she wore low-heeled shoes, or she might have hurt herself. By the time she got to her street, she was tired and thirsty, but her head was still spinning too much to go inside and face her mother's eagle eyes. Iona had a knack for reading faces that was uncanny. So instead of going directly inside, Veronica walked up the driveway, and straight to the chicken coop. The chickens were still wandering around the yard, so she could check the nests, where she found five eggs. Their production was definitely going up now. She grabbed some feed and threw it out for them.

She couldn't believe that she had just followed a colored man down the railroad tracks. Even worse, she had made a point of getting his attention and waving to him. He had probably been terrified, but that wasn't exactly how he had looked. She had been too far away to see his face well, but he had stopped and stared at her. She was also fairly sure that he had waved back when she waved at him, although by the time she did that she was well on the way to a full-blown panic. She had just missed being seen on the tracks with Lazlo by a group of unruly children. That was reckless of her and could have ended very badly for everyone involved. She knew better than anyone the bad things that came from losing control, so she didn't.

Despite her recent reckless behavior, watching the chickens calmed her. They had always calmed her. Most people, including her mother and her brother, thought chickens were dumb, but this had not been Veronica's experience. What she had seen, in the years that their family had been raising chickens, was that the intelligence of chickens varied greatly from bird to bird. Sure, there had been some chickens that were little more than food with feet, but there had been others that had been as smart as any dog or cat that Veronica had seen.

A few years ago, they had a chicken that she had called Betty. When Betty and two of her sisters were old enough, they had brought a rooster from a nearby farm to breed with the hens. All three hens produced fertilized eggs and all three ended up with broods of nine chicks. On the fourth day after hatching, Veronica's mother took all the chicks but four to the market. All of Betty's chicks were sold. That was the day that Betty began trying to kill herself. She refused to eat and didn't drink much. When she was let out of the coop, she would run for the road. Finally, she picked a fight with the neighbor's dog, and it killed her. Veronica's mother thought this was chicken stupidity, but Veronica was convinced it was chicken grief. After Betty, Veronica stopped naming the chickens. Giving them names confirmed their individuality and made it harder to do what needed to be done. This history was why Hank's ugly kill of his chicken had annoyed her. They all raised chickens to provide eggs and to be eaten but as some of them were clearly sentient creatures, their deaths should be as kind and painless as possible.

Watching the chickens had taken her mind off Lazlo for a moment, so it was a good time to go and face her mother. As she walked into the house, she was struck by the sweet smells of baking beans and corn. Her mother was at the stove, stirring a pot.

"Beans and cornbread?" Veronica asked as she stepped into the small kitchen.

"Yes, I got paid yesterday," her mother replied.

Her mother's hair was mostly gray now, but it was a white-gray that looked a bit like snow woven through her dark hair. Her face was worn, and she had deep creases in her cheeks and purplish bags under her eyes. Her mother spent almost every waking hour working. In those rare moments where she had time off, she was either cleaning, cooking, or mending clothes. Veronica had been told that her mother had been a beauty in the days when she had been known as Iona Brackett, the willful middle daughter of the willful Janie Price Brackett. But Iona had married the charismatic but temperamental Deward Crane. According to Grandma Janie, her mother's looks deteriorated shortly after their marriage, along with her life prospects.

"John Sawika stopped by our line today," her mother said, as Veronica sat down on a stool next to their small dining table.

"I thought he was too busy being the plant manager to worry about what happens on the cigarette floor," Veronica replied.

"Normally he is, but he came to ask me about you."

Wow. Her mother normally didn't pull punches, but this was a quick lead in even for her.

"What did he want to know?" Veronica asked.

"He just said that you were approached by one of those colored soldiers and that Tommy had to intervene," her mother said.

Veronica felt the anger rising.

"That's not what happened," she said.

"I suspected as much," her mother said, nodding, "but John Sawika's truth is the only truth that matters in the factory. You know that, right?"

Veronica nodded.

"It's bad enough that the police chief's son is sweet on you, and you don't give him the time of day—" her mother began, but Veronica held up her hand.

"CJ is a horrible person," Veronica said.

"It seems to me that it's Tommy who—"

Veronica cut her off again. "Tommy is CJ's henchman. He isn't smart enough to come up with most of his nastiness on his own. CJ is the one who feeds it to him, and then sits and smiles when Tommy insults the girls, picks fights with colored boys… or makes fun of Franklin."

"Oh, that's what happened," her mother said. "Listen, girl, your brother can stand up for himself. He doesn't need your help. As for CJ Bishop, he's not all he seems, for sure—"

"Oh, there's something underneath the pompous, self-righteous—" Veronica began but her mother whirled on her and pointed her wooden spoon in Veronica's face.

"Hush girl. I know you think you know it all, but there is a lot goin' on here that you don't know a whit about."

Veronica watched as the spoon in front of her face dripped bean juice on the floor. For a moment, neither of them said anything, but then her mother shrugged her shoulders and went back to her pot.

"I ain't asking you to marry CJ, just don't do anything to set him off," her mother said. "That could come back to hurt you… and Franklin."

At the mention of Franklin, Veronica felt fear grab her by the throat. What if someone had seen her talking with Lazlo today? What if that got back to CJ? She had thought he would take it out on her, but the idea that he might take it out on Franklin hadn't occurred to her.

"I understand," Veronica said softly. "I'll be more careful."

"And don't you go talking to any colored people," her mother said. "This town has no love for them and even less for white people who take up for them."

"Shouldn't Franklin be home by now?" Veronica asked, to change the subject.

Her mother offered a rare smile, and it transformed her face. She pulled a bowl off the shelf and ladled some beans into it.

"Franklin came home for a quick dinner before going back to the firehouse," she said. "It seems Dr. Payne has asked if Franklin can walk Nan home this evening as it will be full dark when they get out."

"*Dr. Payne* asked?" Veronica asked.

"Yes, Dr. Payne," said her mother, a smile still playing on her lips.

Dr. Payne was one of the two town doctors and, despite his name, was a genuinely kind and generous man. He treated anyone who came to him, whether they could pay or not. He had even been known to treat people's pets. He had always been courteous to their family. With Nan, the apple had not fallen far from the tree.

"So he's walking Nan home?" Veronica asked.

"Should be…"

Just as the words had left her mouth, Veronica heard whistling. Seconds later, Franklin appeared at the screen door, all smiles.

"Something smells great," he said, as he entered and kissed their mother on the cheek. He said these words out loud, and with no stutter.

"How was Nan?" Veronica asked, smiling at her bowl of food.

Franklin came to sit in front of her.

"Nan was fine, why do you ask?" he mouthed at her.

"You walked her home?"

"Yes, her father asked me to walk her home," Franklin mouthed.

"How was that?" Veronica asked.

"Well, she's pretty good at reading lips, so we could talk a little." Franklin smiled and looked down.

Veronica reached out and touched his arm.

"Nan's great," Veronica said.

"Yeah, she is, isn't she?"

"Well, I need to get to bed because it's another early morning," her mother said. "Ronnie, don't you forget that you have to work the earlier shift tomorrow too."

Her mother's words reminded Veronica that the recruits that she had processed today would be bussed out tomorrow, or at best, the following day. That meant that Lazlo would go with them.

*

That evening as Veronica lay in her bed, she tried to assess the look Lazlo had given her when he saw her on the train tracks. She hadn't seen a look like that on anyone's face before. It looked sort of like shock, but nicer. It could have been the beginnings of a smile, but sadder.

It doesn't matter what look he gave you, you will likely never see him again, she told herself. She also told herself that this was for the best.

So why did her chest feel so heavy and empty?

Chapter Six

A Gift Horse

When morning came, Veronica struggled to get through the basics of her usual preparation. Normally, she got up just as her mother was leaving for work. The factory ran a 24-hour schedule and her mother had worked there long enough to get one of the first shifts. It was the earliest of the first shifts so on weekdays she worked 5 a.m. to 3 p.m., but it was still good. When she worked on the weekends, she only worked ten to six. Veronica herself had not been working at the factory long enough to get the benefit of a constant schedule. So she took what hours she could get. This week, she was working from 8 a.m. to 1 p.m. on Monday, Wednesday, and Friday but from 9 a.m. to 9 p.m. on Tuesday and Thursday. These schedules were posted at the end of every week, so it was hard to plan for things, even if she had something to plan for.

This morning, she didn't wake up until Franklin shook her at almost 7 a.m., as he was leaving for his job at the pig farm. She had dragged herself out of bed, feeling like her head was stuffed with cotton. On the positive side, Franklin had obviously collected the eggs this morning, and somehow her mother had found time to make biscuits. So Veronica was able to have two eggs and a biscuit for breakfast but found herself gazing off into space so much that Lizzie was at her door before she had even finished eating.

"Ronnie, we've got to go, we are going to be late," Lizzie called as she banged on the screen door.

Veronica nodded to no one, and quickly washed her plate and wiped the table before running out the door.

"Did you hear that Mary McGregor found five dead kittens in the bucket of her well yesterday?" Lizzie asked, as they walked swiftly toward the factory.

"No, really?" Veronica said. "That's disgusting."

"I know," Lizzie said. "Ben said that it might be the colored soldiers. I'm really glad they are leaving town this afternoon."

Lazlo.

Veronica stopped in her tracks.

Lazlo would be leaving today. Veronica realized that she had been so slow this morning because her brain had been putting most of its energy into keeping Lazlo from her mind, but at the mention of the colored soldiers, her heart pushed her brain to the background. She would probably never see him again. She felt actual pain in her chest at the thought.

"Come on, Ronnie," Lizzie said, grabbing her arm and pulling her forward. "What's gotten into you this morning?"

"Tommy," Veronica said quickly, covering her silence. "He lied about what happened this weekend."

"Of course," Lizzie said, with a hand flip. "He likes to make himself look grander than he is, but at least he kept you from having to talk to some negro boy."

"That's not the point—" Veronica began, but Lizzie cut her off.

"What is the point, then?" Lizzie asked, throwing her hands in the air with exasperation.

"The point is that Tommy was the one who was bothering me, which is why I was trying to walk away."

"Oh no, you didn't say something nasty to Tommy yesterday, did you?" Lizzie snapped. Lizzie had stopped just at the employee entrance to the factory, her hands on her hips.

"I DID NOT," Veronica snapped back. "But I might next time."

"Listen, you don't want to pick fights with the Sawika family," Lizzie said. "We keep our jobs only if we don't upset Mr. Sawika."

That could come back to hurt you… and Franklin. Her mother's words echoed in her brain.

"I'm sorry, Lizzie," Veronica said. "I just really don't like either of them, but I won't do anything to get you or my family in trouble."

Lizzie put her arm around Veronica's shoulders and gave her a squeeze.

"I know, and I don't like them much either," Lizzie said. "I'm just better at hiding it than you."

"Can you teach me how that hiding thing works sometime?" Veronica said.

"No, 'cause I like you just as you are," Lizzie said, as she opened the door to the factory. "You keep me on my toes."

Veronica smiled, but her heart was not in it. Lazlo and the odd events of the weekend reminded her how small her life was, and that ache was hard to ignore.

*

After clocking in, Veronica went to check the job listings. Once again, she would be working on the factory floor, putting cigarette packs into cardboard boxes of six. She felt shadow pain in her fingers just reading that assignment.

Of course, there were worse jobs in the factory. For example, there were the jobs in building Number 8, where they processed chewing tobacco. Most of the jobs in that building were unpleasant. As the tobacco was treated with rum and sugar, it attracted insects. One of jobs was, ostensibly, to pick the stems out of wet tobacco. In reality, it meant picking bugs out of it. On Mondays, after the weekend fumigations, it was okay, but by Wednesday, you knew the roaches on a first-name basis. It didn't help that all the men working at the plant would be chewing the product and spitting back into it before it got to you. So you were really picking through bugs and spit. Another job was to load empty aluminum cans onto a conveyor belt which would then automatically fill the cans with tobacco. This didn't seem bad until you had to do it for eight hours straight, with few breaks and thirty minutes for lunch. But the worst, by far, was the "camel" job. There was a place in the factory where the tobacco was treated with rum. It ran just below the roof of the building. The factory managers said that this was to keep the smell of the rum to a minimum, but Veronica didn't buy it. The smell was omnipresent throughout the building. Despite its nearness to the roof, someone needed to continually grease the chutes there, or the tobacco would clog and back up. The issue was that there wasn't enough room to stand. So whoever worked that job for the day would spend their time hunched over, looking something like a camel. Most people could only stand about a week of this job at a time, and it was often doled out as a punishment for badly behaved employees.

Compared to building 8, the cigarette floor at Milligan Park was a piece of cake. Many of the top managers of the company had offices in this building. Of course, these jobs were all held by men. Quality Assurance was also housed in this building, and these positions were mainly held by women, but there were only a handful of them. There were only a few jobs for the women there in large numbers, but these were the most needed in the factory, so the workforce at Milligan was at least forty percent women. Most of them sat in booths on the cigarette floor and either packaged cigarettes into boxes or packed boxes into larger cartons. Both were repetitive, but they were seated, and the environment was mostly clean, if loud. The problem for Veronica was that she had joints that were prone to swelling. This meant that any job that involved using her hands in a repetitive fashion was going to be painful for her.

As Veronica made her way toward the seat she had been assigned, she saw John Sawika walking the lines. He stopped at Lizzie's station and put his hand on her shoulder. Lizzie looked up and smiled and Mr. Sawika laughed at something she said. Lizzie was so much better at all of this than she would ever be.

Veronica tapped the woman who was currently seated in her place and placing cigarette boxes into the cartons. This was Mildred Fawkes, a hawk-nosed woman who was around her mother's age and just as worn. Mildred nodded and stood up. Veronica slid into the seat quickly so that she would not interrupt the flow of cigarettes to be boxed, and her day began.

While her hands were busy boxing, her brain was speeding in her skull. Lazlo would be leaving sometime today. She wasn't sure what time. She should have asked Caio when he told her, but she had been too discombobulated by everything that was happening in that moment that she hadn't had the mental clarity. After all, Caio had not only seen the beautiful stranger but also the dark-skinned ghost who accompanied her. Veronica had never known another person, besides herself and her grandmother Janie, who could see ghosts. So Dante had to have been a Furiae, if what Janie said was correct. Caio had been watching the ghost Dante and the woman that he had called Kara. He said that they only appeared when trouble was in the air.

If Veronica had been given to flights of fancy, she might have thought that she had dreamed everything that happened yesterday, but Veronica was not creative by nature. On the occasions that she saw ghosts, her practical brain told her that whether or not they were ghosts made little difference in her day-to-day life… unless she spoke about it or let it affect her actions. Her brain, used to having to operate on less energy than was optimal, was focused, concise, and practical. Grandma Janie had once complained about it.

"You can't even read this child a story without her telling you why this or that is wrong with it," she would say, but then she would hug Veronica tight.

Yesterday, for the first time, her practical brain went on vacation and so the rest of her had used the opportunity to take ridiculous chances. In fact, nothing she had done yesterday had been practical or useful.

Veronica jumped as she felt a hand on her shoulder.

She looked up to see John Sawika looming over her. Even at a distance, John Sawika was an imposing man. Up close, he was extremely intimidating. He was well over six foot tall and probably closer to six-five. Most tall men either become scrawny or overweight as they age, but not Mr. Sawika. He was large and still very muscular. His hair was cropped close to his head, so it was hard to notice that he was balding on the top. He laughed easily and smiled even more easily, but these actions felt more like instinct than expressions of mirth. His close-set, watery blue eyes were never warm, and they moved constantly. Someone had told her that John Sawika had worked in a slaughterhouse when he was young, and Veronica could believe it.

"Veronica, may I speak with you for a moment?" he asked.

Veronica looked at the cigarettes coming off the conveyor.

"Oh, of course," Mr. Sawika said.

"Eddie, send someone over here to cover for Veronica," he boomed in a voice deep enough and loud enough to be heard over the banging of the machines. Almost immediately a girl ran to her, allowing Veronica to leave her station.

"Let's just walk a bit away from the noise," he said, walking Veronica toward the section of the building that held the offices and some of the storage rooms. He stopped outside the Quality Assurance office.

Mr. Sawika knocked at the door, and the door opened. Rather than going inside, one of the line managers came out with Nellie Crowder. Nellie was married and her husband worked at the Number 12 plant. Veronica had seen her occasionally over the years at church picnics and farmers' markets. Her father was the town postman, and he was friendly and chatty. Normally Nellie had been much the same, smiling at everyone, but she was not smiling now. Her face looked worn and ten years older than the last time Veronica had seen her. She was rubbing her hands together nervously.

"Nellie here is going out on maternity leave today," he said. Nellie nodded, even though nothing about her looked pregnant. At least, she didn't look pregnant enough to start maternity leave. Veronica felt a stab of pain in the back of her head, at her knowing spot. Something was wrong here.

"I can stay and train Veronica," Nellie said quickly. "I don't mind."

"No, Nellie. We don't want you on your feet too much, do we, dear?" Mr. Sawika said, patting her arm. The line manager took Nellie by the other arm and began to walk her toward the exit sign. Suddenly, Nellie stopped, turned back, and caught Veronica's eye.

"Veronica, I left some, well, personal girl stuff in the top drawer of my desk," she called out.

Without waiting, Veronica entered the QA office. There were three other women sitting at desks around the room, and there was one empty desk.

"Is that Nellie's desk?" she asked.

"Uh-hmm," one of the women said, without looking up. Veronica opened the desk drawer and saw a small paper sack. She grabbed it and walked quickly back toward the door but not before she had gotten a quick glance at what it was. Sure enough, it had been woman's things—a sanitary napkin.

Why would a pregnant woman need a sanitary napkin?

*

Veronica moved quickly past Mr. Sawika, trotting over to where Nellie and the line manager were standing.

"Thanks, dear," Nellie said, as she gave Veronica a little hug. In her ear, she said, "It's in the snuff room."

"You're welcome," Veronica said pulling away. She had no idea what Nellie was talking about, but her logical brain said that Mr. Sawika was telling her if not outright lies, then half-truths.

"I noticed that you and Nellie had a little conversation over there," Mr. Sawika said, as she approached him. "She didn't happen to mention the snuff storage, did she?"

Veronica didn't know what was safe, but she could tell half-truths too.

"Yes, she told me to be careful of it," Veronica replied.

"Did she happen to say anything else?" Mr. Sawika asked.

"No, just that," Veronica said. She didn't mention that Nellie's arms had been shaking when she hugged her or that her breath had the sour smell of fear.

"I see," Mr. Sawika said. "Can I have a word with you in private?"

He motioned her to move closer to him as he stepped away from the office door and into the shade between two large bins. Alarm bells began to go off in her head. What if he touched her? What if he tried to kiss her?

She moved forward a few feet but stayed an arm's length away.

A dark little smile danced below John Sawika's sharp nose.

"You don't have to worry, Veronica. I won't hurt you."

Her face must have registered the shock she felt at his candor because he laughed.

"But what I am about to tell you, I don't want others to overhear," he said.

Veronica took one step closer.

Mr. Sawika sighed.

"Okay, that's fine," he said. "I wanted to explain the reason why Nellie is leaving and what happened."

"She isn't leaving because of pregnancy?" Veronica asked.

"Oh, that's probably what's at the heart of it," Mr. Sawika replied. "Nellie is normally far from squeamish, but since her pregnancy she has become much more sensitive. She has also become more paranoid."

His eyes darted around the room quickly before returning to Veronica's face.

"The reason that Nellie is so concerned with the room where we store snuff is because things tend to go there to die," he said.

"To die?" Veronica blurted out before she could stop herself.

"Yes, to die," Mr. Sawika said. "Bugs are attracted to the tobacco, but we fumigate the room so most die of the smoke, but it doesn't keep them out for long. But it's not just the bugs. Animals are attracted to the smell of it. So they find ways into the room, but they can't always find their way out. Usually, we find rats and mice, but when Nellie went to check moisture levels two weeks ago, she found a dead dog."

Mr. Sawika stopped for a moment, eyes crawling over Veronica's face.

"She has found dogs before, but I think her pregnancy has made her more sensitive. We could have worked through that, but she had a serious lapse in judgment and called the health inspector."

"Aren't we supposed to report things like that to the health inspector?" Veronica asked.

"Of course, and we do," Mr. Sawika replied quickly. "But it needs to go through the proper channels. Anything that goes wrong in this plant needs to come through me. I need to have a chance to review the situation. If I can assure the health inspector that we have processes to correct the problem, and that it is contained, then we can avoid closing the plant. As a result of Nellie's call, the plant will be closed, starting this afternoon and possibly through tomorrow. That means that there are a lot of people who don't get paid for those days, people like you and your mother."

"Right," Veronica said. Not working part of today and all tomorrow meant there would be less money for food. She felt a twinge of anger at Nellie.

"I'm sorry to be the bearer of bad tidings," Mr. Sawika said. "But I have good news too. I want you to fill in for Nellie. The quality control position pays ten cents more per hour."

"Ten cents!" Veronica gasped. It took her seconds to calculate that this would take her from twenty-four to twenty-eight dollars per week.

"I'm sure your family could use the extra money," Mr. Sawika said with an almost sincere smile.

"Yes, we can," Veronica replied.

"Good, then," Mr. Sawika replied. "Then you should pick up your things and go on home for the day. You can start here Wednesday."

Veronica turned to leave but Mr. Sawika stopped her.

"One more thing, Veronica..."

Veronica turned to find that Mr. Sawika's smile had disappeared, but his eyes were now alive and full of a fierce energy.

"My son told me that a colored boy was bothering you the other day," he said.

Veronica struggled for something to say that would calm the situation while keeping her family safe.

"I wasn't scared, sir," she said softly. Mr. Sawika's eyes widened for a minute but then he nodded.

"You have always been a strong girl, Veronica, but you might not know as well as some of the men do how bad some boys can be. Tommy and his friends told me you had been in danger."

Veronica was concentrating on not snapping at him. She held Franklin's face in her mind.

"I just wanted to let you know that you will have no such problem here," Mr. Sawika said. "Colored folk only work the fields. There will be none in the factory to ever bother you, so you will be safe here. I know safety is important to you."

Ah, there it was, the allusion to her father, presented in a none-too-subtle fashion.

"Thank you, sir," was all she said. Mr. Sawika smiled, took her arm, and escorted her back to her station just as an intercom announcement was made saying that they would all be going home.

It wasn't until then that Veronica realized it was only noon and Lazlo might not have left yet.

She left her practical brain sitting on the cigarette floor as she grabbed her purse and ran for the exit.

Chapter Seven

Desire, Despair, Desire

Veronica froze.

Lazlo began walking the very same path she had walked minutes earlier, although he looked much more graceful than she must have looked. His gate was long and easy. His eyes were down, staring at the track as he walked. Veronica sat as still as she could, terrified that he might see her, equally terrified that he wouldn't.

As he came to the spot where she was sitting, he didn't look up. He walked right past her, as if he hadn't seen her. Veronica felt a stab in her heart. Before she could stop herself, she called out.

"Aren't you Lazlo Fox?"

He turned quickly.

"That's me," he said, and a grin lit up his face.

Now that he was here, Veronica realized that she hadn't planned what she would say if she saw him. For a second, she considered saying that the draft office needed more information about him, but she realized that was both stupid and an obvious lie.

"I have an extra biscuit, if you're hungry," was what she managed to squeak out.

She had hoped to be able to speak with him for a just a moment. She knew that it would be dangerous for him to even be seen with her, but as he walked toward her, she held the biscuit out for him. She knew that he would have to climb up to her to get it, and despite the danger, this is what she wanted.

Instead of scrambling up the broken concrete, as she had done, he gracefully jumped from one to the next, balancing on the ball of one foot as he landed on each one. In less than a minute he was standing on the rock next to her. She expected him to take the biscuit and leave, but she wanted him to stay… how badly she wanted him to stay.

Lazlo smiled and took the proffered biscuit bag gently from her, but his eyes were on her face, not on the bag. For a moment, he paused, and then he sat down next to her. He wasn't so close that she might accidentally touch him but his feet dangling over the edge of the rock next to hers felt weirdly intimate. He opened the bag and pulled out the biscuit. Veronica looked down at her biscuit and took a tiny bite, pretending to be engrossed in eating but her heart was racing so hard, she almost choked on the bread.

"Lazlo, that's an unusual name, is it a family name or something?" she asked.

Lazlo turned and smiled at her. She was suddenly afraid that she had said something wrong or stupid, although she couldn't for the life of her think what it was.

Lazlo's eyes suddenly got wide.

"Well, my mama named me that cause she's a witch," he said quickly, and then winced and shook his head.

"That sounded awful," he said quickly. "I'm not talking bad about my mama. She's actually a witch, so she thinks like attracts like. And if she gives me a rich-sounding name that will draw money to me."

Lazlo then laughed and shook his head.

"I can't believe I just told you that," he said. "I never told anyone that before. Probably because—"

Then he stopped.

Veronica's heart felt like it had grown to take up the whole of her chest. She was frightened of what Lazlo would see if she looked at him, so she took another bite of her biscuit. When she did look up, he was looking at her with eyes that were hopeful and wary in equal measure.

"It sounds like your mother really cares about you," was what she finally said. And that was all.

Looking at Lazlo's guarded yet hopeful eyes, Veronica desperately wanted to tell him that none of this stuff mattered. She wanted to say that they could be friends, or even more. Inside, her crazy heart said that they could just run away together. She longed to say this out loud, but she knew it wasn't true. Neither of them could outrun their class or caste. Lazlo was a colored man. She was the poor white daughter of a single mother. If he was an untouchable, she was barely one step above that. Her brain told her that, even if her heart argued otherwise.

"Do you like working at the draft office?" Lazlo asked, looking back at his biscuit.

"It's okay," she replied, and she realized something she could give him. Something she gave almost no one. The truth of her heart.

"I work because I need the money," Veronica said softly. "I work at the draft office when it is open, but normally I work at the cigarette factory with my mother. It doesn't pay great for me because I am a girl, but I am saving as much as I can. I want to take a course in accounting from the college but… well… we don't have the money. It may take me years to get enough money, because sometimes I go weeks without being able to save a cent, just so we can eat."

Lazlo was silent.

"We're poor," Veronica whispered. It was probably the first time that Veronica had ever said those words out loud.

"The house we live in is owned by the factory, but we are allowed to live there as long as we work there. My brother—well, he works two jobs. One is at a pig farm. Even with that, we don't always have enough food."

She felt her throat constrict and emotion threaten, but she pulled it back in as she always did.

Lazlo's eyes were on her. He reached his hand out toward her but caught himself and pulled it back.

"Growing up, my parents were—still are—working on a sharecropper's farm in Georgia," he said softly. "So we were pretty much dirt poor. I was one of thirteen kids they had to feed. I was the second youngest and the youngest boy, so I had to fight my siblings for what food we had. So I know poor. In the summer months, when I could go to a bit of school, I went with no shoes 'cause they was too expensive. So that was bad. To make it worse, we was black. No, even worse than that, we was half black and half Indian. So I had all the name calling and shit—sorry—stuff that you expect if you're the son of a black sharecropper in Georgia. Plus all the name calling you expect if you was the son of an Indian in Georgia. I came to North Carolina because I had a friend here and he got a job in the fields picking tobacco. It wasn't fun but it paid well. Still, I couldn't see a way out… until the war broke out. I shouldn't be happy about the war, but it gives me a chance for something better. I wouldn't have had that without it. It's a way to escape everything I thought I had to be."

"I wish *I* was a man," Veronica said softly, then started. She shouldn't be talking like this but who could understand that feeling, if not the man beside her.

"I mean, men can go anywhere," she explained. "They can get a job doing anything. I wish it was like that for women, but people don't like to hire women. I mean, for anything besides factory work. We get more work now because of the war, but when the men come back, we will be expected to go back to doing what the world wants us to do."

"And what's that?" Lazlo asked.

"Oh, be wives and mothers," Veronica said with a dark little laugh.

"You don't want to get married?" Lazlo asked, his eyes intent on her face.

"It's not that. I just haven't met anyone I wanted to marry," she replied. With a heartbreaking horror she realized that this might no longer be true.

Lazlo nodded.

"So, if I was a man, I would have more options," Veronica continued. "Even if I was poor, I would be free in a way that I can never be as a woman."

"Not if you was a colored man," Lazlo said gently. "Maybe you and I have some things in common, Veronica Crane."

He knew her last name. Somehow, he had found out her last name. This made her feel both jittery and happy.

"Can't you go up north?" Veronica asked quickly, to cover whatever expression she might have.

"That's what I plan to do. I want to go to New York City… well, that's what I plan to do if I don't die in the war," Lazlo replied.

The longer he spoke, the more his voice took on a softer, richer tone, with longer vowels and a more earthy diction.

A branch snapped behind them, and both of them jumped. It was just a squirrel, but the sound reminded her heart of the danger she was in by just sitting next to this man. No, she wasn't just sitting next to a negro man, she was sitting alone next to a negro man. If anyone saw this, then CJ and Tommy and their like would make sure that she, and her family, would be ostracized from society. She would lose her job. Her mother would probably lose her job. She might be the "victim" of some "random" act of violence, like rape. Her family would have to leave town. But if it was bad for her, it would be worse for Lazlo. The same people wouldn't stop with random violence, they would lynch him, but only after he had been sufficiently tortured. He had to know this, and yet, here he sat, sharing the awful squishy jam biscuit that she made.

How brave must he be? And why would he be risking his safety just to sit with a white girl that he had only met once. Could it be for the same reason that she was risking herself? For a moment, she wondered if he could pass for white. He wasn't much darker-skinned than Caio, but Caio was immediately classified as white by the sergeant. She wondered what the difference was. Both had light caramel-colored skin, both had thin noses and high cheekbones. The only difference Veronica could see was that Caio's hair was obviously straight, while

Lazlo's looked thicker and wavier. Still, it was hard to tell with hair cropped so short.

Veronica realized that she had been silent for too long, just staring at him. He was staring back at her, without guile.

She was about to speak when he said, "What would you do, if you could do anything?"

"I would teach math… at a real university," Veronica replied. "Maybe at a place like Oxford or Cambridge or one of those snobby English universities. I guess I would travel and see how things might be different in other places."

She expected Lazlo to laugh, but he didn't. He just nodded. She realized that he was at the end of his biscuit, but he was taking tiny little bites. They were both drawing this out as long as they could. When they finished eating there wouldn't be any excuse to stay on this rock.

She knew that she shouldn't be here, and yet she couldn't bring herself to leave.

This isn't being brave, it's being foolish, her brain told her. *He will suffer more than you if they catch him.*

"What unit are you with?" she asked Lazlo.

"I don't know yet, but I was sort of hoping to be one of the Buffalo Soldiers," Lazlo replied.

"Who are the Buffalo Soldiers?" Veronica asked.

"It's one of the colored units," Lazlo replied. "But it goes all the way back to the fights with the Indians. The Indians called us Buffalo Soldiers because they thought we looked like buffalos. It was also because they thought we were unusually big, brave, and strong. I like that. Now it's the 92nd Infantry."

"But aren't you afraid of going to war?" Veronica asked him. Lazlo shrugged.

"Not really," he replied. "It's a chance for me. There is this GI bill that will allow me to get my high school diploma and enroll in college. I might even be able to go to school and stay with the army for decent pay. So that's good enough for me. It's a much better chance than I'd have if I'd stayed on the farm. To get a real education would be a fine thing."

She must have looked doubtful because Lazlo laughed.

"Oh, I'm not stupid," he said. "I know that they will say a whole bunch of mess trying to get us to go fight and maybe die in the war. I also know that they might not be as happy to have a bunch of negros getting educated and showing up at colleges… but it's a promise and it's in writing, so it's worth the risk. I ain't scared of risks."

Apparently, Veronica thought.

Lazlo was now holding the paper wrapper. The biscuit was gone. Veronica took the last bite of hers. She didn't want him to go. She didn't want him to be in the war. She wanted to protect him or give him luck, or something.

"Well, it was nice to meet you," she said, sticking out her hand. Women didn't shake hands much, and almost never with a man, but she wanted any excuse to touch him.

He took her hand in his for just a moment. He didn't shake it, he just held it for a moment as his eyes met hers. His were dark and open. Veronica wanted nothing more than to kiss him. For a moment, he leaned forward a bit and she did the same. But then the sound of voices drifted over on the wind. They were male voices.

"I should go," he said softly.

Veronica nodded, as her heart spasmed in her chest.

I choose him, it told her, not in words but in chemicals stronger than any word ever imagined.

Lazlo got up, jumped from the rock, and landed gracefully on the ground. He turned to her, smiled, waved, and then started back down the train tracks.

"Lazlo!" Veronica called out.

He turned around quickly and walked a few steps in her direction.

"Why don't you write me?" she said. "I would love to hear about what you see out there in the world."

Even from this distance, she could see his eyes widen, but he smiled and nodded before turning and running up the other embankment and disappearing.

Not three minutes later, a group of young teenage boys stumbled on to the train tracks, laughing and pushing each other.

It was at that moment that Veronica realized that she hadn't given Lazlo her address.

Chapter Eight

Chasing Cars

Veronica didn't recognize the restaurant. Instead of seeing the inside of the department store and the familiar lunch counter, she was in a carpeted space that contained tables, chairs, and booths. On the wall was a ridiculous clock that looked like a chicken. People were sitting at these tables, eating and laughing. So this must be a restaurant, but it wasn't like any restaurant she had ever been in. As she walked through, she saw that everyone had enough food on their plates to serve two or three people and almost everyone had a steak that was roughly the size of a baby's head.

A distracted-looking young girl with curly, wheat-colored hair was waiting the tables, but she kept cutting her eyes back toward a very good-looking, dark-haired boy who was wearing strange clothes. Actually, everyone around her was wearing strange clothes. Suddenly, Veronica saw a colored soldier sitting at the booth in the corner. He was wearing a hat, and she could only see the back of his head, but his neck was a beautiful caramel color. Sitting in front of him was an extremely large, red-haired woman. Veronica felt a stab of jealously, then felt stupid about it. Surely this man wasn't Lazlo, and even if it was, she had no right to be jealous about anything.

She was turning to go when a voice called out to her.

"Veronica!"

She turned and found that the colored man at the table had turned and was staring at her. It was Lazlo.

"Veronica!" he said, coming forward quickly and taking her hands.

"Who is that woman?" Veronica asked, and cringed at the accusation in her voice.

Lazlo laughed.

"You," he said, smiling. "That woman is you."

Then his smile faded a bit.

"Or at least part of you."

"How can someone be a part of me?" Veronica asked.

"I'm not sure," Lazlo said. "But it doesn't matter, you're here now."

He then took her in his arms. Veronica flung her arms around this neck. His exposed skin was warm against her cold, aching hands. He kissed her gently, his lips barely touching hers, even as his arms held her tightly. Somewhere in the back of her head, she realized that they were standing in the middle of a restaurant. People would see and there would be trouble, but she kissed him anyway. When he opened his mouth to kiss her more deeply, she felt like she might faint. She felt lightheaded, out of breath, and she ached in a pleasant, hungry way. She had never desired a man before, and the feeling was overwhelming, otherworldly, and humbling.

"Won't we get into trouble?" she whispered into his mouth.

"Not here," he whispered back.

"Why?" she asked.

"Because here ain't here. You are in my dream. So I can love you in my own dream."

"But I feel like I am really here," she said, running her fingers over the skin on his neck.

"See, that's what I would want you to say," Lazlo said, laughing. "Me, wishing that you wanted me back. Me, pretending that you might be dreaming of me, like I'm dreaming of you. But why would a beautiful, smart, white girl like you give a boy like me the time of day? I know you was just being nice, but damned if you didn't make me fall in love with you."

"No, I think you were the one who did that to me," Veronica said. He just nodded, laughed, and kissed her again.

She didn't know how long they had been standing there when the dark-haired boy tapped Lazlo on the shoulder. He spun round, and while Veronica couldn't see Lazlo's face, the boy raised both hands. He had dark hair and black eyes, but his expression didn't match his looks.

"Listen, if it were up to me, I'm completely fine with what you two are doing. But you seem to be blocking the path to the salad bar, which some of our hungrier patrons aren't pleased about," the boy said, laughing. "Truth be told, some people just aren't comfortable with public displays of affection."

"And what do you feel about it?" Lazlo asked, his body tense in her arms.

"Me?" the boy asked. "I would be doing exactly the same as you're doing if I were in your shoes. So maybe just sit down in a booth, then no one can complain. Trust me, I won't be the one to kick you out of it. Take as long as you need."

Lazlo smiled at the boy, took Veronica's hand, and led her to a booth.

"If this is your dream, then where are we?" Veronica asked, as they slid into a booth and Lazlo put his arm around her.

"I don't rightly know," he said. "I've been here before, but only in my dreams. I've seen that boy and girl before, too, but I have never seen you here before. Well, not like you are now."

"You said that you were sitting with me," she said.

"Yeah, I think that's me sitting with you when you are older," he said with a smile.

"I'm fat when I'm older?" she asked.

"Maybe that's just me, hoping you're never hungry again. I like you fat. I like you thin too," he said. "I like you 'bout any way I can have you."

He leaned in to kiss her again, and she kissed him back, putting her legs across his lap. He pulled her up until she was actually sitting on his lap. She felt his hardness through the thin material of her dress. Rather than feeling disgusted, frightened, or ashamed, she felt a rush of desire. She did that. His desire for her did that. For the moment, she didn't feel like the plain, smart, practical Veronica she had always been. She felt reckless and beautiful—and she liked feeling that way. In the distance, she heard a train whistle. Her lips were on Lazlo's and the taste of him filled her senses, so what did she care for trains. He had the slight smell of a deodorant she knew, but she couldn't place it. The sound of the train was getting louder. His kisses were sweet and soft. The booth began to shake. Old Spice. It was Old Spice.

Suddenly, the booth fell out from under her, and she felt herself falling in the open air.

*

With a jolt, she found herself standing on the embankment next to the train tracks. She was standing hand in hand with Lazlo. He was wearing a soldier's uniform and army boots. On his arm was a band with a red cross on it.

"You sure you want to do this?" Lazlo asked, turning to face her. He was smiling and his dark eyes were shining. "I can't promise what we'll find on the other side. I can't promise we'll have money or that people will even let us be."

Some people might have replied with some sort of assurance, but Veronica was too pragmatic for that, and Lazlo was too smart to believe it. So she said the thing that she could say, the thing she believed with all her heart.

"As long we're together, we can face it."

"And if they don't accept us?" Lazlo asked.

"We go somewhere else," she said.

"And if—" he began, but she put her finger to his lips.

"We keep going until we find somewhere that does accept us," she said.

"Or some time that accepts us?" Lazlo asked.

"Or that," she said. "As long as I'm with you, I'm happy."

Lazlo nodded, then leaned down and kissed her lips.

"Look!" she heard someone call out. She turned, and behind her she saw CJ Bishop and Tommy Sawika charging toward them, at the head of a crowd of people—all carrying sticks, hammers, and baseball bats.

"Run!' Lazlo yelled, pushing her forward. As she ran down the embankment, she heard the train. It was coming, but it was going so fast. She would have to be running at top speed to have any hope of grabbing on to it.

The driver of the train passed her on her right, the first car, then the second. At the third car, she lunged for the railing at the back and managed to grab hold. She felt like her arm was jerked out of its socket and her body was lifted off the ground, but she grabbed on with the other hand and pull her feet up to the stairs. She then pushed off and threw herself onto the landing at the back of the car. She turned and saw Lazlo running behind her.

"RUN!" Veronica screamed, as she stood and, clutching the railing, reached her hand out to him. He was getting closer. God, he was fast. He lunged forward and grabbed at Veronica's hand, but Veronica couldn't hold on. She fell to her knees, locked one of her arms around the railing and leaned out further. Veronica knew that she wouldn't be strong enough to pull him up unless he was going as fast as the train.

Lazlo was now running full-out with his head down, and he was fast. He was going almost as fast as the train. He was going to make it.

That was when she saw the dogs, running down the embankments on both sides. They were fierce, brown and black dogs. They charged toward Lazlo, teeth bared.

"Lazlo, run! Run! RUN!!" Veronica screamed. He looked up at her, and his eyes widened, then he looked down and put on more speed. Veronica reached out her hand, and Lazlo reached out. She managed to grab his hand. Her whole body was slammed against the railings of the train, but she held on. The bones in her hand felt like they were being crushed but she held on. A dog leaped for the train and made it onto the platform she was lying on. It snarled and bit into her shoulder—but she held on.

Then Lazlo's hand slipped from hers… and she heard a gunshot.

*

Veronica woke to find herself lying in her bed, her eyes wet with tears. It was the same dream she had almost every night now… every night for almost seven months. The sun was rising in the sky, and she could hear Franklin snoring, complemented by the sound of her mother snoring.

She got up quietly and went to the bathroom. She splashed her teary face with cold water. She then splashed cold water on other parts of her body. She wondered how long she would continue to have these dreams. Waking up both aroused and traumatized was not how she wanted to live her life. Every morning, she woke up wishing that she had some way to find Lazlo. She wanted him to be safe. She wanted him to be happy. She wanted him. Either that, or she wanted to be able to forget him, and go on with her life—but her heart didn't seem to want to allow her to do that.

She got dressed and headed outside to the chicken coop. She had to bury all these feelings before her day started. She could share this with no one. She couldn't allow herself to think about it at all during the day, or she was afraid she would say or do something reckless. She needed to find a way to process her feelings.

Or she would end up the human equivalent of Betty the chicken.

Chapter Nine

So Many Monsters

"Veronica, please come in," Mr. Sawika said, beckoning her to enter his office.

John Sawika was sitting behind a very large, dark wooden desk. It looked less like the desk of a factory manager and more like the desk of a lawyer. Behind him was an oversized wreath that his secretary must have put up. Veronica didn't imagine that he was the kind of man who would be bothered with Christmas decorations.

"How are you doing?" he asked, standing and walking around his desk to pull out a chair for her.

Oh no, I am being sacked for sure, Veronica thought glumly.

Veronica had spent almost seven months in the Quality Assurance department. Even though none of the people in that department ever spoke to each other beyond basic pleasantries, it was the best job Veronica had ever had. She had to make eight runs a day to sample tobacco from various areas in the building, and sometimes from other buildings. Each run took about thirty minutes. After that, she tested the tobacco for weight, humidity, and contamination with foreign objects. She could do this in less than thirty minutes, which gave her extra time between runs. Some of the other girls visited friends on the floor during these breaks, but Veronica usually read. This was the first time in her life that she had ever had any reason to visit the public library. Before this job, she had been simply too busy to read.

"Who died?" Mr. Sawika asked, as he sat back down behind his desk.

"Excuse me?" Veronica asked.

"Your expression is far from happy," he said, with a little smirk. "And at Christmas we are all supposed to be happy, aren't we?"

"I'm just worried that you are going to fire me," Veronica said.

"Fire you?" Mr. Sawika said, then slapped his hand on his thigh and laughed.

"That's why I like you, Veronica. You are a straight shooter. You don't try to manipulate conversations with your womanly wiles."

"I don't have womanly wiles," Veronica replied.

"Tommy's friend CJ would argue differently," Mr. Sawika said.

"CJ just likes me because he doesn't really know me," Veronica said, before she could stop herself.

"That's just what I am talking about," Mr. Sawika said. "You are straight shooter. If I were a younger man and unattached, I might just be as smitten with you as CJ is. But not to worry—about that or about your job."

Mr. Sawika leaned forward. As he did so, one of the Christmas cards that had been placed on a side cabinet flew off, even though there was no wind.

"I have spoken with the managers of Quality Assurance in Milligan, Number 8 and Number 17. All of them said that you have done a superb job these past months. I have reviewed your reports, and they are thorough but concise. And we have all been impressed with your punctuality and work ethic."

"Thank you, sir," Veronica said. She was holding herself still. She didn't know where this was going and didn't want to read anything into it. She found that setting her expectations low meant she was rarely disappointed.

"Don't thank me, I consider it a testament to my ability to choose talent," Mr. Sawika said. "Have you felt comfortable in QA?"

"Yes, sir" she replied.

"And you get along with the other girls in QA?"

"As far as I know," Veronica replied. "We don't talk much, but we're friendly."

"And you have found nothing in your rounds that would upset you?"

"If you are asking if I have found dead things in the snuff room, I have," Veronica replied. Mr. Sawika's eyebrows shot up. "I found a couple of mice and a good-sized rat, but that's all. Oh, the rat was still alive."

"What did you do with it?" Mr. Sawika asked.

"I killed it and threw it away,"

"You're not squeamish then?" he asked.

"No, sir. I prepare the chickens at our house," Veronica replied.

Mr. Sawika smiled openly.

"Yessir. I surely would have taken a shine to you, as a young man," Mr. Sawika said, before coughing quickly and looking away.

"So you like your job?" he said, as opened his desk drawer.

"Yes, it's the best job I have ever had," Veronica replied.

Mr. Sawika looked up and smiled again.

"Then I hope you will be pleased that I have just changed your position from temporary to permanent," Mr. Sawika said, as he pulled a piece of paper from the drawer. "I am assigning you to Quality Assurance on a permanent basis."

Veronica gasped and some spit went down her windpipe. For a moment she couldn't breathe, but she quickly took a breath through her nose and was able to get enough air to cough. As she was trying to get her cough under control, Mr. Sawika came around his desk and patted her strongly on the back.

"Better?" he asked, when she finally stopped coughing.

"Yes," she said.

"Can I assume that you will take the position?" Mr. Sawika said, patting her shoulder.

"Yes, sir. Thank you."

"Here, you just take this paper on down to Heddy in Personnel. She should get you all set up," Mr. Sawika said, handing it to Veronica. At the top of the page was one word that immediately caught Veronica's eye. The word was "Contract."

"Excuse me, Mr. Sawika, but what is this?" Veronica asked.

"Oh, did I forget to mention that?" he said, with a wave of his hand. "As a permanent employee you are entitled to paid sick days. Also, if you stay with us long enough, we do pay for additional education, if it is for your work."

Someone could have knocked Veronica over with a feather.

"Would accounting classes be considered educational… for work, I mean?" she asked softly.

"Normally, yes. For QA, not really, but you could make a case for taking math classes or even higher math if you could tie it to quality controls. You like math, then?"

"I love math," Veronica said. Her eyes were still on the paper in her hands, scanning it for contradictions or signs that it wasn't real, but she could find none.

"Well then, just keep up the good work," Mr. Sawika said, turning his attention to a stack of papers on his desk. "We'll see what comes of it. You go on now and take that to Personnel."

Veronica nodded.

"And say hello to Iona for me," he called as Veronica walked out of his office.

Iona? When had he and her mother been on a first-name basis?

She turned back to look at him—and saw five or six black-and-white kittens playing on the floor in front of his desk.

Veronica blinked hard, and the kittens disappeared. She left the office as quickly as possible.

*

The paperwork process had taken longer than Veronica had expected. She had assumed that she would just hand the signed paper over to Heddy, but instead Heddy had walked her through the contract. It turned out that she would not only get paid holidays and paid sick days, but she would also get medical coverage. If she had to go to the doctor or hospital, the company insurance policy would pay for much of it. No one in her family had ever had such a luxury before. Veronica asked Heddy to repeat it three times before she allowed herself to believe it. She would also work a regular eight to five shift, every day from Monday to Friday. She would be making the same salary that she was making now but working fewer hours. In addition to citing her additional benefits, the contract also added restrictions. For example, if she left the company, the contract stated that she agreed not to work at another cigarette factory for at least two years. It also stated that she would not be allowed to discuss anything that happened at work with anyone outside of the company. The penalty for this was immediate termination and a possible fine. Despite looking for it, Veronica could find nothing that struck her as completely unreasonable or out of line.

When she finally signed the papers and left Personnel, it was already 3:10. She wanted to get one more run in before she left for the day, so she quickly ran back to the QA office, grabbed her samples box, and walked out to the cigarette floor. She would pick up samples on fifteen of the thirty machine lines. In truth, she just wanted to *do* something. She had felt an electric sort of energy running through her body since she had seen the kittens in Mr. Sawika's office.

"Veronica!" Lizzie called, as Veronica came to her line.

"Wait for me, and we can walk home together," Lizzie yelled over the noise of the machines. Veronica came to stand next to her.

"What time do you get off?" Veronica yelled back. As all the machines on the line were working today, Veronica had to yell even when if she was right next to Lizzie, although she could yell a little softer.

"Six, same as you."

"I get off at five," Veronica replied.

Lizzie's mouth fell open, even as her fingers continued packing cigarettes into their packs.

Veronica leaned down and put her mouth to Lizzie's ear.

"They made me permanent," she said.

Lizzie shrieked loud enough that a supervisor turned her way, but once he saw that there was no emergency, he went back to his clipboard.

"Ronnie, that's amazing! I'm so jealous," Lizzie yelled. She was smiling but for a moment Veronica saw a flash of something else in her friend's eye—something dark. Veronica noted it and then put it to the back of her mind. She didn't want to have to worry about it right now. She had too many other things to think about.

"You better go, he's staring," Lizzie said, nodding to her supervisor, whose eyes were back on them. "I'll come by your place tonight and you can tell me all about it."

Veronica nodded and placed her hand on Lizzie's shoulder. Lizzie flinched ever so slightly before flashing Veronica a bright smile.

Lizzie has every reason to be jealous, Veronica thought.

Veronica knew that she had done nothing in particular to earn her new job, or her initial move to QA. If she looked at it too hard, Mr. Sawika's comments about her might have hinted at a reason, but she didn't want to linger on that if she didn't have to. In a way, it was darkly humorous that she was the one who seemed to have gotten ahead because of her—well, if not looks, then personality.

By the time she finished collecting samples from the last row of machines, it was 4:30. She could see the fading light through the skylights of the cigarette floor. She wanted to have time to test her samples, so she decided to do one final collection in the snuff room. Normally, she would have gone to collect samples of chewing tobacco in building 8, but if she went all the way over there, she wouldn't have time to test her samples before 5 p.m. She wasn't sure if she was required to leave at 5 p.m. She suspected it wouldn't be a problem, but she didn't want to mess up on her first unofficial day as a permanent employee.

She trotted to the back of the cigarette floor where a short hallway led to a large warehouse, which was segmented into a variety of closed rooms. Each room held aging tobacco, but each was designed for different uses. There were rooms for tobacco that would be chewing tobacco, pipe tobacco, and snuff, respectively. Apparently, each product required different sizes, age, and quality of tobacco leaves. Veronica knew nothing about how this process worked. Only the top bosses knew the precise criteria and aging process. This was because the process chain was spread across different units that didn't interact with each other. The people who picked the tobacco, and knew its type, had no idea where it would be stored. Those who stored it didn't know where it came from. Only the line managers knew each step in the process and there were fewer than ten such managers.

As Veronica reached the infamous snuff room, she set her box on a wooden table by the door. This table had once held an antique moisture reader but now it served to hold an air hose. Veronica picked up the hose and used her full body weight to pull the heavy wooden door open. It creaked and scraped against the floor as she pulled it full open. The sweet, salty smell of drying tobacco assaulted her nostrils. It was a pleasant smell in moderation, but this was not in moderation. The smell was so strong that it made her eyes water. She wiped them quickly with the back of her hand.

On the inside of the door were thousands, or tens of thousands, of tobacco bugs. It was normal for this room, and one of the lesser things Mr. Sawika had warned her about. It was supposed to be procedure to use the hose to blow these bugs back into the snuff room, so they would not get out onto the factory floor, but Veronica thought this was stupid. Instead, she blew them out into the center of the warehouse, where they scattered across the floor. What she knew, that her predecessors apparently didn't, was that these bugs would quickly be eaten by other bugs, mice, and rats, and it was better to draw these things away from the tobacco itself, where they could do damage.

She picked up her sample box and stepped quickly into the room. Just inside the room was headless broom. Veronica had removed the head, which had revealed a large nail where the head had been. She had used this on more than one occasion to spear bugs, mice, and even rats. Most of the time they would run away from her but from time to time they would come toward her. She made the broom spear after the first of such incidents.

Around her, rows and rows of tobacco were hanging from wooden beams that rose up almost to the top of the high ceiling. Unlike the cigarette factory, this room had no skylight. It also had very dim electric lights. Veronica walked through the rows, pulling bits from leaves on different rows.

She was trying not to think about the kittens she had seen in Mr. Sawika's office. They had been ghosts, of course. There had been no kittens when she arrived. In that moment, she saw them in faded black and white. They looked like something that had been taken from a movie. On top of that, John Sawika was not the sort of man who would own pets, let alone bring them to work. These were not the first ghost animals she had seen. In the past nine months, not a week went by without her seeing the spiritual remains of some animal. She suspected that they stayed near the spot where they died, as she often saw them near or on the paved roads of the town. Once, she thought she saw the specter of a chicken near their coop. The spiritual implications of this were terrible. If animals could be ghosts, then they had souls, not unlike human souls. If that were true, then how was killing them any different from killing another human?

Veronica tried not to think about this. She didn't get enough food to begin with, she didn't need to start getting picky about what she did get.

There was a rustling sound on the row to her right. She could see movement in a pile of tobacco leaves. She moved carefully toward the sound. She assumed it was a mouse or rat, but what came tumbling out of the leaves was neither. It was a small raccoon, and not a healthy one. Its fur was matted and dirty with tobacco dust, and its skin seemed to hang on its bones. It started to run forward but its back legs were not coordinated with its front legs, so it fell to the side.

"Okay, little guy, let's not get any further," Veronica said, backing up and holding the broom handle out in front of her, nail pointed at the raccoon.

The animal twitched and flailed. Its head pulled back toward its spine at an impossible angle.

It's either been poisoned or it has rabies. Either way I need to get out of here and warn someone.

She began to move slowly backward. For a moment, the raccoon lay still but then it began rolling and using its front paws to try to push itself up to a standing position.

"I know you're tired," Veronica said in a soft voice. "You just rest there, and I'll go get you some help."

At the sound of her voice, the raccoon sat up and bared its teeth in her direction. Its eyes were clouded so it probably couldn't see her, but clearly it heard her voice. The creature fell forward, pulling itself toward her with its front paws, dragging its back legs behind it. The lower half of its body was twitching, as if it was having muscle spasms.

Veronica was backing away slowly and was almost at the end of the row when she saw a dark shape appear next to the raccoon. Like the kittens, it looked like a black-and-white image superimposed on the world. Unlike the kittens, it didn't have the form of an animal. It had the vague form of a human, and its shadow arms reached out across the floor toward her. Veronica jumped back just before those shadows reached her feet. The image flickered for a moment before its arms were pulled back from her. It then turned away and the whole of it rushed toward the raccoon. For a moment the shadow was superimposed upon the animal but then it disappeared, and the raccoon lurched forward. It stumbled for a moment, but then its eyes turned toward her. At that moment it began to run toward her, with no hesitation and no stumbling.

She dropped her box and ran full-out toward the door. She could hear the scrabbling run of the raccoon behind her, getting closer. She turned the corner and came in view of the door but the last thing she needed was for that thing to get loose on the factory floor, so rather than run out the door, she turned down another row, where she stopped suddenly and crouched. It was only a few seconds until the raccoon ran around the corner. As it did so, Veronica used her broom to knock its legs out from under it. It fell and its momentum caused it to tumble forward and into one of the wooden beams, resulting in a cascade of tobacco falling on top of it. Veronica ran for the door, grabbed it, and pushed it closed with all her strength. It felt like forever before she got it moving, and the very second she got it shut, she heard something slam against the door—and keep slamming.

Veronica ran to the phone on the wall and called the emergency number listed there.

"John Sawika's office," his secretary said.

"This is Veronica Crane. Can you please tell Mr. Sawika that I found a rabid raccoon in the snuff room?"

The sound of the raccoon banging against the door was becoming less sharp, and flatter. It sickened Veronica to think why.

"Veronica, are you okay?" Mr. Sawika said on the phone. "Did it bite you?"

"No, sir," she replied. "But it's trapped in the snuff room."

"Of course it would be the snuff room," Mr. Sawika muttered. "Stay right there and I'll come get you."

As Veronica hung up, she heard loud chattering and screeching sounds coming from the door.

She didn't know what that thing was, but she knew that she didn't want to be there when they opened the door again.

Chapter Ten

Unseeing the Veil

Mr. Sawika arrived within minutes and immediately escorted Veronica out of the tobacco storage area. He had his arm through hers as he walked her across the cigarette floor. At every machine they passed, people looked up but quickly turned their eyes back to their work—a bit too quickly. Despite his size, his normal demeanor, and the fact that his arm was linked in hers, his touch was light and delicate.

When they entered the management area of the factory, he immediately turned toward the Quality Assurance offices. He coughed loudly.

"Excuse me, ladies, but I am going to need to ask you all to take a little break," he said to Veronica's coworkers.

All three of them immediately stood up and left the room without question. Once again, their eyes were averted. Veronica wondered if this sort of thing had happened before.

"Sit down, Veronica," Mr. Sawika said, pulling out a chair for her. "You must have had quite a scare."

Veronica nodded. She had been very scared, but probably not for the reasons he would think. She had already been nervous when she entered the snuff room. Seeing the ghost kittens playing by his desk had unnerved her. Maybe that was why she had seen the ghost in the snuff room. If so, it wasn't a bad thing because knowing it had given her a couple of seconds warning of an impending danger.

"I have asked animal control to meet us here," Mr. Sawika began, "so they can get your story, but perhaps you should tell me first, in case I need to go back and check something before they get here."

Veronica nodded.

"So can you start at the beginning…"

Veronica's brain was trying to re-form what had just happened to her into a digestible bite for someone in management.

"I went into the snuff room. I was collecting samples when I heard a noise at the end of one of the rows."

"You didn't happen to notice what row?" Mr. Sawika asked.

"I did. It was row 26. I took a sample from that row, and I logged it."

"Very good. Do continue."

"So I noticed a sound," Veronica replied. "I thought it was a rat but that didn't bother me because I had my spear."

"You had what?"

Oh no. She hadn't meant to say that.

"Oh, it's just this broom with a nail on the end," Veronica replied, waving a hand. "I have used it to kill rats that I found in the snuff room."

"What did you do with the rat bodies?" Mr. Sawika asked.

"I threw them in the trash bin with the bad tobacco."

"You didn't write about this in any of your reports?" Mr. Sawika said.

Veronica had not done so because people who worked in factories knew that rats were normal and expected but health inspectors seemed to have different opinions.

"I didn't think it was important, sir," she replied.

"You thought just right," Mr. Sawika said, patting her on the arm. "But you don't have to be a rat hunter. Of course, you can if you want to, but you don't have to do that."

Veronica got the distinct impression that he liked that she had killed the rats. The picture of him working in a slaughterhouse was becoming clearer in her mind.

"So back to what happened," he said, as he pulled up a chair and sat next to her.

Veronica focused on the facts.

"Well, it wasn't a rat. It was a raccoon, and it was making very strange noises."

She did not mention that it could not use its back legs in the beginning because then she would have to explain how it came to use them later without the help of a possessing ghost.

"When it saw me, it came straight for me. I knew that no normal raccoon would do that, so I ran. It chased me all the way down the aisles, but I managed to get out before it caught me."

It was best not to give too many details.

Mr. Sawika furrowed his brow for a minute.

"Do you think it was rabid?" he asked.

"Yes, sir. I have seen a rabid raccoon before, and it had all the signs. It was scrawny, its fur was matted, and it was making noises that you don't usually hear raccoons make."

"Yes, that sounds like it was rabid," Mr. Sawika said, his brow still furrowed. "Did you see anything else? Anything out of the ordinary?"

You mean like a ghost? she thought.

"You mean like other dead animals?" she asked out loud.

"Or anything," he replied. "Anything that might have seemed out of place, no matter how small."

Veronica pretended to consider this, avoiding thinking about the ghost in the snuff room, or the ghost kittens playing beside his desk earlier.

"No, sir."

Mr. Sawika smiled and patted her arm.

"Perfect," he said. "I feel even more confident about promoting you to permanent full time. You have showed good judgment and composure in a stressful situation. Would you like to go on home now, or are you okay with staying a little while past five to answer questions from animal control?"

"I'm fine to wait," Veronica replied.

"Good. Thank you," he said. "Of course, you might want to leave out the bit about the rats."

"Of course."

The phone on one of the desks rang. Mr. Sawika got up and answered it.

"Yes. Well, at least that's good news," he said with a sigh. "Oh, they are? Good. Veronica is here but I will come and escort them myself."

"They opened the snuff room, and it looks like the raccoon is already dead," Mr. Sawika said to Veronica as he hung up the phone. "It's good timing because the animal control men are here, so it will be less dangerous for them. It's never a good thing to have a government employee injured by something in your factory."

Veronica nodded, as was expected of her.

"Are you okay to sit a few minutes by yourself while I escort the animal control people up?" he asked.

"Of course, sir. I'm fine."

Mr. Sawika smiled at her. It was different from his normal, toothy smile. It was closed-mouthed and for a moment his eyes looked almost sad.

"Yes, I suppose it would take more than a rabid coon to unsettle a girl like you," he said. The words could have been sarcastic, but they weren't.

As he left the room, Veronica wondered what he had meant exactly, by "a girl like you." Of course, that was the least of her problems. A more pressing concern was the fact that she had just been chased by a raccoon that was possessed by a ghost... a ghost that looked like it might have been human.

*

It was 6:15 p.m. by the time Veronica left the factory. The animal control specialists had grilled her about every possible detail of her encounter with the raccoon—except the one detail that really mattered. Of course, rabid animal possession by a human ghost probably wasn't something they encountered on a typical, or even atypical, case.

The sun had already set when she began her walk home. There were streetlights on the main road home, but they were few and far between. The nighttime frightened some people, but it had never frightened Veronica. She knew from experience that the dark was an equalizer. Physical strength meant less when you couldn't see your opponent. In the dark, smart won more often than strength.

A crescent moon was hanging low in the sky with Venus shining like a beacon beneath it. For a moment, Veronica stopped and just stared at the sky. She had studied astronomy from books when she was small. Janie had told her that planets had meaning. Venus was a symbol of love. The moon was a symbol of things we hide. That pretty much summarized Veronica's life right now. She was in love, and it had to be hidden.

After Lazlo had left, Veronica had spent weeks trying to convince herself that she would get over it. As the weeks turned into months, it was her practical side that forced her to acknowledge her love for Lazlo. The rational part of her recognized and acknowledged that the feeling she was trying to suppress was not going away. In fact, it got deeper as time went on. As this emotion represented a possible threat to her, it was important to acknowledge it, so that it could then be controlled. She had trained herself not to think about Lazlo while at work or at home with her family. She allowed herself to entertain thoughts of him, and the changes he had brought to her life, only when she was completely alone. So she thought of him every night as she drifted off to sleep. He was the shape of her prayer. It seemed that this prayer must have gone to Nyx, or Morpheus, as Lazlo returned to her every night in dreams. These dreams were not like fantasy. Most of them had elements of fear or tension but in all of them she was with Lazlo... and that was enough. More and more, her daylight hours were a distraction, helping her fill her time until she could see Lazlo again. Some might have given in to this and refused to leave their bed, but Veronica was too grounded for that. She needed her daylight world because she was a physical creature and she had physical needs. She needed food and a place for her family to live. Her day job provided this, and she had managed to keep her days and nights separated most of the time… except for the ghosts.

A chilly wind rustled what few leaves remained on the trees. The moist air whispered of mystery and an upcoming snow. Veronica kicked a stone, and watched it roll through the circle of light created by a streetlight, before hearing it strike a bush by the side of the road. A bush shrouded in darkness.

Seeing animal ghosts had started a few weeks after Lazlo left. A few weeks after that, she had begun to see the shadows that looked more humanoid. At first, these had unnerved her, but she learned that they would disappear if she acknowledged them. She didn't have to speak to them, a longish look or a nod was usually enough. She wished that she had someone she could talk to about these ghosts, but she didn't know anyone else who had this ability. Grandma Janie could see these things, but she said that she only saw the ghosts of Furies. Veronica was pretty sure that animals wouldn't count. Occasionally she thought about asking Franklin about it, but she knew he didn't see them. She knew this for two reasons. The first was that Janie had once told her that these gifts were passed down through the womenfolk of a family. The second was that she was sure Franklin would tell her if he was to see shadows or ghosts. For a moment, she felt a twinge of guilt, but she quickly buried that feeling. It was better—safer—for Franklin to know as little as possible about anything that could further stigmatize him.

Besides, the shadows she saw didn't really amount to much in daily life. They had seemed to only want acknowledgment, and they had been benign. At least, that had been true until today. What happened in the snuff room put things into a new light. The shadow that had possessed the raccoon had not been benign, in its actions or obvious intent. It had come for her in a very real way.

"Veronica Crane!"

A voice startled her out of her thoughts. Ahead of her, under the glow of a streetlight, Veronica saw Tray Crowder, the town postman.

"What are you doing out so late, little girl?" Mr. Crowder said, as she approached. His voice was gruff, but he had always had a heart of gold.

"There was a—" Veronica began, but stopped herself. She was supposed to keep quiet about the raccoon. "There was a lot of work at the factory. I was late on my run, and I needed to do the testing before I left."

It wasn't exactly a lie.

Mr. Crowder's face seemed to draw into itself in the moonlight.

"You be careful at that factory," he said. "You know they ain't fair there."

"I know," Veronica replied, immediately changing the subject.

"How is Nellie? Has she had her baby?"

Mr. Crowder snorted.

"Nellie wasn't ever pregnant," he said. "They used that as an excuse to fire her. They was angry at her for calling the health inspector is all. So they laid her off, and gave that worthless husband of hers his notice."

"Doug was fired?" Veronica asked. She had a sick feeling in her gut.

"Yeah," Mr. Crowder said. "He was furious about it and took it out on our Nellie. She came home to stay with us for a few weeks after that. He hit her jaw and it was swole up so bad that she couldn't eat proper for two or three days. She should have just stayed with us, but when that good-for-nothing came calling for her, with flowers, and his hair all slicked up—well, she went back to him."

She and Mr. Crowder were standing in a circle of light beneath the streetlight… and they were not alone. They had been joined by a tiny, jittery shadow, one that would disappear and reappear at different spots within the circle of light. Mostly it was staying close to Mr. Crowder but sometimes it would stray toward her.

"How is Nellie now?" Veronica heard herself ask, not really wanting an answer.

"I don't rightly know," Mr. Crowder said. "She and the good-for-nothing left town a few weeks after she went back to him. I ain't heard hide nor hair from them since, and that ain't like my girl."

"Did you tell Chief Bishop about it?"

Mr. Crowder snorted again.

"You know as well as I do that Chief Bishop has his favorites. The good-for-nothing was one of them, but my Nellie wasn't. I think that group thought that she wasn't good enough for him 'cause of the rumors that we have Injun blood in our family."

"So he didn't check about them?" Veronica asked.

"Oh, he said he did. And he said he didn't find nothing, but I don't believe him."

Mr. Crowder moved a bit closer to her.

"I'm on my way right now to meet some friends in the mail service from other cities," he said softly. "We're doing some checking around, but I ain't found nothing yet. I'll be honest with you, I'm scared for my girl."

"I'm so sorry, Mr. Crowder," Veronica said, trying to keep her eyes off the shadow dancing around at his feet. In her heart, she knew who and what that shadow was, but she didn't want to allow herself to think about it right now.

"If you find out something—anything—you will find me and tell me, won't you?" Mr. Crowder asked.

"Of course," Veronica lied. She already knew something, but she just couldn't tell him.

"You get on home now," Mr. Crowder said, with a worn little smile. "Your mama will be worried."

Veronica nodded, and gave him a quick hug, before turning to take her leave.

"One more thing, Veronica," Mr. Crowder called, coming closer, but now out of the glow of the streetlight. "There have been some letters come through the office addressed to you," he said. "Thing is, they had no address, just your name and the town."

Veronica felt her heart jump in her chest.

"Some of the fellas sorting mail was taking a bit too much interest in them, and I didn't want them opening them, so I told them to give me all those letters. So I have been delivering them to your mailbox."

"I didn't get any letters," Veronica said softly.

"Hmm, maybe your mama picked them up before you," Mr. Crowder said. "I wanted to tell you because I ain't sure if I got all the letters. For all I know, some of the fellas might have took some and read them. I ain't got no way to know. I got another one today though."

Fear and excitement were battling in Veronica's gut for supremacy.

"Mr. Crowder, could you put it in our mailbox after 5 a.m. tomorrow?" Veronica asked, her heart pounding.

Mr. Crowder looked at her for a moment. It was hard to see his face, as he was backlit by the streetlight, but he nodded his head slightly.

"I will do that, but you be careful, girl," Mr. Crowder said quietly. "I'm quite fond of you and your family, and I wouldn't want no one to get the wrong ideas."

"That's why I need to see a letter," Veronica said. "If I don't know what they are, then I don't know how to—well, how to handle myself about it."

Mr. Crowder nodded, more vigorously this time.

"That's just so," he said. "You've always been a smart one, Veronica Crane."

He then gave her a chaste little kiss on the cheek and turned away. His walk seemed slower than she had ever seen it. Slower and less steady.

As he passed through the circle of light from the streetlight, she saw that the small darting shadow was still at his feet.

*

When Veronica approached her house, she saw Franklin and Nan sitting on their porch swing. As she got closer, she realized that they were holding hands. This was the first time that Veronica had seen them holding hands in the open. She felt a little glow of warmth in her chest.

If love had been unkind to her, at least it had decided to bestow its blessings on one member of their family. Franklin and Nan had been almost inseparable since he began working at the firehouse. They worked together in the evenings, and about half the time, Nan would eat with them, or Franklin would eat at the Payne house. Veronica's mother cooed over Nan, which was amusing for both Veronica and Franklin. When Franklin and Nan were together, they laughed a lot and smiled more. Even CJ and his friends left the couple alone, probably because Dr. Payne was so respected in town. This must have been very painful for Tommy, who had decided that Nan was worthy of him shortly after she developed from a skinny girl into a thin but shapely woman. As it was, Nan had eyes for only Franklin, and he had been in love with her since he was a boy. It was good to know that love could be kind, and not always malicious.

"Hi there," she called to them as she started up the driveway. She wanted to give them the opportunity to move apart or drop hands. When she rounded the corner to the back porch, she was happy to see that they had done neither.

Nan caught her eye and then looked down with a small smile. Franklin beamed and raised his right hand, the one not holding Nan's hand. Nan had always reminded Veronica of a delicate flower. She was pale, blonde, and small-boned. She was beautiful, but people weren't likely to notice it because she was shy and a bit guarded on first meeting.

"Have I missed dinner?" Veronica asked as she stepped up onto the porch.

"No, not yet," Franklin mouthed. "Ma is making dinner for the four of us, so I think she is trying to rustle up something special."

"Well, we can make it a celebration then," Veronica said, pulling a copy of the contract out of her bag and handing it to Franklin.

"I got hired for permanent today," Veronica said.

"In Quality Assurance?" Nan asked.

Veronica nodded.

"Oh Ronnie, that's so great," Nan said, jumping up to give her a hug. The use of her family nickname would have annoyed her if most people said it, but it sounded normal and right coming out of Nan's mouth.

This girl may just end up being my sister-in-law, she thought to herself.

When Nan released her, she saw Franklin staring at her with wide eyes.

"Did you see the part about the house?" he said.

"No, was there a part about the house?" Veronica replied, shocked that she had missed something, and scared. What if that was the catch that she had overlooked? There wasn't anything she could do now, she had already signed it.

"It's ours," Franklin said. "It says here that from this date onward, the house is in your name. It says that the deed will be delivered to you by the company attorneys within a week."

"What?" Veronica said, taking the paper back. She saw it, there in black and white. It had been in the same paragraph as her new hours, shoved in the middle as if it meant nothing. What it meant was everything for them. You couldn't be evicted from a place you owned.

Veronica felt her eyes welling up in spite of herself. She looked up to see that Franklin's eyes were wet as well… and Nan was looking at him with unmistakable love.

"I guess your dad was right, giving Mama some roses," Franklin mouthed to Nan.

"My father gave Iona some roses to thank her for allowing Franklin to walk me home all these months," Nan explained.

"Allowing him?" Veronica asked, trying hard not to laugh. She felt like a boulder had been lifted from her shoulders, and it made her feel giddy.

"Ronnie…" Franklin warned.

"I'm just thinking that I am kind of hoping that one day, I might have a sister named Nan." The words left Veronica's mouth without her mental consent. Franklin's face went white, but Nan smiled and looked down.

"I hope that too, Ronnie," Nan said softly.

Franklin's eyes went back and forth between Nan and Veronica in such a comic manner that Veronica laughed out loud.

"I'm gonna go on inside now," Veronica said. "I'm guessing you two have something to talk about."

Veronica didn't hear her brother's words because he would be mouthing them to Nan. Around her, the night was close, silent in the way that only winter nights can be. Despite the silence, Veronica could feel energy heating up the air.

Finally, one word broke through the quiet. It was Nan's soft voice, and it was trembling with emotion. She said only one word.

"Yes."

Chapter Eleven

Here Comes the Rain Again

Veronica had just sat down at their table when Franklin burst into the kitchen, hand in hand with Nan.

"She said yes!" Franklin mouthed to his mother.

Iona dropped the spoon she was holding and put her hands to her mouth. Her eyes began to water. Nan stepped forward shyly and Iona pulled her into a hug.

"I'm so happy for you," Iona said, letting go and taking Nan's face in her hands. "I had hoped—well, I had hoped that you could be friends... but this is so much better."

Veronica stood and pulled Franklin into a hug.

"Thank you." He whispered the words out loud—with no stutter. He pulled back and ruffled Veronica's hair and mouthed, "I would never have had the courage if you hadn't forced my hand. You are such a pain... and the best sister anyone could ever have."

"We aren't the only ones with good news," Nan said suddenly, turning to Veronica.

"I got on permanent with the factory," Veronica said. Her mother closed her eyes for a moment, smiled and nodded.

"Is that in QA?" her mother asked.

"She got a contract and everything," Franklin mouthed. "And we get the house."

Her mother put her hand to her mouth for the second time in five minutes. "What?"

"It's in the contract. They are going to deed the house to us," Veronica said softly. Her mother came over and drew her into an embrace. This was probably the first time her mother had hugged in several years.

"That's good news, sure enough," she whispered in Veronica's ear. She then gave Veronica a little squeeze and Veronica returned the gesture.

"Well, I wish I had something more to celebrate with—" her mother began, but Nan interrupted her.

"Whatever you cook is always delicious," Nan said.

"This girl has been raised right, sure enough," her mother said, with an open, unguarded smile for Nan and Franklin. "So sit yourselves down like you plan to stay a while."

In the next few hours there was more laughing in the Crane household than there had been since her Grandma Janie had been alive—and maybe even more. Her mother served beans, spinach, and cornbread with a bit of salt pork on the side. Veronica didn't know when her mother had bought salt pork but didn't question it. Sometimes Iona came home from work with certain food items and the family had learned not to question.

Just after dinner, as Franklin and Nan were discussing possible dates for their ceremony, Veronica excused herself.

She went to the restroom where she opened the door and closed it. She then moved quietly to her mother's room where she pushed the door open enough to allow the light from the hall to enter it. Postman Crowder had said that he had delivered several letters here. Her mother had to have been the one to have picked them up. Of course, she could have just thrown them away, but her mother wasn't big on throwing things away. Veronica quickly checked under her mother's bed, but she saw nothing but her mother's slippers. She then looked under the mattress, where she found a few envelopes with money stuffed inside. The envelopes had the factory seal on them. There wasn't a lot of money but there was probably twenty dollars spread across them. This was perplexing but not what she was looking for right now. She moved to the door and listened. She could hear Franklin starting to sing a song that he had learned as kid. It was peculiar that Franklin could sing with no stutter at all.

Veronica moved back into her mother's room and went to her sewing cabinet. It was an old machine that had belonged to Grandma Janie. She never really looked at this thing, as she despised sewing. Her mother did all the sewing that was needed in the house. As Veronica examined it, she saw nothing and was about to leave when, just to be thorough, she ran her hand along the back of it. Her hand hit a rough patch. She couldn't see what it was, but it felt like a drawer. Why would there be a drawer on the back of a sewing cabinet? As she traced her finger around the edges of it, she became convinced that it was a drawer, but she could not feel a knob or indentation to open it.

"Hi there everyone!"

Veronica heard Lizzie's voice booming through the house. She quickly moved from the room and into the restroom. She waited for a few moments and then opened the door and walked down the hall.

"You got on permanent!" Lizzie squealed as Veronica entered the room. She gave Veronica a hug that was just a little too tight for comfort. "You lucky, lucky thing. Is it in Quality?"

"Yes, Mr. Sawika told me today," Veronica said.

"What shift will you be on?" Lizzie asked. There was something in the way that Lizzie's eyes were glinting that made Veronica want to change the subject… but she found that she didn't want to talk about Franklin and Nan's news either. She looked to her mother and found that her expression seemed to reflect her own reticence.

"I'll be on eight to five," Veronica replied. "But I don't want to get too excited, I mean, they could decide to take it away from me at any time, so I want to enjoy it while I can."

Franklin gave her a puzzled look but said nothing.

Lizzie laughed and hugged Veronica again.

"You should enjoy it while you have it," Lizzie said with a little laugh. "No more going hungry for ya'll."

Veronica tensed up. Her mother's face closed in on itself. Nan looked down and Franklin put a protective arm around her. If Lizzie noticed that the temperature in the room dropped, she didn't show it. Even three months ago, Lizzie would have noticed the reaction to her statement. Six months ago, she wouldn't have said it. Lizzie had changed, and Veronica wasn't quite sure why. Her eyes had taken on a cold, hard look when she thought she wasn't being watched.

"Have you heard anything about Nellie Crowder?" Veronica asked, to cut the silence.

"You mean Nellie Ferguson?" Lizzie asked.

"Yes," Veronica replied. "Her dad stopped me on the way home and asked if I had seen her."

"Oh, that," Lizzie said. "Ben told me that she had skipped town. Apparently, she was pregnant, and Doug found out that the baby wasn't his. He went after her anyway, to take her back, but he couldn't find her. He just got back yesterday."

"What?" Veronica gasped.

"I know, it was horrible for Doug," Lizzie said. "On top of all that, when he came back, he found out that some colored men stole and ate his dog."

There were so many things wrong with that statement that Veronica was momentarily speechless. Mr. Crowder had told him that Nellie wasn't pregnant.

Doug Ferguson was a well-known bully, so why was Lizzie now so close to him that she knew his feelings about his wife's supposed infidelity? And the thing with the dog was ridiculous.

"Well, anyway. I just wanted to drop by to say congratulations on your new permanent position," Lizzie said, moving toward the door. "But I need to go because I'm meeting Ben and he hates it when I'm late."

"Tell Ben we said hello," Nan said.

"Oh, I will if he can hear me," Lizzie said, rolling her eyes. "He's dragging me to one of those rallies. It's always too loud and at the end everyone starts just yelling. It's at the football field again, so it will be super-cold."

"Why are you going then?" Veronica asked.

"Oh, Hugh asked Ben to come and then asked him to bring me," Lizzie said. "And, you know, a girl's gotta do what a girl's gotta do."

Lizzie was still trying to get Ben to propose. It had been eight or nine months since she had subtly broached the topic with him, and she had been dropping larger and larger hints as the months went on. When they first started dating, Lizzie had viewed him as a "possible" suitor but somehow the thought of dating another boy seemed to have flown from her head when she found out that Ben was not going to simply give in to the power of her beauty. After that, Lizzie's behavior had gone from vain but playful, to vain with not-so-buried elements of resentment. It didn't suit her, but Veronica could never have brought that up.

"Be careful out there," Veronica said.

Lizzie smiled and waved before sweeping out the door, but not before she caught Veronica's eye. There was something dark and twisty in her gaze.

For a moment everyone was quiet.

"It's those rallies," Nan said suddenly.

*

"Well, that wasn't Lizzie at her best," mouthed Franklin.

"She's being influenced by the Knights of Harrisville," Nan said. "That's the sort of garbage they spout at their rallies. And Lizzie's been going to a lot of them."

"But they haven't had that many, have they?" Veronica asked.

"Yes, they have. There is one almost every week," Nan replied. "And when they don't, they have meetings at someone's house."

"How long has that been going on?" Veronica's mother asked.

"Five months at least," Nan replied. "I know because my father always ends up having to treat people afterward. They either get themselves worked up and start fights among themselves, or they find someone they can gang up on."

Nan's fists were clenched at her side.

"They often try to find a colored person to scare or beat up. They know that colored people will be too frightened to complain. Then they sneak into my dad's office late at night because they are afraid to come during the day. They are afraid that it will look bad for my father—or me. That's why my dad wanted Franklin to walk me home."

Franklin put a protective arm around her shoulder.

"From now on, I will always be there," Franklin mouthed.

"I just don't understand the way they think," Nan said. "No matter how strong we are, as a town or even as a country, we aren't any stronger than our weakest people. As long as we feel like we have to keep a person down, some part of us will have to hold him down. So we'll never be able to rise to what we could be."

"You are a very wise girl," said Iona, patting Nan on the shoulder. "But most folks ain't. So you need to be careful what you say and who you say it to."

Nan smiled.

"I know," she replied. "I would never speak like this outside of family."

Iona practically beamed.

"Well, now, we should let Franklin take you back to your other family, so you can share the good news," she said. "But don't you stay out too long, either of you. And stay away from the high school."

As Nan and Franklin put their coats on, her mother gave Veronica a strange look.

"You be back here before midnight," her mother said to Franklin as he walked out the door. He threw his hand over his head in response.

Once they had disappeared, Iona turned to Veronica and caught her eye, before turning to the sink and beginning to wash up.

"Maybe you should follow them," she said softly. "Nan is angry, and we both know that Franklin won't back down from a fight."

Veronica nodded and grabbed her coat. Maybe she wasn't the only one who saw shadows tonight.

"Don't let no one see you," Iona said, then reached into one of the kitchen drawers and pulled out her father's old Zippo lighter. "Take this."

"I don't want to—" she began, but Iona raised an eyebrow in warning. "I am still your mother, and you will be doing what I say."

"Why do I need to take Deward's old lighter?" Veronica said, snatching it and shoving it in her pocket.

"Because it belonged to your Grandma Janie before he took it from her,"

Iona replied, turning back to her washing. "I suppose I don't have to spell it out for you, do I, girl?"

Veronica stared at her mother, wondering if she was really referring to the things that Janie had taught her.

"You go on and get back just after Franklin," Iona said, turning back to her sink.

*

Nan's family's house was closer to the town than anyone else's that Veronica knew, but it was also closer to the high school. On normal occasions, that was a good thing, but Veronica suspected that the recent rallies had made it a less desirable location.

Veronica followed Franklin and Nan at a distance. To avoid being seen, she walked slowly and in the shadows, just outside of the streetlights. She knew she was probably walking among and through the shadows of animals and people past. While she was sure that most of what comprised the souls of these people had passed on to wherever we all went after death, it seemed that they had left slivers behind. Maybe they were the manifestation of the memories of them held by their loved ones. Maybe they were thoughts or dreams they had had, that had never been fulfilled. Or maybe tragedy ripped part of their souls loose and lodged those remnants in the physical world. She let her mind drift along with these esoteric thoughts because they were focused on things outside of herself, and were therefore safe. She didn't want to turn her thoughts to the fact that her mother just gave her Janie's lighter, as if she knew what message that would send to Veronica… as if her mother knew that it could be a weapon in Veronica's hands.

Should you ever be threatened, or if your loved ones are ever threatened, remember that the flames that kill others are your friends. Don't hesitate to call them, if you are scared, no matter who makes you scared.

Her Grandma Janie had said that, all those years ago. Veronica had never completely understood what she meant. If Janie meant that Veronica was capable of setting fire to a person as easily as she could set fire to wood, then Veronica wasn't sure she wanted to believe that. An ability like that came with a high price tag of responsibility. Plus, Veronica was fairly sure that she wasn't ethical enough to control what she might do with this kind of ability, if she knew for sure that she could use it that way. So she chose to keep herself in the dark. There was a danger to the light of knowledge.

She saw that Franklin and Nan had turned the corner that led to the high school, so she picked up her pace a bit. If they were going to get in trouble, it would likely be when they were closest to the rally. By the time she made it to the corner, Franklin and Nan were several streets past the high school. Veronica felt the knot in her belly relax when they turned down Maple Street.

As Veronica approached the high school, she could hear someone yelling into a microphone. The distance and distortion made it impossible to make out the words, but she recognized the tone of voice. It didn't matter the mode of amplification or even the language, the sound of hate was always the same. The sound of the crowd cheering and whooping might sound like a football game or a pep rally, but it didn't feel that way. Veronica felt the air get warmer around her as she approached. The high school buildings were dark shadows against a glowing, flickering light coming from behind. This told Veronica that they had lit bonfires. She knew that it wasn't legal to do this on public property, but as she suspected the chief of police's son was present, any complaints filed would not be followed up on.

Veronica stayed on the opposite side of the road as she passed. When she reached Maple Street, she made her way into the woods that lay behind the houses on the left-hand side. At this time of year, it wouldn't be much cover if Franklin or Nan looked her way, but she doubted that they would.

Sure enough, when she arrived, Nan and Franklin were standing on her front porch. Veronica crouched down behind some bushes, even though that was unnecessary. Franklin and Nan had eyes only for each other. Franklin reached out and brushed a hair off Nan's face, and she lifted her chin up toward him expectantly. Most of the time, Veronica didn't notice how handsome her brother was—he was her brother, after all. But now, as he took Nan's face into his hands and bent down to gently brush her lips with his own, he could have been mistaken for a movie star, and Nan was the perfect girl to receive such a tender kiss. Veronica had always thought that Nan was beautiful, but not in the glamorous way that Lizzie was beautiful. Lizzie's beauty would fade. In fact, it was already fading. Nan's beauty was gentle, soft, and ethereal, the sort that doesn't fade. It came from a mix of good bone structure and a good heart.

Nan put her arms around Franklin's neck and pushed her body against his as their kisses became more heated. Veronica felt bad invading their privacy, but it was such a beautiful thing to watch. This was love made physical, not simply lust. Franklin stepped back, and then kissed Nan on the forehead. Nan then took his hand, opened the door to her house, and stepped inside.

Veronica smiled to herself as she turned and began to make her way back through the woods to the street. She would wait for Franklin near the school.

Chapter Twelve

Midnight with the Morons

Veronica stood at the entrance to the high school. It was getting colder out. She wrapped her arms around herself and stamped her feet. Her coat was thick but worn in spots, and when it was bitter cold, she became well aware of where those spots were. The color of the night sky above her was not uniform. In some spots, it was a velvet navy blue twinkling with stars. In others, wispy clouds drifted across the sky. Where they touched, the sky was a milkier blue and the stars were muted. She could see more clouds gathering to the north. The breeze that rustled the dead leaves in the trees smelled of snow.

It would be easy enough to get warmer. All she had to do was to join the rally. From the intensity of the glow of light behind the high school, she knew that there were at least a couple of big bonfires burning. There would also be the heat generated by people—drunk people. So there would be heat aplenty. Veronica hoped that Franklin would be quick enough that she didn't need to resort to that for warmth. Still, she could get a bit closer and perhaps that would drop the chill factor.

She could hear the speakers from here, so it wasn't like staying in the cold was helping her shut out their nonsense.

"Here in Harrisville, we are all friends, we are all neighbors," boomed the current speaker. It was a voice that toggled her memory. She had heard this amplified voice before.

"We help each other out. We look after each other's children. No one here goes hungry if a neighbor has food."

Really? What about if nobody has enough food? We aren't so neighborly then, are we? Veronica thought.

"We are a community, and we are a TEAM," shouted the voice.

Oh, it was the football coach. That was how she knew the voice.

"And if our community is threatened, then I, for one, will fight back."

Veronica had walked a little further up the street until she was at the corner of the gym. She could see a surprisingly large crowd gathered on the football field. A bandstand had been set up, and half a dozen people were standing on it. Two bonfires had been set, one on the far side of the bandstand, but the other, on the near side, was strong enough to have raised the temperature, even from where Veronica stood. She moved a bit closer. The light from the bonfires danced and rippled across the people standing in the crowd. This light made it look like people were moving in slow motion. It made everyone look both more beautiful and more demonic.

A large form moved forward toward a microphone. Even from here, Veronica recognized the form of Don Bilbo, the town mayor.

"Thank you, Coach Villar," he said, clapping the football coach on the back.

"So good evening, everyone," he bellowed into the microphone, causing a ferocious whine of feedback.

"You don't need no damn mic, Don," someone bellowed from the crowd. The crowd laughed and Don laughed with them.

"You're surely right, Bill, I don't," Don yelled back. "At least not for ya'll to hear me."

He then stepped back up to the mic.

"But it might not be good enough for people across town," he said into the mic. "And there are some people 'cross town that should hear what some of these folks have to say."

Don Bilbo's voice was softer now but much more threatening. The crowd roared its approval.

"I know we have been celebrating the fact that some of our boys are coming home from the war safely."

There was universal applause and some hoots.

"And Christmas is coming up."

This produced distinctly less enthusiastic applause.

"And, of course, our football team's win over Gastonia last week."

The thunderous applause came back.

"But now, I'm afraid that we need our community's help, so I would like to ask our Police Chief Bishop to talk to you all," Mayor Bilbo said. "But before he speaks, I want to recommend that some of our gentlemen escort any of our particularly delicate ladyfolk from the area. Any mothers-to-be or teenage girls should be escorted on home by their menfolk. We can let you men know about this later. We will send round leaflets."

People started moving away from the bonfire. Shadows of men in the firelight, connecting to shadows of women. There were other shadows dancing between the human ones. Veronica looked away from that and quickly stepped into the shadow of the high school building so that even if she was seen, she wouldn't be recognized.

"Good evening, my friends," boomed the dark, raspy voice of Chief Bishop. "I wish I was here with better news. Even no news would be better than what I have to tell you."

All voices had quieted. All eyes were on the short, squat form of the police chief.

"There is no way to say this gently, so I will just say it," Chief Bishop said. "This afternoon we found the body of a woman in the woods."

The crowd was completely silent.

"It was a white woman."

The tired, drawn face of Nellie Crowder came unbidden to Veronica's mind. *Oh no.*

"Who?" someone in the crowd called out.

"We haven't completely confirmed her identity yet. Our next step will be to contact a few people in the hopes of identifying her, which we will do later this evening. I wanted to come here tonight to warn you. Her body was found in the woods near the cigarette plant."

"That's near where the coloreds live!" someone yelled.

"We want to make sure that we keep our womenfolk safe, so please make sure that your wives and daughters do not go out walking alone until we get more information about this," Chief Bishop continued.

"Are we going to let them get away with this?" someone yelled.

There was a roar from the crowd. Veronica could see Hugh McBrayer at the back of the crowd. One arm was raised in the air. The other was tightly around the waist of Missy.

"We believe that this may be the same individuals who have been killing cats and dogs for months now," Bishop continued. "Those events began seven months ago, in May of this year."

This was a flat-out lie. The dead cats had been showing up for over a year now. Why would he say that?

"That was when the army brought those colored bastards that they drafted here to process," yelled someone from the crowd. This person was certainly a plant.

"We don't know that there is a connection with that," Chief Bishop said, but there was a dark smile in his voice. "But we are investigating it. This is very important because we received notice today that we will be receiving a group of injured soldiers in our hospital."

He waited and looked around. The crowd had pushed itself closer to the platform.

"Many of these will be colored soldiers," Bishop said.

Colored soldiers returning here. Veronica's heart began to race at the same time as fear ran in shivers up her spine.

A low, discontented rumble ran through the crowd. There were a few shouts of "No" as well as a few boos.

The police chief said nothing but glanced back at the mayor and nodded his head ever so slightly.

"We don't want any of our citizens taking the law into their own hands," Bishop continued. "We will handle this. We just wanted to alert you to the situation and ask that you all take precautions. Keep your eyes and ears open. Protect your womenfolk and your daughters. Thank you."

Mayor Bilbo stepped back up to the microphone.

"I hate to end this on such a somber note, but we have only booked the football field until midnight, and it's going on 11:30. I want us to have a few minutes to finish up the wonderful snacks provided by our ladyfolk. We also have some sodas, and something a little stronger, at the tables we set up over by the building. Let's make sure we finish all this, so we have less to bring home."

From what Veronica could see, many of them had already been drinking and more than a few without reserve. Chief Bishop had played these people well. Drunken bullies would spread out from here and into the streets. They wouldn't remember that he had told them not to take the law into their own hands. They would be fired by alcohol and ego to "protect" their "womenfolk and daughters" and they would do so with violence against anyone who wasn't just like them.

Franklin.

Veronica turned and saw a wave of people moving from the football field and toward the road. She ran along the side of the building until she reached the front. To her horror, she saw that her brother had just emerged at the end of Maple Street. He glanced over at the high school and crossed the road to the other side before continuing. When Veronica saw Tommy Sawika pass by her, roughhousing with some other young men she didn't know, she felt her throat close in fear.

No, no, no, no. Franklin, walk quicker.

*

"Well, look who it is. It's the moron," Tommy called out.

Veronica's prayer that Franklin would manage to make it past this mess without incident was definitely going unanswered.

"What are you doing on this side of town? Did you want to join the rally, boy?" Tommy guffawed. Franklin refused to acknowledge him. He just shoved his hands in his pockets and kept walking.

"No, man, he's over here seeing his girlfriend," yelled Charlie Cazort, son of Dick Cazort, one of the richest and snobbiest business owners in town. Charlie was clasping his hands together and batting his eyes. "She's the doctor's daughter. Maybe he is hoping Dr. Payne can fix his brain."

Tommy's face turned stormy. He whirled on the boy and punched him hard in the gut. Then he turned back toward Franklin, snarling.

"Nan is making a big mistake, wasting her time with you," he yelled, walking toward the road. "I'm sure she just feels sorry for you, so she doesn't see that you are sniffing after her. Oh, you are on her scent for sure, but you ain't getting any. I'll make sure of that, moron!"

Franklin kept walking. Veronica knew he was smart enough to know when he was being baited. It would do him no good to get into a fight with Tommy when Tommy was surrounded by idiots who thought the same way, but Tommy wasn't going to let this go. He sauntered out on the street toward Franklin.

"Hey, idiot!" he called out in a sing-song voice. "I know you can hear me, dummy. Hey, why don't you go and get yourself a dark girl. I'm sure she'll give you a place to put your thing, and then you won't have to spread whatever is wrong with you to some nice white girl."

Franklin kept walking but he had removed his hands from his pockets. His fists were clenched by his sides. Veronica prayed that Franklin would walk faster but she could read his body well enough to know that the likelihood that this would end without a fight was decreasing by the minute. All it would take was a shot at Nan, and Franklin would throw caution to the wind. There was nothing she could do to intervene here; in fact, she was sure that her presence would make things worse, as Tommy wasn't overly fond of her. The only reason he left her alone was—

Veronica turned and began to scan faces in the crowd, muttering a little prayer as she did.

"Maybe something's wrong with the Paynes too," laughed Phil Villar, son of Coach Villar. "I mean, her dad treats them coloreds. Maybe they got some infection."

That was it. Franklin stopped walking.

"Hey, dummy, I'm talking to you," Tommy said, grabbing Franklin by the arm. Franklin whirled on Tommy and clocked him hard enough that Tommy hit the ground before he saw it coming.

Veronica found the face she was looking for.

"CJ!" she yelled, coming out from the shadow of the building. The lower pitch of her voice allowed it to carry better than she had hoped. CJ had stopped in his tracks, but even better, Tommy turned to face her. Franklin, sadly, was not moving away but standing in a boxer's stance with his fists up. When his eyes caught hers, she saw the fury in them. Franklin had put up with just about enough.

"Ronnie!" CJ called back. He didn't exactly run toward her, but he walked plenty fast. "I didn't know you were coming. If I had known, I would have introduced you to some people."

"Well, Lizzie told me that she was coming, so I sort of decided to drop by on a whim," she said, trying as hard as she could to act like Lizzie did with boys. She even flipped her hair. She felt stupid and awkward, but CJ beamed.

"Tommy, for god's sake, get up off the ground and leave Veronica's brother alone," he called.

"What?" Tommy said, scrambling to his feet, face full of suppressed rage.

"I said leave him be," CJ snapped. "Get on over here now!"

At that moment, Hugh and Missy came walking up. Hugh still had his arm tightly around Missy's waist. It was so tight that it looked more like he was pulling her rather than walking with her. Missy smiled at Veronica, but then quickly looked away. Missy's arm was in a sling.

Veronica saw that Franklin had not moved from where he was standing. He motioned to her and then pointed to his watch.

"Go on, Franklin. I'll be behind you in five minutes, I promise," Veronica called out. Franklin glared but Veronica flipped her hand at him. He got the message but was none too happy about it. He stepped backward a few paces, staring at her, before turning to continue on his way.

"Sorry about Tommy," CJ said. "He's just drunk and acting stupid."

"At least you aren't," Veronica said, with real feeling. For a moment, she was worried about how that came out, but CJ was still beaming.

"Did you hear what they said about finding a woman's body?" Hugh asked. "It's horrible. I hope it isn't anyone we know."

"How could it not be, everyone in this town knows each other," Veronica said.

"Ronnie's right," CJ said. "We know about each other, and we care about each other. Whoever did this must have been an outsider."

Veronica said nothing. It was hard to agree with such a caring sentiment looking at Missy with her splinted arm, and Hugh's possessive grip on her waist.

"So we need to be even more careful and watch out for each other," CJ said, parroting the mayor and his father.

Veronica saw Lizzie from a distance. The last thing she wanted right now was to have Lizzie show up and go on a tirade about colored people.

"Well, I should get home. I have work in the morning," Veronica said. "Thanks so much for—"

She stopped. She was thankful that CJ had stopped Tommy, but she couldn't say that out loud. CJ removed the need for it.

"I'm happy to help in whatever way I can," CJ said. "Also, you shouldn't be walking home alone, so would you allow me to escort you?"

In that moment, CJ Bishop sounded shy and almost likable. It would be almost impossible to say no at this point.

"Yes. Thanks, CJ," Veronica replied. CJ looked up with such shock and happiness that Hugh laughed.

"Didn't expect that, did you CJ?" he said.

"Shut up now, Hugh," CJ replied. His voice had returned to its normal soft but menacing style.

"Come on, Ronnie. Let's get you home," he said.

As they walked, Veronica kept a respectable distance from CJ. She had agreed to have him walk her home because she couldn't find a good way out of it without putting CJ in a position where he would lose face. Given the drinking, the rally and the hate bubbling just beneath the surface, Veronica had thought it was the safest option. But now that they were alone, she hoped she had not miscalculated.

"I'm going university next year," CJ said suddenly.

"Really?" Veronica asked. "I thought your father wanted you to join the police force."

"He does, but that's not what I want to do," CJ responded. "It took a while for me to decide, but I think the world has bigger problems. Police have to get involved when things are broken. When communities are broken. I want to get involved in helping to keep our communities thriving."

"How would you do that?" Veronica asked.

"I think I'd like to be involved in government, somehow," CJ replied.

As he was speaking, Veronica noticed that a few small shadows had appeared in the glow of the streetlight. These were shadows without owners. The thought of CJ in a position of power made Veronica's skin crawl.

"Well, here we are," Veronica said, stepping quickly onto her driveway to increase the distance between them. "Thank you for walking me home."

"I am here whenever you need me, Ronnie," CJ said. "I always have been."

Veronica forced herself to smile as she waved and turned her back on him.

"Ronnie," he called.

Veronica turned.

"Did you hear the part in the rally about the colored soldiers being housed in our hospital here?"

Veronica's heart began to pound.

"Just a bit of it," she replied.

"My father heard that they will be arriving on the eighteenth or nineteenth of December," CJ said. He was standing at the bottom of her driveway with his hands behind his back.

"That's next week," Veronica replied. "Why are they sending them here?"

And who *are they sending here?*

She couldn't ask that out loud.

"That was exactly what I asked," CJ said. "Why do they have to come here? But apparently our hospital is one of the newest in the area, and all North Carolina soldiers are being spread out among the best hospitals. So we will get soldiers, both black and white. They wanted to get some of them home for Christmas. I understand for the white soldiers but—well, we don't need any more trouble, do we?"

CJ met Veronica's eyes and held her gaze. For a moment there was something in that gaze. It could have been hope, accusation, sadness. Then he looked away.

"Okay, just be safe, Ronnie," he said, as he turned and walked away, hands stuffed in his pockets.

Veronica turned and began to walk up her driveway. She could hear her mother inside, talking to Franklin. Her voice was unusually soft and melodious. It was the voice that she used when she was trying to calm him down. Veronica knew that Franklin would be angry at Veronica for being there, and for then interfering. He would also probably suspect that Iona had suggested that Veronica follow him, or if she didn't suggest it, she had at least condoned it. So Veronica knew that she would be walking into an argument with Franklin. Arguments were always uncomfortable because in those moments his inability to speak without a stutter was all the more frustrating for him. When he was upset, he often tried to speak, it was like he couldn't help himself. Of course, these were the exact moments that made words difficult for normal speakers. For Franklin, this usually deteriorated into him making one sound over and over. So most serious arguments ended with Franklin stomping from the room and Veronica left to sort things out with her mother. She understood this, but today had been dramatic enough already. She didn't need the added drama.

Veronica was just at the top of the driveway and about to turn to the back door when something caught her eye.

Something was twinkling, just beside the henhouse.

Chapter Thirteen

Will-o'-the-Wisp

The little light was dancing in the air. All the hens were currently asleep but were very easy to wake. This meant that whatever the thing was, it wasn't something that they sensed.

Veronica moved slowly up the drive and toward the henhouse. As she did so, the little light moved back, away from her. It was a bluish-green and it was hovering only an inch or two above the ground.

It's a will-o'-the-wisp, she thought.

Will-o'-the-wisps were not unknown in their community. Their town was close to a river and most wisps were seen in the muddy, swampy areas near the water. Most of the town officials said that they were really little bursts of gas from the ground that caught fire on sparks coming from plants. A few people claimed that they were ball lightning. The more common folk claimed that they were mischievous fairies or discontented spirits. The one thing that everyone agreed on was that they were not safe to approach.

So what did Veronica do? She followed it into the woods behind their house. The air around her was getting both colder and wetter, which was making her hands ache. It was also filled with the smell of sulfur. She knew that she probably shouldn't be out here in the dark. The brambles from the bushes were pulling at her coat and scraping her already irritated hands. On top of all that, she was sure she was getting her shoes dirty.

Just as she was turning around to head back, the light in front of her flashed brightly, sending out sparks of red and gold. It then returned to its bluish-green color but this time the shiny ball had a different shape. It was chicken-shaped and something about its energy felt familiar.

"Betty?" she asked softly.

The shimmering light glowed more brightly for a moment before spitting forth four sparks, which then grew into smaller glowing orbs that skittered around her.

"Your babies, Betty?" she asked. The shiny, glowing, chicken cloud spun before moving forward again. Veronica now followed without hesitation. The glowing ghost of Betty moved forward, in the direction of the thick woods near their house. Given what she had just seen and heard, it probably wasn't the smartest idea to go digging around in the woods by herself. Franklin would be even angrier with her if he knew she was back doing this.

She was so lost in thought that she didn't notice that the ghost of Betty had stopped and was just standing, with her chicks pecking around her. Veronica moved slowly forward, but her stomach lurched when she saw what Betty was pecking at. On the ground was a pig—or what was left of one. The animal had been sliced open from throat to anus, but its throat had not been slit. This thing had been killed by having its guts pulled out. Said guts were lying in front it, now rotting, and probably teeming with maggots—or at least she hoped that was the reason that she could see its innards moving. To make things worse, the pig had been a female and pregnant. The baby pigs had been hacked to pieces and scattered about.

Why would someone slaughter a pig? Or more accurately, why would someone slaughter a pig and not take the meat? And killing a pregnant sow was wasteful in the extreme. From the corner of her eye, she saw another shiny blue ball. It wasn't Betty or her chicks. They had wandered away from the pig carcass. This blue ball was moving toward it. As she watched, she saw the blue ball form itself into the shape of a tiny pig. The blue pig snuffled around the carcass, moving forward to sniff at it, only to jerk away. It didn't notice Veronica at all. In fact, it moved very close to her in its explorations. At some point, it moved toward what might have been the pig's uterus, and violently jumped away, moving through Veronica's body. As this happened, an image flashed before her eyes—a face twisted with a furious sort of glee. A face with dark hair and bright green eyes.

"Thanks, Betty," Veronica whispered to the glowing bird. The bird flashed and then disappeared, along with her chicks.

"You can leave now," Veronica said to the tiny pig before it too disappeared.

Veronica turned to head back to her house. She had a new worry, and a potential new threat.

Tommy Sawika.

Tommy killed this pig and dragged it here, behind her house. Veronica had a sinking feeling that this had something to do with Franklin. She didn't give

Tommy credit for the brains to come up with a plot against Franklin, but CJ could.

*

"I only asked Veronica to follow you so that someone would know if those idiots started something," her mother was saying, as Veronica stepped into the kitchen.

"So what would happen if something did happen? How could Veronica help? Before she could find help, whatever was going to happen would have happened," Franklin mouthed. He was sitting at the table, his eyes bright and jaw set. "You just set up a situation where I might have had to fight to protect two women rather than one."

Iona caught Veronica's eye and shrugged.

"I need to change the topic for a minute," Veronica said, sitting down at the table across from Franklin.

"That's convenient," Franklin mouthed.

"I found a pig carcass just out back in the woods," Veronica said. Her mother whirled.

"What? What kind of carcass?" Franklin asked.

"An ugly kill and a wasted carcass," Veronica said. "The pig was slit from throat to anus, and its insides had been yanked out. All the meat remained. It wasn't the remains of a slaughtered animal."

"Do you think it was dead before, hit by a car or something, and dragged into the woods after?" Franklin asked.

"No, I think it died from having its guts ripped out."

"Could it have been an animal attack?" Iona asked.

"No, Mom," Veronica replied. "It was a straight cut—no animal could do that. It was killed by someone with a sharp, big blade. It hadn't even been bled out. Whoever did it either wanted the pig to suffer or didn't care if it suffered."

Franklin's blue eyes were fiery.

"What did it look like?" he asked.

"If you are asking if it looked like it could have come from your workplace, it did. It was well-fed and clean. I couldn't see any markings on it, because it was night, but you should check in the morning."

"You need to tell them about this at the farm," her mother said, as Franklin stood up.

"Yeah, I know," he said. "If it's okay with you, I'm going to bed now."

Veronica walked over and gave her brother a hug.

"Don't let this ruin your day. The nicest and prettiest girl in town just agreed to marry you."

Franklin smiled and nodded, but his face wasn't calm. He knew the implications of the pig behind their house as well as she did. It was either a warning or a setup.

Veronica sat back down.

"Is there something you ain't saying?" her mother asked.

"The pig was a sow. It had been pregnant," Veronica said softly.

"Oh, dear Jesus," her mother muttered. "What sort of person would do something like that?"

"Someone with a lot of hate inside," Veronica replied. "Or someone with a plan."

"What sort of plan?" her mother asked.

"To kill one of the pig farm pigs—and blame it on Franklin," Veronica said.

"That's ridiculous. No one in their right mind would believe such a thing of Franklin," her mother replied, as she cleaned up the stove.

"I saw the rally while I was waiting for Franklin. A lot of people there didn't seem to be in their right mind. The police chief announced that they had found the body of a dead white woman."

"Who?" Iona asked.

"He said that they didn't know but that they would be calling on people to try to identify her," Veronica said. "What sort of policeman announces something like that before they find the identity and notify the family? He said it to rile the crowd up. When they left, there were probably several of them happy to rip the guts out of more than pigs."

"Did he blame anyone?" Iona asked.

"Not directly, but he insinuated that it was the colored people near the factory," Veronica said.

"No colored person would waste a good pig like that," her mother muttered.

"The only people who would do that are being fed regularly," Veronica said.

"Listen, don't you go sticking your nose in where it oughtn't to be," her mother snapped.

"CJ walked me home tonight."

Her mother turned to face her.

"I got backed into a corner. I needed Tommy away from Franklin, and CJ is the only one Tommy listens to, so I had to be friendly."

"Not too friendly, I hope. You don't want to be leading him on if you have no interest."

"No. I was just friendly and kept my distance. Besides, I haven't led anyone on in my entire life," Veronica said.

Her mother gave her a sad little smile.

"I know that's what you think, but some men see the ghosts of desire wherever they look," Iona said. "So you be careful who you go talking to…"

The letters.

Veronica stood up.

"I'm tired, so I'm going to bed," Veronica said. "Do you need me to do anything before I go?"

"No, you go on and get some sleep. You are permanent now, so they will expect more of you. Congratulations, Ronnie. It's thanks to you that we got our own house now. I never thought we would be that lucky."

"Well, let's wait until they send us the deed. I don't count my chickens…"

"I know. You learned that lesson early. I wish I had."

Veronica turned to see her mother wipe at her eye. She turned away to give Iona her privacy. She hadn't mentioned her other concern to her mother, that the pig was left as a message to Franklin. Tommy was none too happy with Franklin's relationship with Nan, and most of his friends would be more than willing to butcher a pig as a warning. Some of them would be more than happy to butcher Franklin if they could, and could get away with it.

She went to the bathroom to brush her teeth and spot bathe. She then snuck into the room she shared with Franklin. He was already asleep on his bed when she entered—or was pretending to be.

Nellie's disappearance weighed heavily on her mind. Someone who got pleasure from kittens, cats, dogs, and pigs would surely get bolder if they got away with it. She prayed that Nellie wasn't that next step.

As she lay down on her bed, she felt a warmth spread from her belly to her throat. She closed her eyes, and finally allowed her brain to go where it wanted. As usual, it went to the same place.

It went to Lazlo.

Chapter Fourteen

Darker Stars

In the months since Lazlo had left town, Veronica's bedtime routine had been the same. She washed her face and spot bathed her body. Afterward, she crawled into her single bed. Her brother and her mother both snored, so she waited until that symphony began before she allowed herself to cry. For a girl who had never given in to the luxury of tears, even in the worst moments of her childhood, she was now crying on a daily basis.

She missed Lazlo, which was crazy. She had seen him only twice, spoken with him in any depth only once. Yet in that short period of time, she had fallen in love with him. It was a feeling that she had never had before and the depth and power of it left her feeling like she was drowning, unless she buried it way beneath the surface of her everyday life. She allowed herself only the time before bed to release it, and it always brought tears of sorrow and regret.

Today was different. So much had happened in twenty-four hours that it had been easy to distract herself. She had been made permanent. Ghost kittens appeared by Sawika's desk. The company was giving them their house. She had been chased by a possessed, rabid raccoon. She found out that Nellie Crowder had disappeared. Franklin had proposed to Nan, and she had accepted. She had intervened to keep Tommy from jumping Franklin. CJ had walked her home, and Betty, the ghost chicken, had led her to the carcass of a massacred pig. But the thing closest to her heart was what she had been told by Postman Crowder. Someone had written her letters addressed only to her name and the town, and her mother had apparently intercepted them and hidden them from her.

A flame was now burning wildly across her chest. Someone had written to her. Someone who didn't know her address. Everyone in this little town knew where she lived or could have easily found out. Only someone from out of town, or someone afraid to ask, would have written to her without an address.

Her brain tried to bank her hopes, but her heart was pounding in her chest. After all, why would her mother keep such letters from her without a reason?

Could it have been Lazlo? To do this, he would have had to have written her a letter and then taken it to a post office, where he would have had to explain why he didn't know the full address. If anyone knew that he was writing to a white girl, then he would surely be in danger. Would he be that bold? Surely not. And yet he had sat with her on a rock above the train tracks, knowing that if he had been caught, he would have been lynched. So, clearly, he was brave. But why would he go to all that bother for a poor white girl he had only spoken to twice? Is it possible that he dreamed about her as much as she dreamed about him? She was tempted to sneak into her mother's room again, as her mother was a deep sleeper, but what would she say if she was caught? No, that wasn't prudent.

Well, she would know one way or another tomorrow. Her mother had to go to work at 5 a.m. and Franklin had to be at work by 6:30. She would make sure that she was the one who picked up the mail tomorrow. Mr. Crowder had promised he would bring the letter tomorrow.

Could it be from Lazlo? Veronica closed her eyes and willed sleep to come.

*

This time, when her dream came, it was gentler. She found herself sitting on the rock that jutted out over the train tracks. The sky above was cloudless and bright blue. She was wearing a sleeveless dress, and she could feel the heat of the sun on her shoulders. She had a sandwich in her hand, but it was not a normal sandwich. It was long and thin and stacked full of different fillings. It looked like it could feed two people easily. It was wrapped in brown paper. For a moment, she was alone there, but then she heard a cough.

Lazlo was sitting next to her, holding a sandwich in similar paper. He was wearing a soldier's uniform, but his trousers had been rolled up and his feet were bare.

"Do you like it?" Lazlo asked, nodding at the sandwich.

"It's huge," she said.

"Only the best for you," Lazlo said, with a grin that Veronica didn't understand.

"This is what I live for," he said suddenly, putting the sandwich down.

"What is?" Veronica asked.

"Nighttime. When I can be with you," he replied.

"What's happening during the day?" Veronica asked.

"War... war is happening," Lazlo replied.

"What's it like?"

"Horrible, but I expect it always is."

"How are you, I mean, in the war—" Veronica began, but Lazlo interrupted her.

"Oh, I had been meaning to tell you 'bout a crazy man in our unit. We're in tanks. So this one man, his tank was destroyed but he stole a truck with a machine gun. He killed all the Germans who were firing on us from the front. Another time, his tank got stuck in the mud and damned if he didn't jump out with another machine gun, without cover or protection, and force the German infantry back, all by his damn self."

"Please don't do anything like that," Veronica said with a little laugh. "Someone like that is going to end up getting killed."

"Not him," Lazlo said. "There was something 'bout him. He had fire. He was very quiet and soft-spoken when we was just sitting around. But in battle, he was different. He was a demon. And I swear, it was like the bullets couldn't hit him."

"Well, just don't let them hit you," Veronica said. Lazlo scooted closer to her and put his arm around her waist. "If you die, I'll be angry with you."

Veronica said this lightly. She was trying to laugh at shadows. Lazlo didn't laugh.

"What's real can't die," he said, kissing her forehead. "Oh, a friend of mine will be heading your way."

"Who?" Veronica asked.

"Do you remember a boy named Caio?" he asked.

"Yes! Missy thought he was handsome," Veronica blurted out.

Lazlo laughed.

"And you? Did you think he was handsome?"

"I suppose so, but I didn't really notice." Veronica looked down and smiled.

"Why would that be?" Lazlo asked with a smile.

"I met someone more interesting just after that," Veronica said. She was staring at her feet hanging off the edge of the rock.

When Veronica looked up, Lazlo's eyes were staring into hers.

"He must be really something, if a girl as beautiful as you noticed him."

"He is," she said.

"I don't know about that, but he loves you inside and out, that's for sure," Lazlo replied. Veronica wanted him to kiss her lips. She wanted that badly, but he had closed his eyes and his expression looked pained.

"Is Caio okay?" she asked.

"No, I don't think so. He was busted up bad when I saw him. He took a hit in the guts. It tore his stomach right open. I couldn't believe he survived it, but they treated him and sent him back. I thought he wouldn't make it home, but, apparently, he did."

"When will you be coming back?" Veronica asked.

"I wish I knew," he replied softly, as he pulled her into his arms. "But I'm here with you now." Then he kissed her nose, her forehead, and eventually her lips. She became lost in his kisses.

The sound of air raid sirens brought her to her senses.

"What's that?" she muttered.

"It's the new hospital. It's on fire," Lazlo replied. "The old one will be on fire soon enough."

"Why? How do you know that?" she asked, but Lazlo pulled back from her.

"You need to leave your town," Lazlo said, putting his hand under her chin.

"What? Why?" Veronica said.

"Bad stuff is happening there and I'm afraid you might get hurt. Things are dying."

"Like the cats and dogs and pigs…"

"And people," Lazlo replied. "Lots of people in that town are mighty afraid of anyone who ain't like them."

"Afraid enough to kill?" Veronica asked.

"Afraid enough to kill repeatedly," Lazlo said. "Your brother and his girl are in danger. You are in danger for being too close to them. You are in more danger from being too close to me. I might have put you in danger without meaning to. So you need to get out and you need to use your smarts to talk your family into leaving."

"But how will you find me, if I move?" she asked.

"I will always find you," Lazlo said, pulling her to him again and holding her tight, like he was trying to press her into his heart.

Suddenly there was a crash, and holes began to open in the air around them. Actual holes, like it was a painting, and someone was ripping the paper. Inside the holes, it was black and green—and it throbbed. To her horror, she saw that the holes were sucking things into them. Rocks, trees, even earth. A giant hole opened just above her and air from it felt hot and smelled of rotted milk. Suddenly Lazlo was sucked upward. Veronica grabbed his hand, trying to pull him down, but instead she was lifted off the ground. Lazlo shook his head and pulled her hand loose.

She felt herself falling… and much further than she had been lifted.

*

Veronica woke up as she usually did—desire crawling in her belly and tears in her eyes.

It wasn't yet light outside, but she heard Iona in the kitchen. Franklin was washing his face in the bathroom. By the time Veronica had finished washing her own face and getting dressed, Iona had left for work, but had managed to bake biscuits before she left. It was almost 6:00 a.m. when Veronica went out to check the chickens. Franklin was still in the kitchen eating a jam biscuit. After Veronica collected the eggs, she walked to the end of her driveway to check the mail. Before she could open the mailbox, she saw Postman Crowder down the street. He was five houses away. At that moment, Franklin appeared at the top of the driveway. Veronica felt her stomach drop slightly. It wouldn't do to have Mr. Crowder mention letters, or worse, give her a letter, when Franklin was there.

"You're going to be late," Veronica called up to Franklin. He walked down the driveway until he was close enough for her to see his lips. This close, she could also see anger in the lines of his face.

"I checked the pig this morning, when I first got up," he mouthed. "It's one of ours."

Veronica shook her head.

"You have to tell them," she said.

"I know," Franklin said. "Or else someone will let it slip that they 'found' a dead pig behind our house. If a setup is what the person was going for, and it wasn't a threat."

"And if it was a threat?" Veronica asked, her eyes on Postman Crowder. He was walking much slower today than usual. He was now four houses away.

"Then good luck to them," Franklin said—out loud. He didn't stutter, but she heard something like a growl at the end of the words. "But I don't want you to take any chances right now."

You need to use your smarts into talking your family into leaving.

Veronica's dream descended on her brain in full Technicolor. She shook her head to dislodge it.

"You need to take care too, Franklin. You and Nan need to keep away from Tommy, CJ, and their clan. Avoid them, don't provoke them."

"I think I already provoked them by loving the girl that I love," Franklin said.

"Well, don't make it worse, okay?" Veronica said, giving her brother a quick peck on the cheek. Mr. Crowder was nearing now.

"Go on to work, and I'll see you this evening. Nan can come over for dinner this weekend and we'll celebrate proper."

Franklin smiled and nodded, before taking off down the road.

Mr. Crowder was just walking up toward their driveway, and Franklin waved at him. Mr. Crowder threw up a hand, but his head was down.

"Hi, Mr. Crowder," Veronica said as he approached.

"Oh, right," Mr. Crowder muttered, reaching into his mailbag and yanking out some letters.

"These are for you," he said, holding out a handful of letters, but several fell from his hand. He didn't seem to notice.

"Are you okay, Mr. Crowder?" Veronica asked.

At her words, Mr. Crowder's body began shaking and he dropped his mailbag.

"No, honey, I'm not," he whispered. "The police came to see me this morning. I had to go to the police station. My-they-I had to-I-I-I..."

"Did they find Nellie?" Veronica asked softly, putting her hand on his arm. When his eyes met hers, Veronica understood for the first time the real meaning of the word "damned."

"They killed my baby girl," he choked out. "They beat her and strangled her... they-they-they tore her right open. From her neck to her belly."

Just like the pig.

He covered his face with his hands and dropped to his knees.

Veronica dropped next to him, throwing her arms around him. He grabbed her around the waist and held tight, his body shaking like he was having a seizure.

"Nellie... my little Nellie," he sobbed. "I should never have let her go back to that bastard. He did it. I know he did. That bastard cop... he said that sh-sh-she went to some colored encampment for-for-for-sex... and they-they-they-they-they did... that to her. But he lies. He lies, he lies, he lies. My Nellie would have never gone off on her own."

In her mind, Veronica could see the faces of the people at the rally. The faces of her friends and neighbors, ugly and contorted by rage, followed by the smug face of Chief Earl Bishop. He knew that Nellie had been killed, he had to have already known by that point, and yet he showed no sorrow, no concern, instead he used her death to manipulate the crowd.

Mr. Crowder's sobs had stopped. He pulled back from Veronica and wiped his nose with his sleeve.

"I'm sorry, Veronica, I shouldn't put my problems on you," he said, as he collected the letters he had dropped and shoved them back into the mailbag.

"Wait, these are the ones for you," he said, handing her two letters. "Some others done already been picked up. I don't rightly know by who."

Mr. Crowder stood up. Veronica stood as well and held out her hands to him.

"Why don't you come in for some coffee?" she asked.

Mr. Crowder gave her a little smile.

"If you got coffee left during wartime, you should save it for someone besides the likes of me," he said. Then he gave Veronica a quick hug, before grabbing his bag from the ground.

"Are you sure?" Veronica asked.

"Work is the best thing for me right now, it keeps my mind—" Mr. Crowder stopped and shrugged.

"I understand that at least a little bit," Veronica said softly.

He turned and walked a few steps before turning back to her.

"You be careful out there, Veronica. You are a good girl with a good heart. Don't let that get you in trouble."

With that, he turned and began shuffling down the road again.

Chapter Fifteen

Curse of the Camel

"Ronnie!"

Veronica jumped and shoved the letters into her jacket pocket.

She saw Lizzie walking down the road toward her. Lizzie passed Mr. Crowder with not much more than a brief wave. Six months ago, she would have stopped to talk, but not today.

"You're out early," Lizzie said, as she walked up.

"Well, I'm used to getting up early," Veronica said, "so I just wanted to see Franklin off."

"I heard that Tommy gave him some trouble last night," Lizzie said. "I also heard that you were at the rally and that CJ walked you home."

"News travels fast." Veronica snorted.

"Oh, don't be like that, Ronnie," Lizzie said, putting her arm around Veronica's waist. "Go grab your lunch and walk to work with me. I'm only starting a half hour earlier than you today, so you'll just be a little early."

"Okay," Veronica said, turning to head up her driveway. She was hoping to get the opportunity to shove the letters into her purse, but clearly she couldn't do that with Lizzie around.

"So what was the story with CJ?" Lizzie asked, as she followed Veronica into her kitchen.

"There isn't much of one," Veronica began but then realized that she didn't want to have to explain why she was at the rally. "I just decided to stop by the rally. Franklin came to look for me, and Tommy went after him. CJ called Tommy off, so that Franklin could go home without getting into a fight. I let him walk me home, so I would have the chance to thank him."

As she said this, Veronica grabbed a biscuit and slapped some jam on it before wrapping it and putting it in her lunch box. She was aware that the letters were in her pocket and that her jacket pocket was very shallow. So she kept her arm against it as much as she could.

"That's great, Ronnie," Lizzie said. "CJ's not so bad, you'll see."

"You used to think he was a cad," Veronica replied, as she pushed through the screen door and onto her driveway.

"That was before I knew him," Lizzie replied. "I've gotten to know him much better since Ben has been going to the rallies."

"And?" Veronica asked, as they started down the main road to the factory.

"And he really cares about the community," Lizzie replied. "He wants to make things better. He's going to university next year."

"He told me that."

"Exactly, so he's planning for his future."

"Mm-hmm." Veronica didn't like the direction this conversation was headed in.

"CJ really likes you, Ronnie," Lizzie said. "He always looks out for you, and even for Franklin, just because he's your brother."

"If you're referring to him calling Tommy off Franklin last night, I already thanked him," Veronica replied.

"It's not just that, I heard that CJ told Tommy to lay off Franklin permanently," Lizzie said.

"Well, that doesn't seem to have worked."

"Yeah, but that's because Tommy likes Nan. In fact, he is planning to ask her out," Lizzie said with a little laugh. "So Franklin might have some competition."

"Well, seeing as how Nan accepted Franklin's proposal yesterday, I don't think Franklin needs to worry," Veronica snapped, and immediately regretted it.

"REALLY?" Lizzie asked, stopping. She was smiling but only with her mouth. That hard, cold look was back in her eyes. "Why didn't you tell me?"

"It didn't happen until after you left," Veronica lied, hating herself for giving Lizzie this information.

"That's SO GREAT," Lizzie said, coming to give Veronica a big hug. "Tell Franklin that I'm SO happy for him."

"You can tell him yourself, next time you see him," Veronica said. She started walking again but Lizzie was standing still.

"What's this?" Lizzie asked, picking something up off the ground. With horror, Veronica realized that it was one of the letters. She quickly felt in her pocket. One was still there, but the other was now in Lizzie's hands.

"It's addressed to you," Lizzie said, laughing. "It looks like a boy's handwriting. And no address, so a strange boy…"

"Stop, Lizzie, give that back," Veronica said, lunging forward.

Lizzie danced backward, ripping open the letter as she did. She actually opened the letter meant for Veronica. Veronica lunged forward again, but Lizzie ran ahead, holding the letter up.

"My oh my, look at this… it looks like it's from a soldier. He's talking about being at the front."

"Lizzie, give that back right now," Veronica yelled, running at Lizzie, but Lizzie laughed and dodged past her.

"Oh, and he says, 'but no landscape can compare to a beautiful woman.' I wonder who he's talking about?"

"Lizzie, stop! That's not yours to read."

"Why didn't you tell me that you had met a soldier?" Lizzie laughed, turning to the last page. "And his name is…"

Lizzie suddenly stopped, staring at the page, her eyes wide and unblinking.

Veronica used this to snatch the letter back from her.

"Ronnie, is that the colored boy?" Lizzie whispered.

"His name is Lazlo," Veronica replied, shoving the letter into her purse. Veronica's heart was hammering in her chest and everything around her looked sharper and more contrasted.

Veronica turned and continued walking toward the factory. She knew that she should explain things to Lizzie. She should tell her that this was the first letter and that she hadn't written Lazlo back. She should tell her that the postman delivered the letter to her without her address. These would be the practical and prudent things to say, but she couldn't force these words out because, despite their literal truth, they were a lie. They would make it seem that she was an innocent receiver of Lazlo's attentions, not the instigator that she was.

Lizzie suddenly caught up with her and grabbed her by the arm.

"What were you thinking?" she whispered, as she squeezed Veronica's arm hard.

"I wasn't thinking anything," Veronica said, yanking her arm away and continuing to walk. "I haven't even had the chance to read the letter yet. You've read more of it than I have."

"Is that the boy that Missy thought was handsome?" Lizzie asked, walking briskly beside her.

"No, that was Caio," Veronica snapped.

"Caio, Lazlo, why do you remember these people's names?"

"Wait," Veronica said, stopping to face Lizzie. "How do you know that Missy thought Caio was handsome? I never told you that."

Lizzie stepped back a few feet.

"Missy told Hugh, and Hugh told Ben and the others," she replied, looking down. "It's a good thing Caio left when he did or Hugh might have killed him."

"Missy would never have admitted that to Hugh," Veronica whispered, taking a step closer to her friend. "Never. Missy can be loose-lipped but not about something like that—and not with Hugh."

"That doesn't matter," Lizzie said, waving her hand. "What matters is that Missy paid too much attention to that boy, and the Knights were none too happy about it."

The truth sprang up in Veronica's brain like a fungus.

"Missy told you, didn't she?" Veronica asked. "She told you, and you told Ben and Ben told Hugh. And Hugh punished her. That's right, isn't it?"

Lizzie took a few more steps back, her eyes darting around her.

"Why would you do that, Lizzie? Why would you rat out a friend?"

"You have some nerve, accusing me," Lizzie suddenly snapped. "After all I have done for you. After all of your family secrets I have kept. I never judged you for having a deadbeat father. I've always been nice to Franklin even though—"

"Even though what?" Veronica snarled, she could feel a mixture of fury and sorrow fighting for dominance inside her. It was easier to let fury win.

"Even though what, Lizzie?" she asked, taking a step forward. Lizzie took an instinctive step back. "Even though he is a 'moron'?"

"I didn't say that, you did," Lizzie said, hands up.

"But you told Ben that Missy had found Caio attractive?"

"So what if I did?" Lizzie snapped. "It's not like I did anything wrong."

"So she deserves to be hit?"

"No, but she was acting like an idiot." Lizzie was now getting red in the face. "But Missy should never have been looking at a colored person like that. Maybe she needed reminding that there are some things that just aren't said or done in a polite society."

"I see," Veronica said. "So do you think that I am acting like an idiot?"

"I don't know, Ronnie," Lizzie said. "That letter wasn't sent to your address, so you obviously didn't give him your address. There was no return address, so he doesn't seem to be expecting a response. So I don't think there is anything between you now."

Lizzie was backing away. Her face was now both bright red and weirdly expressionless.

"But you might have done something to lead him on while he was here," Lizzie said. "Knowing you, I could see you doing something like that just to annoy people like Tommy and CJ. So, yes, I could see you being stupid that way. You do this stuff, and you don't think about how it will affect the people around you. Your brother, your mother, me."

"You're worried that if this gets out, people might think less of you, right?" Veronica asked.

"Yes."

"Particularly the Knights of Harrisville will think less of you," Veronica said quietly. "So you are a spy now."

"Watch your mouth, Ronnie. You don't want to say things that you'll regret," Lizzie said.

"Like Missy regretted it," Veronica replied. "You were supposed to be her friend and you sold her out just to make inroads for Ben with the Knights of Harrisville. He gives them information from you, and they let him in their little club, is that how it works?"

"They aren't like that," Lizzie snapped. "They just want to make our community better. They want to keep us safe."

A thought suddenly popped into Veronica's brain.

"You knew that Nellie Crowder is missing, didn't you?" Veronica asked.

"Yes," Lizzie said. "And that's exactly what I was talking about. Her husband said that he thought she was taken by some colored boys."

"And you believe that?" Veronica snorted. "I always thought you were smart."

"I am," Lizzie said. "I am smart enough to know that what is true is decided by those in power. I'm smart enough to know that I can't change the rules alone, whether I like them or not. I am smart enough to know that the world isn't all sunshine and that it is hard, so hard, to rise above the station assigned to us in life. But I think I am smart enough to do it. And I'm smart enough not to end up like Missy—or even Nellie. You, on the other hand, might end up just like them if you don't straighten up and fly right."

Fury churned in Veronica's gut as she moved quickly toward Lizzie, who flinched backward. That was fulfilling, but Veronica just walked past her.

"Goodbye, Lizzie," Veronica said.

"Ronnie, wait," Lizzie said, but Veronica kept walking. She had to get to work, and she needed to come up with a mitigation plan to deal with Lizzie—and she had to come up with it fast.

*

At work, Veronica did her runs with her head down. She didn't want to catch Lizzie's eye as she made her way across the factory floor to collect samples. Lizzie had seen more of Lazlo's letter than she had, so she felt lost on how to respond to Lizzie's accusations. Veronica's brain was circling around this problem, trying to find ways to shut Lizzie down before she started something, ways to deflect the attention to other matters, ways to use Lizzie's vanity to downplay everything. Her brain told her that she had been stupid in her reaction to Lizzie. She should have shrugged and told Lizzie that she had just received the letters that morning and had no idea what they were about. She should have said that she had no idea why Lazlo would have written to her, but that was a lie that she wasn't sure she could pull off, because her heart was screaming inside her chest.

He wrote to me. He wrote more than once. He wrote me letters. He cared enough to address them to my name alone, not knowing if I would get them. What did he say? What did he say? What did he say?

Her need to see his words ate at her insides. It was a new sort of hunger, one she hadn't experienced before. It was horrible and sweet in equal measures. Several times in the morning, her heart forced her to excuse herself to the restroom to read them. Once there, once she held them in her hands, she realized that she might not be able to hide her feelings to his words. If she left the restroom with wet eyes, that would surely be noticed and commented upon. So she would need to wait until she got home to read the letters. She would just need to avoid Lizzie until tomorrow, which would be difficult if she was always on the factory floor.

Around 11 a.m., luck favored her when one of her coworkers asked if someone else could take the runs at Number 8, because she wasn't feeling too well. Veronica volunteered immediately. This would mean that she would make fewer runs during the day, but she would be away from the factory floor. So Veronica spent the rest of the day running back and forth between her building and Number 8. It was on the second-to-last run of the day that she saw Missy— doing the camel job. Missy was crouched over the tobacco chutes, greasing them, her arm still in a sling.

Why would they put Missy in that job if she had an obvious injury? That was when Veronica remembered that the factory manager of Number 8 was none other than Hugh's father. She felt her stomach drop.

As she walked through the factory collecting samples, she kept her eyes on Missy. When she saw her begin to climb down the ladder, probably to take her break, Veronica moved quickly to that side of the factory.

She got to Missy just as she was at the bottom of the ladder. When Missy turned around, Veronica felt her stomach lurch rather than drop. The skin around Missy's eye was yellow-green and swollen.

Missy's eyes went wide at the sight of Veronica. She smiled, but immediately dropped her gaze to the floor.

"Missy, what happened?" Veronica asked.

"Nothing, I just fell down," Missy replied.

The memory of shame washed over Veronica again. How many times had she been forced to make up those lies as a child.

"Are you on your break?" Veronica asked.

Missy nodded.

"I need to take a break as well," Veronica said.

"I don't have much time, just enough to go to the restroom and get some water," Missy said.

"That's okay, I'll go with you," Veronica replied.

The sound of the machines prevented them from talking as they headed toward the women's restroom. Veronica noticed that Missy was walking with a slight limp. She suspected that her arm and her face weren't the only parts of her that were injured. Hugh was turning out to be a real gentleman.

When they got into the women's restroom, Veronica scanned the room for others, but they were alone. As Missy was trying to wash her hands, she had difficulty turning the faucet on.

"Let me help with that," Veronica said.

Missy gave her a quick, sad smile.

"I need to learn to be more careful," Missy said.

"Or maybe Hugh needs to learn to be more careful," Veronica replied.

"No, it's my fault," Missy said. "I've been careless and reckless. This is what happens when a girl like me is careless."

"That's not true—" Veronica began, but Missy interrupted her.

"Look, Ronnie, truth doesn't matter," Missy replied softly. "What matters is what other people believe. Hugh told me that he had reservations about marrying me, since the Caio thing. He said he didn't want to marry anyone who would find a colored person attractive. Then he got mad, because he said that he still loved me, and he couldn't stop. When I tried to calm him down—well, I shouldn't have said anything when he was that mad."

"Missy, that wasn't your fault," Veronica said. "There's never an excuse to hit someone. Wait, did you say anything to Hugh that might have made him think you found Caio attractive?"

"No! Of course not," Missy whispered. "I would never do that."

"Did you talk to anyone, besides me, about it?"

"No—wait. I think I mentioned it to Lizzie, but I didn't say much," Missy said. "Wait, you don't think—"

"I don't know. Have you noticed Hugh spending more time talking to Lizzie?" Veronica asked.

Missy was quiet for a moment.

"Yes, he has," Missy replied. "I didn't want to think about it. Actually, it's more like Lizzie has paid more attention to him."

Of course, if Ben wasn't going to marry her—well, Hugh's dad wasn't as far up the social ladder, but he was a factory manager here at Number 8. He would either go to university or take a management job here at the factory. He wouldn't be a bad catch for a girl at the bottom of the social ladder. These townie boys should have been drafted and in the fight for their country, but their parents had obviously found ways around that.

"Missy, you need to break up with Hugh," Veronica whispered. "And then you need to stay out of sight for a while."

"I can't," Missy replied. "Look, I know what you are thinking. I know you are afraid for me, but it's just a bad patch Hugh and I are going through. Normally, he's the sweetest boy in the world. It's just a bad patch."

"Missy, no. It's not a bad patch. It's a pattern," Veronica said softly. "One I've seen before."

Missy gave Veronica a little one-sided hug, protecting her arm.

"I know you mean well, Ronnie," Missy said. "But not all men are like your dad. I'll be okay. I love Hugh, and he loves me. This really is just a bad patch."

Missy then smiled, walked away, and returned to the ladder back up to the camel position.

Suddenly, Veronica realized that Mr. McBrayer had not put Missy into the camel job to punish her, but to keep people from asking questions.

Out of sight was out of mind.

Chapter Sixteen

Fearless

When Veronica came back to Number 8 for her last run of the day, Missy was nowhere to be seen. Veronica felt the back of her head begin to tingle in an unpleasant way, so she finished her run quickly. Lizzie's shift ended at 4 p.m., and Veronica didn't want to accidentally run into her on the way back into the factory.

She was worried about Missy. Missy's family had always been even worse off than her own. Missy was one of five children and was the middle child to boot. From a young age, Missy had known that she would have to make her way through life without any help from her mother, financial or otherwise. It wasn't that her mother was a bad mother, she was just trying to raise five children on her own, with a part-time factory job. She didn't have time to focus on any one child. So when Missy began dating Hugh McBrayer, it was a relief to her whole family. Hugh had always been a fringe member of CJ's group, and a bit spineless in Veronica's opinion, but to Missy he hung the moon.

Veronica walked briskly across the Milligan Park cigarette floor, which was just in the middle of a shift change. She stuck close to the factory wall to avoid people. As she neared the QA department, she glanced up toward the management offices. Mr. Sawika's window was open, and Veronica saw that Tommy was standing in his father's office. Tommy was gesturing wildly. The door to Mr. Sawika's office was suddenly thrown open and Tommy came charging out, followed by his father. Mr. Sawika grabbed Tommy by the arm and almost threw him back into his office. He then slammed the door shut. Veronica saw Tommy get up in his father's face.

She dropped her eyes and walked quickly into the QA office. The last thing she needed today was a confrontation with Tommy. With horror, she realized that Tommy being in the factory meant that he was in proximity to Lizzie. She wasn't sure if Lizzie would be willing or even able to keep her mouth shut about the letter from Lazlo if she was confronted with Tommy. The temptation to earn brownie points by throwing Veronica to the wolves might be too much for the new Lizzie to resist.

On top of that, the letters from Lazlo, now in Veronica's purse, were calling to her, and their call was becoming more insistent. She thought the best thing might be to find a hidden spot on the way home to read them—although, given the recent death of Nellie Crowder, it might not be good to be alone.

Veronica did her quality check on the chewing tobacco and snuff as quickly as she could. She was picking up her things to leave when Mr. Sawika walked into the QA office.

"Veronica, may I have a word with you?"

Veronica stepped out and Mr. Sawika closed the door behind them.

"I wanted to tell you that your mother will be working late tonight. I asked her to do a double shift, for additional pay, and she agreed. She asked me to let you know."

Her mother wouldn't be home, and Franklin would be at the firehouse. She would have time to search for the letters.

"Veronica, may I ask you a question?" Mr. Sawika asked, in a lower voice.

"What is it?" Veronica said. Mr. Sawika gave her a wan little smile.

"Tommy said you were at the rally last night—and that CJ walked you home."

Veronica froze. She wasn't sure what angle she should take. She should probably pretend an interest or something. She opened her mouth to say this but something else came out.

"I was following Franklin to Nan's house, just to make sure that there was no trouble," she said.

"You might have been putting yourself in harm's way," Mr. Sawika said.

"My mother suggested it," Veronica replied. Mr. Sawika's eyes widened slightly.

"And my boy gave your brother some trouble?"

"He tried to, but CJ stopped him."

"To please you, I assume," Mr. Sawika replied. Veronica said nothing.

"That was well played on your part, but be careful of CJ," he said. "Don't lead him on if you have no interest. His feelings for you are old and intense. Words like those spoken at those rallies can twist minds like his."

"Weren't you at the rally?" Veronica asked.

"No, I try not to go to those unless I have to," Mr. Sawika replied. "It's usually a bunch of drunk, stupid people acting like drunk, stupid people."

"Tommy went," Veronica said. She knew this wasn't smart, but she was still angry about how Tommy attacked Franklin.

"I don't have as much control over Tommy and Tommy's actions as I would like," Mr. Sawika said. "One day, you'll learn the pain of being a parent. You can dislike what your child has become but that doesn't keep you from loving them. I'm probably to blame. I should have let him get drafted. Being in combat tends to make or break people, but I wanted to protect my son. In life, Tommy hasn't wanted for much, and he may have grown to be a lesser person because of it."

"I think Tommy is old enough to be responsible for his own actions," Veronica said. "You can only blame your parents for so long."

Mr. Sawika laughed.

"There you go again, being a straight shooter," he said. "Listen, you should get home, but before you do, I wanted to warn you. The Knights of Harrisville boys are getting whipped up. I've seen this before and it never ends well."

"I thought you were one of them," Veronica said before she could stop herself.

Mr. Sawika smiled.

"I was when I was a young man, but I did a lot of stupid things back then. I don't regret any of it, because I was always just trying to do the best I could. I got out when I realized what they really were. I don't regret it though... what I regret are the things that I didn't do."

Veronica nodded, thinking of Lazlo. Now she wished more than anything that she had kissed him as they sat on that rock eating biscuits.

"I knew your mother, when she was young," Mr. Sawika said suddenly. "She was a whip-smart, fiery, and no-nonsense girl. At the time, I was sure she would marry some town businessman. I wouldn't have been surprised if she had left the town, the state, or even the country. She was wild and willful, that one."

He was smiling as he stared right through her. Then his eyes focused back on her.

"She was a bit like you, but that was before she went and married Deward Crane," he said, spitting out the name like it was a bad taste. "I'll never understand why she would pick him. He was no good and headed nowhere fast."

"Because she thought she was pregnant, but nothing came of it," Veronica said softly.

"What do you mean, nothing came of it?"

"She either wasn't pregnant, or she lost the baby," Veronica said.

"She told you that?"

"No, my mother doesn't tell us much, but my grandmother hinted at it."

Veronica paused, weighing the impact of her next words.

"My Grandma Janie also hinted that she might have lost the baby because my father beat her."

Mr. Sawika's eyes widened and the veins in his next began to stick out and pulse.

"Then he got what was coming to him," he snarled, then spit on the ground. His fists were clenched, and face was getting dangerously red. "Pity it didn't happen sooner. If I had known—"

He stopped himself, let out a sigh, and began flexing his hands.

"Well, that's ancient history," he said. "You go on home now. Go straight home. This isn't a good time to be out past sundown, for you or any of your family."

Veronica nodded.

To her shock, Mr. Sawika pulled her into a quick hug, but immediately released her as if she had been on fire.

"Git, girl," he said, as he turned and strode back into the factory. She watched him walk up the stairs. As he moved toward his office, she saw a face appear in the office window. At first, she thought it was a ghost, but the pale face in the window was that of Tommy Sawika.

*

Rather than going out through the main entrance, Veronica chose to leave by the side door. If she left via the main entrance, she might run into Lizzie, Tommy, or any number of other people that she didn't want to talk to this evening. What she wanted to do this evening was get home and ransack the house for more letters. She had noticed that Lazlo had dated the back of each envelope, so she wanted to find the first ones. Anyone wanting to speak with her would decrease the time she had alone at home.

The side door to the factory was located just off the snuff room and down a mirrored hallway. Veronica had never understood the need for mirroring in this corridor but supposed that it must serve a practical purpose of some sort. She trotted through the snuff room, shoes clacking on the wooden floor. She could smell fresh air, coming from open windows in the snuff area. This air diluted the overwhelming smell of tobacco that lingered in this room by just enough to make it bearable.

She had just turned into the entrance to the mirrored walkway when she stopped dead in her tracks. Walking through the hallway in her direction was the ghost that Caio had called Dante. He was wearing the same stovepipe hat and codpiece, and looking around him with an expression that could have been wonder. A surreal feeling washed over her when she saw that Dante was casting no reflection in the mirrors of the hall.

"This place is amazing," he said, in soft voice.

"What place?"

"This place... this factory," he replied, moving toward her. She took a step further back into the snuff room.

"All this was imagined by man, made by man, and it will be improved upon by man. There was a time, not so long ago, when such a thing was unimaginable."

She was sure that she couldn't outrun this ghost, so she decided to stand firm in her spot. Maybe he would be like some predators and be unlikely to attack something that seemed like it might fight back.

Dante walked toward her but then stepped aside at the last minute. He was examining the snuff room.

"Yes, it's sad that it will be lost," he said.

"What do you mean, it will be lost?" Veronica asked.

"This place is blighted," Dante said, his eyes scanning the roof. "It will be razed to the ground."

"Are you a minister?" Veronica asked.

"No, I am most assuredly not that. Why do you ask?"

"You said 'blighted' and 'razed'." No one uses words like that, except for ministers," Veronica replied.

"Really?" Dante said, cocking his head. "Well, that's good to know. Still, I like these words. It gives the connotation not just of punishment but of deserved punishment."

"So you think this place deserves punishment?" Veronica asked.

"Not the place."

"But the people?"

"Do you think the people deserve punishment?" Dante asked.

"My brother wouldn't think so, even if he should," Veronica replied. "Nan doesn't. I want to be able to agree with them... but the fact that others are nasty to both Franklin and Nan says something about this place, doesn't it? I just can't close my eyes or train them to see only good things. I wish I could."

"Yes, ignorance is bliss much of the time, but some of us don't have that luxury," Dante said with a sad smile. Veronica knew that she should be scared. Other people would be scared. Dante was a ghost, and she was pretty sure that he wasn't a benign ghost.

"Are you the devil?" she heard herself ask.

Dante laughed.

"My, you're direct."

"So I have been told," Veronica replied.

"No, I am not the devil. Strictly speaking, the devil is my brother. But he isn't what you think he is."

"You are a fallen angel then?" she asked.

"No, I'm not an angel and there is nothing fallen about me. Or, at least, I am no more fallen than you."

"That's not saying much," Veronica muttered.

Dante smiled. "You don't think a lot of yourself then?"

"I try not to," Veronica replied.

Dante's smile softened.

"Is this why you have run from your gifts?"

Veronica felt like someone had blown a hole in the center of her forehead.

"I'm not sure I can be trusted with them," she said quietly.

"You are afraid of killing people accidentally?" Dante asked.

Veronica nodded. This ghost's voice was so soothing that it felt like she was being hypnotized.

"You wonder if you might have killed your father?"

"I wanted him dead," she said. "He disappeared. Maybe I made it happen."

"You have gifts, but dealing death by mere thought isn't one of them," Dante replied.

Despite how oddly he was dressed and his slight transparency, Dante was handsome. He had high cheekbones, a fine nose, and full lips. His coloring was not unlike Lazlo's, despite a grayness to his pallor. Veronica was finding herself liking him more by the minute, which was neither logical nor particularly safe.

"I suspect stubbornness is another of your gifts," Dante said softly. "I may not be able to convince you of the need to leave this place. I'm afraid I don't have the time to do so, but as I like you, I may ask others to help. It's almost Christmas, after all."

"So you are planning to send Jacob Marley or Tiny Tim to visit me?" Veronica asked. Her practical side was getting churlish and angry at herself for liking him.

I should not be insulting him. He just admitted to being the brother of the devil.

But Dante just smiled at her.

"Yes, I do like you. Kara would like you too. I like you enough that I already sent one ghost your way. I believe you named her Betty. She was supposed to warn you and suggest that you should leave."

"You sent Betty and her chicks?" Veronica gasped.

"Yes. I assume she led you to the gift that was left for you?" Dante replied.

"A rotting pig carcass. Did you leave that?"

"You know that I didn't because you know who did. What you may not know is that he is sick. That sickness is contagious and it's spreading," Dante said, his dark eyes beginning to glow orange in their depths. Veronica felt a heat coming off him and liked it.

"Are you and Kara Furies?" Veronica asked.

Dante laughed again.

"You may think of me that way if you like. It's close enough."

"And Kara?"

At the mention of her name, Dante's expression became so intense that it was hard to watch.

"Kara is everything."

Veronica remembered them sitting on the tree branch together and how it had felt to watch them.

"You are so beautiful together," Veronica whispered.

"If that is what you see, it says more about you than us," Dante replied. "Yes, I do like you a lot. In my mind, you have more than earned your existence."

Dante began to glow slightly, with a dark red light.

"So, Veronica whom I like, I will give you some advice. You have maybe five days at most to leave this town. If you stay longer than that, you and yours will get hurt. So what was it your boss said back there—'Git, girl'?"

"Thank you for the warning," Veronica said. She wasn't sure if he was what he said he was, but her gut told her that he was right about things going downhill here.

"Oh, and don't worry, I will send you no living people," Dante said… and then he was gone.

Veronica ran down the hallway and into the fading light.

Chapter Seventeen

Love Letters

Veronica ran the whole way home. She was afraid that if she stopped, she would take Lazlo's letters out of her pocket and read them. The air was cold around her, and a few snowflakes were beginning to fall. The smell of snow and woodsmoke mixed in her nostrils and triggered a long-held memory of sitting by the fire with Janie at Christmas. Janie had shown her an old pocket watch that had been given to her by her father. It was beautiful and had a stag engraved on the back. Veronica had known that it must have cost a pretty penny, but when she asked, Janie just smiled.

"Cost is just what someone's willing to pay," she said. "But it will be yours when I'm gone. If Iona forgets that, you remind her."

"You could just give it to me now," Veronica remembered saying, but Janie had just laughed.

"No, child. I'd be afraid your papa would take it from you and sell it. No, I will keep it safe for you until it's your turn to carry it." Veronica had never seen it again.

The snow was coming down properly when Veronica got to her house. She ran up the driveway and straight inside. As she had predicted, Franklin had already left for work. She took off her shoes and left her coat by the front door. She then went to her mother's room. Before she moved the sewing cabinet, she marked where it was on the floor. She didn't want to tip off her mother that she had been digging around in her room.

When she pulled the sewing cabinet from the wall, she saw that there was indeed a small drawer there. It had no knob or handle, but she was able to get her fingernail hooked into it well enough to pull it out. Inside, she found what she had been hoping to find. There were two letters folded up, and underneath them were two rings. One was her mother's wedding ring. The other was a man's ring, which she assumed was her father's wedding band. She didn't know, as she had never seen him wearing a ring. Veronica removed the letters, gently closed the door, and moved the sewing cabinet back into place. She then moved quickly to her bedroom.

Once inside, she closed the door. It might look odd if her mother came in, but she could pretend that she was napping. She then opened the two letters. Sure enough, they were written in the same hand as the letters that she had pulled out of her purse. She looked at the dates that Lazlo had written on the back of each.

The earliest one was dated October 12, 1944. The second was November 11, 1944.

Veronica opened the first letter carefully. It looked like it had been folded for some time, and the places where the paper had been creased was thin. When she opened the letter, she saw that Lazlo's handwriting was much better than she might have expected, given what he had told her about his schooling. His penmanship was fine and the strokes strong. She sat down on her bed and began to read his words.

Oct 12, 1944

Dear Veronica,

I am guessing that you weren't really expecting to hear from me. Still, I wanted to tell you about what I've seen.

You won't believe it, but I'm in France now. We landed a couple of days ago on a place called Omaha Beach.

They didn't give us much training, in fact, we were only in training for a few weeks in the heat and the sun. We were sent to Camp Claiborne in Louisiana, to an all-colored unit. Most of the soldiers had already been there for up to a year, but they needed more men so we was trained fast and hard. To be honest with you, I wasn't even quite sure where we were when we first got there, and there was some white soldiers that weren't happy to have any of us there. On the radio, the president of the Chamber of Commerce here was speaking and, in his speech, he kept calling us ugly words. The white soldiers do the same here. I tell myself that maybe that's because they don't know that it's ugly, but I'm probably just fooling myself. Still, I don't want to think about this, and I don't want to bother you with it.

We were trained on tanks. I was shown how to work the main gun and machine guns only, because I didn't have time to learn much more. Well, I say I didn't have time, but it felt like we were there forever. The heat of Georgia is one thing, the heat of North Carolina was another. The heat of Louisiana... that is a thing the devil himself couldn't imagine. It was hard to get enough water to make up for what you lost every day. I'm sorry, that's not the sort of thing I wanted to tell you about. I wanted to be able to find pretty things to tell you about, but we haven't seen much of that. We trained in swamps and in the heat there, so there isn't much to describe, at least that I would want to describe to you. Maybe you will think fondly of me if you know that I got through it without too much complaining.

A little over a week ago, we was sent on a ship to come to France. A lot of the fellas got sick, seeing as how there were storms, or it felt like they were storms to me. I didn't get too sick, but that was probably just my pride refusing to allow myself to admit to it. I shouldn't admit it to you, probably, but you would guess anyway, I'm pretty sure. Some of the soldiers are saying that the trip is the most dangerous part of the war, but maybe that's just hopeful thinking. I can tell you that I never imagined so much water in all my life. It went on for days and days with nothing but ocean. When you saw any land at all, you wondered if you were just imagining it.

We landed at Omaha Beach. Yes, Omaha Beach, where the allies won the battle. They made up a whole harbor here for moving in men, supplies, and all sorts of things. I've met lots of people already. The French soldiers treat us differently than the American soldiers. They don't seem to care so much that we are colored. Maybe it's different in other places.

I know this ain't much of a letter, but I am writing it sitting in my little tent. I will send more letters to you when I can. They seem to have pretty good mail service for the soldiers here and they don't seem to care much about color. I don't have your address so I will just address it to you and the town. If the powers that be want you to have it, then it will find its way to you.

I hope with all my heart that you are doing well,

Lazlo Fox

Veronica closed the letter. Her eyes were moist, and she didn't want to drip tears on the paper. Lazlo had written to her. He had taken time out of fighting an actual war to write to her. She didn't know what this meant, but, surely, he cared about her at least a little or he wouldn't be writing. She wondered how many other letters he had written. She had four and it would be better if the four she had were the only four that existed, for his safety and hers. He had taken a real risk writing to her. If he was brought back to this town, and someone knew of these letters, then he would be at serious risk of being lynched. She would need to find out from Postman Crowder how many other letters he had seen.

Outside, it was now pitch black. The snow was coming down heavily enough to be blanketing the ground. Veronica wondered if it was snowing where Lazlo was; she wondered if he was thinking about her. She wondered if, maybe, when she dreamed about him, he was dreaming about her as well. Her practical brain told her that this was a ridiculous thought, but she held on to it anyway. She wished that she could see him, in whatever tent he was in. She wondered if there was any way that she could send him a letter without putting anyone at risk.

She had felt a surge of shame when he described being referred to with ugly words. She knew the type of words he was talking about. With a certain horror, she realized that although she had sensed that these terms were offensive, she hadn't known how offensive until she read Lazlo's letter. Now, the shame she felt in her own ignorance was sticking in her throat as she understood the dehumanizing effect of the word. In how many other ways had Lazlo been shamed and dehumanized? And how many times had it gone unnoticed by most white people? How often had they just gone about their business, ignoring the inhumanity of man toward man?

Suddenly, Caio came into her mind. Caio, who had stepped between Tommy and George, and had taken the hit because of it. Caio, who had known her feelings for Lazlo almost before she knew them. She wondered if people from Brazil were just more sensitive or less prejudiced than people in North America. Maybe that was a place where a white woman and a black man wouldn't stand out so much.

What am I thinking? Surely Lazlo is not interested in risking his life by running off with a white woman? And it wasn't like either of them had the money to go to Brazil.

Veronica could tell by the light that Franklin would be coming home soon, if not her mother. She didn't have much time left on her own. So she opened one more letter.

Nov 11, 1944

Dear Veronica,

I'm sorry that it took so long to write you again. We've been in combat, and it's been pretty hard.

I also realized that I forgot to tell you some things in my last letter. Before we came to France, we landed in Dorset, England. That was in September. I should have written you from England, but it took me a long time to work up the nerve to write a second letter. Something I saw in England gave me the courage to finally do it. Some of the colored soldiers went on dates with white girls here. And the English people didn't seem to care. Of course, the white American soldiers didn't like it, and one of the boys got beaten up pretty bad coming back to base after being out with a white girl.

It seems that the Germans are wise to things like this, because a buddy of mine showed me a flyer that the Germans are dropping out of planes. It is addressed to "Colored Soldiers of the US Forces." It says "the white people in the USA do not allow you to pray in their churches, although you are American citizens. Colored people living in Germany can go to any church they like. There have never been lynchings of colored men in Germany. They have always been treated decently." It goes on like that, trying to tell us that we should defect. I know that the Nazis aren't too keen on colored people. That's pretty clear from what they believe, but it shows that they know what we are feeling. Still, I was surprised to discover that both England and France seem to care less about the differences between colored people and white people. Also, the fact that white women were dating colored men in England—well, it gave me something to think about, to be sure. I would sure love to live in a place like that.

I'm talking about all this because I don't want to talk too much about the combat. I have to tell you that even though we are in a Sherman tank, I have been in situations where I was forced to crawl on my belly for what felt like hours as bullets were whistling past my ears, seeming to come from every direction. You'd be surprised how often tanks get stuck in the mud. I would never have thought something like that would happen, but it does. So I've seen my comrades torn open by gunfire and mortars. Every day, I am surprised that I managed to live through it. I try to just get on with it and not think too much during the day. I can say that, despite all that, my dreams at night are good.

I can't tell you where we are now, I'm not allowed, but we are supporting an infantry unit. I can tell you about where we been, though. We went through a little town called La Pieux. It's this little village with stone houses. I know this will sound very stupid to you, but I was surprised by the fact that all the road signs were in French. I saw a street called La Fleurs, someone told me that this means 'Flower Street.' I can't tell you why, but something about that just made me happy. The French people have been very kind to us. One night, a French farmer and his family told us that we could *stay in their farmhouse, as long as we kept it clean. They left us food and told us to collect eggs from the chickens. The French have this bread called Baguette. It's like a long, skinny sandwich loaf but it's very crusty on the outside and soft and chewy on the inside. When I took a bite, I just knew that you would love it. One of the boys told me that a French girl in the village was flirting with me, but I don't believe him. I couldn't understand her anyway, so she could have been saying anything.*

Oh, and I met George, a young, colored man who told me he had met you. He had a friend name Caio, who is in another unit but close by. George told me that you had been kind to him when he was registering and that you had tried to step in when some white boy took a swing at Caio. I didn't tell George that I was writing to you, because I didn't know what he would think about that, but what he said made me worry a bit. I don't like the idea of you putting yourself in danger when it won't do no good. I guess that's none of my business, but it still worries me.

I don't know if you got my other letter, but if you did, I hope it found you well. I will keep writing you, just in case you happen to get them.

I hope with all my heart that you are doing well,

Lazlo Fox

Veronica had just finished reading when she heard a knock at their back door.

She had no idea who would be knocking. Her mother, Franklin, or even Lizzie would come right in. She got up quickly, wiped the tears from her eyes, and shoved the letters into her purse. She would finish reading them tomorrow when she could find time alone at the end of the day.

The knock came again at her back door. Veronica walked down the hall. When she saw who was standing at her screen door, her stomach dropped. It was Stella, Missy's mom.

"Hi, Mrs. Sewell," Veronica said, opening the door for her.

"Hi there, Veronica. I'm sorry to be bothering you so late, but Missy hasn't come home. I went by the McBrayers' house as well, but they hadn't seen her. Mr. McBrayer said that she left the factory this evening, just like usual. I was hoping you had seen her."

This place is blighted. That's what Dante had said. It was blighted and the blight was getting bolder.

"I'm sorry, Mrs. Sewell," Veronica replied. "The last time I saw her was this afternoon at Number 8. She was doing the camel job, and her arm was in a sling."

Mrs. Sewell winced and lowered her eyes. She knew what Hugh had done to Missy, then, but she had chosen to turn a blind eye to it. Perhaps it was because that was what Missy wanted. Or perhaps because the McBrayers were well-to-do townies. Or perhaps it was that she had four other children to worry about, and she had been happy to have Missy taken care of—at least in her mind.

"Well, I guess I had hoped that she went home with you," Mrs. Sewell said. "I'm probably getting all nervous about nothing. Missy's probably already home by now."

Behind Mrs. Sewell, Veronica saw a glowing blue chicken appear near the henhouse. It was Betty. She was surrounded by her chicks, all scratching their ghostly feet and pecking with their ghostly beaks. But darting between them was a small shadow. A shadow that was moving tentatively closer to Mrs. Sewell.

Missy isn't dead yet... but she is dying.

The thought came to her as if someone else had whispered it into her ear. She felt her stomach tremble. If she knew where to find her, if she could find out from Betty... but Betty didn't seem inclined to move, even if Veronica could get Missy's mother out of the way.

It's too late for Missy, you can't save her. But you can save others.

The voice in her head sounded like the voice of the ghost Dante. Suddenly, the faces of Franklin and Nan appeared in her head.

"I'm sorry, Mrs. Sewell," Veronica said. "But I'll let you know if I see her—and you'll do the same, okay?"

Mrs. Sewell nodded and then backed out of the house without another word. As Veronica watched her walk down the driveway, she remembered Dante's statement.

This town will be razed to the ground.

Chapter Eighteen

What the Spider Said

"Missy Sewell has gone missing," Veronica's mother said, as Veronica stumbled into the kitchen Saturday morning. She had slept badly, and her dreams had been of Lazlo in trouble. He was caught in some sort of tornado, and she couldn't save him. In the dream, she had decided to go into the tornado herself to find him.

"I know, Mrs. Sewell came by last night," Veronica replied. "When did you hear about it?"

"This morning," her mother said. "Postman Crowder told me when he brought the mail."

Her mother gave Veronica a quick glance. Veronica ignored it.

"What time did Franklin get in last night?" Veronica asked.

"He spent the evening at the Paynes' house. So he got back late," her mother replied. "I would rather the two of you not stay out too late right now. What with Nellie's murder and Missy now apparently gone missing. You should always be with someone else."

"Tell that to Franklin," Veronica mumbled. "See how he responds."

"I'm his mother, he will listen when I talk," her mother said.

Veronica felt the twinge of anger she always felt when her mother tried to take an authoritative stance. She couldn't help remembering how her mother hadn't protected her or Franklin from her father.

"Mr. Sawika stopped me as I was leaving last night," Veronica said.

"Yes, I know. I asked him to tell you that I was working a double," her mother said, as she cracked two eggs in the pan.

"He told me that. He also told me that I needed to be careful right now because of the Knights of Harrisville."

"He's not wrong," her mother said.

Veronica was about to ask more when her mother took her apron off.

"I'm going into work this morning. I was able to get a few overtime hours," she said. "I asked and Mr. Sawika said that you could come in from noon to three. A lot of people are taking time off for Christmas shopping. It's not many hours but it's at time and a half."

"I'll do it," Veronica said. "But you've been working ten days without a break."

"Folks like us have to take what work we can get, when we can get it," her mother said. "Franklin picked up a few extra hours at the pig farm today as well. If we are lucky, we might be able to sock some money away for—well, for the future."

Veronica looked at her mother. Her face was as drawn and weary as it had always been, but her eyes looked different. There was a slight sparkle in them.

"I need to get going," her mother said. "There are a few more eggs for Franklin, and here—"

Her mother put a couple of dollars on the table. Veronica was shocked.

"Go downtown after work and get something for us to cook tomorrow lunch. Franklin told me that Nan is coming over, and maybe her dad as well. Don't scrimp. If you need more money, come find me at work."

Her mother put her hand on the screen door but then stopped and sighed.

"You know, I'm not the sort of woman who don't know when someone's been snooping in my room," she said softly. "Have a care on what you do with what you find."

The screen door slammed behind her before Veronica had a chance to respond. She got up quickly and went to her bedroom. Franklin was still in the bathroom, but she saw with horror that the letters she got from Lazlo were no longer in her purse. They were sitting on her bedside table. Veronica grabbed them quickly, and saw that her mother had scribbled something on one of them.

Your purse ain't no hiding place if you ain't with it. Do better.

Veronica's fingers were trembling, as she took the letters and shoved them back into her purse. Her mother was right, she would need to find a better hiding place, or both the letters and her feelings might escape.

*

When Veronica walked into the factory that afternoon, she had a new place for her letters. She had cut a small hole in the lining of her skirt and had slid all four letters between the lining and outer fabric. The fact that her mother had rummaged through her purse bothered her, but it wasn't like she could say anything about it. After all, she had rummaged through her mother's bedroom.

As she was only working from noon to three, Veronica only had time for three runs. Unfortunately, as she was leaving for her second run of the day, Tommy Sawika swaggered into the factory.

"Hey, Ronnie," he yelled, after she pretended not to see him.

"Hi Tommy, what are you doing here?" she asked, as he came toward her.

"My dad runs this place, or had you forgotten that?" He smirked.

"Yes, but you don't," she said, but then saw Tommy's green eyes narrow. "So why would you want to hang out in a place like this?"

At this last sentence, Tommy smiled. She had openly acknowledged his superiority by alluding to the fact that he didn't have to be here. But when he turned his gaze to Veronica, it was far from friendly.

"Did you tell my dad about what happened with your brother?" he asked.

"No, I don't talk to your dad that often, and never about anything not related to work," Veronica said.

"Well, somebody told him, and your brother better not have been the one who told him, or he'll be sorry," Tommy said.

"Were you the one who left the pig behind our house?" she asked.

"Oh, you got it—I mean, what pig? I don't know anything about a pig," Tommy replied with a grin.

"That was a waste of good meat," Veronica said.

"Maybe you should save it then."

"It had maggots."

"So what's a few maggots?" Tommy laughed.

"Clearly you're new to slaughtering," Veronica replied.

"Maybe, maybe not," was Tommy's response. His eyes were now too bright, and his skin flushed. Veronica was toying with the idea of luring him to the snuff room and stabbing him with her broom when she heard a voice behind her.

"Boy, I told you to come straight to my office."

Veronica turned to see Mr. Sawika approaching them. His face was already red. She turned back to see that Tommy was no longer smiling, but the gleam in his eyes was still there.

"Excuse us, Veronica, but I have something to discuss with my son."

Veronica nodded and quickly escaped. Tommy was going to be a problem. Her daydream of stabbing him with her broom had been a reaction to his disgusting comments, but now, with a cooler head, she wondered if she could get away with it. There had already been a killing, others were probably now expected. No one would ever suspect her. She was a woman—she was a white woman. But then who would be blamed? Some innocent, colored man. Some innocent, colored man like Lazlo.

Like Lazlo. His face came to her mind. His intelligent dark eyes, the small mustache that sat gently above his lip, his thick, arched eyebrows. He had made her feel intelligent, worthy, and beautiful. Yes, not only had he made her feel beautiful, but he also made her feel okay about wanting to be seen as beautiful. There were still letters that she hadn't had time to read.

Veronica dropped her sample box on the ancient scales as she pushed open the door to the snuff room and hosed the bugs into the center of the room. She felt a slight twinge in her stomach. Even though she had been in this room several times since she had been attacked by the possessed raccoon, this was the first time she had been back in the afternoon. Since the incident, she had made it a point to make snuff runs in the morning. She felt a tingle in the back of her neck but shrugged it off. She wanted to leave so that she could find somewhere to read Lazlo's last three letters. The first letter had made her cry, and the second one had made her cry more. Therefore, she could not trust herself to read them anywhere that she might run into people. That meant that she needed a few hours alone in the house, or she needed to find a place away from the house.

Veronica set her sample box down on one of the wooden tables that sat at the end of every other tobacco row. She then took a couple of small collection bags, and her spear broom and began pulling samples from every other row, starting with the second. The further in she walked, the stronger the sweet-sour smell of tobacco became. The smell of the leaf was stronger than usual today. Veronica wondered if they had forgotten to open the air vents near the roof. When she looked up, her heart leaped to her throat.

A shadow was stretched across the entire length of the roof. Its torso and head were just above her head, and its limbs stretched out to all four corners of the rectangular roof. It looked like a giant daddy longlegs perched just above her. The shadowy oval-shaped ball that must have been its head was turning this way and that, as if sniffing. As Veronica began to back up slowly, she saw that there was something shining on its torso, as if there was a jewel hanging from its neck. The shadow had the same general body contour as the one that had possessed the raccoon. She heard a shuffling sound coming from the tobacco leaves further down the row she was standing in, so she dropped her samples and held the broom with both hands. She started to back away when she heard more rustling just behind her. She whirled and saw the tobacco leaves shaking, but not just in the row she was standing next to—the shaking was moving across the room, like a wave. The soft rustling was becoming louder as she backed toward the entrance.

"Roooonnnnnniiieeee," a voice said, from above her head. She looked up just in time to see the shadow on the roof pull itself into a ball and launch itself down at her. Veronica screamed and crouched, throwing her hands over her head. A cold, dank wind blew over her, along with the smell of whiskey and piss. Veronica knew this smell. It was the smell of sloth and sexual deviancy. It was the smell of her father. Her throat closed up and began to burn, and then—well, she felt love embrace her. When she looked up, the air around her was shimmering with heat. The shadow had skittered away to the end of the nearest row of tobacco. As a stream of that shimmering hot air touched it, it curled up and launched itself back to the ceiling. Veronica got to her knees and was about to stand when she saw something lying on the floor in front of her.

It was a silver pocket watch. She touched it gently and, as it was cool to the touch, picked it up. On one side was the clock face. On the other was a faded engraving of a stag. It was her grandmother's pocket watch.

What the hell was it doing lost in the snuff of the cigarette factory?

*

As Veronica was walking back to the QA office, she looked up to see that Tommy and Mr. Sawika were still in his office. Not only were they in the office, but they were also clearly having another heated conversation. They were standing face-to-face, closer to each other than was normal or comfortable for two men who weren't about to get into a fistfight. Veronica turned her eyes downward. She hadn't really thought much about the relationship between Tommy and Mr. Sawika until recently. She had assumed that Tommy was simply a reflection of Mr. Sawika until he had approached her yesterday about the rallies.

She glanced up at the office just in time to see Mr. Sawika smack Tommy. Tommy's head rocked to one side, and he stumbled. When he stood back up, he looked out of the office window, and straight at her. Veronica dropped her eyes and scurried to the QA office. Once there, she set up her samples and began to test them. As she ran the tests, she kept her eyes on the window where she could see the stairs leading from the senior managers' offices to the factory floor. Sure enough, ten minutes later, Tommy charged down the stairs and stomped across the factory. As Veronica didn't want to encounter him as she was leaving, she took her time with her last tests. When she clocked out for the day, Mr. Sawika had left his office and Tommy was nowhere in sight. Still, as she left, she kept to the main roads for her walk home.

Veronica had hidden the watch in the same hole in the lining of her skirt where Lazlo's letters were hidden before she left the snuff area. She knew that this was Grandma Janie's watch. She recognized it. She had also recognized the shadow in the snuff. The smell of her drunken father's breath was something that she wished she could forget, but she suspected she never would. Olfactory memories had always been the hardest ones for her to shake.

So now she knew that a scrap of her father's spirit was trapped in the snuff room. She had known he was dead. Dante had confirmed his death, and yet, to her, this was the greatest proof that his body was dead. Even better, she knew that she could hurt whatever part of him remained. Knowing this meant that he would never be able to hurt her or anyone she loved ever again. There were times, even now, when she looked at Franklin and wondered what might have happened if she had killed her father before he had a chance to beat her brother so badly that he lost his ability to speak fluently. She hadn't killed him for a very simple reason—he had been her father, and she had no other.

As she walked home in the mid-afternoon sun, Veronica pondered the connotation of what happened. If a slice of her father remained in the cigarette factory, there had to be reason for that. Ghosts or memories usually congregated around places they had loved or the place they had died. Her father had never worked at the cigarette factory so there was no emotional reason for his spirit to be tied there. The only reason she could think of was that he had either been killed there or his body had been placed there for a while shortly after death.

Which brought her to John Sawika. He had made it clear to Veronica that he hadn't liked her father, but could he have been the one who killed him? And why had her grandmother's pocket watch been in the snuff room? Of course, her mother might have brought it to work and lost it there, but that seemed particularly unlikely. The watch was an expensive thing, and her mother would have kept it hidden somewhere if it was valuable.

She would need to talk to her mother about this when she got home, but not directly. Her mother had always avoided talking about their past in any way. Even mentioning Grandma Janie could result in Iona leaving the room. She never acted angry, she just simply wouldn't engage in these conversations. It might have been shame, or anger, or the desire to maintain a selective memory. Whatever it was, she knew that she wouldn't be able to just ask her mother about anything from the past without a good reason.

The one good thing was that it would be a while before her mother or Franklin got home. This meant that she might risk reading Lazlo's letters. She knew that this wasn't particularly smart, but the letters were calling to her. Lazlo was out there, somewhere, in the world. He may even be on his way back to America. She wondered if he would write and tell her where he was when he got back. She wondered if she would have the nerve to go looking for him. She wondered if he would be happy if she did.

Veronica was lost in these thoughts as she walked up her driveway. It wasn't until she reached the top that she saw that the screen door was open. For a moment, her heart went to her mouth—until she heard the sound of washing dishes.

Chapter Nineteen

The Boy Who Would Be King

"I need to talk to you," Veronica's mother said, the minute she walked in the door.

"About what?" Veronica asked. She knew that this would be about the letters, but she didn't know what her mother knew or guessed.

"I want you to know why I kept those letters," Iona said, now washing the kitchen counter. "And it's not for the reason you think…"

"It's not because they were letters written to me by a black soldier?" Veronica snapped.

"No, it's not," her mother said. This completely took the wind out of Veronica's sails.

"I was trying to save you some pain, is all," her mother said softly.

Veronica snorted. It was soft, but her mother turned and raised her eyebrows. Then she sighed.

"I know what you think of me," her mother said. "And if it makes you feel any better, you don't think any worse of me than I do of myself. I should have stood up to Deward all those years ago, but… I didn't. I can't even tell you why now. There's no good reason. But love dies slowly, and it poisons everything around it before you realize it's no longer love. At first, Deward was all loving and thought I was a goddess. He even called me his wild goddess." She laughed darkly.

"There was nothing I could do that was wrong in his eyes. It was such a wonderful feeling, to be loved like that. So I guess I overlooked it when he started making little jokes about things I did, or comments about the way I looked. We were married by then, and I didn't want to believe that he was changing. But by the time he slapped me for the first time, I had already had you. He acted all upset about it and swore it would never happen again. He said it was because he had been drinking and he was gonna stop, but he didn't."

Her mother had stopped cleaning and was staring off into space.

"By the time Franklin was born, my mother used the birth as excuse to come live with us. She knew what was going on. But what I am trying to say is that by that time he did nothing but tell me how useless I was… by his words and his actions. And I believed him because I had stayed. I had to be useless if I had stayed and put up with it. I thought I deserved it. I thought I was weak. It took his disappearing to prove to myself that I wasn't what he said I was."

Her mother stopped cleaning, threw the towel she had been holding over her shoulder and sat down at the table.

"Now we're poor but we're safe," she continued. "It took us years to get there, and to live without fear in your house is a fine thing. So when I saw those letters you got, all I could think about was how you could get hurt. I don't care that he is colored. If you were happy with him, it wouldn't matter to me. But no one would let you be happy with him, not round here at least."

Veronica pulled the pocket watch from the lining of her skirt and dropped it on the table. Her mother gasped.

"Where did you find that?" she whispered.

"I found it buried in the snuff room at the factory," Veronica said. "Yesterday, John Sawika came to find me to tell me that you were working late. He asked me if I had gone to the rally and told me that it wasn't wise for me, Franklin, or you to be out after sundown. He told me that he knew you when you were young and that you were wild and willful. He said that he thought you would leave this town and that he had been shocked when you married Deward."

"He said that?" Iona asked, taking the watch into her hands, and tracing her fingers over the surface.

"That was Grandma Janie's watch," Veronica said. "She showed it to me when I was little. Why would I find it in the snuff room at the factory?"

Her mother said nothing, she held the watch to her chest and closed her eyes.

"This watch was supposed to be for you," she said. "I guess it found its way back to you."

"Did John Sawika kill Deward?" Veronica asked.

Her mother opened her eyes. She put the watch on the table and stared at it. There was silence for what felt like hours.

"I met John Sawika when he was ten years old," her mother finally said. "He was sent here to live with his auntie because his mama had caught sick and died.

His pa had died under what the law men said was 'questionable circumstances' or something like that. John was small for his age then. He was smaller than me, and we were the same age. So some of the older boys decided to rough him up a bit, but that didn't turn out so well for the older boys. Pretty quick, people stopped bullying him. John was little but fierce and he fought like a wild thing. He fought like he didn't feel pain or fear. After that, rumors started going round the school that John had killed his papa. Apparently, his father worked slaughtering pigs and brought him to work there too. His father disappeared and they found his remains in a vat of pig slop. I guess no one accused him, maybe 'cause his father was a hard-living bastard who liked his drink and his whores."

Veronica had no idea where her mother was going with this, but there was a churning in her gut—no, it was more of a burning.

"No one would talk to him at school," her mother continued. "He sat by himself when we were allowed out for lunch. All the kids said he was dangerous. I told Mama the stories about him, and she just laughed.

"'The difference between the strong and the weak is being able to do what needs to be done, even if it's ugly,' was what your grandmother said. So I went to sit with him the very next day. I sat next to him for the rest of that year."

"You were friends with John Sawika?" Veronica asked.

"Yes. We were ten and it was before I knew much about people. I liked him. He worked harder than anyone else at school—at least, when he was there. The law said kids had to be in school four months a year, and I think that's all his auntie allowed him. He started at the factory part time when he was ten. It wasn't allowed, but as long as he put in four months of education, no one said much. But I never saw anyone work harder than that boy. He grew when he was fourteen. He was almost as tall as he is now. He and I had stopped talking much to each other. He was too busy at school and his auntie made him earn his food and board by working. He was strong, healthy, and worked like a demon. By the time he was seventeen, he was a line manager at the factory. When I got married, he was the one that gave me my job."

Her mother shook her head.

"That watch... your grandmother's watch," Iona said. "It was given to her by her daddy. It's silver and it was probably worth a month of wages. I don't rightly know where her papa got it, but I know she cherished it. She had always planned to give it to one of us kids. Since all the others moved away, it would have been me. While she was living with us, it disappeared. Mama told me that she thought Deward took it and sold it for drink money. She wanted to confront him about it, but I begged her not to. By then, I knew what confrontation with him would mean for me. She was disappointed in me, but she understood. That young, strong girl that I had been was gone by then… she died the first time he beat me unconscious."

"Grandma hated him for what he did to you," Veronica said. "I'm sure she didn't blame you."

"You loved my mother," her mother said softly. "And she you. I think she saw herself in you. I was like her too, when I was young, and we were close until I married Deward. She saw that as a weakness, my marriage. My papa died when he was only forty-five, so she was left to raise all of us alone. Raise us and run the farm, and she did it all alone. But I thought I was in love.

"When she moved in with us, Deward didn't want her, but she didn't give him no choice. I'm guessing she figured that he wouldn't hit me if she was around. And she was right, for the most part. Deward was scared of her, for sure. Most people were scared of Janie Price Brackett. She was full of spit and tar, my mother. That's why I didn't believe, why I don't believe, that she died in her sleep. That, and the fact that it didn't look like a peaceful death when I found her that morning."

Veronica's heart dropped to the pit of her stomach.

Her mother was sitting at their table staring out of the window, presumably at the chickens, but her eyes were unfocused.

"Dr. Payne came by and confirmed her death. Deward shook his hand, shaking his head but smiling when he looked down. Doc Payne took my hand, and when he looked in my eyes, he gave me this tiny shake of his head. That's when I was sure. Janie hadn't died natural. Deward had suffocated her in her sleep."

"Why didn't you go to the police?" Veronica asked.

"The police then was same as the police now. Crooked through and through. And when Dr. Payne left, Deward grabbed me and told me that if I made any trouble, I would end up the same as Janie. He then said that you were coming into womanhood, and you suited him just fine. My blood run cold when he said that."

"Did you kill him?" Veronica asked softly.

"No, child. But I did the next best thing. I told John."

"Mr. Sawika?" Veronica asked.

Her mother nodded.

"We hadn't said much to each other in years, but I was a right mess when I showed up at his office. See, Deward had smacked me around a bit for good measure before he took off to meet his friends to get drunk. Before he left, he told me to get myself off the floor and get myself off to work. He wasn't working at all by that time. He was drinking full time. Then damned if he didn't pull Janie's watch out of his pocket and open it. He grinned at me and told me I was going to be late if I didn't hurry. Then that bastard walked off down the street whistling. You came down but I sent you back to your room to watch Franklin. It was horrible.

"I made it to work and went straight to John Sawika's office. He was a senior manager by then. He didn't ask anything, he just brought me into his office and closed the door. I was torn up. I couldn't believe Mama was gone. I knew that Deward had done it now. He told me as much with that watch. So when John asked me what was happening, I told him everything."

"What did you tell him, Mama?" Veronica whispered.

"I told him that I thought Deward had killed Janie. I told him that he had threatened me… and I think I managed to hint at what he was doing to you."

"How did he respond to that?"

"John? He didn't say much," her mother said softly. "He was doer, not a talker. So he told me not to worry about a thing. He sent me home and told me that, as I was on his line, he wouldn't dock my pay. That evening, his wife Kate came by with a casserole. She helped with the funeral arrangements."

"What did Deward do?"

"Your papa stayed drunk for a whole week after that. He missed the funeral. Then, the second week, he just disappeared. Everyone said he ran off, but he had only been gone for two days when my job was made permanent full time by the factory."

When her mother looked up at Veronica, her eyes were wet.

"I will be thankful to John Sawika for the rest of my life," she said, picking up the pocket watch. "I know what he did. He did what needed to be done. But he's a person who either has a lot more of something than most of us, or a lot less. For John, that difference has made him strong and fair in his own way. His son Tommy might have inherited this difference, but his life has been too easy to force him to become what his father became."

"Did you… do you… love John Sawika?" Veronica asked. Her mother snorted.

"I don't believe in love," she said, wiping her nose with the wet towel. "People are in the way of saying they love to excuse lust. I made that mistake with Deward, and I paid for that one mistake with my future and yours and Franklin's. So, no, I'm not in love with John. I was his friend when no one else was. He returned the favor. This is how it is for our kind."

"So you think John Sawika killed Deward?" she asked.

"I don't know if he did or he didn't, but I know he had it in him to do it. But I guessed that someone must have killed Deward. He was too lazy and too mean to just run off, particularly once your grandma was out of his way. I know

John smoothed the way for me to get a permanent job. I know that he gave you a job when you were old enough… when there were others crying out for one. The fact that you found your grandma's watch at the factory—well, that tells its own story, doesn't it?"

Veronica nodded.

"Don't you go saying anything about this," her mother said sharply. "You hide those letters you got, and the ones you took from my drawer. If more come, you say that you don't know nothing about them. There are people in this town mean enough to try to get ahead by climbing on your back, and your old friend Lizzie is one of them."

"She knows, she found a letter," Veronica said.

"Sweet Jesus," her mother whispered, closing her eyes. She put her head in her hands and leaned on the table. Then she sighed.

"All right, then," she said. "You do whatever you need to do to calm things down with Lizzie for now. You lie if you have to, and you lie well. Tell her whatever she needs to hear."

Outside, they heard whistling. Franklin was walking up the driveway. Her mother picked up the watch and put it in her apron.

"Not a word to Franklin," her mother said. "And don't you breathe a word of this to John Sawika."

"There's only one thing that I would want to say to Mr. Sawika about this," Veronica said, standing up to go to her room. "And that's thank you."

*

Veronica heard the screen door slam and immediately headed back to the kitchen.

"You're home early," Veronica heard her mother say.

She had just stepped into the kitchen when she saw Franklin mouth.

"It's nearly Christmas, so they have more people taking extra hours besides me."

"Is Nan still coming for lunch tomorrow? And her father, is he coming?"

"Yes, they're coming, but Nan told me to tell you not to go to too much trouble. She says your regular meals are always delicious."

Her mother smiled but shook her head.

"I want to make a stew with beef for once," she said. "So can both of you go down to the butcher and get me three pounds of stew beef?"

Franklin shook his head. "No, we don't need to try to impress the Paynes."

"We're not doing it to impress the Paynes. We are doing it because I got this at work today," Iona said, taking something from her apron pocket. She handed it to Veronica. It took a moment for Veronica to realize what it was, then she smiled and passed it to Franklin.

"The deed to the house?" Franklin asked.

Her mother nodded.

"Mr. Sawika called me to his office when I got to work. He had a notary there and someone from the courthouse. I signed the deed, and then the lawyer took it, and I went to work. A couple of hours later, Mr. Sawika called me back to his office and gave me this. He told me to go on home and celebrate. I wanted to ask him a few questions, but I saw Tommy talking to you, and I figured he was there to see his father. So I came on home."

"Do we need to do anything with this? I mean besides hold on to it," Veronica asked.

"I don't think so," her mother said, smiling. "But I want for us to have a big proper meal tomorrow. A big proper meal in our own house. So I want you two to go buy some stew beef, potatoes, and some good rolls. Veronica has some money."

"I can go by myself," Veronica said.

"No," her mother said. "John Sawika warned you about being out alone."

"But it's daytime."

"I wouldn't trust that matters to someone who would slaughter a pig and throw it in our backyard," her mother said. "You told your work about it, right?"

Franklin nodded.

"They were shocked," he mouthed, "and more than a little upset. But no one thought it was me, so that was good. Still, I think Ma is right. You shouldn't be going out alone."

"And neither should you," Veronica said. She toyed with the idea of telling them about her run-in with Tommy but decided against it.

"Fine," Franklin said. "Let's go then."

Franklin kept to himself on the walk toward Main Street. He kept his eyes on the road, not making eye contact with her.

"Okay, what's wrong?" Veronica asked.

"What?"

"What's wrong, and don't go saying nothing, because I know better," Veronica said.

Franklin sighed and turned his head slightly so she could read his lips.

"Some of the guys at work said that Tommy Sawika was planning to ask Nan out," he said.

"Okay. If anyone can let him down gently, it will be Nan," Veronica said.

"I'm not sure he will take no for an answer," Franklin replied. "He's the one who left the pig."

"How do you know?" Veronica asked. Franklin made eye contact with her and smiled a sad little smile.

"I just do," he said. "He's hated me long enough for me to predict what he'll do. I don't why he hates me so badly. That started long before Nan. I sort of think that he wants to go out with her just to get at me."

"Maybe, but if he was the one who killed the pig, then there is something wrong with him. And you should stay away from him."

"I try! I don't search him out, he searches me out."

"I know," Veronica said, as they turned onto Main Street. The Christmas decorations were up, and it gave the normal shops a bit of color. It was crowded with the usual Saturday crowd, plus the Christmas crowd. Since the rations on meat and cheese had been lifted in February, people were celebrating more at holidays. They had had an actual run on turkeys at Thanksgiving. Veronica was surprised that there were people, people in this town, who thought nothing of buying a bird much larger than their family could eat.

Franklin touched her on the arm.

"I'm kind of tired," he said. "There are lots of people here, so how about we split up? I'll go get the vegetables if you go to the butcher."

Veronica nodded. She knew the real reason that Franklin didn't want to go to the butcher's. Fred, the butcher, was a nasty person who hid his nastiness with outward friendliness. He always insisted on speaking to Franklin on the rare occasions that he went in. Then he would slap his head and claim to have forgotten that Franklin was "dumb, you know, he can't speak." Fred said the word "dumb" loud and with purpose, using it to offend without having to take responsibility for the offense.

Franklin had already left for the vegetable market stands as Veronica started toward the butcher's shop. She was examining the various Christmas decorations as she walked. In the butcher's shop she bought three pounds of beef, like her mother had instructed. Fred raised his eyebrows at her, but simply shrugged when she was able to produce the money.

As she came out of the butcher's, she saw trouble.

Chapter Twenty

Where Beauty Sleeps

Tommy was standing with Nan, who had just come out of the bakery. She had what looked like cakes in her arms. Tommy had put one hand against the building and was blocking her path. Veronica felt a surge of heat in her belly, as she quickly looked behind her. She couldn't see Franklin, so hopefully he wasn't seeing this.

"Hi," Veronica said, as she walked up to them as casually as she could.

"Hi Ronnie," Nan said, relief flooding her face.

"Veronica, this would be a good time for you to get lost," Tommy said, reaching out and brushing Nan's hair off her shoulder.

"I'm sorry, Tommy. I need to leave now. Please let me pass," Nan said sternly.

Tommy just laughed and stepped directly in front of her. When Nan tried to step around him, he moved back in front of her.

"I'm not going to let you go until you agree to let me take you on a date," Tommy said.

"So you have to bully people into dating you now?" Veronica asked, the heat in her belly spreading outward to the rest of her torso.

"Shut up, Ronnie," Tommy said. Veronica opened her mouth, but then closed it. At that moment there was a flash behind them in the butcher's and the sound of someone swearing.

"What the hell just happened to the grill?" he yelled. "Who threw something on it?"

Veronica felt the warmth in her belly abate a bit.

"Tommy, I'm not going out with you. I have a boyfriend," Nan said.

"Oh, right, the d-d-d-d-d-dummy," Tommy said, laughing and taking Nan's arm. Nan jerked away.

"I've never liked you," she said, her voice calm but sharp. "You are a rich, spoiled, bully. You are a little boy who pouts when he doesn't get his way. What's worse is that you are terrified of everything. You're afraid of people who aren't like you. You're afraid of people who are smart. You're afraid of people who are strong. You're afraid of people who are richer than you. So you spend all your time trying to bring other people down so that you can feel better about yourself. I'd never consider dating someone like you in a thousand years—not in a thousand years."

Tommy stood, his mouth hanging open and his cheeks pink and getting pinker. His green eyes were shinier than usual.

"You should leave now," Nan said. Tommy winced so slightly that he probably didn't even feel it, but that small moment registered real pain. Then his eyes turned hard and cold. He grinned at Nan, reached out and put his arm around her waist, pulling her to him. Nan quickly turned her back to him and pushed him away with her shoulder.

"Well, I guess you're in love with the coloreds too," Tommy hissed, turning toward Veronica. "Yeah, Ronnie, we know about your little soldier friend and his letters to you. CJ knows too, so you won't be able to count on him helping you anymore."

Veronica suddenly saw Franklin appear down the street. His eyes were scanning the market.

"My brother is just down the street," Veronica said. "He hasn't seen you yet, so you should go before he does."

"I'm not scared of your dumb brother," Tommy snarled.

"Well, then you're stupid. Do you really want to fight Franklin Crane? All by yourself? After you just laid hands on his fiancée?"

"Fiancée?" Tommy spat out.

"Yes, Franklin asked me to marry him, and I accepted," Nan said, standing straighter, pale blue eyes flashing.

Veronica saw Franklin's eyes scanning for them in the crowd. When he saw them, his eyes widened, and he started running toward them.

Oh no!

"Nan, Franklin's coming, stop him!"

Nan's eyes went wide, and she shoved the cakes at Veronica and began running toward Franklin.

Veronica could see her brother's face now, and there was death in it.

"For the love of god, Tommy, get out of here," Veronica hissed. "Or he's gonna kill you."

"You're gonna regret this—all of you," Tommy snarled, but he stomped off plenty fast. She suspected he had seen the look on Franklin's face too.

Veronica turned, throwing her weight forward, preparing herself to stop Franklin with her body, if need be, but Nan had beaten her to it.

Nan was standing with Franklin in the middle of the market. She took his face in her hands and kissed him, in front of god and everyone. At first, Franklin froze, but then he took her in his arms and kissed her back. This moment, with the whole street staring at them, told an honest story of their town. About a quarter of the people were smiling, eyes soft and misty. Most people looked away, embarrassed but not displeased. However, a good portion of the white men looked on with hostility. Veronica needed to get her brother out of there. If anyone mentioned that Tommy had laid his hands on Nan, Veronica wouldn't be able to stop Franklin from chasing Tommy down.

"I've got your cakes, Nan," Veronica said, walking up to them. It took a moment for her words to register with Nan, who was lost in Franklin's kiss.

"Oh, I'm sorry, Ronnie," Nan said, turning in Franklin's arms. "I wanted those to be a surprise for tomorrow's lunch."

"You don't need to bring things like that," Veronica said. She and Nan were both making meaningless small talk, to avoid talking about what had just happened.

"Well, I saw you at the butcher buying beef and I know what beef costs these days," Nan replied.

"Look, some of my favorite people all together," came a voice from behind Veronica. She turned to see Nan's father, Dr. Payne approaching. Dr. Payne was a handsome man, a widower, and a doctor. He would have been a wonderful catch for a widow, but up until now he had been too busy with his practice and looking after Nan. Now that Nan was engaged to Franklin, some of those women might finally get their chance. From the look on several older women's faces around them, Veronica suspected that these women had already considered this.

"Papa," Nan said, extracting herself from Franklin's arms and giving her father a hug.

"Good afternoon, Dr. Payne," Franklin mouthed.

"Franklin, I hate to burden you, but I was wondering if maybe you and your sister could stop by our house on your way home. There is a leak in our kitchen sink that I haven't been able to fix."

"I'd be happy to, Dr. Payne," Franklin said.

"Good man," Dr. Payne said, clapping Franklin on the shoulder. The two of them walked toward the Paynes' house, with Veronica and Nan walking a few paces behind them.

"That was good thinking," Veronica said to Nan.

"It was the only thing I could think of," Nan replied. "Franklin looked like he was going to kill him."

"I've never seen him that angry. That would have been a bad fight. Tommy's an idiot to start up with Franklin, particularly after bothering you."

"I love him, Ronnie," Nan said. "I love him so much, sometimes I can't breathe. So I don't want him to do anything that will get him hurt. Do you think agreeing to marry him put him in danger?"

"If it did, I don't think he cares," Veronica replied. "And I don't think you should let what a bunch of idiots think keep you from being happy."

"I know, but thanks for telling me that," Nan whispered. "Sometimes I don't know how straight I can think when it comes to Franklin."

Veronica smiled at her, and Nan responded with a smile, but then her brow creased.

"Oh, about what Tommy said, I should warn you. Just before you got here, Lizzie was at the market telling Tommy and his gang that a colored soldier has been writing to you. I won't ask you if that is true or not. I don't care. But CJ did not take that rumor well. He walked off without another word."

"Great," Veronica muttered. "Okay, if anyone asks you, a soldier sent letters to me that were just addressed to my name and the town. He didn't have my address but—"

"But that's all I need to know," Nan said, taking Veronica by the arm. "I'll stand by you no matter what you do, or what they say."

Veronica felt her eyes tear. This sweet girl loved her strong, loyal brother. If that could happen then maybe the world wasn't as hard and factual as she had always thought. Just as she thought this, she saw Missy's mother wandering through the market stalls.

*

When they got to Nan's house, Dr. Payne immediately engaged Franklin in looking at the pipes under the kitchen sink. Nan took Veronica into the living room, which felt huge to Veronica but was small compared to the number of objects it held. On one side of the room was a piano, a phonograph player, and an old harp. On the other side was the fireplace and a couch covered in rose-colored fabric. The walls were covered in wallpaper depicting roses, and displayed multiple photos of a pretty woman with blonde hair. This was the first time that Veronica had been inside the Paynes' house proper. Of course, she had been to Dr. Payne's office before, but it was a separate small building just behind his house. Veronica assumed that it was in the back to give patients some privacy while they were being seen. This might be why some of the colored people in the town took the risk of coming to see him.

Nan sat on the couch and motioned for Veronica to sit next to her.

"Thanks for saving me back there," Nan said, speaking softly so that the men would not overhear them. "I was afraid of Tommy, and then I was afraid of what Franklin would do to Tommy. I don't know how you are always able to be so calm and cool around those people."

"I'm not," Veronica replied.

"Well, you look like you are. And you always seem to know what to do. I wish I was like that. I wish I could stand up to bullies better than I do."

"You did a perfectly decent job of standing up to Tommy," Veronica said, patting Nan's hand. Nan took Veronica's hand.

"Is that your mother?" Veronica asked, looking at the photos.

"Yes, you know she died when I was very young. She was beautiful, and she played so many instruments. It's sad, but I inherited none of her talent." Nan laughed and shrugged.

"You inherited her beauty though," Veronica replied.

"That's kind of you," Nan replied.

"It wasn't a compliment, it was a statement of fact," Veronica said. "But it's who you are that Franklin fell in love with, not what you look like."

Nan smiled.

"People think that my father hasn't remarried because of me. I wondered that too, until I fell in love with Franklin. Now I understand it. He can't remarry because he will never love anyone like he loved my mother. He keeps her pictures on the wall, and he keeps things the way she decorated because it's a way to stay close to her. I don't think he is willing to change that and he doesn't want to have to put some other woman second in his life."

"My brother worships you, you know," Veronica said. "I've known that for a long time. He will be true to you until he dies. It's nice to hear that you feel the same."

Nan blushed.

"Listen, I was thinking that you might want a few moments alone. Maybe you should go to my bedroom and lie down for a bit. Or just rest. Whatever you need to do. In fact, if you ever need somewhere private, you can always come here. If we aren't home, you can use Dad's office. He leaves the key in the flowerpot near the door."

Nan stood up and led Veronica to her bedroom. It had wallpaper decorated with pale yellow daisies rather than roses. Her bed was small and soft as Veronica sat down.

"Stay here as long as you want to," Nan said. "I won't let the men disturb you."

Nan then leaned forward and kissed Veronica on the forehead.

"I always wanted a sister, and it seems like I'm getting the best."

With that, she turned and closed the door behind her.

Veronica immediately pulled up her skirt and took out the letters she had hidden there.

Nov 14, 1944

Dearest Veronica,

I hope you are getting these letters. I know I shouldn't be wanting that, but I do. I'm not sure if I'm being considerate or if I'm being a coward by—well, I wish things weren't in such a state that I have to worry about things like that.

So today the Germans had put a log to block the way into the village and all the tanks were getting stuck. We was in the front, and being from the country, I knew the setup for a turkey shoot when I saw one. So I got my ass out of that tank, out in the smoke and the shrapnel, and got a line on the log—we used the tank to pull it out the way. I didn't think much about it at the time, but looking back I guess they was all shooting at me. This got us through, and we got into the town. My commander told me that was the bravest thing he ever saw and the stupidest. He asked if I was trying to get myself killed. I laughed when he said that, but tonight, I have to wonder if it might be true.

You see, I have these dreams at night. I used to only have dreams during the day. I had dreams of getting an education. I had dreams of moving up north, getting a job and having a house. I had dreams of what it would feel like to really be a free man. Since I have been in England and

France, I've learned what that feels like, and I want it even more, but not as much as I want something else. The dreams I have at night now are what I want. I can't write to you about them because it would be impossible to describe. I don't have the right words for it and my writing isn't good enough. I've never had dreams like these before. I've never felt dreams that were so real—and so perfect. So when my commander asked if I was trying to get myself killed, I wondered if maybe I'm just trying to find some way to stay in those dreams. I'm sorry, I shouldn't put these thoughts on you, but if I can't tell you, I don't know who else I could tell.

Anyway, we took the town of Wuisse a few days ago. It's funny, but I feel very at home here. Most of the villages are small and out in the country. It reminds me of being at home with my family. I guess I was expecting things to look completely different, but they don't. The trees still look like trees. The lakes look like lakes. The grass and the bushes look like grass and bushes I would see at home. The people, even though they speak a different language, all seem to be wanting the same things we all want. They want to have food to eat and a place to live in. They want to raise their kids in peace. The big difference here is that they don't seem to care as much about the color of a person's skin. I could see myself living in a place like this. Travel is a fine thing after all. I wish... well, I wish a lot. I will say that some of the landscapes here have been very beautiful, but no landscape can ever compare to a beautiful woman. I guess every man knows that in his heart. I might try to sketch one anyway, just to send to you.

We have been on the move since October 7. I don't know how much longer we will be on the move. General Patton, he gave a speech to us, and he said that we were representing all colored people in America. I'm not sure that he really meant that, but I know it's true. The white American soldiers didn't like us much at first, but it's getting a little bit better. I think that's because of how the French and the English see us. I've been getting a name for being able to stitch people up. I used to work with animals on the farm, and I was the one to tend them when they was sick. I stitched up donkeys and dogs when they got cuts that were too deep. Stitching a person isn't too much different, except they don't kick or bite you. That was a joke—some of the people try to kick and bite you too. As we don't have a medic in our division, and the medic in the other regiment was killed, quite a few people end up coming to me. Sometimes I can help, but sometimes all I can do is hold their hand as they pass on. I have to say that's one of the hardest parts, holding the hand of a man who just wants to get back to his wife and kids… and knowing that he will never see them again. It's an ache in my already aching heart.

I hope you are doing well. I hope you can save some money for school. I hope you get these letters. I hope…

All my best,

Lazlo

Veronica put her lips to the letter where he had signed his name. He was trying to speak to her without telling people that she had been alone with him. He mentioned dreams. No, he mentioned dreams good enough to make him want to die to stay in them. She ached to think that he might be dreaming about her the way she was dreaming about him.

She was just pulling out another letter when she heard Franklin and Dr. Payne's voices coming closer. They must be done with the plumbing, and they should get home as they still had the meat with them.

Veronica wiped her eyes with the back of her hand, folded the letters and put them back into their spot in her skirt. As she did this, she shoved all her feelings back deep inside her, leaving the security of Nan's room, the Paynes' house and a love that was just out of reach.

Chapter Twenty One

Traces of Life

When Veronica and Franklin got home it was 5:30 but the sun had already set. She had been expecting a torrent of questions from Franklin about what had happened with Tommy, but no such questions were forthcoming. In fact, he didn't communicate much at all. He walked staring at his feet. At first, Veronica was afraid that he was angry, but when she asked him about the work he had done on the Paynes' kitchen sink, he opened up with all the details. As he mouthed information about U-bends and grease, Veronica didn't pay so much attention to what he was saying as to how his face was moving. When Franklin was angry, his face closed down, as did his body language. But right now, he was speaking with his hands, as he often did. When he finished describing the sink repair, he went back to staring at his feet. His face looked not so much angry as preoccupied. What had happened at the market had been dramatic, even for Franklin's life. He had seen Tommy possibly threatening Nan, and when he came to help her, she had thrown herself into his arms. In this one move, she had announced their relationship to the entire town. To be acknowledged in public would a big deal to Franklin, but, surely, he would sense the danger in it as well.

When they got to the house, her mother was in a blind panic about how to sit the table for five rather than four for dinner tomorrow. Veronica offered to eat in the living room, but this earned her a glare from Iona. Franklin immediately went to the bathroom to take his shower. As she had no interest in watching Iona fret about furniture, she went to the bedroom she shared with Franklin. She wouldn't be able to read the last letter from Lazlo before Franklin finished his shower, and even if she could, she doubted that she would be able to keep her face in control afterward. Franklin had already given her an odd look when she had come out of Nan's bedroom.

Reading Lazlo's letters had left her heart aching. After meeting him, and up to this point, she had been successful in separating her feelings. She thought about her basic needs and family during the day and she thought about Lazlo at night. The difficulty began when she learned that Lazlo had written to her, and now that she had read his letters, the practical side of her brain was turning against her. Her heart told her that she needed Lazlo. Her practical brain told her that, now that she knew that her feelings for him were reciprocated, it was reasonable to pursue them, so she should try to find him. It was only the part of her that lived through her father's violence that prevented her from charging into the draft office and demanding that they find him for her. This part of her knew that the world around her was neither logical nor practical, and that world would not be likely to mind its own business. She hated feeling this way. It felt like someone put a plate full of food in front of her, and she was being prevented from eating. Even worse, she was forced to watch it being thrown away. The pain in Veronica's heart was turning to anger. With that anger came a burning inside.

Franklin walked into the room. His hair was wet, and his face was a storm of emotion. He sat down on Veronica's bed next to her. Then he put his arm around her and pulled her into an embrace.

"Th-th-thank you," he whispered in her ear.

"For what?"

Franklin pulled back enough for her to read his lips.

"I saw you at the market. I saw you send Nan and I saw you bracing to stop me," he mouthed. "I was so angry, I might have killed him if the two of you hadn't stopped me."

"Well, you have a fiancée who isn't afraid to let people know that she cares for you," Veronica said, "and who isn't afraid to stop you from doing destructive things."

"I have a sister who has done that for my whole life," he replied. "I don't want to go off my head and cause more trouble for Nan. Do you think being married to me will hurt her?"

"Funny, she asked me if you marrying her would hurt *you*," Veronica said. "Besides, you can't keep people from getting hurt, you can only be there to help pick up the pieces after life pulls them apart."

Veronica felt the burning in her eyes that meant tears were threatening.

"I know," Franklin said. "I know about the soldier writing to you."

"How do you know?" Veronica asked.

"Lizzie spilled her guts, and Hugh McBrayer told me about it in not the nicest terms."

"I'm sorry, Franklin," Veronica said.

"Don't be. You love him. I know that. I've known that you loved someone for a long time now, I just couldn't figure out who."

"How did you know?"

"You're my big sister, how could I not know?" Franklin said. He then laid down on her bed and pulled her down. She settled her head into his shoulder. They had slept like this sometimes as children, but it had been a long time since they had been particularly physically affectionate with each other. Once Franklin grew into looking like a man, it had felt strange, but now she was grateful for his embrace. She let the tears fall from her eyes, wetting Franklin's shoulder.

If he noticed, he didn't say anything.

*

The following day, Nan and Dr. Payne arrived for Sunday dinner at exactly 2 p.m. Nan brought the cakes for Iona. She also brought some flowers. It would have been awkward for Dr. Payne to present Iona with flowers, him being a widower and her being a widow. Instead, he brought some oranges and peppermint sticks. After all of Iona's worry last night, they managed to squeeze all five of them around the table, and the food was set out in the kitchen buffet-style. In fact, Nan had been the one who suggested that they just leave the food in the kitchen and serve themselves. She positioned it by saying that it would mean that they could all sneak back into the kitchen and get seconds, which she knew she would want to do. Iona had positively beamed.

Her mother served Brunswick stew, but it was her own recipe. She insisted on simmering the beef at a low temperature for the evening before and starting again first thing in the morning. She only added the potatoes, tomatoes, beans, corn, and okra a couple of hours before. On the side, she prepared squash casserole, collard greens, and cornbread. Also, even though Veronica had told her mother that Nan would be bringing cakes, Iona insisted on making a pecan pie as well. Veronica had only had this much food once or twice in her life. Of course, this was their official celebration of Franklin and Nan's engagement, and this was as happy as she had ever seen her mother.

"Have you two set a date yet?" Dr. Payne asked, as he dipped a corner of cornbread into his stew.

"As soon as possible," Nan said.

"We want to do it early next year," Franklin said. "I should be able to get on full time as a fireman. I'll get a good salary there, and I can still work at the farm. I promise that Nan will never go hungry."

Veronica felt her eyes begin to burn again. Dr. Payne was smiling at Franklin kindly, but he didn't really understand what Franklin was saying. Veronica did. Franklin was saying that Nan would always eat before him. He was saying that if there was nothing to drink but his blood, he would gladly provide that for her. He was also saying that he would endure whatever discomfort, pain, humiliation, or torment to keep Nan happy and healthy.

"New Year's Day," Nan said softly. "I want to get married on New Year's Day."

"That's so soon, I won't have enough money yet," Franklin said.

"I agree with my daughter," Dr. Payne said. "We are happy to have Franklin move into our house. We have the space, and I would be happy to have a son-in-law to help with things around the house."

"You might have trouble organizing a wedding so quickly," Iona said.

"We don't need a wedding to be married," Nan said. "We can just go to the courthouse."

"You might regret that later," Iona said.

"Not for one minute," Nan replied, looking at Franklin, eyes shining.

"Well, she told all of us," Dr. Payne said.

"New Year's Day it is," Franklin said. "And if it's not open?"

"January second," Nan said. "I'll wear Ma's white suit."

"I'll make sure that Veronica and I aren't working, or can take the day off," her mother said. Her voice was softer than usual, and her eyes were on her plate. Veronica thought she might be trying to repress tears. Nan reached out and put her hand on Iona's arm.

"Can I go cut us some of your delicious pie?" Nan asked. "I know it's rude to ask, but I've been smelling it all evening."

Iona looked up and smiled.

"No, let me get it for you," Iona said. "The rest of you can take your plates into the kitchen."

The pie was delicious, just as Nan had said it would be. After they finished eating and cleaned up, they spent a few hours playing cards at the table. As the gloaming faded into night, Nan tapped her father on the arm.

"Right, we don't want to overstay our welcome," Dr. Payne said, but didn't move to stand.

"It's not possible to overstay welcome with family," Veronica said. "Family is where you go when you've overstayed your welcome somewhere else."

"Ronnie's right," Franklin said.

Nan smiled and started to stand, but her father shook his head.

"Before we go, I wanted to share some information with everyone," Dr. Payne said. "I don't know if you noticed that yesterday felt a bit tense around town. If you did, then there may be a reason for it. Some of the wounded soldiers were brought into the hospital yesterday evening."

For a moment, Veronica felt like she couldn't breathe.

"They're trying to keep that information secret for as long as they can. A few military doctors came as well, to help take care of them."

"Why haven't we heard anything about that?" Iona asked. "I would have thought that people would want to know. Don't the church ladies and the PTA usually bring food baskets or other such stuff?"

Her mother was trying, but her disdain for these organizations bled through. Dr. Payne smiled.

"Well, I'm not sure how they would feel about distributing baskets to these soldiers," Dr. Payne said. "About half of them are colored soldiers."

Veronica felt her heart begin to slam in her chest. She had a million questions that she wanted to ask, but she didn't trust her voice.

Dr. Payne had paused and was looking hard at his hands which were folded in his lap.

"What is it, Papa?" Nan asked.

"Nellie Crowder was not the only person murdered in our community this year," Dr. Payne said. "There have been seven murders of colored men and women in the past nine months."

Nan gasped, putting her hand over her mouth. Veronica felt Franklin put his hand on her leg.

"Why didn't Chief Bishop tell us?" Franklin asked.

"Well, at first he didn't know," Dr. Payne said. "The first was a young man. His body was brought to me in secret by his relatives. I told them that we needed to tell the police, but they begged me not to say anything. They were afraid that it would make them the target of the police. I told them surely not, but they begged me. So I did the best I could to clean up the body and gave it back to them."

"Did you tell the police chief?" Iona asked.

"No, I told them I wouldn't, so I honored my word—until another colored family showed up. This time it was a young woman. She was—well, her family was extremely distraught, but this was the second time. So I told them that I had to tell the police. They made me promise that I wouldn't give her name or tell the police what they looked like. Then they said their goodbyes to their daughter and left her body with me."

"You told Chief Bishop?" Franklin said.

"Yes, I did," Dr. Payne said, biting his lip. "After that, the bodies that came, came from the police department. No more bodies were brought to me. I'm afraid that the police department might have gone into the colored neighborhood a bit roughly."

"Papa, I still don't understand why we wouldn't have been told about this," Nan said. "That means that someone has killed eight people."

"I suspect that there have been more deaths than that," said Dr. Payne. "I think we haven't been told about all of them."

"Why didn't you tell me?" Nan asked.

"Because you didn't need to know, and I was afraid of how you would react," Dr. Payne said. "You can get very stubborn when you feel strongly, and you have that need to do something."

A little smile played at the corners of Franklin's mouth before disappearing. He took Nan's hand.

"She's just like her mother that way," Dr. Payne said to Franklin. "Good luck to you, my son."

Nan snorted.

"But Papa, people are getting killed. Shouldn't we do something?" she asked.

"We have done something. We have alerted the police. That's all we can do, anything else is interfering with law enforcement."

"That's just so," Iona said, eyeing Veronica.

"The only reason that I am telling you about this is because I don't want you going around the hospital right now," said Dr. Payne. "I don't know how long it will be before the news of the colored soldiers being treated there gets out, and I don't expect some people in our community will be too happy about it."

Franklin's eyes did not leave Dr. Payne's face, but his hand tightened on Veronica's leg under the table.

"You think that people are going to cause trouble?" Nan asked. "These are soldiers who served their country… surely they wouldn't."

"I wish I could have your optimism, dear heart, but I don't," Dr. Payne replied.

For the first time, Veronica noticed that his face was pale and drawn. Was it always that way?

"As a doctor, it is my job to keep people's secrets. I know who is sick and with what. I know who is likely to die before their next birthday. My job is to treat people and to keep their health between them and me. Cause of death is something that is not discussed unless there is very good reason to suspect foul play. Sometimes I am suspicious, but I don't have enough hard evidence to say anything unless the family brings it up."

He looked at Iona, and she nodded ever so slightly.

"So I have kept some secrets about this town, even from you. The fact that Chief Bishop has asked me to keep these things quiet is almost as disturbing as the events themselves. It has gone against my beliefs, but Police Chief Bishop claimed that he wanted time to investigate before the community was informed."

Dr. Payne ran his hand across his forehead.

"I questioned his judgment, but I said nothing. Now—well, now I'm afraid of what I think."

Veronica had listened quietly while Dr. Payne told his story, but her mind had not been quiet. Flashes of Betty the ghost chicken and the slaughtered pig kept inserting themselves into her brain. She turned to Dr. Payne and caught his eye.

"How were they killed?" she asked. Franklin's hand squeezed her leg harder.

"Veronica, this might not be an appropriate question to ask over dinner," her mother said.

"How, Dr. Payne?" Veronica asked again, ignoring her mother.

"I think they should know, Iona," Dr. Payne said. "I think Veronica and Franklin might already guess."

"They were butchered, weren't they?" Franklin asked. Dr. Payne nodded.

"Yes, Franklin, they were cut open. Some had their limbs cut off. Some had other bits cut off. Whoever did this wasn't right in the head. Chief Bishop said that he thought it was someone in the colored community, so we shouldn't let them know that we know. He said it would make the person easier to catch."

"He's lying," Veronica said.

"Don't you go accusing anyone without knowing," her mother snapped. Veronica glared at Iona, but Iona glared right back.

"I think it would be extraordinarily dangerous to accuse anyone of anything right now," Dr. Payne said, "But I think that whoever is killing these colored people will be incensed by the fact that there are colored soldiers in our midst."

"Dr. Paaaaynnnnnneeeee!"

The owner of a high, shrill voice was running up their driveway.

"Dr. Paaaayyyy... uh—" There was a thud. The owner of the voice seemed to have slipped on the snow and ice.

Everyone jumped to their feet and ran out the back door. Stella Sewell was on her knees in their driveway, scrambling to her feet.

"Stella! What is it, dear?" Dr. Payne ran to help her up.

"The police found the boy—" she began, panting. Her hair was all over the place. Her clothes were askew, and her face looked like she hadn't slept in days. She grabbed Dr. Payne's shoulders.

"Just calm down, Stella," Dr. Payne said. "Tell us what is happening."

"The police, they caught the colored boy that they think killed Nellie… he's at the police station," she gasped.

"That's good then," Dr. Payne said but she shook her head furiously back and forth.

"No… no… you don't understand. My Missy's still gone. What if he is the one who took her, what if he knows—" Stella gasped out.

"Then the police will surely find out—"

"No, they've got him in the police station. There won't be anything left of him to ask. I went in… and they're beating him… they're going to beat him to death. Help me—"

Dr. Payne whirled.

"Franklin, go! Distract them until I can get there."

Her brother didn't need to be told twice. He sprinted down their driveway, sure-footed as a goat, even on the ice and snow.

"I'm going with you," Nan said, taking her father's hand.

"Ronnie, go with them," her mother said, but Nan shook her head.

"No, this is not a fight Ronnie needs to be in, let us handle it."

Her mother started, but then nodded.

"That girl has a good head on her shoulders, and she's right. Let's go inside."

Veronica wanted to be able to argue but she knew they were right. These women knew her, maybe better than she knew herself. What would she do if she saw the police beating a colored man to death? Or maybe the question was, what control would she have left?

Chapter Twenty Two

Worlds on Fire

Franklin didn't get back for another three hours. Veronica sat at the kitchen table while her mother paced back and forth across the kitchen probably five thousand times. Every thirty minutes she would ask Veronica if she thought that everything was okay. Her mother was usually stoic, so Veronica was more nervous about her change in behavior. Therefore, every half hour she got up to go find Franklin only to be told to sit back down by her mother. They were on their sixth cycle of this when the screen door opened, and Franklin entered. His normally tanned face looked pale and there were dark circles under his eyes.

"Well?" Iona asked.

Franklin just shook his head. Veronica stood and took her brother into her arms. His body was tight and buzzing with energy. She tried to absorb some of that energy back from him.

"What happened?" her mother asked.

Veronica pulled back and looked at her brother's face.

"Did they kill him?" she asked.

Franklin nodded.

"But it gets better," Franklin said. "When I got there, a crowd was standing outside. There were probably twelve people—no, twelve men, just standing there. A few of them were carrying rifles. I thought that I was going to have to fight my way in, but they just stepped back so I could get to the door. When I opened the door, a group of five police officers were posing over what looked like a lump of clothes. One had his foot on top of the lump and was holding a rifle. He was posed as a hunter poses with a body of a lion on safari. At first, it didn't register what they were doing—how could it? It wasn't until the police kicked the clothes, and I heard a groan, that I realized that the pile of clothes was a person. It was a colored boy—he was just a kid. He couldn't have been more than thirteen, at least, that's what his body looked like. His face was so bruised and swollen that I couldn't tell. He was so beaten that he didn't even look human. He was just lying there on the floor in the middle of the police house. Policemen were drinking coffee and taking pictures with him."

"What did you do?" Veronica asked.

"I went after five policemen," Franklin said, with a wan little smile. "Well, at least it was the distraction that Dr. Payne asked for."

"Franklin, why would you do that? They were armed," her mother said, hands over mouth.

"You hardly have a scratch on you," Veronica said, examining his face.

"I know, I don't think any of them got a blow in," Franklin said. "Yesterday, when I saw Tommy with Nan. Well, I thought that was the maddest I could ever get. But today it was worse. And again, it was Nan who showed up and kept me from killing anyone. Without her, I might be a police killer by now."

"Did you beat up Chief Bishop?" his mother asked.

"No, he wasn't there, and I think that was planned. He came back just about the time that Nan and Dr. Payne showed up. He just brushed the whole thing off. He said it was a shame about the boy, but that the officers got a confession. He confessed to murdering Nellie Crowder AND Missy Sewell."

"They haven't found Missy?" Veronica asked.

"No, but I got the feeling that they might know where she is," Franklin said. "I think they knew—and I know that kid didn't kill anyone."

"Did Chief Bishop speak to you?" her mother asked.

"Oh, he said something about how he understood how it might look, that I didn't understand interrogations. He was mad, of course, but he wasn't mad that I beat up his cops. He was mad because I saw the boy. He was madder that Dr. Payne and Nan saw it. And Nan… oh god… you should have seen her face. She went on her knees next to the boy and just started sobbing. I got her out of there. I went home with her and held her until her father got back."

"What happened with the boy, do you know?" Veronica asked.

"Dr. Payne said that the boy was barely alive when he got there, and he died within thirty minutes. Apparently, Chief Bishop kept Dr. Payne there afterward to 'explain' to him what had happened. The story was that they caught the boy carrying a sack with a cat inside it. He was near the colored encampment on the far side of the tobacco fields. The officers who brought him in said that he resisted arrest. So the officers 'subdued' him and brought him in for interrogation. Dr. Payne said that they didn't tell him how long the boy had been there, or how long he had been beaten, but given the state of him, it must have happened over the course of several hours. He said that they must have continued to beat him even after he was unconscious. How could someone do something like that? How could you listen to the sounds of that sort of beating and keep doing it?"

Franklin turned his eyes to Veronica.

"Ronnie, his face... what they did to his face. His head was swelled up like a pumpkin and his whole face was flat. They beat his nose flat against his face, his brows were beat flat against his face. It looked like a tray. He was just a baby, Ronnie... just a kid."

Franklin began to shake and he buried his face in Veronica's hair.

"Come on, let's get you to bed," Veronica whispered, taking him toward the bedroom. Veronica noticed that Franklin's hands were covered in dried blood. Suddenly she remembered Tommy hitting Caio in the face and his blood splattering.

"Mama, lock the door tonight," Veronica called back to her mother.

*

The night was the inverse of the night before. Veronica lay with Franklin on his bed as he sobbed. She had only seen him this upset once before. It had been when he had come home from the hospital after Deward had beaten him unconscious only to discover that he couldn't speak without a stutter. There had been many times in those early years that Veronica had felt furious that she wasn't a boy. Franklin had been small, and she couldn't protect him. When he grew, he began to protect not just himself, but her. Franklin's goodness was beyond question in Veronica's mind.

At some point, both fell asleep. Veronica woke some hours later. She could tell by the pattern of Franklin's breathing that he was sleeping soundly. She had fallen asleep in her clothes—she was still wearing the skirt that hid the letters from Lazlo. The house was dark, and she could hear her mother snoring. She got up quietly and padded out into the kitchen. In the kitchen, she dug in a drawer until her hand found the flashlight. She then sat down at the kitchen table and pulled Lazlo's letters from the lining of her skirt and taking out the fourth letter.

Nov 18, 1944

My Darling Veronica,

I'm watching the world burn all around me, but all I can think about is you. I'm so sorry. I tried not to feel this, but I couldn't. Then I tried not to tell you, but I can't keep it to myself anymore. I love you, Veronica Crane. I dream of you every night. I fight to survive each day, just so I can spend my evening dreaming of you. So you are giving me a reason to stay alive. That's crazy, isn't it?

I fell in love with you when I met you at the draft office. I fell in love with the way you talked to me, like I was just the same as the white boys. I fell in love with how smart you are, and how you aren't ashamed of it, or trying to hide it, like most women. I fell in love with the tight, stubborn way your mouth sets itself when you don't like something. I'm in love with the way you laugh suddenly, as if it's escaping you in spite of yourself. But I knew that I would never love anyone else the day that you met me on the rock. I knew how dangerous that was for you, and how brave you had to be to risk it. Listening to you talk about your family, and the way that you listened to me about my family... I could never have hoped to find such a person. I am in love with you, but it's more than that. I am impressed by you, by the fact that your goals are to learn and travel, not just marry some rich man. I'm impressed with how you spoke about being poor when I knew that hurt you. I know your life hasn't been easy, but I love how you don't let that kill your dreams.

I've been trying to write these letters with the best grammar and spelling as I can, because I know that this matters to you, but I'm not that educated. I want to be, but I never got the chance. One of the boys in the tank division had some schoolbooks. He's been trying to educate himself too. So I borrowed one of them, so that you might like what I say better. You see, you are making me better even if you aren't here. So I will keep writing these until I come back, or I die.

I need you to know that I will never forget you. I never loved no one before. It was like I couldn't. My friends fell in love. My brothers and sisters fell in love. But I never felt nothing more than friendship. I was beginning to think it was something people was just making up. But when we were sitting on that rock, it was like the rest of the world stopped. It was like water was closing all around me, but in a good way. It felt like a glove holding me. Love found me and damned if my heart didn't pick someone impossible for me to be with. I know that, and I knew it while we were sitting on the rock. So if I could have chosen a place to die, it would have been there, sitting right next to you. Now, I suppose I'm likely to die in the mud in some country I don't know, but I will think of your face as I go. I will love you with the last beats of my heart. I will hope that your life is wonderful and that you meet a man who can love you even a tenth of the way I do.

Of course, I know that you can't feel the same. I know that, and I'm sorry to put this on you, but the fighting is getting heavier, and I just couldn't stand dying without telling you. If anyone intercepts this letter, they need to know that this is only on my side. You were just being nice to me because that's who you are. You are all tough on the outside, but you really care about others. You are not pretending. I saw it when you were checking people in at the draft office. You looked everyone straight in the eye, colored or white. You have a good heart, Veronica Crane, and the bravery of a Buffalo Soldier. Everything about you glows like a firefly.

Now, I will go to bed and dream of what might have been if the world was different. If I had been born a white man or you a colored woman, or if we lived in a time or place where our color didn't matter. I can dream of how I would *court you, if I was allowed to do that, and if you was allowed to see me that way. I can imagine coming home from work and bringing you a box of flowers. If you wanted to work, I wouldn't mind. If you didn't want to work, I wouldn't care either. To have you in my life... I would have done anything. Anything at all. Even now, if I knew that... no, I won't say that. I won't put that on you. I respect you too much and I care for you too much.*

So I will keep fighting. If there is even the tiniest hope that I might see your face again, I will keep fighting. I will fight as the smoke fills my eyes and the ash burns my lungs. I'll will crawl on my knees through all the barbed wire in the world if means ending up at your feet. Even if you reject me, just seeing your face as you do it is worth whatever heartbreak comes.

I will post this letter tomorrow and then I will do my best to help our army win this war. Then I will come find you. Even if you don't, or can't, love me, then at least I can go to school and try to become someone that I know you would be proud of. If I don't live, then I will die being glad that fate gave me the chance to meet you.

With all my love forever,

Lazlo

Veronica's tears were now dripping on the letter and smearing the words. She refolded it carefully, then put her head down on the table and cried. She had not cried when her father disappeared nor had she cried when Janie died, but she cried now. Her father's disappearance had been a blessing. Her grandmother's death had made her angry and determined in equal parts. But if Lazlo died, it was nothing but a waste. She wouldn't even been allowed to properly grieve him, which made the grief sharper and more poignant. There was one letter left. Veronica was afraid to read it, and yet she needed to read it. She needed to be with him.

Nov 18, 1944

My Dearest Love,

    I hope you aren't shocked that I addressed you this way, but maybe I can explain why I would be so bold, and why I am happier now than I have ever been in my life. Today, I met up with George and Caio again when we stopped. . We started talking about the difference in how we felt here in Europe compared to how we felt back home, and we discovered that we was all registered in Harrisville on the same two days. I was excited to meet people who might have met you. I'm that crazy about you, but I guess you know that from my last letter. So I asked if they thought that the ladies who registered us was nice. George said that he thought the ladies were much nicer than the other townsfolk. Then Caio smiled and said that he thought the nicest lady they met was a red-haired lady named Veronica, who made jokes with them. George nodded and said that you looked at colored people and white people just the same. That's when I knew they was talking about you. I tried to listen to the rest of the things they said as we sat and ate, but I couldn't focus on anything. I kept trying to find ways to bring the talk back around to the draft office and you. So I asked them if they had gone out with anyone in England, but both said no. George said that he had a girl that he was partial to but that he hadn't done nothing about it. Caio just shook his head. George laughed and said that there was a little girl in the draft office that seemed taken with Caio. Caio smiled and said that she was just being nice. I told them that you registered me and that I thought you were the nicest person I met in the town. I wanted to say more, but the way they looked at me and smiled made me shut up right then and there.

When we finished our food, and I was about to leave, Caio asked if he could talk to me. I thought it would be about the girl that registered him, but that's not what he told me.

He asked me if I knew you. He said "Veronica Crane." I was shocked that he knew your name and your family name at that. I said yes. He then asked me if I was in love with you. He asked that right out. I didn't say nothing for a moment 'cause I didn't know what I could say. He then told me that he was the one who told you how to find me on the train tracks. He said that you was looking for me. Then he said the most incredible thing that I had ever heard. He said that you loved me. He said it like it was fact and all. I asked if you had told him that, but he just smiled and said that he knew what a woman in love looked like. I asked him how it would be possible for a pretty, smart, white lady like you to love an uneducated colored man like me. Then he asked if I had seen you more than once and, I couldn't help myself, I told him. He told me that a woman as brave as you wouldn't be put off by something like color. I couldn't believe it but, well, I've been having dreams about you that feel so real that I'm becoming sure that we are really seeing each other in them. I touch your hands, I see your eyes. Your eyes are gray but with a little bit of gold right round the center that you can only see when you are up close. Are they like that? If they are, then how could I have known that?

When I got back to my tent, there was three or four soldiers with minor wounds waiting. So I fixed and stitched as best as I could, but my mind was on you the whole time. If there is even a chance that this is true, then I have to survive this war. I have to find you. We can move up north. We can find a life for us. I am getting crazy now, just thinking about all this. If someone reads this, they need to know that you said nothing. This could all just be the imagination of a bunch of lovesick soldiers, and none worse than me.

Still, I will look forward to seeing you in my dreams tonight and every night.

With all my love, today and forever,

Lazlo

Veronica sat staring at Lazlo's signature. Her tears were gone. There was no longer a need for them. Lazlo loved her and he knew that she loved him. There was nothing left to hide. There was no more need to protect herself. After Franklin and Nan's wedding, Veronica would do whatever she had to in order to be with Lazlo. He said that he would come find her, so she would need to be prepared to leave with him when he did. Dante had told her that she needed to leave this town, but now she would stay and save money until Lazlo returned. Her heart felt like it was blooming in her chest, but there was nothing fragile about it.

It was a bloom of fire and iron.

Chapter Twenty Three

Ghosts and Machines

The next day, at work, Veronica tried to concentrate on doing nothing but keeping her nose down and getting through the day. She didn't want to focus on the events of last night, because any memory was likely to trigger feelings of rage, fear, or loss. She needed to stay out of trouble until Lazlo could return to the town. She wished that she had a way to contact him so she could warn him about the situation in Harrisville, but asking about him would mean sharing his name. If the wrong person got ahold of his name, that could be dangerous for him. Lizzie had read his name, but Veronica was sure that she had forgotten it. It wouldn't be helpful to remember the name of the colored soldier because his name wouldn't matter to anyone Lizzie would share this with. In fact, knowing his name might reflect badly on her.

At the factory, Veronica was going to volunteer to do runs at Number 8 but one of the other girls beat her to it. Even though it was snowing outside, the lure of fewer sample runs was strong around this time of the year. If you organized your day right, you could get done almost an hour before everyone else. That had not been why Veronica wanted to do the Number 8 runs. She wanted to stay off the cigarette floor where everything was brighter, there were more people, and Lizzie would be able to watch her.

However, circumstances didn't seem to want to help her at all with this. At the beginning of her day, on her first run, she saw Tommy standing at Lizzie's station, chatting with her while she boxed cigarettes. Lizzie couldn't watch him while they were talking, but smiled, laughed, and raised her shoulder enough that Tommy would have to be stupider than he was not to read her cues. Veronica walked by them quickly, but not quickly enough.

"Oh, look, there she is," Tommy called. Veronica refused to take the bait.

She moved quickly across the cigarette floor in a zigzag fashion, taking samples at random machines as she went. She was just walking back toward the QA office when a group of black-and-white kittens ran out from under one of the extruder machines. Veronica jumped and almost dropped her box of samples. A second later, she heard the sound of muffled barking, and a gray dog appeared, running after the kittens. She recognized the kittens as the same ones she had seen in Mr. Sawika's office last week, but she hadn't seen the dog before. Mr. Sawika had told her that dead dogs had been found in the snuff room, so she suspected that this might be the spirit of one of them. She looked around and found that a few of the machine operators were staring at her, along with a significant number of people sitting next to the window in the break room. She shook her head and continued her run.

As the day progressed, she saw the kittens five or six times. She also saw the original dog, plus three or four new ones. In the early afternoon, a dog about the size and shape of a Great Dane charged at her and through her body. It felt like ice going through her. She had jumped when she saw it, and once again, people stared. She went quickly back to the QA office but when she walked in, she heard one of the girls saying "... from a colored soldier..."

She shut up the moment she saw Veronica, but it had clearly been a conversation about her. News traveled fast in a small town, and even faster when it was something this shocking. Both women turned back to their work without acknowledging Veronica. If she had been a more social person, this might have bothered her, but as it was, she didn't care as long as they didn't start asking her about it. She dropped her box on her desk. Before starting her tests, she headed toward the restroom.

Just her luck, Lizzie was there washing her hands as Veronica walked in.

"Oh, hi Ronnie," Lizzie said, smiling, as if nothing had happened. Veronica nodded at her and immediately went into a stall.

The noise of running water stopped, and Veronica listened for the sound of retreating footsteps, but she didn't hear them. When she came out of the stall, Lizzie was waiting.

"I wanted to talk to you," Lizzie said.

"I don't think we have anything to talk about—at least, nothing that you haven't already shared with the whole town," Veronica said, as she began washing her hands.

"I didn't tell anyone anything that they didn't already suspect," Lizzie said. "In fact, I made a point of telling everyone that the letters were addressed to the town, and not your house. So that meant that you hadn't given him your address."

"Great, thanks," Veronica said. As she walked past, Lizzie grabbed her arm. "Don't be like this, Ronnie," she said. "I've known you all my life."

"And apparently I haven't known you all mine," Veronica said, yanking her arm away.

"Come on, Ronnie," Lizzie called after her, as she walked quickly back to the QA office.

When Veronica opened the door, she saw that her sample box had been thrown into the middle of the room. Her samples were scattered across the floor in all directions.

"Who did that?" Veronica asked.

"Who did what?" asked Sandra, one of the two other girls on shift today. Francine was the other one.

"Who threw my sample box into the middle of the floor?" Veronica asked. She was feeling a heat radiating around her throat.

"No one, it just fell," replied Francine, and giggled.

"It fell fifteen feet from where I left it?" Veronica asked.

"I guess so," replied Sandra. Veronica felt something like pleasure as the heat in her throat began radiating up into her head. She walked to the door and locked it. When she turned back, she saw that Francine and Sandra were looking at her with shock. This pleased her.

"Well, as the two of you are only ones here, and as your explanation is ridiculous, I have to assume that one of you threw it. As neither of you is pointing fingers, then I can only assume that the one who didn't throw it approved of it."

Veronica moved to stand only a few feet away from them. She leaned against one of the desks.

"So I should warn you. I'll let this one go, but if happens again, I will find a way to get both of you fired," Veronica said. She could hear embers in her own voice. "If you think I can't do it, you know nothing about me. I'm smarter than you, I'm meaner than you, I don't care what anyone thinks of me, and I hold grudges for a VERY, VERY long time. Given all those things, do you think it's smart to make an enemy of me?"

"Sandra did it," Francine said. Sandra whirled around and glared at her.

"So, Sandra, do you have something to say?" Veronica asked.

"I don't want to share an office with a girl who likes—" Sandra spat out.

"Okay, let's go then," Veronica interrupted, stepping toward her. Veronica felt the burning in her throat spreading into her stomach. Sandra flinched back.

"I don't want to go anywhere with you," she hissed.

"Very well, I'll go by myself," Veronica said, turning for the door.

"Go where?" Francine asked.

"I'll go tell Mr. Sawika that Sandra is unwilling to work in the same office as me," Veronica said. "I'm sure he will want to come down here and ask you about it, and that's a bit of a waste of time for him. And he will, of course, probably move one of us back out on the floor. I wonder who he will choose?"

Veronica smiled at them and both of them cringed backward. She couldn't see herself, but she suspected that some of her deep desire to kill both of them was showing in her face.

"Never mind," Sandra spat out.

"Oh, no. It has to be dealt with," Veronica said, moving toward the door again.

"I'll redo your run," Sandra said.

"Do you think I would trust you to do that?" Veronica asked. "If you do, then you must be even stupider than you look."

Sandra looked like a cornered rat. Still, it was probably better to keep her enemies close.

"Okay, I'll let it go, but if it happens again, I'm going straight to Mr. Sawika. Does everyone understand that?"

The two other girls nodded.

"Can I suggest that you inform the others because if one of them starts up with the same stuff, I'm not giving any of you another pass," Veronica said, picking up her sample box.

"And someone clean up that mess," she said, as she closed the door behind her.

*

When Veronica stepped out onto the cigarette floor, she momentarily thought that the fire and brimstone church people were right—the apocalypse was upon them. Everywhere she looked, she saw ghostly animals. A pack of twenty or so dogs were running around and through the line of machines. Pale gray rodents were crawling all over the machines, the walls and some were even just floating through the air, in various orientations. Small black orbs filled the air. As one passed Veronica, she recognized it as one of the tobacco bugs that she regularly blew off the door in the snuff room. Well, it was part of one—the one passing by only had the front half of its body. Fewer in number, but more disturbing, were the smaller shadowy humanoid figures that would occasionally skitter out from between machinery, only to run back as soon as the light hit them. As she surveyed this chaos, everyone else on the cigarette floor continued on with their jobs, unseeing and unfeeling, even when an apparition ran right through them.

A wind began blowing through the factory, originating from the roof. When she looked up, she saw Dante standing on one of the exposed rafters. He had one arm on a cross beam and the other arm around Kara. She was wearing a pale yellow dress that was floating all around her. The air around them looked rippled and even from this distance, Veronica could feel the heat coming from them. This was probably what was causing the air currents.

Suddenly, a familiar figure scampered past her. It was none other than the rabid raccoon from the snuff room. Rather than being purely black and white, it had a blue glow to it. It stopped a few feet ahead of her and turned to look at her. Veronica let out a long breath and began to follow it, acting as if she were not walking through ghosts and ghost remains.

The raccoon led her to the far end of the factory floor, where there was a steel door. This was the door that led to the non-visible part of the factory. Most of the people who worked at the factory worked on the floor. Only very few had reason to go beyond it, and those were employees dedicated to working in that area. Veronica had been there a few times when special runs were made to check moisture from the tobacco running through there, but that only happened when other readings were off, and they could not find a reason for it. She had always thought it was creepy-looking.

The raccoon stopped for a moment and turned back to her. Then it disappeared into the steel door. Veronica looked around the floor. No one saw the ghost chaos around them and they weren't paying attention to her. She walked with purpose toward the door and entered quickly.

Once inside, she dropped her test box by the door. It took a moment for her eyes to adjust.

This room was part of the internal guts of the factory. It was filled with pipes that moved tobacco from the storage areas and onto the cigarette floor. There were small doors built into the pipes at various points along their length, to give people access to pipes blocked with tobacco. The room was dimly lit only by gold/red lights interspersed around the area. Veronica had no idea what occurred here that required the lack of lighting, but even on normal days, this room looked haunted. Today, it actually was. The spirits that were overrunning the factory floor had bled into this room as well, with the addition of a few things that looked like snakes wrapping around the tubing.

The raccoon had stopped just next to one of the larger machines, and immediately one of the lights began flashing and an alarm went off. The raccoon didn't move.

"Okay, you are trying to tell me something, right?" she asked. The raccoon remained annoyingly silent.

"Well, what?" she said.

With something that might have been a sigh, the raccoon turned and began weaving its way between machines, with Veronica following. It wasn't particularly easy, as it required climbing over low pipes and under high ones. Finally, the raccoon stopped at large wooden booth. These booths existed around the room, and they were big enough to hold one or two people if they were standing up. They had once been used by QA employees to test moisture but now they were unused. This particular one was buried so far behind rumbling machines that Veronica was sure no one ever went there. The alarm was still blaring, and the flashing light was casting shadows across the room.

"What?" she asked the raccoon.

It scratched at the door to the booth. Veronica moved forward and, as she did so, the back of her neck began to tingle. As she placed her hand on the door handle, a dread swept over her.

Do I really want to open this? Do I want to see whatever a rabid ghost raccoon would lead me to?

Veronica dismissed this thought as weakness and cowardice. She yanked at the door. It did not open easily. She had to put her full weight into it before she could get it open. Once opened, she saw that it contained nothing but an ancient weight machine, a bench to sit on and a moth-eaten blanket that looked like it had been there for forty years or so.

"Nothing here," Veronica said to the raccoon, even as her brain registered something wrong. She turned to look at the booth more closely. She suddenly realized what was wrong. Everything she had walked through to get here had been covered in a fine layer of tobacco dust, but there was no dust in the room. The blanket, although old, had no dust on it. Veronica reached out and picked up the blanket. It felt stiff and scratchy in her hands, but it felt more solid than she would have expected. As she threw the blanket back in the booth, something caught her eye. Something that glinted on the floor near a small vertical pipe that ran the length of the booth. Veronica crouched down and saw that it was a set of handcuffs. The tingle in the back of her neck turned into a fire. She picked them up and noticed dark brown stains on them. With a dawning horror, Veronica realized that these stains looked like dried blood. She threw them back into the booth as if they had been alive.

Her hands suddenly began to scream at her. The normal burning pain that she felt in her fingers had been transferred to her wrists, where it felt like her bones were grinding together.

Something moved behind her, and she jumped. The raccoon was moving again.

"More fun?" she asked as she followed it back through the pipes.

The raccoon led her back to the blinking and buzzing machine. The machine had six pipes leading into it and twelve leading out. This was a place where tobacco was sorted to distribute to different extruders on the factory floor. There were six windows in the middle of the machine. Each of these corresponded to a pipe. Each of these windows allowed an employee to open it and unclog whatever was clogged there. The light and alarm were coming from the top of the fourth pipe. The raccoon crawled up the stepladder and sat next to that pipe. Veronica followed suit, although she didn't want to.

She opened the window on pipe four, sticking her hand into the sticky clogged tobacco. At first, she felt nothing but loose tobacco, but then, as she reached down, she found the clog. She pushed her arm into the window until it was almost up to her armpit. It was hard to dig the thing loose, as pressure from the falling tobacco was pressing on her arm. Finally, she managed to free something that felt familiar, in a sickening way. When Veronica pulled her arm from the window, she immediately dropped what she was holding onto the ledge.

It was a severed hand.

A different sort of woman would have screamed, but Veronica realized that where there was a hand there might be other body parts, and it would be unwise for her to be associated with them. The hand wasn't too decomposed, so it could not have been there long. She quickly picked it up again and was about to drop it back in the tobacco chute when she felt something on the hand. She turned it over and found that there was a ring on the fourth finger.

It was a Claddagh ring… like the one Hugh McBrayer had given Missy.

Chapter Twenty Four

The Woods Speak

Veronica quickly dropped the hand. Fear and anger were sending chemical messages throughout her body. Her heart was hammering. Her breath was fast and shallow. Her muscles were contracted. Her body was pushing her toward fight or flight, but neither would help her in this situation. Veronica closed her eyes and took a deep breath, fighting her fear that someone might walk in at any minute. She needed to get her wits together before she acted.

Her first instinct was to take the hand to Mr. Sawika, but her practical side nixed this idea. She wasn't sure how much Mr. Sawika knew and whether he was indirectly, or even directly, involved in whatever end had come to Missy Sewell. Missy, with her sad doe eyes and slightly pudgy hips. Missy, who was so desperate that she continued to believe that Hugh loved her even after he had beaten her and broken her arm. Missy, who had a heart that didn't see color, only people. Fear and fury threatened to overwhelm her again, but Veronica pushed them aside. She couldn't afford to act rashly, especially now. Everyone in town knew, or would know soon, that a colored soldier had been writing personal letters to her. This would make her a prime candidate for scapegoating. She had to keep her head down until Lazlo returned, and she didn't know how long that would take.

As much as she hated it, her best and safest course of action for the moment was to do nothing and say nothing—at least, not until she could further assess the situation. So she gently picked up Missy's severed hand and dropped it back into the tobacco chute. She heard it bang against the metal of the tube before it was swept away by the flow of tobacco. Veronica's heart spasmed in her chest, but not in fear. This time, what she felt was a deep sorrow. Missy had been a kind girl, and if not a close friend, she had still been a true one. Veronica felt a burning in her stomach, it came with a sudden mad urge to burn this place down. She clamped down on that thought. She wasn't capable of that sort of thing, and it would be dangerous for others if she was.

Veronica's throat constricted. She climbed down from the humidor machine to find the ghost of the raccoon still standing there, regarding her with its unnaturally black eyes.

"Is there anything else?" she asked it.

It immediately turned and waddled across the tobacco-strewn floor leading to the door to the cigarette floor. It turned and regarded her briefly before disappearing through it. Veronica moved quickly to follow, opening the floor, and stepping out into a cigarette floor that was no longer being overrun by ghosts. The raccoon started forward, but rather than moving back toward the QA office, it turned toward the snuff room.

"Oh no, not the snuff room," Veronica thought. She had had just about enough of this room.

Instead, the raccoon waddled past the snuff room and into the mirrored hallway that led to the side entrance. Just like Dante, the raccoon had no reflection in the walls. There was a cold breeze blowing down the hallway. Veronica looked up to see that someone had left the door open. Outside, she saw a blanket of snow beneath a slate-grey sky, but that wasn't the only thing she saw. In the distance, where the woods met the parking lot, a man was sitting on a wooden log.

It was a colored man.

Before she could stop herself, Veronica was running down the hallway. She ran right through the raccoon without slowing down, but as she exited the building, she realized that the man sitting on the log wasn't Lazlo. Her heart sank and she pulled up short. She was about to turn back when the man stood up and waved at her.

"Miss Veronica," he called, then glanced around him. She recognized his voice better than his face. It was George.

"I don't know if you remember me," he said.

"Of course, you're George," Veronica said as she approached him.

"Yes, ma'am."

"Please don't call me ma'am." George's eyes widened.

"Yes, ma—I mean, Miss Veronica."

"Veronica is fine."

"Is there somewhere I can talk to you that is more private?" he asked very softly. Veronica felt her throat constrict but she smiled.

"We can talk in the woods," she said.

George gasped.

"No, no, no. They would lynch me if they found me alone with you."

"They would lynch you if they saw you talking to me here, and probably me as well, and I'd rather not have that happen to either of us. Come on," she said, as she stepped into the overgrowth of the snow-laden forest. George followed but with a very tentative step. It was shocking to realize that he was so much more scared of her than she was of him, even with the town's story about colored men killing women in the woods. But Veronica knew this wasn't true. Still, if they were caught, she would likely be killed, at the minimum, and George would be tortured and lynched after being blamed for her death.

She came to a small clearing. There were some logs laid around the remains of what looked like a campfire. She sat down on one of them.

"I'm not sure this is smart," George said, but he sat down anyway.

"The logs haven't been moved in a while, you can tell by the build-up of snow," Veronica said. "And the fire pit there is at least a week old, by the lack of sticks."

George nodded but he kept glancing around him anyway. Veronica noticed that he was carrying an army rucksack.

"How did you end up back here?" she asked him.

"I was injured so they sent me back with the others who were injured. But my injuries were so small that they healed on the way. I think they just sort of grouped me with the others to come back. My friend, Caio, was sent to the hospital here. I was going to come see him, but I wasn't sure I would get here in time. He was busted up bad, so I don't expect he'll live."

"I'm so sorry, George," Veronica said, but when she heard her own voice, it sounded like she was hearing it from the end of a long hallway. The world around her started to feel muffled. She felt herself staring at the rucksack that was sitting on the ground next to George.

"I'm not here for that, though, Miss Veronica," he said. "I came for something else. I was in a squadron with another colored man, name of Lazlo Fox."

Veronica felt the world around her begin to spin. The dreams she had been having—the ones that felt so real—suddenly took on an ominous meaning. He had felt so real in those dreams but in the same way that Janie had felt real when Veronica saw her at her funeral.

"Is he dead?" she whispered.

"Are you all right, Miss Veronica? You look awful pale."

"Is Lazlo dead, George?" Veronica asked, knowing the truth before he spoke.

"Yes, ma'am."

The world suddenly closed, and Veronica left it.

*

"Wake up, darling."

Veronica opened her eyes, to find that Lazlo was kneeling next to her on the forest floor. He was wearing his army uniform and his combat boots. She could see his breath coming as fog in the cold air. How could that be? He looked like he was really there—but he wasn't, he…

"Lazlo?" she whispered.

"Yes, my love," he said, taking her hands in his.

"You died?" she said, voice trembling.

"I did, I'm sorry," he said, taking her into his arms.

"You left me." Veronica buried her head into his chest. His body felt so warm and real. She could even feel the blood pulsing in the veins of his neck. It felt like life was mocking her. She wanted to be able to cry but she felt dead inside, and the dead don't cry.

"I didn't have no choice," Lazlo said, stroking her head. "I was trying my hardest to get back to you, but I got blown up by a mine. But if I had known for sure what you felt for me—well, I couldn't have guessed it. Even now that I am dead, it's hard for me to believe."

"I won't let you be dead," she muttered into his chest.

"I'm afraid we can't change that, my love," Lazlo said. "I'm so sorry. I tried. I was stupid. I should have—I should have just left to come find you. I should have told you how I felt before I left."

"I don't want to live without you," Veronica whispered. As the words came out, she realized they were true. It wasn't drama. She quite simply did not want to live without him. Her heart had finally shown her who she wanted, and he had been taken from her. Of course, she would go on living, she was too practical about things not to. And she knew that she needed to survive for the sake of others, for her mother and for Franklin. But it was not what she wanted.

"We can talk about that later," Lazlo said, kissing her head. "But the most important thing now is that you leave this town. Bad things are coming here, and I don't want you to get hurt."

"I don't care," Veronica replied.

"That's just your grief talking," Lazlo said. "I didn't think I was able to love you more, but the fact that you would grieve for me makes me feel… well, I can't even explain it. But for now, you need to get out. You need to save your mama and your brother and his girl. You need to get them and get out. Strong people are coming for these people, people who make turning people into pillars of salt seem trivial."

Dante and Kara.

"Wake up now and get you and yours out of that place, however you have to do it," Lazlo said, as he softly kissed her lips. The kiss started gently but Veronica grabbed him and pulled him tightly to her. As she kissed him, she felt the fire in her build in her throat. She refused to lose him. She heard someone calling her name from a distance, but Lazlo was holding her tightly and kissing her with a passion that made her want to be dead to stay with him.

"Veronica."

She heard her name, and pushed it aside, clinging more tightly to Lazlo. He did not push her way, in fact, he pulled her closer.

"Veronica."

Suddenly she felt someone pulling her away from Lazlo and she lashed out.

With a shock, she found that she was now on her knees in the snow, with George sitting in front of her, his hands held up.

"Miss Veronica?"

"Did I push you?"

"Yes ma'am. Are you okay, Miss Veronica?"

"No, George, I'm really not okay," Veronica said shakily, sitting down on the cold, wet earth. Her skirt was going to be a sight, but she had bigger worries. "Tell me what you are here to tell me."

"Are you sure?" he asked.

"Yes, I'm sure now. Don't worry, I won't faint again."

George picked up the duffel bag.

"I'm sorry, and I know this ain't proper here. But my friend Lazlo. He made me promise that, if he died, that I would get this to you. I told him that it wasn't proper, but he begged me."

"It's okay, George," Veronica said. "I loved him."

George's eyes got wide.

"Sweet Jesus," George muttered. "I knew he loved you."

"He told you that?" Veronica asked.

"In the beginning he didn't have to, it was in his eyes every time he said your name. And he said it as often as he could without looking suspicious. Finally, he came out and told me. If he had known... if he had known you felt that. I'm not sure what he would have done. Probably killed Hitler himself to get back to you. Did you get his letters?"

"Not until last week," Veronica whispered. "I didn't know. If I had known, I would have written back."

Her voice caught. She reached out and took the duffel bag from George.

"What's in this?" she whispered.

"What's left of his uniform. He also left one more letter for you. Before I left, I saw that Caio had left a letter that Lazlo wrote to be given to me. I don't quite know what that is about but maybe you can ask Caio if you go see him. I'm so sorry Miss Veronica."

"Please just call me Veronica," she said.

"He said you were a special lady, but I didn't know what he meant. Now I do. I don't think I've ever met anyone as brave or as true. If only other people were more like you."

"I'm not a great person, George," Veronica said. "I just loved Lazlo. That might be the best and truest thing I have ever done."

"If I was you, I would leave this town," George said. "There's lots of bad going on around here. I'm going to look in on Caio and then be gone. But now I need to leave just in case someone happens to wander into these woods and sees us together. I'm not as true as Lazlo, nor as brave as you. So you take care and get out as soon as you can."

With this, George stood up and began making his way through the underbrush, toward the factory.

Veronica sat down on the log and opened Lazlo's duffel bag. She pulled out his uniform, which looked just like the one he had been wearing when she just saw him in her dream. She buried her face in the fabric. It smelled of dirt and ash, but it also smelled of him. In the draft office and then again on the rock, she had gotten only the slightest hint of his smell. Now, she was drowning in it. It was all that was left of his physical body, and it made her ache and burn in equal portions. Flashes of his face danced in her memory. She didn't cry. She realized that she had feared this for months, and that had been the source of her sensitivity. Now that the worst had come to pass, she felt a numbness creeping over her.

She took out his letter and put her lips to it before opening it. She sniffed it, but it had no traces of his scent. Then she opened the envelope. For the next five minutes, Veronica sat on the log. At first, she was motionless, but the more she read, the more she began to shake. Eventually she had to put the letter on her knees to keep from dropping it. She didn't cry, she barely breathed. When she was finished, she folded up the letter gently, and put it back into the duffel bag.

The sun was low on the horizon when Veronica left the forest. She didn't bother trying to move quietly. Quiet was probably a thing best left behind her now in favor of speed. She needed to find her mother, Franklin, Nan, and Nan's father and she had to do whatever was needed to get them to leave this place tonight. Any doubt in her mind about everything she had felt, everything she had seen, and everything she had learned was no longer a luxury she could afford. Whether she liked it or not, she would no longer be able to hide, and she didn't want to.

As she left the forest, she left behind a blazing fire in the abandoned campsite.

Chapter Twenty Five

Missed Messages

"It's past visiting hours," said the skinny, hawk-like woman sitting at the hospital's reception desk.

"Oh, when do visiting hours begin and end?" Veronica asked.

The woman plastered on a toothy smile sitting beneath blood-red lips.

"It's seven a.m. to seven p.m.," she said. "It's written just there."

She pointed to a large sign on the wall.

"Okay. I'll come back tomorrow," Veronica said, but the woman had already turned her back. A tall, handsome doctor had just arrived at the reception desk.

"Good evening, Gladys, how's your night going?" he asked, winking at her.

"Oh, it's fine. Just the normal issues." The woman laughed, running her hands through her salt-and-pepper hair.

"I know that you have your hands full, but I was wondering if you could file some paperwork for me…" the doctor said, putting his hand on Gladys's shoulder. They began to speak to each other in hushed tones. These two were just a little too close, their gaze just a little too long, and the heat between them too palpable to be a simple colleague relationship. They had clearly forgotten that Veronica was in the room.

She saw her moment.

George had told her that Caio was in this hospital. The letter from Lazlo had told her to find Caio, and damned if she was going to let "hospital hours" stand in her way. She crouched below the line of sight of the desk and moved quickly into the stairwell.

She didn't know what floor Caio might be on, but she would go floor by floor if that's what it took. George had said that Caio had been badly injured, so she didn't know if he was even still alive, but she was sure that she would remember him. Missy had thought him handsome. At that thought, Veronica felt her heart twinge. Poor Missy. She deserved so much better than what had happened to her. If Veronica had followed Dante's advice and left the town earlier, would she have been able to convince Missy to come? Would she have even thought of it? Probably not.

The hallway that Veronica stepped into was long and covered in tile. The nurse's station was just in front of her, and if a nurse had been present, Veronica would have had to have come up with a lie, and at the moment, she was too wired to think of one. She peeked into the first door on her right. It was a long, narrow room with a checkerboard tiled floor. Between fifteen and twenty beds were arranged along the walls. All of them were filled with patients, but even from here, she could see that all the patients were white. The second room looked much the same as the first except for having chairs arranged around the room.

As she looked into the third room, she froze. On the bed closest to her, she saw Caio. His hair had grown out and it was dark and wavy, and it lay against skin that was paler than she had remembered. He was motionless and a pretty, young nurse was sitting beside his bed, staring at him. Veronica needed to talk to him, and she couldn't do that if she just stood there in the doorway.

She stepped into the room. The nurse looked up.

"Can I help you?" she asked. The girl had white-blonde hair and pale skin.

"I'm here looking for someone," Veronica said softly, so her voice wouldn't be heard outside the room.

"It's past visiting hours," the nurse said, turning her eyes back to the boy in the bed. The nurse was holding his hand. She didn't bother letting go of it for Veronica's benefit.

"You should go," she said quietly.

Veronica stepped further into the room. She saw that this room, like the others, was filled with soldiers. All of them were white or some version of white.

"I know him," Veronica whispered.

"Who?" asked the nurse. She was wearing a badge that said *Bennett*.

"The boy in the bed. I came here to see him."

The nurse's eyes snapped to her.

"Are you his girlfriend, or wife?" she asked, quickly removing her hand from his and looking away.

"No, I'm not his wife or girlfriend," Veronica said. "I met him in May when he registered here."

"Do you know who he is? Or where he comes from? Or—anything?"

"His name is Caio," Veronica said "Caio Silva, I think. I think he was from Brazil."

"When he was brought in, you could hardly recognize his face for the injuries. His nose was smashed and bloody… but look at him now."

Veronica looked and saw that Caio's face was without scratch or blemish.

"How long has he been here?" Veronica asked.

"Thirty-six hours."

"That's not possible," Veronica said, looking at Caio's face.

"There's even more to it than that," the nurse said. "His chart said that he had been shot in the gut in France. But there's no wound on his stomach—nothing."

"Are you sure?"

"Yes, I checked." The nurse blushed and looked away.

"I mean, are you sure he was really shot in the gut?"

"Yes, it's on his file. There are notes from the field doctor, and the field nurse. The doctor who looked at him for transport back to the US said that his injury had almost healed but when you read the description of it from the field doctor—well, he shouldn't have even survived it."

"How is that possible?" Veronica asked.

"I don't know, but here he is," the nurse said, turning back to him. She put her hand back over his. "I'm sorry, I shouldn't be troubling you with this."

"That's okay," Veronica said. "By the way, I'm Veronica Crane."

"Suzanne Bennett," the nurse replied. "I'm from Atlanta, but I got called here to help with the transfer of the soldiers. Why did you come to see Caio?"

"He…" Veronica began to fabricate a lie but looking at Suzanne's open, honest face, she couldn't, at least, not completely. "He knew Lazlo. I loved Lazlo, but he died. Caio was in a unit with him, so I just wanted to—I don't know, to know if he knew anything. I wanted to see if he had seen Lazlo before he died. George, another friend, had said that Caio knew Lazlo pretty well."

Seeing Caio lying there on the bed somehow brought back memories of the physicality of Lazlo. How his shoulders had looked. The way the small mustache shadowed his well-formed lips. Veronica took a deep breath and let it out, feeling a sense of loss welling up inside her.

"I didn't even know Lazlo very long," Veronica said, closing her eyes. "How can I fall in love with someone that I only spoke to a couple of times? But I did."

She was shocked to feel arms around her.

"I think you were sent by an angel," Suzanne said softly, as she hugged her. Normally, Veronica would have pulled away but something in Suzanne's embrace felt warm and familiar.

"I've been thinking the same thing," Suzanne said softly as she stepped away, turning back to Caio. "When they brought him in, with his smashed-up face, I felt like the rest of my world just went away. I could only see him. So I've been coming in to visit him whenever I get a chance. When I came in tonight, I saw his face for the first time. Now that I've seen it, how can I forget it?"

"So you fell in love at first sight?" Veronica asked.

"No, I don't believe in that," Suzanne said. "I'm a nurse. I'm a battlefield nurse. I see people ripped apart. I see the ugliness of mankind. I see what humans are willing to do to other humans. I love my parents and my sisters, but—well, I never believed in romantic love. And here I am, just staring at him… worrying about him."

"What are you worrying about?' Veronica asked. "He's healing, right?"

"Yes, but the doctors have noticed—of course they have—and they are a bit too interested for my comfort. He hasn't regained consciousness, but they are already talking about running tests on him and sending them to the military research center in DC. There was something about his blood that they found unique. He has some sort of strange unknown virus or something."

A vision of Caio with his nose bloodied flashed in her mind, followed by a vision of her own hands, sticky with his blood.

"An unknown virus doesn't sound good," Veronica muttered.

"I think they are wondering if the virus is what's healing him, but if the military gets the government involved—well."

"My Grandma Janie used to say that the best way to be involved with the government is not to be. She said that there's always a danger if you get noticed by people in power."

"Your grandma was right," Suzanne said, then she turned to look up at Veronica. "I don't know why I trust you, but I do. I need to find a way to get him out of here before they transfer him."

"Do you need help?" Veronica asked, but Suzanne shook her head.

"I get the sense that you have enough troubles," she said. "You can't take on mine, and you should probably leave before the doctor on duty shows up. Besides, there is something about this town that feels wrong. I don't know why but I know it's true."

"You aren't the first one to say so," Veronica said, reaching out her hand to Suzanne. "Stay safe."

"You too," Suzanne replied.

When Veronica left the building, there was an emptiness that felt deeper and more menacing than a normal hospital at night.

*

As Veronica walked quickly toward home, she made plans. They had to leave, and they had to leave within the next few days. It was going to be hard to convince her mother to leave the house, particularly since it was just deeded to them. So Veronica would need to present it as a temporary thing. She didn't want to have to tell anyone about what she had been seeing but if she had to in order to get them out, she would. Even without that, she had a feeling that Nan might side with her, if she could get Nan in a room alone. They would need to take a train or bus to get far enough away to wait out whatever was going to happen. Maybe she could position it as an early wedding present. They could go up to visit her mother's sister in Winston and then take a trip to Hanging Rock.

She had just come to the corner of Main Street and Maple when she heard the noise. It was coming from the high school. Light was coming from behind the school, making it look black, like the sun during an eclipse. The noise was cheers and clapping, almost as if it were a pep rally.

"Oh great, it's another rally," Veronica muttered as she sped up to get by. She could hear a deep male voice, but couldn't make out words, it was just a cacophony of voices and the whining of amplification being overstressed. Yet as she got closer, she realized that this was not just another rally, at least not to her senses. She felt a hate pulsing in the air before she was able to distinguish words. As she neared, she stepped quickly into the shadow of the school. It was worth seeing what they were up to, as it might influence the timeline of her plans.

The firelight made long shadows on the side of the building, stretching and twisting human shapes into shapes of birds, beasts, and demons. Rivers of energy flowed above the stage and the audience, and swimming and twisting in these rivers were the blue-gray forms of ghosts—but these were not the sort of ghosts she had previously seen. These were no animal ghosts, or humanoid ghosts. No, they looked unnatural, stretched and twisted like the creations of a sadistic god.

The energy that these creatures were swimming in was thick and lumpy like curled whey or vomit. The last time she had seen a rally was only a few days ago, and the hate had been present but was nothing like this.

Veronica recognized the voice she was hearing. It was that of Don Bilbo, the mayor. As Veronica moved into the football field, keeping to the shadows, she saw that the crowd was easily twice, maybe even three times, as large as it had been before. Quite a few of them were wearing their stupid white robes, but no hoods—at least, not yet. She supposed that they didn't feel the need to hide their faces in this crowd.

"So up there in Salem, they had a problem like ours," said Bilbo. "They set up some draft office and recruited some of them coloured boys for the war. And you know what happened?"

The crowd went ominously silent.

"Well, white women started going missing, just like here in our town. Yes, they did. Two women went gone in two months. Two white women. Two mothers. Two families destroyed. Two husbands now widowers."

A sound came from the crowd. It sounded like a growl.

"So they found the bastard that did it," he continued as the wind began picking up. Veronica saw gray shadows dancing in that wind.

"And you know what happened?" he asked.

"No," the crowd muttered.

"Nothing... NOTHING!" he shouted into the microphone, and it began to whine. "That colored boy was put in jail and he's now awaiting *his* trial. The lawyers are worried about *his* rights. What about the rights of those husbands putting their children to bed best they can, while the children cry for their mothers?"

Veronica looked at the faces of the people standing there. The faces of the men were alight with hatred. But if the men's faces were filled with anger, the women's raged. Every mother there was thinking of her own children, abandoned.

"So just after the colored soldiers left, the women stopped disappearing. And just one month after a few of them came back, another woman disappeared. I don't think that is a coincidence... do you?"

"No," the crowd said as one.

"Well, now, I don't want to scare you or upset you, but they have already brought those same type of colored soldiers to our town. They are sitting up there in the hospital, right now. They might be the same as the one we caught who killed Nellie Crowder."

"You took care of him good, Don!" someone yelled.

Veronica saw a group of young men jumping around imitating monkeys.

"I don't know what you are talking about, Paul," Mayor Bilbo said. "Our police brought him in and interrogated him. Unfortunately, he fell when he was being led to his cell and hit his head. He hit it in just the wrong place, so he died. So I guess god gave him justice, that's all. Just like we hope god will give justice to whoever took Missy Sewell."

"Let's give all them bastards justice!" someone yelled.

"Of course, we want to take the law into our own hands, but we are law-abiding citizens. No matter how much we want to make things better ourselves, we owe it to our police department to let them handle these situations. But what we can do is help the police department in whatever way we can. Chief Bishop, is there anything we can do?"

Earl Bishop strode up to the microphone. When he spoke, his voice sounded soft and weary. Like a lone warrior fighting to protect his town from the barbarian hordes. A wave of disgust washed over Veronica.

"First, I want you all to know that we will be doing our very best to bring criminals to justice."

"Justice!" yelled someone in the crowd.

"But how you can help us is to be our eyes. Keep an eye on what's happening around you. You all know that there are now colored soldiers sheltered in the hospital. If you see any nigg—colored people—in places where they shouldn't be, let us know. If you see any white women being addressed by a colored man, let us know."

These last words felt like a cold wind in Veronica's face, and she quickly fell back into the shadow of the school building. A blast of hot air blew her hair back from her face, and she was momentarily worried that it came from her, but she heard a voice beside her.

"Humanity at its best, isn't it?"

Dante was leaning against the building with his knee up and his foot propped against the wall. His head was cocked to the side, and he was smiling, but there was nothing warm in his smile.

"I see you've wandered into the belly of the beast," he said.

Suddenly a thought slashed across her consciousness, blocking out the horror of her surroundings. Dante was a ghost; would he know about Lazlo?

"This is neither the time nor the place," Dante said, as if reading her thoughts. She was about to argue when she noticed that his eyes were glowing orange in the darkness. "I will try to give you twenty-four hours to leave here, but these idiots are trying my patience. If Kara were to see this, there would be no stopping her from acting immediately."

"Where is Kara?" Veronica asked.

"I helped her rest for a few hours, but when she wakes, this will begin. Be gone before it does," Dante said. For a moment, he appeared as a black flame, and then he was gone.

Veronica turned and ran for home.

Chapter Twenty Six

The First Flame

Veronica was winded by the time she got back to the bottom of her driveway. Unfortunately, she wouldn't have time to catch her breath, at least not emotionally, because Lizzie was sitting on the swing of her front porch. She slowed to a walk.

"Ronnie! I need to talk to you," Lizzie called, as Veronica walked up the driveway.

Veronica ignored her and walked past the porch. Her hand was on the back door when Lizzie said, "I know you're angry with me, but this is about Franklin and Nan."

"What about Franklin and Nan?" Veronica asked, returning to the porch. She stood with her arms crossed against the cold.

"There was a rally tonight," Lizzie said.

"I know, I saw it. Why aren't you there?" Veronica asked. She shouldn't have asked. She should just find a way to get Lizzie out of here, but Lizzie sucked her in with the mention of Franklin and Nan.

"I left before it was over," Lizzie said. "I know you're mad at me, and I guess you have reason to be. But I love Ben, and I've been doing whatever I had to do to get him."

"Missy said something similar, just before she disappeared," Veronica snapped before she could stop herself.

Lizzie jumped up and put her hand over Veronica's mouth.

"Sssssshhhhhh," she whispered, looking around her into the dark. "That's why I'm here. When I was at the rally, I saw Tommy. He was surrounded by a group of fatheads but they were brand new fatheads. I recognized a few of them as being a couple years younger than us in school. I heard Tommy grandstanding about how Nan was no better than trash if she was willing to marry an idiot like Franklin."

Veronica felt a surge of heat in her throat and Lizzie suddenly stepped back and put her hands up.

"I didn't say it, Tommy did," Lizzie replied, but her eyes were wider than Veronica had ever seen them before.

"I thought that you had decided that Tommy was your new goal—or it sure looked like that," Veronica said, surprised that her voice could sound so icy when her insides burned.

Lizzie sighed.

"I thought about it, I admit it. His father runs the factory and Tommy has certainly never gone hungry, but when I saw him at the rally tonight, well, I changed my mind."

"Uh-huh," Veronica said. At that, Iona opened the back door and stuck her head around. She caught Veronica's eye, but Veronica nodded. Iona disappeared.

"I guess I'm no longer welcome at Iona's house," Lizzie said. For the first time in a long time, Veronica heard real pain in her voice. "But I didn't come here to talk about me. I came to tell you what happened."

Lizzie let out a long sigh, and it sounded shaky.

"While Tommy was acting like a fool with his new friends, Hugh McBrayer came up, with some new girl. I'd never seen her before, but she was very pretty. No, she was very, very pretty. She looked a little like Lauren Bacall. Missy has gone missing not a week and he already has another girl."

"I thought they said that the black man they beat up had confessed to killing her?" Veronica said.

"Yes, that's what they said yesterday but apparently they've changed their minds about that now. Now they are saying that Missy is just missing, and that the gorgeous new girl is 'consoling' Hugh. Anyway, Tommy looked at Hugh and slapped him on the back.

"CJ was there, but he's been really quiet for the past few days. Everyone thinks it's because that soldier was writing to you. Anyway, when Hugh came up, CJ turned to Hugh and asked, 'what happened to your Claddagh ring?'

"So then Hugh says 'What Claddagh ring?' like none of us knew that he and Missy had identical rings. Like we hadn't heard him refer to it as a 'pre-engagement' ring. So, CJ said something like 'the one you and Missy wore'."

"You know, Hugh didn't even flinch, he just looked at CJ all stony-eyed and said, 'I lost it,' like it was nothing. This made Tommy and his new boys hoot and laugh. Then Tommy slapped Hugh on the back again and said, 'Well, looks to me like Hugh traded up. Missy was useless, I think we'll be losing a few more useless things in the next week or two.' Then he starts jumping around and his idiots follow. They start chanting 'Move 'em... out of town.'" Lizzie's voice was low and trembly. "I couldn't believe it. They pretty much openly admitted to having something to do with Missy's disappearance."

"Her death," Veronica whispered.

"They don't know—" Lizzie began, but Veronica cut her short.

"I do."

Lizzie raised her eyebrows the slightest bit but then shrugged.

"If she's not dead, she better stay away. Tommy is not going to stand for her being in town."

"When did Tommy become the one to decide something like that?" Veronica asked.

"When they made him the head of the Knights of Harrisville. Apparently, it happened yesterday, and his dad was none too happy about it. Tommy is changing the name to the White Knights of Harrisville. Now that he has some power, he doesn't feel like he has to listen to anyone, including CJ."

The fire burning in Veronica's belly flamed.

"I'm telling you this because he *is* going to come for Franklin and Nan. He said as much. He said that ret—well, mute people were inferior and that the town needed to be cleansed of them."

"He said 'cleansed'?" Veronica asked.

"Yes, so he is going to come after your brother and Nan."

"Let him come," Veronica said. "He will have to go through me."

Lizzie reached out and gently touched Veronica's arm.

"You are just a girl, you can't stop them all by yourself, Ronnie."

"You don't know me, Lizzie."

With this Veronica turned and went inside her house.

*

"What did Lizzie have to say?" Iona asked, as Veronica stepped inside. Iona was washing up in the sink. Veronica considered lying but an idea suddenly bloomed in her brain.

"She said that Tommy was elected the president of the Knights of Harrisville," Veronica said. Her mother dropped a dish into the sink.

"Why the fool hell would anyone go and do that?" she snapped.

"I think the words fool and hell sort of cover it," Veronica said. "Lizzie also said that Tommy pretty much admitted to killing Missy."

"You shouldn't be throwing accusations, girl," her mother said.

"I wasn't the one accusing. That came from Lizzie."

"Lizzie said that?"

"She did," Veronica replied. "She also said that Tommy was going to come after Franklin and Nan. He said that Nan was no better than me if she was willing marry a 'moron like Franklin.'"

Her mother's eyes widened in alarm, and she sat down suddenly at the table.

"I walked by the rally. Mayor Bilbo and Police Chief Bishop are getting people riled up because there are colored soldiers at the hospital. They're going to do something. I think we should go away for a few weeks. We can go to Aunt Ester's house in Winston. She's been asking you to come for years."

"We don't have the money for the bus," her mother began.

"You do—it's under your bed," Veronica said. Her mother looked up and Veronica was surprised to see tears in her eyes.

"What about work?"

"I'll talk to Mr. Sawika."

"Franklin won't want to go without Nan."

"We'll bring her. In fact, let's offer to have their wedding in Winston. We can do it at Aunt Ester's house, that way we have an excuse to bring Dr. Payne."

"I understand why we should leave, but why should Dr. Payne leave?"

Veronica said nothing.

"Is there something I don't know, girl?"

Veronica hesitated but behind the anger, fear, and exhaustion on her mother's face something else lurked… something like expectation.

"A man I met told me that this town is going to be… razed to the ground. Except he wasn't really a man."

Iona's eyes went wide for a moment, but then she closed them and sighed.

"I had just gotten used to having my own house," she whispered. "But you're right, we should go. I'll talk to John in the morning. If you can get the bus tickets, we can leave tomorrow evening."

"You think Franklin will agree?" Veronica asked.

"If we tell him the truth, that Nan is in danger," her mother said.

"And tell Nan that Franklin is in danger. Okay, I'll talk to Nan. You can talk to Franklin," Veronica said.

"First thing in the morning," her mother replied. "But for now, let's get us some sleep."

Veronica went to her room and fell onto her bed, asleep before her heart could remember that it had been ripped apart.

*

It was around two in the morning when Veronica woke to a pounding on their door. She jumped to her feet and threw on a robe. As she ran out of her room, she met her mother in the hall. When they got to their door, they found Dr. Payne standing there, his eyes wide and his hair wild.

"Is Nan here?" he asked, voice trembling.

"No, she's not here," her mother said. Dread, like a ball of molten lead, fell from Veronica's heart to her gut.

"Do you think she could be with Franklin?" he asked.

"I don't know," her mother said. "Come in, Allen, come in."

"No, I can't. I need to find Nan," he said, turning to leave, but Veronica took his hand.

"Slow down," Veronica said. "Let's think this through, otherwise you're just wasting your time."

And this could be precious time.

She led Dr. Payne into the house and pulled out a chair for him. Her eyes were crusted with sleep and her hands were throbbing from the cold, but she sat down in front of Dr. Payne. Her mother put her hands on his shoulders. Veronica could see a strange shine in her eyes.

"When was the last time you saw Nan?" Veronica asked.

Dr. Payne blew out a puff of air.

"A colored family came to my back door just before bedtime," he said. "Nan told me she was going to bed. I spent an hour with the family. They brought in their teenage son who had been badly beaten by some of our local Knights. He was lucky to have survived it. The parents said that he was jumped down by the plant earlier this evening."

By the plant.

"The cigarette plant?" Veronica asked.

Dr. Payne nodded.

"When I finished, I stuck my head in her room and saw her asleep. So I went to bed. But I woke about an hour ago. I just had a feeling something was wrong. I checked Nan's room. At first, I thought it was fine but then I realized that the lumps in her bed didn't look right. When I went in, I saw they were pillows instead of Nan."

Iona gasped.

"So, you think someone took Nan?" Veronica asked.

"I hope that she and Franklin just decided that they couldn't wait. Maybe they eloped," Dr. Payne said.

"Allen, Franklin would never do such a disrespectful thing to you," Iona said.

Dr. Payne put his head in his hands.

"Who would do something like this?" he whispered.

Veronica caught her mother's eye. Iona shook her head gently.

"What do I do?" Dr. Payne said, looking up.

"We go now and report her missing," Veronica said.

"I think you'll be reporting it to the people who did it," her mother said, shocking her.

"No, they wouldn't—" Dr. Payne started, but Iona cut him off.

"They would, Allen. They are getting right off their heads. Something needs to be done. I'll take you to the police station to report her missing. That way they can't say they didn't know."

"Do you need me to come?" Veronica asked.

"No, wait here for Franklin. He needs to know but you are the only one likely to keep him from tearing down the town. That won't help find her."

Her mother took Dr. Payne by the hand and helped him to his feet.

At that moment, the air raid sirens pierced the night air.

"Take him to the police station," Veronica said to her mother. "I'll take care of whatever needs to happen here."

"You do what you have to do," her mother said, leading Dr. Payne down their driveway.

Her mother and Dr. Payne had just disappeared across the street when Veronica heard the fire truck. She saw it speed past on the main street, lights flashing and horn bellowing. Franklin would be on that truck. She needed to get him and get them out of here.

Veronica took off down the road chasing after the fire truck. The sound of an explosion ripped through the air around her. It didn't take her long to realize where it was coming from—she had heard these sirens and explosions in her dream of Lazlo what felt like years ago.

It had come from the hospital.

Chapter Twenty Seven

Play With Us

When Veronica arrived, the hospital looked like a fire monster. The right half of the building was mostly gone. The only things remaining were steel girders that were glowing white. A hot dry wind hit her face... kissed her face.

Love.

Suddenly, Veronica saw a body crash through the second-floor window and hit the ground. A fireman ran toward it. Veronica didn't need to see the fireman's face to know it was her brother. No one else moved with that same mixture of grace and strength. He covered the man with a blanket and rolled him. He then picked the man up, carried him away from the flames, and laid him down in the grass across the street, a few feet behind the fire hydrant that was in use.

Veronica ran forward. She could see two firemen standing next to Franklin, but they were doing nothing, just staring at the man on the ground.

"He said that there were other men trapped on the first floor," Franklin said.

For a moment, Veronica hesitated. Nan was missing, and she needed to get Franklin out of here, but could she really do that at the cost of other lives? Franklin moved slightly and Veronica really saw the man on the ground. A horrible suspicion chewed at her stomach. The two other firemen backed away as Veronica dropped to her knees next to the man. At first, she thought he was burned all over, but she quickly realized that the man before her was one of the colored soldiers, and not just any soldier. It was George, who she had seen healthy and whole just that afternoon. Now, he looked thinner, and he was covered in ash. His lips were dry and cracked and his face was blistered.

"George," she said, leaning forward and placing her hand on his cheek.

"Veronica, you need to get on home now," said one of the firefighters. It was Fred Morton, the father of Lizzie's Ben.

"I need some water," Veronica said.

"You need to get on home, girl, if you don't want to end up getting hurt," Fred said. Franklin turned on him and was starting to stand when Veronica put her hand on her brother's arm and pulled him down. She could feel a tingling heat flare in her belly. It felt like that medicine that Dr. Payne put on hurt muscles, cool and hot at the same time.

"No, you might be the one that ends up getting hurt tonight, Fred," Veronica said softly. She had just enough time to see the shock on his face when George grabbed her arm.

"In there—" he began, but a coughing fit took him. Even as he was hacking, he was struggling to sit up.

"… building…" George forced out between coughs.

Veronica turned to see a group of firefighters with a water hose, aiming the spray at the second floor of the building. Three other firefighters were connecting a hose to a fire hydrant further down the street.

As Franklin was checking George's vital signs, Veronica hurried to the nearest fire hydrant. She returned with water in her cupped hands. She held her hands to George, and he took some sips from her hands, but even in these circumstances, he paused first to look around him before taking the water. The water triggered another coughing fit.

He then grabbed Franklin's arm as he was coughing.

"They… have… girl trapped," he sputtered.

"What do you mean?" Veronica asked.

"Girl… nice… took her…"

"What girl?" Franklin asked, minus stutter.

"On… the… second floor. I saw them… dragging her in this evening. Had… her… in handcuffs."

Franklin looked up with horror dawning in his eyes.

"George, did you see her? Did you see where she was taken?" Veronica asked.

"No," George said. "But… she was… trying to reason with them. They was police. She kept saying her father… was… a… doctor."

"N-n-n-n-" Franklin said, jumping to his feet and taking off across the street.

"Franklin, no!" Veronica screamed, running after him. As he got to the building, a blast of heat threw him to the ground.

"She's in there… Nan," Franklin said to Veronica as she caught up with him. "Th-th-th-they t-t-took her—"

The fire is your friend.

Suddenly, a strange sense of calm settled over Veronica, and along with it, a knowing.

"Nan's not going to die Franklin—not today," Veronica said, taking his hand. Her practical brain told her that what she was about to do was insane but, in this moment, she chose to shut off that voice completely.

With Franklin's eyes on her, pleading with her, Veronica began to lead Franklin toward the building. Once inside, it would be difficult to orient themselves, so she needed to have a path in mind. Franklin's hand was crushing hers, but she blocked that out.

George had jumped from a second-floor window. If he had seen Nan, it meant that there was a chance she was still on the second floor as well. But they wouldn't want her near the front of the building, so she was probably in a room at the back, but even knowing that, how would they find her?

The flames that kill others are your friends.

Veronica remembered sitting with Janie in front of the fire. She remembered how she had felt about the fire—how she still felt about fire. She closed her eyes and focused her energy in her throat. As she did, a fierce love bloomed and spread from her throat all the way to the tips of her fingers and toes. When she opened her eyes, the fire was no longer a fire. It was simply another living creature but made of flames. It had windows for eyes and its mouth was the opening of the hospital.

Come inside, said a hissing voice in her head. It sounded like water hitting hot stones.

"I need to find a girl—a girl being held inside," Veronica said aloud to the flames. Franklin turned to stare at her, tears streaming down his face. "I need safe passage."

A strip of blue flame appeared at the edges of the broken window. The blue flame moved across the hospital building and began dancing just over the entrance. Veronica moved forward, pulling Franklin. She knew what she had to do.

Veronica picked up a fire blanket that someone had discarded on the lawn and turned toward the building. As she advanced toward the door, she felt a blast of heat that stole her breath and singed her lungs. She forced herself forward, and as she did so, the heat faded. The further forward she moved, the cooler it became.

Suddenly, Franklin yanked his hand away from hers. He turned back and fell to the ground, coughing.

"I need safe passage for him as well, I can't carry her by myself," Veronica said out loud.

There was a sound of glass breaking. A bloody body fell from the upper floors of the hospital, hitting the ground less than a hundred feet from her. This building wouldn't last much longer. If she was going to do anything, it had to be now.

Your blood, said the hissing voice. *Passage through your blood.*

Veronica ran back to Franklin.

"Franklin, give me your knife," Veronica yelled to him. He was doubled up coughing, but standing. Veronica saw the knife in his belt. She grabbed it, and without thinking, sliced the blade across her palm. She then grabbed Franklin's hand and sliced his palm. She then grabbed his hand in hers, their blood oozing together and mingling.

The expression on Franklin's face was something that had no business being on the face of her brother. Horror, grief, anger, love, fear, all fought for dominance over his facial muscles.

"Come on, Franklin," Veronica said, pulling him forward. At first, he resisted, but as Veronica pulled him past the first step of the hospital entrance, he stopped for a moment. He looked at Veronica and his eyes widened. Then he rushed forward into the blaze, pulling Veronica behind him.

"Follow the blue fire," Veronica screamed over the roar. She and Franklin were surrounded by blue and green dancing flames.

Come play with us.

"I will... later."

Set us free, play with us.

They pushed forward through the bright flames and billowing black smoke. By all reason, she shouldn't have been able to see in all this, but she could. It was as if the flames and smoke were a transparent overlay, and underneath she could still see the structure of the building, or what was remaining of it. She didn't know if Franklin saw the same, but he must have. He was dragging her down the hallway, looking into rooms as they passed. Most of these rooms were empty, but some were strewn with blackened bodies. They looked as if they had been burned by a nuclear blast.

We kill quickly. They felt no pain.

Franklin saw Nan in a back room before Veronica did. Nan was on the floor, her wrists handcuffed to a metal chair that had tipped over. She was wearing a dress that might have been white but was now ashy gray. She looked like a piece of paper that someone had crumpled and thrown away. Fire was dancing all around her, tiptoeing its way toward her hair.

Letting go of her hand, Franklin grabbed the blanket from Veronica. He rushed to Nan and threw the blanket over her body. He then demolished the chair to which Nan had been bound. Even from here, Veronica could see Franklin's skin turning an angry red.

At least it's not blistering, and he can still breathe, she thought, as she rushed forward, reconnecting her hand with his.

"Franklin, cut her hand," Veronica yelled to Franklin. He immediately grabbed Nan's hand and sliced it. Veronica held out her other hand for Franklin to cut, but he shook his head. He gave her Nan's hand instead.

"Franklin, take my hand!" Veronica yelled.

"I have to carry her. If we run now, I can make it."

Just as he finished his words, there was a horrible creaking sound and then the far side of the room crumbled away in a cloud of hot rubble. The flames around her flashed blue and moved in a straight line toward the new hole in the wall.

"There," Veronica cried, pointing to the hole. Franklin scooped Nan up off the floor, and they ran toward the hole in the wall.

Are you insane? screamed her rational brain.

"Yes," she screamed back as she jumped.

*

She was surprised when she hit the ground. First, that she hit almost immediately. Second, that she landed in a bush. Unbeknownst to her, the hospital had been built on a gradient, so there was only about a six-foot drop from the second floor. She turned quickly to see that Franklin was falling backward from the window, holding Nan protectively in front of him. He landed in the bushes as well, but quickly rolled over, still cradling Nan in his arms.

Veronica ran to Franklin's side. He was struggling to his feet with Nan. Even in the light of the moon, Veronica could see that Nan's face had been badly burned.

Franklin ran across the street, Nan in his arms.

"We need a doctor!" Veronica yelled as they ran up. "It's Nan Payne."

Franklin laid Nan gently on the ground. The right side of her face was ugly red and blistered.

Dr. Payne suddenly appeared and dropped to the ground next to Franklin.

"You found her!" he gasped, as he began to check Nan's pulse at her neck. His face was streaked with tears, but his hands were steady and sure.

"What was she doing in the hospital?" he asked.

"The police took her there," Veronica replied.

"Our police? Our town police?"

Veronica nodded.

"Why would they do that?" he asked. "Never mind, write this down on her other wrist."

Dr. Payne took Nan's wrist and held it quietly. Franklin ran toward one of the firemen, who had a pen. He grabbed it away and ran back to Nan's side.

"Blood pressure, 124 over 76," Dr. Payne said. "Respiration rate, 20 beats per minute. Heart rate, 85 beats per minute."

Franklin wrote this on Nan's arm.

"What happened? What did you see when you found her?" Dr. Payne asked. His face was a wreck, but his movements were steady and his gaze razor-sharp.

"She was in a room, by herself—" Veronica began.

"Was she on fire when you found her?" Dr. Payne asked.

"No, she was lying on her side, handcuffed to a metal chair. There was a ring of fire all around her."

"But you are sure she wasn't on fire?" Dr. Payne asked again.

"I'm sure."

"How did you get her out?"

"Franklin broke the metal chair into pieces and freed her."

"Franklin, show me your hands," Dr. Payne ordered.

Franklin held up his hands, and sure enough, his palms were raw red and covered in blisters.

"You need to get those treated now, go on over to Fred Morton. He has some bandages, and you need to get them covered."

"No, n-n-n-"

"I got her," Veronica said. "Nothing will happen to her while I am here. Go, Franklin."

"Was it smoky in the room where you found her?" Dr. Payne asked.

It must have been, but she hadn't seen it.

"Yes," Veronica said.

"Right. Then Nan, your brother, and you are in danger of inhalation injury. You and Franklin need to go to—you know the old hospital on the other side of town?"

"Baptist Hospital?"

Dr. Payne nodded.

"Why would they do this to my little girl?" he whispered, putting his hand on Nan's face.

"I hope to never know," Veronica replied, taking his hand. "But she'll be okay. She's fierce."

"She's bad. We will have to take her to Charlotte," said one of the firemen, squatting next to Nan and gesturing for help.

Franklin had returned. He touched Dr. Payne on the arm and tapped his chest.

"I want to go with her," he said, eyes filled with tears.

"I'm sorry son, we only allow family with patients," replied one of the firemen, as Franklin moved forward to help lift Nan and move her into the ambulance.

"I'll go," said Dr. Payne.

"You can, sir," replied the fireman. "But, respectfully, sir, you won't be able to help her much just sitting in the car—but you may be able to help other people here. We only have the old hospital left and damn few doctors anywhere."

For a moment, Dr. Payne's face hardened.

Veronica put her hand on his arm. As she did so, her fingers began to throb.

"There are still good people in this town," she said. "And some of those people lying there probably won't get much, if any, medical care from some people."

Dr. Payne looked around him. Veronica hoped he saw what she saw—a lot of white firemen and volunteers taking care of white victims, while most of the colored people lay unattended. The triage system was clearly based on race, not injury.

They fought for their country and managed to survive the war, only to die from negligence and hate at home.

"I'll go with her," said a voice from behind her. Veronica turned to see the nurse who had been sitting next to Caio's bed.

"Suzanne Bennett," she said, putting her hand on Dr. Payne's arm. "I'll make sure she is receiving the best care that we can give."

Dr. Payne paused for a moment, then he took out a handkerchief and wiped his glasses. He then picked up his medical bag and walked across the street toward the colored men lying on the lawn.

Some of the firemen around them started muttering.

"We can go now," Suzanne said sharply to the nearest one. He glared at her but then nodded and moved toward the front of the ambulance.

Suzanne crawled into the back of the ambulance and sat next to where Nan was lying. She looked calm and strong, nothing like how she had looked sitting next to Caio.

Caio.

"Oh god, is Caio still in there?" Veronica asked.

Suzanne shook her head.

"They came for him just after you left," she said softly. "But he wasn't there. Apparently, he left on his own when I was in another ward."

"So do you think he is all right?"

"I think he's healed. I think he did it himself… but I don't know how," she said. "They won't search for him because they have nothing to go on. In fact, I saw them sign his death certificate."

"I guess that's good," Veronica said.

"It's good for him, and that's all that matters."

"Is it good for you?"

For a moment, Suzanne's face registered shock, but then she shrugged.

"He lives. I'll never see him again, but he lives. I guess that has to be enough," she replied.

A fireman standing next to the ambulance banged the side of it.

As Veronica closed the ambulance door, Suzanne gave her a small, sad wave. Veronica saw Franklin was standing stock-still in the street, staring at the retreating ambulance with his fists at his side.

Veronica pushed her sleeves up. At least she could go help Dr. Payne if no one else would. As long as Franklin and George were okay…

She suddenly whirled around. George was no longer lying next to the fire hydrant. She felt her stomach drop.

"Excuse me, there was a colored man lying here, just near the fire hydrant. Where did he go?" she asked one of the firemen who was tending to an older white man.

"I don't rightly know ma'am," the fireman said. "But if he was near the hydrant, I suspect that some of the volunteers moved him out of the way."

"What volunteers?" Veronica asked.

"Probably half the town is here now," the fireman said, gesturing around him. "Some of the police are helping out, as well as the fellas from the mayor's office and the courthouse."

As Veronica looked, she saw that people were indeed appearing to help with the wounded. But most of the people she saw were women. The only men to be seen were the firemen, the injured white men, and the injured colored men. Not one member of the Knights of Harrisville was present. Usually this was exactly the sort of thing that would bring out the white male community in full numbers.

Unless something more important was going on.

Oh no. George.

"Franklin!" Veronica yelled, turning back to the street.

But Franklin was nowhere to be seen.

Chapter Twenty Eight

Strange Fruit

Veronica ran back across town toward her house. She was desperately hoping that Franklin had gone home to get some money for a bus or train ticket to Charlotte. She didn't have much hope for that, but she had no idea where else to look. The fact that George had gone missing, along with all the Knights of Harrisville, didn't bode well. When she got home, her mother was in her bedroom with a suitcase.

"What's happening?" Veronica asked, as she bent to catch her breath.

"We're leaving this town tonight," Iona said. "I got us bus tickets."

"We can't. Franklin's gone missing."

"Tell me what happened." Her mother sat down on her bed. She seemed calm but her face was the color of the robes those morons wore at their rallies.

Veronica told her about the hospital fire, and George and Nan and Franklin. Her mother's lips were tight, but she nodded.

"CJ came round here, looking for you. He said all of this was happening because of the colored soldier who was love with you," her mother said.

Veronica stood straighter and looked her mother in the eye.

"Yes, his name was Lazlo. He loved me and I loved him, but he died in the war," Veronica said, her voice breaking at the end. But she didn't look away, and she let the tears come, the ones she had been keeping inside since Lazlo went away. They rolled down her face, and she felt no shame.

Her mother nodded.

"Did CJ threaten you?" Veronica asked.

"No, but he said that Tommy was coming for Franklin and you. He also said something about Tommy taking a colored soldier to 'pay the price' for one of them loving a white girl. You need to find Franklin and Dr. Payne. If you find that colored soldier, you can bring him too."

"How do I find them?"

"How did you find Nan in the middle of a burning building?"

The flames.

"I'll go looking too," her mother said, standing up.

"No, you stay here. We can't split up too much," Veronica said, grabbing her coat. "Let me find them."

Veronica ran back through the kitchen and grabbed the lighter out of a drawer. She ran down her driveway, where she sheltered the lighter from the wind and flicked it.

"Show me where Franklin went," she whispered. Immediately, the tiny flame flared into a much larger one and turned blue. It rose from the lighter and became a small, blue, fiery ball that glittered in the air. She expected to see the form of Betty the chicken, but instead she saw the rabid raccoon. She was afraid that it would be too slow to help her, but it turned and began to run down the road so fast that she had trouble catching up. She followed it down the main road, past the line of factory houses, past the cigarette factory… and then beyond and into the fields.

By the time she made it to the first bare field, she could already see the burning cross in the distance. Her heart seized in her chest. She ran at full speed across the dirt field. The soft earth made it hard to run and she fell more than once, scrambling to her feet in the red mud. As she got closer, she saw that there were no people in the field. Or no living people. The remains of a body were visible, hanging from the cross.

Veronica's throat closed up. The smoke from the fire set beneath the cross was drifting toward her, making her lungs burn and her eyes water.

Please god no. Please god no. Please god no.

When she got closer, she realized that the body on the cross belonged to neither Franklin nor George. While the fire had obliterated his clothes, the frame and features of the body were that of a smallish man. His flesh was charred and his body was bowed backward, telling a story of death in unbelievable pain.

Veronica fell on her knees in the dirt, her face in her hands. The horror in front of her was beyond measure. She couldn't believe anyone could be capable of this.

Why did you bring me here? Veronica whispered, staring at the raccoon. She heard a sizzling voice in her head whisper. It was not the voice of the raccoon, but of the flame.

We killed him with smoke. We killed him as quickly as we could. Others won't be so lucky.

The flame surrounding the man turned blue and the flames began to reach toward a patch of trees and shrubs between fields a few yards away. The raccoon turned and began to wobble toward it.

You need to know and then go quick, if you want to save your brother.

Veronica jumped up and ran after the raccoon. She saw the body when she was still 20 feet away. It was carelessly thrown at the edge of the trees, as if it were a child's rag doll. A jacket had been thrown over it. As she got closer, Veronica saw that it was an expensive leather jacket. It had been thrown away as if it meant as little as the body it covered. Veronica knelt by the body, already knowing what she would find when she removed the jacket. She pulled the leather back to reveal Missy's sad face. Her eyes were swollen, and her neck was black and blue with bruises, but she looked like the Missy Veronica had always known. She was missing both hands.

Why bother to cut off her hands? She looked back at the blue flaming raccoon.

He did her like the pig, whispered the sizzling voice. *He cut off her hands and feet before she died. He wanted to see her in pain. Her pain excited him.*

"Why were her hands in the tobacco?" Veronica asked.

Because that's where he killed her. He didn't manage to get all the parts because he was afraid of being caught doing it.

Veronica didn't pull the jacket further off. She knew what she would find, it would be like the pig. Tommy Sawika did this. She recognized his jacket. If he was now so crazy and brazen that he would cut up Missy's body and then drag the remains out here, with his jacket on top of it, then he had to be pretty sure that he wouldn't be held accountable—CJ and his dad would cover it up. And if he would cover this up, he would cover everything up. She needed to find her brother, but she would need help to get out of here, from the only person who might possibly have some control over Tommy. There was only one person…

The flaming raccoon turned and pointed her in the direction that she already knew she needed to go. She just prayed that she would be in time. As she ran toward the cigarette factory, she prayed to the fire gods that John Sawika was working tonight.

*

Veronica ran through the side door of the plant and into the mirrored hallway. She saw herself running, and she saw several shadows running behind her. She prayed that these shadows were no one she knew.

John Sawika was on the cigarette floor, and he spotted her the moment she ran in.

He ran toward her and pulled her into the snuff area.

"The Knights... they set the fire at the hospital," Veronica panted. "They kidnapped Nan and left her in there. Franklin... Franklin and I found her... Franklin ran off. I can't find him. The Knights... they burned a man on a cross just behind the factory... and... and... and... Tommy killed Missy. Her body is in the trees next to the burning cross. It has Tommy's jacked on top of it."

John Sawika's face turned to stone. For a moment, he closed his eyes. When he opened them, they were burning.

"We need to get you home fast, and you and your ma need to get out of town," he said.

"We can't leave without Franklin."

"Where is Nan?" Mr. Sawika asked, leading her quickly back through the mirrored hallway and toward the parking lot. The small shadowy figures had been joined by small fiery ones.

"She was taken to a hospital in Charlotte," Veronica replied.

"Good, then she is safe for now, but your family isn't," Mr. Sawika said. "CJ told me about the letters you got from a colored soldier. I don't give a damn about that sort of thing. In my mind, any man who fights for his country willingly is a man. I don't know what your relationship with him might be, but any suggestion that you did anything at all to encourage his letters will likely get you killed on a night like tonight."

"I don't care what they think, they killed Missy," Veronica spat out.

"I'm just asking you to keep quiet for tonight, while I try to get things calmed down and get you, Iona, and Franklin out of here," Mr. Sawika said, opening his car door for her. "Lizzie has done you harm spreading rumors. I'm just asking you to stay silent for this night."

Veronica nodded, as she got into Mr. Sawika's car.

"I've known that Tommy had a problem for a while now," Mr. Sawika said, as he started the car up. "When he was little, he used to like to kill bugs and use his slingshot to kill birds. I didn't think much about it then. When dogs and cats started showing up dead and tied to telephone poles, I didn't let myself think about it either. I guess I suspected, but I didn't want to think about it Since they nominated him for the Knights of Harrisville, it's all gotten worse. He decided that he wanted Nan Payne only after she became taken with your brother. I think it was partly because it was your brother, and that might be my fault."

"How is that your fault?" Veronica asked as they drove.

"I have a lot of time for your brother," Mr. Sawika said. "He reminds me of myself when I was young. He's smart, tough, and he's made something of himself despite what other people have thought. I would have hired him in the factory if he had ever come to me. Nan is lucky to find a man like that. And you, you should have been my own daughter, if I had been man enough to tell Iona my feelings for her before she went off with that good-for-nothing Deward."

Suddenly, things became clearer to Veronica. The money under the bed in the factory envelopes. The way Mr. Sawika always asked after her mom.

"Is that why you killed Deward?" Veronica asked.

"You think I killed Deward?" Mr. Sawika said, with a dark laugh. "I wish I had been the one to do it. And I would have done it, if CJ Bishop hadn't beat me to it."

"CJ?" Veronica gasped.

"Yep. After your mother told me what had happened to your grandmother, I called Chief Bishop and told him to go pick up that good-for-nothing before I killed him myself. I guess CJ heard this because by the time Chief Bishop made it to your house, CJ was already there, standing over Deward's body, holding his daddy's gun. I don't think much of that boy, but he cared enough for you to remove your daddy from your life."

"I didn't know," Veronica whispered.

"Of course you didn't. We covered it up," Mr. Sawika said. "Even Tommy doesn't know. We hid his body in the snuff for a while, until we found the time to take it out to the river. I had no problem throwing that asshole into the water. I just wish that I had been the one to shoot him. CJ wasn't ever really right after doing it. Knowing that you have that inside you, that you can kill a man, changes you. That's why I told Tommy that he should never provoke CJ, and to be respectful of you and your family. So Tommy taunted your brother as a way to get back at me, I guess."

Mr. Sawika was flying down the roads. As they approached her house, Veronica saw that a car was already parked in their driveway. Her mother was on the ground, and she was cradling Franklin in her arms.

Tommy Sawika, Hugh McBrayer, John Bilbo, Charlie Cazort, and Phil Villar were standing with a group of other young men that Veronica had known most of her life. All of them were wearing white robes. Tommy was brandishing a shotgun at CJ Bishop, who was standing in front of Franklin and her mother.

"Stay in the car," Mr. Sawika said, as he screeched to a halt.

*

"Tommy!" John Sawika called, getting out of the car. "You need to put the gun down, now!"

Tommy whirled on his father and smirked. He kept his gun trained on CJ, who had his hands up as if he had been trying to reason with Tommy. Reasoning with Tommy Sawika wouldn't work, didn't work, and had never worked. Tommy didn't operate by reason. His only driver was power and violence. It had always been so.

"Do I? Why should I do that, Papa? CJ has gone and lost his mind over this. Even knowing that Ronnie loved some colored bastard, knowing that she might have let him put his dirty dick inside her, he still wants her."

CJ started forward but Tommy pointed the gun at his face.

"I'm just saying what's true, CJ. You need to let us find you a nice white girl."

"Tommy, I told you to put that thing down. Guns don't make you a man, I would have thought you might know that," John Sawika said, as he moved toward him. Tommy whirled and turned the gun on his father. CJ once again moved but Hugh McBrayer also had a shotgun and aimed it at CJ.

"What do you know about being a man?" Tommy snarled at his father. "You think this moron is a man. Well, at least he won't be able to make more morons."

"What did you do?" Mr. Sawika asked, horror apparent in his voice.

"Well, Hugh here is handy with a knife, so we just took out one of his baby makers. We gelded that moron. He still got one, so we gave him a fighting chance."

Veronica opened the car door and jumped out. Franklin was lying on the ground, and Veronica saw with dawning fury that there was blood on the crotch of her brother's pants and on his hands. Her mother looked up and caught her eye. Iona's gaze was strange. It showed no fear, no anger, not much of anything. A hot breeze broke through the cold air.

"Get out of here, Ronnie!" CJ called to her.

"Oh, you brought a date, did you? After Mom dies, this is what you replace her with?" Tommy spat out at his father, but then turned to Veronica and laughed. Something was playing behind his eyes that wasn't strictly Tommy, nor strictly sane.

"So, Ronnie. Was he good, your colored boy? I heard he died though. At least that's what his friend told us," Tommy indicated behind her. Veronica turned to see that a black man had been tied by a rope to the back of the car. He had been dragged to death. His skin was ripped off in multiple places on his body and his face, although turned upward, was an unrecognizable mask of blood. His head was lumpy and misshapen. It was beyond sickening and yet there was something even worse. It took a few seconds to register that she knew some of the scraps of clothes left on the body. It was George.

"Oh no, looks like he got stuck on our car, trying to catch a ride." Tommy laughed.

Veronica grabbed a baseball bat that one of the men was carrying and ran toward Tommy. Hugh turned his shotgun toward her and fired just as CJ lurched forward to protect her. The blast hit CJ in the side of the head and threw him backward. He hit the ground, his head now nothing but a mass of blood and bone.

For a moment, there was silence. Everyone froze where they stood. Then Tommy laughed, a shrill, high-pitched giggle.

"Well, I guess CJ paid for the sin of his lust," Tommy said. Hugh nodded and smiled.

"There must be something about Ronnie worth dying for, I'm guessing," Tommy said, grabbing Veronica and pulling her toward him.

"You best be letting go of that girl, and heading on home," John Sawika growled.

"I best be doing whatever the hell I want to!" Tommy shouted. "I'm the president of the Knights of Harrisville, in case you don't remember."

"So you're the president of a bunch of inbred rednecks. Is that something to be proud of, son?" John Sawika asked.

Tommy suddenly pulled Veronica to him and pushed his lips against hers. His breath was a mixture of alcohol and something sour—maybe fear.

As Veronica struggled against the force of Tommy's body, she began trying to pull up the fire in her throat, but she was too shocked and horrified by what she had seen to raise it. George's body looked like shredded meat and CJ had half his head missing. When realized that she still had the bat in her hand, she used it to hit Tommy in the thigh. He grunted, fell back, and then, without any hesitation, punched her in the stomach.

As Veronica slumped to the ground, she saw John Sawika grab Tommy from behind. Tommy swung round and there was the sharp retort of a shotgun. Veronica fell back onto the driveway. As she scrambled backward, toward her mother and Franklin, she saw John Sawika lying on his back on the ground, blood blooming across his chest.

His expression was not one of surprise.

It was more of anger and disgust.

Chapter Twenty Nine

White Candles

For a moment Tommy said nothing, then a strange gagging sound came from his throat—but at the same time, he began jumping up and down.

"See, Papa, I don't have to listen to you no more," he yelled. "You don't rule me. You don't own me. You couldn't even keep yourself alive, so what's so great about you?"

He yelled this down at his father, but John Sawika was no longer capable of hearing his son.

Suddenly, Veronica felt a gentle warm breeze blow through her. Not over her, but through her. Tommy turned, and the expression on his face changed from a dark glee to confusion. The breeze was now getting warmer—a lot warmer. She could feel intense love surround her and she understood this love. Veronica reached out to put her arms around Franklin. Whatever was happening here was not coming from her, but the love in the breeze told her that while she would not be hurt, she needed to protect her brother. The hot breeze sparked the fire inside Veronica that had been doused by horror. She felt her own flames awaken and kiss her blood. She used these flames to make a bubble for herself and her semiconscious brother.

Suddenly Tommy's face froze. At the same moment, the hem of John Bilbo's white robe burst into flames. All the other boys jumped away as John screamed and swatted at the fire.

"Drop and roll," one of the boys yelled, but John was jumping up and down, batting at his robes.

"Help–help–help me, someone help me," he screamed as the flames rose quickly up his robes and toward his face, setting the white hat ablaze as if it were tissue paper. John Bilbo, the son of the mayor, who had bullied both her and Franklin in grade school, was shrieking. Then Veronica heard what might have been the most frightening thing she had heard all evening. It was the sound of her mother's laughter. Iona was standing over her and Franklin. She was smiling, and she looked forty years younger.

"Won't have a tongue to do that much longer," Iona said with a smile.

Phil Villar had yanked off his robe and now tackled John Bilbo with it, rolling him over on the gravel of the driveway, his once-white robe becoming milky gray from the wet snow and dirt. Another wave of heat passed through Veronica, this heat felt like the flames she had felt at the hospital. Instantaneously, Phil Villar's clothing burst into flames as well. These flames combined with the flames consuming John Bilbo as if they were lovers. Phil began to shriek and stood up to run but a thin line of blue flames sped around Veronica and Franklin. Rather than following on the ground of the driveway, these flames leaped through the air and attached themselves to Phil Villar's screaming face. His voice was immediately silenced.

All the boys, with the exception of Tommy, broke and ran in all directions. Tommy stood stock-still, as if rooted where he was. His eyes were wide and his mouth open.

"What pretty little white candles," Iona said, still smiling. At these words, Charlie Cazort, who had just made it to the end of the driveway, exploded.

"That was a bit too hard," Iona muttered. "I gotta do better."

Tommy seemed to wake up from his daze. He took a few steps back, eyes wide and spittle on his lip.

"You're a witch!" he yelled, pointing at Iona.

"Maybe I am," Iona replied, stepping around Veronica and Franklin. "But boys who like to play with fire are likely to get burned."

A line of blue flames escaped her and quickly formed a circle around Tommy. He turned to flee toward the street but the flames on that side of him roared and flared up at least twenty feet into the air.

"No, no," Iona said, shaking her head and approaching him.

"Get away from me you witch, my papa will—"

"Your papa is dead," Iona replied, voice suddenly harsh. "You killed him. You killed your best friend." She was now only inches away from Tommy, who seemed unable to move through the circle of fire. Iona reached her hand through the wall of blue flame.

"You tried to kill my children," she said, as she touched her finger to Tommy's lips. A tiny ball of blue flame appeared, which sunk into the skin of Tommy's lips, sealing them shut to the screaming his throat was producing.

"But you won't hurt no one no more" Iona said softly, her voice sweet-sounding again, her face beautiful and her expression almost kind.

Tommy was still trapped inside the circle of fire.

Why isn't he running? Veronica thought, until she noticed that his feet and ankles had been melted and fused to the ground beneath him. His arms had melted into his torso. The flame that had closed his lips was now moving gently over his face and head, marking him in blistering flesh. The smell of singed hair and burned skin filled the air. For a moment, it smelled like barbecue. Tommy was thrashing his head from side to side as all the skin of his face began to melt like candle wax. Somehow, he managed to rip his lips apart. His scream rose into the night for a brief moment before Iona shook her head. The air around him shimmered for a brief second, and then blood exploded from his mouth just as his entire body burst into flames.

Neighbors had come out from their houses, and were standing there, as if transfixed. No one was moving to help anyone. The other boys, the ones who had come with Tommy, were scattered in all directions, running for their lives. One by one, each erupted in flames, bathing the street with light and smoke. Iona was smiling as she stood still in their driveway. Hank Price's old truck suddenly exploded in his yard.

"We need to stop her, or she'll kill one of our neighbors."

Franklin had pulled himself out of Veronica's arms. His nose was split open, and his lips were badly swollen. He was covered in blood. It was all over his shirt and pants. His hair was matted with it. His eyes were blue-black and mostly swollen shut. Watching her beautiful, caring brother worried about the people on their street made her heart ache and her eyes burn. Veronica would be happy to see them all burn. Her neighbors had stayed in their houses while Tommy and his idiots did this to her brother. They must have seen the car drive up, dragging a body behind it. At that thought, Veronica stood up and stumbled to the back of the car.

She bent down, hoping, but there was no life in the body of George. She ran back and grabbed her mother's hands. Iona was staring off into the distance with a serene smile on her face.

"Ma, stop. We need to get to the hospital."

Her mother's face had a serenity that Veronica had never seen there before. Despite the blood and horror around her, she looked beautiful.

"You best be sure I won't let you do what you did to my son and my girl. So you all be best getting on home now, before you and yours get hurt," she said softly, as if those boys were still around to hear her.

Down the street someone shrieked as his white robes burst into flames. A line of blue flames ran from her mother, through her, down the driveway where it splintered and raced off in all directions at a speed as fast as any car. Veronica heard more screams coming from further away.

"Mom, Iona, you have to stop now. We have to get Franklin to the hospital," Veronica said, as she took her mother's arm. Her mother just continued to smile, eyes far away. The heat was building up around them. Not knowing what else to do, Veronica pulled her mother into her arms. The heat radiated through her, but rather than let it go through her, Veronica pulled at it. Pulled it into her throat, into her belly, into her sex. She pulled it with a fierce love—the love that she realized she was feeling for her mother. Her mother, who had just seen the only man she might have ever had the chance to love shot in front of her.

Suddenly her mother slumped in her arms and let out a ragged breath. A small sob escaped her.

"We have to stop our crying now, girl," Iona said, seemingly to herself. She then stepped away from Veronica with a small nod. "We ain't got time for it. I need you to help me get your brother to the hospital."

Veronica nodded and went to John Sawika's car. The keys were still in it. She and her mother helped Franklin into the back seat. There was a lot more blood than she wanted to see. The word *gelded* flashed in her head, and she was suddenly fiercely happy that her mother had melted Tommy. She only hoped he was still alive to feel it as she had melted his muscles and bones.

As they drove through the town, toward the old hospital, Veronica saw that her mother's flames had traveled for at least a mile from their house. Blue flames were jumping from roof to roof.

Maybe Kara and Dante were not the ones who were destined to destroy this little town.

The thought didn't displease her.

*

Veronica drove as fast as she could but the ride to the hospital seemed like a lifetime. Her mother sat in the back with Franklin. His head was in Iona's lap and Veronica could hear him snuffling to breathe through his blocked nose.

When they drove to the hospital entrance where Veronica jumped out of the car and handed her keys to her mother. Even though there must have been a shortage of doctors due to the fire at the main hospital, two attendants ran out and got Franklin onto a stretcher.

"Franklin, what happened?" a voice called from inside. Dr. Payne appeared at the side of Franklin's gurney. Apparently, they had thought he was more needed here.

"Tommy and his gang got to him," Veronica said as they wheeled Franklin down the hall to a room. "They said something about gelding him."

"Sweet Jesus," Dr. Payne whispered. "Will this night ever end?"

"It will, but not well," Veronica said, taking Dr. Payne's arm. "Listen, after you see to Franklin, you need to go to Charlotte to check on Nan."

"I want to, more than anything, but there are a lot of people here who need my help right now," Dr. Payne said.

"What's happening here?" asked another doctor who ran up.

"This is Dr. Lira," Dr. Payne said. "He is a surgeon. Veronica just said that the boys who attacked her brother claim to have gelded him."

Dr. Lira said nothing more, he just grabbed the gurney and ran with it down the hall.

"He'll be okay," Dr. Payne said. "Dr. Lira is a friend of mine from Charlotte. He has been keeping me up to date about what's happening with my Nan. One of his friends is following her."

"If he's a good guy, he needs to leave too," Veronica said.

"Why?" Dr. Payne asked.

"I can't explain, or you wouldn't believe me," Veronica said. "But I can tell you that you will be getting a lot more burn victims coming from near our house You need to leave. If you don't, Nan may lose you when she needs you most."

Dr. Payne's eyes were wide, but then he nodded.

"I've never known you to be prone to exaggeration or drama, so I believe you. I've done a full shift, so as soon as Franklin has been tended to, I'll go to Charlotte."

"Plan to be gone a few days," Veronica said.

Dr. Payne nodded and walked swiftly in the direction that Dr. Lira had gone in.

Veronica saw her mother come in the front door. Her eyes searched the room. When she found Veronica, she ran awkwardly toward her.

"How is Franklin?" her mother asked. Her voice was now shaky, and her face looked drawn and tired. She looked twenty years older than she was and sixty years older than she had looked thirty minutes ago.

"The doctors are looking at him," Veronica said. "As soon as they finish stitching him up, we need to leave. Even if they want him to stay, we still need to leave."

"I know," her mother replied. "Apparently some of the injured colored soldiers were brought here. Some of the Knights of Harrisville are collecting outside."

"You mean the ones still alive."

"Yes, the ones still alive. And others that weren't at our house—more's the pity," her mother replied, and a small smile fleetingly transformed her face into something younger and fiercer.

"I'm sorry about John Sawika," Veronica said. "He told me that he loved you."

"He said that? Out loud?"

"Yes, he said he had loved you since high school."

"If he had only told me that, after you and Franklin were born, so much of this could have been avoided. But despite how horrible Deward was, he gave me my children, who I wouldn't change for anything."

She reached out and took Veronica's hand. Veronica blinked back the wetness in her eyes. She needed to cry. She needed to grieve all the things that would now never be—her life with Lazlo, her mother's possible happiness with John Sawika, their own house, enough food, and hands that didn't hurt all the time.

At that moment, Dr. Lira wheeled Franklin out in a wheelchair. He was pale as a sheet, but he was awake. Dr. Payne was leaving out of the back door.

"How is he?" her mother asked.

"He'll live," Dr. Lira replied. "One of his testicles has been ruptured and will probably not be able to produce sperm. But the other seems in good working order. It just needed a quick stitch up. We need to make sure that he doesn't get any infection, so I am giving you some strong penicillin."

"Here are some painkillers as well," the doctor said, handing her two small bottles. "Keep the wound clean and change the dressings once a day."

A nurse came out and whispered to the doctor, who immediately went back into the room he had come from.

Iona went and put her arms around Franklin.

"How are you?" she asked.

"I'll live. I may be half a man, but I'll live."

Veronica bent down and put her arms around Franklin's neck.

"You are ten times the man of any other man in this town. I would never have been able to believe that any man could be good and decent if it wasn't for you."

Franklin gave her a wan smile. "I just wish that I had managed to take down one of those monsters before they got me. They killed Missy, they killed some poor colored man and dragged the other and Nan—"

He stopped and his eyes welled with tears.

"I know," Veronica said, "but Nan will be okay."

"How do you know?" Franklin asked.

"The fire only kissed her, it didn't consume her," Veronica replied.

"How do you know?"

"It told me," Veronica said. "The scars she carries will just show the world how beautiful she is inside."

Veronica heard angry voices—a lot of angry voices—from the front of the hospital as someone came through the front door.

"I would suggest that you go out the back door," Dr. Lira said, appearing at the door with his bag and car keys.

"But our car is out front," Veronica said.

"Then you might consider walking," Dr. Lira said. "The crowd out front does not look friendly."

"I suspect some of the people in that crowd did this to my boy," Iona said, quietly. Her eyes looked unnaturally bright again.

"Even more reason to avoid them," the doctor said, before heading down the hall toward the back door.

"I'm going to get our car," her mother said to Veronica. "Take Franklin out back, and I will meet you there."

"Those people won't hesitate to try to kill you," Veronica said.

"I'm not the one who is going to be killed," her mother replied softly, starting down the hall. Veronica started after her when she saw Kara appear in the lobby at the hospital entrance. Her mother didn't hesitate. She approached Kara, who was just as shockingly beautiful as she had been every other time Veronica had seen her. Kara opened her arms and gave her mother a hug.

"You should go now and take your brother out back," said a voice. Veronica jumped and turned to find herself face-to-face with Dante. He was also just as handsome as she remembered him.

"But my mother—"

Dante interrupted her. "—will never be better protected than she is right now. Kara has marked her as one of her own, so no god will save the soul of whoever tries to hurt her."

Veronica looked at her mother. She was standing straight and proud next to Kara, but her frame was so small, and her bones so delicate. Had she always been this way?

The fire in Veronica rose again, and this time she didn't try to push it back down. Instead, she let it rise.

"I'm tired of this, this town, these people, their stupid ideas. I'm tired of making myself lesser just to try to fit into a town that will never accept me, my family, or the man that I love and could have had a life with. I'm done."

Dante smiled at her.

"Then go and be what you are, and be proud of that," he said, before disappearing.

Veronica turned back to face the front of the building, her mother, Kara, and whoever was threatening them outside the building. With each step she took toward them, she felt the heat grow, dancing inside her blood and filling up her brain. It felt good. It felt so very good. She felt no pain in her hands, no hunger in her belly, just a warmth that filled her body and began seeping out of her skin.

Her mother must have felt her approach, but when she turned and saw Veronica, her eyes widened.

"You need to get out of here, child. You need to get your brother out back and wait for me. I will get a car..."

"There are cars out back," Veronica said. "Take Franklin and get in one."

"I won't have my child tell me what to do—" Iona began, but Veronica cut her off.

"I'm not a child. Strictly, I may not be a girl either, but you know that," Veronica said.

She saw that Kara had turned to her. This was the first time she had seen her face this close, and Veronica realized that she had the sort of beauty that would drive people mad. If this was the face of god, Veronica would be honored to worship at her shrine for the rest of her life. The power that radiated from Kara made the fire inside Veronica blaze brighter.

"Iona, you should listen to your daughter," Kara said. "I can certainly handle a group of rowdy idiots all by myself, but I think that Veronica needs to step out of the shadows and into the fire. You've had your time, give her the same."

As her mother walked away, Kara took Veronica by the hand, and they walked toward the entrance of the hospital. Suddenly, there was an explosion and the building shook. The front of the building exploded outward, spraying concrete and glass in all directions.

There was a crowd of fifty or more Knights of Harrisville in the parking lot, wearing their white robes, their mouths hanging open like trout. As she and Kara stepped out through the rubble, she saw Police Chief Earl Bishop standing, gun raised. There were other people she recognized standing in the rubble—Mayor Bilbo, Coach Villar, and much of the police department. These were the people in power who presided over the evil in this place. The ones who were supposed to protect the people, but who had instead separated and divided them.

"There she is," a male voice yelled, voice cracking. "She's the one that killed Tommy Sawika."

The voice belonged to Hugh McBrayer. In Veronica's mind she saw the pretty, sad, doomed face of Missy Sewell.

"You go do what you do," Kara said softly, touching her arm. "Let it all go. I will make sure the innocent aren't touched."

Veronica closed her eyes. On the black-red screen of her eyelids, faces appeared: Missy Sewell, Nellie Crowder, Tray Crowder, Caio, Suzanne, George—and Lazlo, smiling his beautiful smile. She had loved him, and could have loved him for a lifetime.

Veronica took a deep breath and let it out. With that she felt a different kind of love bloom in her chest. They wouldn't let her have her love of Lazlo, but this was a love that she could share.

As she walked into the parking lot, the air began to shimmer all around her.

*

An hour later Veronica was sitting in the passenger seat of a stolen car as her mother drove them out of Harrisville. Franklin was lying in the back seat. He had taken a few pain pills and was dozing. His beautiful, bruised face was sweet even now. This was a town that had done this to her perfect brother. It was a town that had allowed her friend George to be dragged to death—and it wouldn't be punished. Sure, Iona had killed some of the men who did it. Veronica herself had delivered death to a hundred or so people in front of the hospital. But the town was still there, still sick, still evil. Kara said it would be gone by morning, but the land still existed. It lay there, uncaring of what had been done on top of it. Suddenly the cigarette factory appeared on their right.

"Stop the car," Veronica snapped.

"Why?" her mother asked.

"Just stop it," Veronica yelled.

Her mother stopped and Veronica jumped out of the car and turned to the factory. She just stood. On the other side of the factory was forest and fields. This land was fertile and teeming with life.

"What are you doing?"

"As long as the earth is good here, they can replant," Veronica whispered, her voice shaky with rage. "They can bring the factory back. The same people who did this, the same people who created this horrible culture, the same people who grew rich and fat on the backs of people like us, like Lazlo—well, they can just bring it all back."

"Yes, Ronnie, but that's what happens. You can't prevent that from happening," Iona said.

"No," Veronica whispered, tears in her eyes. "But maybe we can prolong it. We can take away the food, the water, the energy, and the jobs."

"How?" her mother asked.

Veronica's eyes turned to the city off to her right, its lights still shining through a haze of smoke. It still lived. She turned to the field in front of her, in the distance the charred remains of a burning cross still stood, bearing the body of an unknown man who had been crucified. In a group of trees next to it Missy's body had been dropped as if she were a badly used broken doll.

"We scorch the earth," Veronica said, as she felt her throat open to the fire that she saw in the distance. Her body began to heat up ever so slightly. Her mother came to stand next to her and took her hand.

"I've never said it, but I want you to know how proud I am of you... how proud I have always been," Iona said, fiery tears running down her face, making blood rivers that immediately healed.

"We burn it all to the ground."

Standing hand in hand, a wave of fire rose from the two of them. It rolled outward in a semicircle around them consuming everything in its path: trees, buildings, grass, and any living creature unfortunate enough to be in its path. When Veronica saw the flames crest over the outskirts of Harrisville, she closed her eyes and thought of Lazlo.

It didn't take long to accomplish. When Veronica came back to her senses, the factory was ablaze and filling the sky with light and smoke. All the trees were gone. The empty fields all around them were smoldering. Veronica didn't know how hot a fire had to be to scorch the actual earth, but she suspected it was much hotter than a normal fire. The air around them was hot and dry, even in the dead of winter. She heard the song of the fire, and it was beautiful.

On the other side of the factory, the natural gas that seeped out of the earth near the river was now alight as well. The city in the distance looked like one monstrous flame, as if a meteor had hit there. Her mother was smiling, as she squeezed Veronica's hand.

"Good riddance to bad garbage," she said.

"I'm just sorry for whatever innocent people got caught in that," Veronica said.

"Not to worry, I feel sure that the innocent will have already left or been protected," Iona said. "Let's go now. We need to find a place to sleep tonight, and I want to be far enough away. Tomorrow we can go to your Aunt Ester's house. She has rooms ready for us."

"How did she know?" Veronica asked, getting into the car. Franklin was lying on the backseat, muttering in his sleep.

"I have been planning this for about a month," Iona replied.

"Why didn't you tell me?" Veronica asked. Iona started the engine and pulled back onto the road. She was silent.

"Mama, why didn't you tell me that you were planning on leaving?" Veronica asked again.

"Because I wasn't sure myself," Iona said. "I just wanted to have things in place in case it was true."

"What was true?" Veronica asked.

"I also met a man who told me that this town would be razed to the ground," Iona said.

"Dante."

Her mother glanced at her and nodded before turning her eyes to the road.

Veronica was staring out the window when she saw something in the distance. It was the town's water tower.

"Slow down," she said to Iona.

"What do you want to do?" Iona asked.

"I want to make things worse," Veronica replied, rolling down her window.

She focused on the water tower in the distance. Her throat opened and a line of fire jumped from her, racing across the fields and toward the tower. She felt it when it hit the water. It felt like a tug in her gut, draining something inside her. As the tugging got more intense, it was both painful and pleasant, like lancing and draining a boil. A few moments later, the city's water tower exploded, spewing water and steam into the air.

Epilogue

Veronica sat on her front porch, waiting for the arrival of her children, grandchildren, and her new great-grandson. Her house was on a lake, and it had six bedrooms and three stories in addition to a carriage house, an apartment that would hold six more people. They had a boathouse as well, with all the Jet Skis, canoes, and boats that came with it. Yes, the house was very large for just two people, but it allowed her and Nan to have their kids and grandkids stay. The only concern was maintaining the grounds, but Nan had insisted on being the one to hire a landscaper and gardener. Franklin's company had grown so large that Nan was now a very rich woman. Veronica was less rich, but none of that mattered to her. If a person had the basics, that was enough.

Veronica's kids and grandkids were coming to celebrate the birth of her new great-grandchild. She had suggested that she simply come visit all of them, but they seemed to be under the impression that she was feeble, so she would play the part for them. The truth was that Veronica was far from feeble. She was eighty, if you used her birth certificate as the reference, but she looked like she was in her fifties, and she had the reflexes and hormones of someone even younger. Her family doctor would have been shocked if he had taken any blood tests—if she had a family doctor, which she didn't. She tried not to see any one doctor more than once or twice—at least, that was until this year. Just this year, she got something from a new "doctor" who prescribed something to heal her heart rather than her body.

On that fateful evening in December 1944, she and her family had driven to Winston and Aunt Ester had been waiting. Ester and her husband welcomed them with open arms. The next morning, Harrisville, North Carolina became the unexpected epicenter of a magnitude 7.2 earthquake. As if that wasn't enough, somehow the earthquake triggered storms, birthing several tornadoes which further devastated the town. These things, on top of the fires that had already been in progress, did not go unnoticed by the religious and the superstitious. Pastors from the pulpit talked about the supposedly "wicked, wild ways" of Harrisville that had caused god to strike them down. Harrisville had been wicked, all right, but not in the way that they meant it. Superstitious people had said that Harrisville was cursed. Even to this day, the ground remained parched and dry. Nothing grew there, and no one lived there.

Dr. Payne left that night and never returned. At first, no one knew where he and Nan had gone, and Franklin had been frantic. It took him a year to find her. Then it took him another six months of letters and calls to talk her into letting him visit her. She was ashamed of her scars, but Franklin didn't care. Veronica knew her brother, and she knew that Franklin wouldn't even see the scars. He asked Dr. Payne for her hand in marriage again. Dr. Payne once again gave his blessing and then some if Franklin could talk Nan into it.

Franklin did more than that. He talked her into it with his own voice. He had started seeing a speech doctor in Raleigh, who helped him with his stutter. When Franklin finally proposed proper, he did it on one knee, in his own voice. He went back to school and became an agricultural engineer. If Nan needed any proof that Franklin loved and desired her, she needed only to look at the daughter and two sons that he gave her. Nan overcame her self-consciousness and went to nursing school. It was there that it became evident that Nan's beauty had never been about her appearance. It had been about the sound of her voice and what that voice said. Most people were shocked when they saw the scars on Nan's face—for about two minutes. Once she began speaking, none of that mattered. She was smart, kind, and empathetic. Patients who were lucky enough to get her as a nurse got better faster and with fewer complications.

A cool wind came up and blew flower petals across the porch. A few pink and white ones settled in Veronica's lap, and she felt that flush that she always felt when Lazlo was around.

Her life had been comparatively easy since that winter in 1944. There was a cigarette factory in Winston-Salem as well, and she got on second shift almost immediately. This allowed her to go to school during the day. So she got a Bachelor of Science degree in math in 1949. In that same year, she met William "Billy" Bissett on a trip to the beach. He had just taken a job in the Foreign Service. After corresponding for six months, they got married. His job required that they move every three or four years. Her son Nathanial was born in Crete, in 1953. Her daughter Violet was born in Hawaii when Veronica was thirty-four. Both her children were beautiful, and both had dark hair and skin that was slightly but noticeably more tanned than either Veronica's or her husband's.

Veronica gained quite a bit of weight when she was pregnant with Nat. She gained more when she got pregnant with Violet. By the time her children were in grade school, she was officially classified as obese in the weight charts. She didn't care. Despite all the pressure on TV and in magazines to be skinny, Veronica knew the value of holding a bit more weight. She had been hungry and would never be that way again, if she had any choice in the matter. Billy began having affairs on her by the time the kids were teenagers. She hadn't really cared because, in truth, she hadn't really loved him. She hadn't hated him, but she hadn't loved him. She had only loved once. But she wanted to stay with Billy until the kids were out of the house. It was when Billy slapped her that she decided she had to leave him. It turned out that this had not been necessary. A tree branch fell on Billy's head less than twenty-four hours after that. So Veronica became a widow at the age of forty-eight. She moved back to Winston-Salem and applied for a job teaching math at the local school, and fate must have been on her side, because she got the job.

But fate is a fickle monster. Her beloved brother Franklin died of a heart attack when he was only fifty-five. Franklin, the man with perfect health, seemed to have had a weakness in his heart. Her mother Iona, although remarried to a good man, died a week later. Veronica deeply believed that this was from grief. After Franklin's death, Veronica moved in with Nan. Their kids were mostly grown by then, but Nan's heart was broken bad, and if anyone could understand that, it was Veronica. Eventually, the two of them bought this house. Two old spinster women. Veronica ended up telling Nan her whole story. At the end of it, Nan asked if Franklin had gone on. Veronica told her that she didn't think so. In truth, she knew that he hadn't. He had become another ghost in her life, watching over Nan and his kids. She didn't know if Lazlo and Franklin met each other as ghosts, but she hoped they did.

As she got older, it didn't seem to show in her body—or at least not in the same way that it showed in other people. She was still spry enough to take care of her grandkids, which was a good thing because her daughter Violet had dropped out of college to marry a less-than-educated, less-than-intelligent and less-than-responsible man. Violet had to get a job and support him. Veronica could not hide the fact that she despised Violet's husband, and Violet was too proud to ever leave him. So they drifted apart but Veronica was still very close to Nat and his family. Nat's children, Jason and Iona, were her pride and joy. She was also extremely close to Nan and Franklin's kids.

The air was getting warmer now. It was probably close to 10 a.m. She should get up and start something for lunch. Although she could afford any food she wanted now, she had become a strict vegetarian. This had started all those years ago when she began seeing the ghosts of animals. Any lie that she might have told herself about animals lacking consciousness had been destroyed that year. When she saw chicken in the grocery store, she was reminded of Betty. When she saw bacon, she saw the dead pig in her backyard surrounded by ghost piglets. As a result, Veronica often ate the same things that she ate when she was young and hungry—beans, cornbread, and collard greens. She just ate a lot more of it.

She told herself that she would get up in ten minutes. In the meantime, she sat in her rocking chair. In her lap she held Lazlo's last letter to her. The paper of it was now getting thin and the words were smudged in some places. Despite that, it was her most treasured possession.

She looked down at it, re-reading the words for the hundredth, thousandth, ten thousandth, time.

My Dearest Veronica,

I'm so sorry that I went and died. If I had been more confident, I would have believed the love I saw in your eyes when we last spoke, sitting on that rock over the train tracks. No, love is too small a word. If I had been more confident, I would have seen something more profound in those beautiful gray eyes. I would have seen the heat of your desire. I would have seen the strength of your feelings. I would have seen the stubborn heart that wouldn't let you rest without me. I'm so very sorry that I didn't have the confidence to see all that… until after I was already dead.

I know you must be confused now. I met this boy, Caio, here. It seems that he can talk to ghosts. So I have asked him to write for me, with my words and his hands. He will give the letter to George, who I hope will bring it to you.

What I want you to know is that I will be watching over you, and I will do this for the rest of your life. I made a pact with an angel to make this happen. I couldn't go on without you. I tried but I felt like it was cleaving my heart in two, and I was bleeding out. I was afraid that the only thing that would be left of us would be cold and resentful. I couldn't let that happen to me but, even more, to you. So I will watch over you. If you are cold, I will keep you warm. If you burn, I will cool you. I know more of your past now. I know how your father hurt you, but I will make sure that no harm comes to you. I know you won't be able to see me. The angel said that my silence and invisibility to you was the price I had to pay to stay with you, but I gladly accepted it. So I will be here. I will do whatever I have to do to help you make your way through life. All I want is to be able to walk with you through this life, invisible though I may be.

It will be very tempting to find people to allow me to write to you, but that's not allowed either and it wouldn't be good for you. I want you to have a life. I want you to have a husband and children if you want them. It's crazy but the idea of that don't even make me jealous. I guess I never got it in my head to hope that I could be with you anyway, besides in dreams. I feel happy to be able to be in your life, and I want you to be happy too. I'm afraid if you see me, or if you hear from me, then you won't do those things. Besides, the angel made that a part of the bargain.

I hope that I can still see you in our dreams though. I know now that when we met in our dreams, it was real. People can go to other levels of existence when we dream. When we dream, you can tell me your truths.

Your heart and your soul are as strong as any soldier, my love. And you have an ocean of feeling inside of you. Your feelings are as deep and as perilous as the sea. I can see them better now that I'm dead. I can love you more now than I could have done while I was living. I would have felt too inferior to you in life. Now, I know you better and love you more. I love you as a whole but also in parts. This is hard for me to explain, but I've learned that every piece of a person's soul carries all their soul. There may be pieces of you spread throughout the universe and throughout dimensions, but they are all you and they are all connected. I love all of them. I can't see the future, exactly, but I believe that a time will come, even in this life, where I will be better able *to see you and touch you. I have to believe that, or that we will be connected in the next lives.*

I have asked Caio to deliver this letter to you. You should speak with him. I believe he can help you.

I love you without limit and I will be with you now and forever,

Lazlo

Veronica sighed as a breeze caressed her.

Lazlo had been as true as his word. He had stayed with Veronica throughout her life. Even after she married, he stayed. He had been in the room during the birth of her children, even if her husband hadn't. She felt him around her all the time. Sometimes, in special moments, they met in dreams where they laughed and loved for as long as that time and space allowed. But Veronica could also see him when she was awake —if she used the fire in her as a magnifier. When she did, he looked just as he had when they met. Handsome, tall, with kind, laughing eyes. He would look at her, smile, and then look away. They weren't supposed to be able to see each other, but she saved and cherished that secret.

Veronica suspected that Lazlo had found ways to help her even in the physical world. When things seemed to come too easy for a girl who had never had things come easy, she suspected. There were even moments, during the times of the year when the veil between the worlds was thinner, when Lazlo had stepped into her husband when they made love. Veronica couldn't acknowledge it, but when she looked into her husband's eyes in those moments, she saw Lazlo staring back at her, with all the passion and love that they had been denied in the physical world. She knew it was him, and he knew that she knew but they weren't allowed to let on. That would be breaking the rules. When her husband died in an accident the day after striking her, she had known that Lazlo had been responsible. She didn't hate him for that, she loved him more. After her husband's death, she didn't take another man. Instead, she found other ways to bring him close to her when she took her pleasure alone.

Despite everything, her life had been good. It was still good. In fact, she was hoping it was about to get much better. A few months ago, she had received a strange package with no return address. When she opened it, she found a video game, of all things. On it was a Post-it Note, which had read:

It seems that my blood might have traveled further than I thought. Let your kids or grandkids get the correct platform to play it on. I think that you'll find a couple of the players inside interesting to you. Keep healthy.
    Yours truly,

Dr. Caio Silva

When Veronica had read those words, her heart had pounded in her chest, although she didn't know why. She had immediately called Nat and asked him for the equipment needed to play the game. They would be bringing it today.

Veronica was startled out of her reverie by the sound of cars approaching down the long road. The family was almost here, and she hadn't even started the meal. She quickly got up and went into the kitchen to put some beans and greens on the stove.

"Hey, Mom!" Nat called from the door.

"Bring that great-grandson in here right now," Veronica called from the kitchen.

"It's just us for now," Nat replied.

"Aunt Iona's coming with him later," her grandson Jason called. "But I got the console you wanted. I'm surprised you knew about it, let alone got the game. It's got some cool—whoa, wait a minute. Is this why?"

"What are you talking about?" Veronica asked.

Jason was standing in front of a photo that Veronica had up on her wall. It was from a newspaper clipping. It was the only photograph of Lazlo she had ever seen. Someone had taken it on the day they met when he had been sitting on his field pack in front of the draft office.

"What are you on about, Jason?" Veronica asked, giving him a hug. Her grandson hugged her back distractedly.

"That guy... the one in your photo. He looks exactly like one of the NPCs in the game," Jason said.

"What's an NPC?" Veronica asked, her heart fluttering dangerously.

"Non-player character. It's a construct of the game. Listen, you won't believe the similarity. I'll set it up for you this evening."

Veronica's head felt like it was about to explode, so she shook it quickly.

"You all go put your stuff into your rooms, and I'll finish up lunch here. Nan will be home in thirty minutes or so, so we can all eat then."

"Don't overcook, Grandma," Jason called as he started up the stairs with bags.

"I most assuredly will," Veronica replied.

*

That night, after the rest of the family had gone to bed, Veronica sat in front of the fire she made herself, with her great-grandson, Hudson. As she gently rocked him, her heart was full to the brim. Caio had given her and Lazlo a new way to meet. It was a much more physical one. In fact, she suspected if she stayed in that game with him too long, it might kill her—but she couldn't think of a better way to die.

The fire in front of her crackled. Her gift had been passed down not only to Violet but also to Nat. It seemed that it had changed somehow and it was no longer confined to the women. She had taught her grandkids how to use it when they were young. This gift—this power—would keep her family safe long after she was gone.

As she sat watching the fire, she felt Lazlo all around her. Wrapped in the embrace of a ghost, her family all under her roof, she felt blessed.

Love, whispered the flames.

"Forever," Veronica whispered back.

Acknowledgements

As always, my deepest thanks to those who helped in the creation of this book. So big hugs to Tessa, Addie, Myra, Hassy, Leo, Valerie, and Ian, for all their insights, help and support. Also, thanks to all the folks at LiterallyPR. It's so great to have people who believe in my work.

Most of all, thanks to my family: Sebastien, my loving and perfectionist dev editor and film maker; Lucas, my paradigm shifter and master of blurbs; and Julien, my husband, best friend, and partner for all of our life's craziness.

* * *

For Those Who Enjoyed this Book

Amelie, Lazlo, Hudson, Kara and Dante will return in "The Ghosting Academy".

***

As most people know, reviews make or break authors, so if this book made you feel anything, do please share it, and connect with me at the following:

Webpage: *Lsdelorme.com*
Tiktok: *@lexyshawdelorme*
Insta: *ls_delorme*
Twitter: *@lexyshawdelorme*
Facebook Page: *Lexy Shaw Delorme*

Printed in Dunstable, United Kingdom